Jo's Boys

Louisa May Alcott

was born in Germantown, Pennsylvania, in 1832. She was the second of four daughters of Abba May Alcott and Bronson Alcott, a prominent transcendental thinker and social reformer whose idealistic preoccupations left him little time or interest for his family's practical needs. In Concord, Massachusetts, where the Alcotts settled, Louisa enjoyed the skating in winter, the berry picking in summer, and the melodramas she and her sisters performed for the neighbors. Those neighbors included Ralph Waldo Emerson, Nathaniel Hawthorne, and Henry David Thoreau, the great writers of New England's flowering. Louisa early began to shoulder her family's financial burdens—as a domestic, as a teacher, and as a writer, producing everything from sketches of her Civil War nursing experiences to pseudonymous lurid thrillers. Fame and fortune came with the publication of *Little Women* in 1868/1869, a domestic novel based upon her childhood experiences. This was followed by other books in the Little Women Series, all of them enormously popular: *An Old-Fashioned Girl* in 1870, *Little Men* in 1871, *Eight Cousins* in 1875, its sequel *Rose in Bloom* in 1876, *Under the Lilacs* in 1878, *Jack and Jill* in 1880, and finally, in 1886, *Jo's Boys*, the sequel to *Little Men*. Among other books from her pen was the autobiographical novel *Work: A Story of Experience* in 1873. The last decade of her life was spent in caring for Lulu Nieriker, the daughter of her dead sister May, in literary activity, and involvement in the woman's suffrage and temperance movements. Louisa Alcott died in 1888, two days after the death of her father who had influenced her life for better and for worse.

Jo's Boys

by
Louisa May Alcott

WITH AN AFTERWORD BY

Madeleine B. Stern

Mattituck, New York
Amereon House

TO THE READER

It is our pleasure to keep available uncommon titles and to this end, at the time of publication, we have used the best available sources. To aid catalogers and collectors, this title is printed in an edition limited to 300 copies. ——— Enjoy!

To order contact
AMEREON HOUSE, the publishing division of
Amereon Ltd.
Postal Box 1200
Mattituck, New York 11952

Contents

Chapter 1

Ten Years Later

IF ANYONE had told me what wonderful changes were to take place here in ten years, I wouldn't have believed it," said Mrs. Jo to Mrs. Meg, as they sat on the piazza at Plumfield one summer day, looking about them with faces full of pride and pleasure.

"This is the sort of magic that money and kind hearts can work. I am sure Mr. Laurence could have no nobler monument than the college he so generously endowed; and a home like this will keep Aunt March's memory green as long as it lasts," answered Mrs. Meg, always glad to praise the absent.

"We used to believe in fairies, you remember, and plan what we'd ask for if we could have three wishes. Doesn't it seem as if mine had been really granted at last? Money, fame, and plenty of the work I love," said Mrs. Jo, carelessly rumpling up her hair as she clasped her hands over her head just as she used to do when a girl.

"I have had mine, and Amy is enjoying hers to her heart's content. If dear Marmee, John, and Beth were here, it would be quite perfect," added Meg, with a tender quiver in her voice; for Marmee's place was empty now.

Jo put her hand on her sister's, and both sat silent for a little while, surveying the pleasant scene before them with mingled sad and happy thoughts.

It certainly did look as if magic had been at work, for quiet Plumfield was transformed into a busy little world. The house seemed more hospitable than ever, refreshed now with new paint, added wings, well-kept lawn and garden, and a prosperous air it had not worn when riotous

boys swarmed everywhere and it was rather difficult for
the Bhaers to make both ends meet. On the hill, where
kites used to be flown, stood the fine college which Mr.
Laurence's munificent legacy had built. Busy students
were going to and fro along the paths once trodden by
childish feet, and many young men and women were
enjoying all the advantages that wealth, wisdom, and benevolence could give them.

Just inside the gates of Plumfield a pretty brown cottage, very like the Dovecote, nestled among the trees,
and on the green slope westward Laurie's white-pillared
mansion glittered in the sunshine; for when the rapid
growth of the city shut in the old house, spoilt Meg's nest,
and dared to put a soap-factory under Mr. Laurence's
indignant nose, our friends emigrated to Plumfield, and
the great changes began.

These were the pleasant ones; and the loss of the dear
old people was sweetened by the blessings they left behind; so all prospered now in the little community, and
Mr. Bhaer as president, and Mr. March as chaplain of the
college, saw their long-cherished dream beautifully real-
ized. The sisters divided the care of the young people
among them, each taking the part that suited her best.
Meg was the motherly friend of the young women, Jo the
confidante and defender of all the youths, and Amy the
lady Bountiful who delicately smoothed the way for needy
students, and entertained them all so cordially that it was
no wonder they named her lovely home Mount Parnassus,
so full was it of music, beauty, and the culture hungry
young hearts and fancies long for.

The original twelve boys had of course scattered far and
wide during these years, but all that lived still remembered old Plumfield, and came wandering back from the
four quarters of the earth to tell their various experiences,
laugh over the pleasures of the past, and face the duties of
the present with fresh courage; for such home-comings
keep hearts tender and hands helpful with the memories
of young and happy days. A few words will tell the history
of each, and then we can go on with the new chapter of
their lives.

Franz was with a merchant kinsman in Hamburg, a

man of twenty-six now, and doing well. Emil was the
jolliest tar that ever "sailed the ocean blue." His uncle sent
him on a long voyage to disgust him with this adventurous life; but he came home so delighted with it that it was
plain this was his profession, and the German kinsman
gave him a good chance in his ships; so the lad was happy.
Dan was a wanderer still; for after the geological researches
in South America he tried sheep-farming in Australia, and
was now in California looking up mines. Nat was busy
with music at the Conservatory, preparing for a year or
two in Germany to finish him off. Tom was studying
medicine and trying to like it. Jack was in business with
his father, bent on getting rich. Dolly was in college with
Stuffy and Ned reading law. Poor little Dick was dead, so
was Billy; and no one could mourn for them, since life
would never be happy, afflicted as they were in mind and
body.

Rob and Teddy were called the "Lion and the Lamb";
for the latter was as rampant as the king of beasts, and the
former as gentle as any sheep that ever baaed. Mrs. Jo
called him "my daughter", and found him the most dutiful
of children, with plenty of manliness underlying the quiet
manners and tender nature. But in Ted she seemed to see
all the faults, whims, aspirations, and fun of her own youth
in a new shape. With his tawny locks always in wild
confusion, his long legs and arms, loud voice, and contin-
ual activity, Ted was a prominent figure at Plumfield. He
had his moods of gloom, and fell into the Slough of Despond about once a week, to be hoisted out by patient Rob
or his mother, who understood when to let him alone and
when to shake him up. He was her pride and joy as well as
torment, being a very bright lad for his age, and so full of
all sorts of budding talent, that her maternal mind was
much exercised as to what this remarkable boy would
become.

Demi had gone through College with honour, and M̶
Meg had set her heart on his being a minister—pict̶·
her fond fancy the first sermon her dignified y̶
would preach, as well as the long, usef̶·'
life he was to lead. But John, as she ̶
firmly declined the divinity school, say̶

enough of books, and needed to know more of men and the world, and caused the dear woman much disappointment by deciding to try a journalist's career. It was a blow; but she knew that young minds cannot be driven, and that experience is the best teacher; so she let him follow his own inclinations, still hoping to see him in the pulpit. Aunt Jo raged when she found that there was to be a reporter in the family, and called him "Jenkins" on the spot. She liked his literary tendencies, but had reason to detest official Paul Prys, as we shall see later. Demi knew his own mind, however, and tranquilly carried out his plans, unmoved by the tongues of the anxious mammas or the jokes of his mates. Uncle Teddy encouraged him, and painted a splendid career, mentioning Dickens and other celebrities who began as reporters and ended as famous novelists or newspaper men.

The girls were all flourishing. Daisy, as sweet and domestic as ever, was her mother's comfort and companion. Josie at fourteen was a most original young person, full of pranks and peculiarities, the latest of which was a passion for the stage, which caused her quiet mother and sister much anxiety as well as amusement. Bess had grown into a tall, beautiful girl looking several years older than she was, with the same graceful ways and dainty tastes which the little Princess had, and a rich inheritance of both the father's and mother's gifts, fostered by every aid love and money could give. But the pride of the community was naughty Nan; for, like so many restless, wilful children, she was growing into a woman full of the energy and promise that suddenly blossoms when the ambitious seeker finds the work she is fitted to do well. Nan began to study medicine at sixteen, and at twenty was getting on bravely; for now, thanks to other intelligent women, colleges and hospitals were open to her. She had never wavered in her purpose from the childish days when she shocked Daisy in the old willow by saying: "I don't want any family to fuss over. I shall have an office, with bottles and pestle things in it, and drive round and cure folks." The future foretold by the little girl the young woman was rapidly bringing to ass, and finding so much happiness in it that nothing ld win her from the chosen work. Several worthy young gentlemen had tried to make her change her mind and choose, as Daisy did, "a nice little house and family to take care of." But Nan only laughed, and routed the lovers by proposing to look at the tongue which spoke of adoration, or professionally felt the pulse in the manly hand offered for her acceptance. So all departed but one persistent youth, who was such a devoted Traddles it was impossible to quench him.

This was Tom, who was as faithful to his child sweetheart as she to her "pestle things", and gave a proof of fidelity that touched her very much. He studied medicine for her sake alone, having no taste for it, and a decided fancy for a mercantile life. But Nan was firm, and Tom stoutly kept on, devoutly hoping he might not kill many of his fellow-beings when he came to practise. They were excellent friends, however, and caused much amusement to their comrades, by the vicissitudes of this merry love-chase.

Both were approaching Plumfield on the afternoon when Mrs. Meg and Mrs. Jo were talking on the piazza. Not together; for Nan was walking briskly along the pleasant road alone, thinking over a case that interested her, and Tom was pegging on behind to overtake her, as if by accident, when the suburbs of the city were past—a little way of his, which was part of the joke.

Nan was a handsome girl, with a fresh colour, clear eye, quick smile, and the self-poised look young women with a purpose always have. She was simply and sensibly dressed, walked easily, and seemed full of vigour, with her broad shoulders well back, arms swinging freely, and the elasticity of youth and health in every motion. The few people she met turned to look at her, as if it was a pleasant sight to see a hearty, happy girl walking countryward that lovely day; and the red-faced young man steaming along behind, hat off and every tight curl wagging with impatience, evidently agreed with them.

Presently a mild "Hallo!" was borne upon the breeze, and pausing, with an effort to look surprised that was an utter failure, Nan said affably:

"Oh, is that you, Tom?"

"Looks like it. Thought you might be walking out to-day"; and Tom's jovial face beamed with pleasure.

"You knew it. How is your throat?" asked Nan in her professional tone, which was always a quencher to undue raptures.

"Throat? Oh, ah! yes, I remember. It is well. The effect of that prescription was wonderful. I'll never call homoeopathy a humbug again."

"You were the humbug this time, and so were the unmedicated pellets I gave you. If sugar or milk can cure diphtheria in this remarkable manner, I'll make a note of it. O Tom, Tom, will you never be done playing tricks?"

"O Nan, Nan, will you never be done getting the better of me?" And the merry pair laughed at one another just as they did in the old times, which always came back freshly when they went to Plumfield.

"Well, I knew I shouldn't see you for a week if I didn't scare up some excuse for a call at the office. You are so desperately busy all the time I never get a word," explained Tom.

"You ought to be busy too, and above such nonsense. Really, Tom, if you don't give your mind to your lectures, you'll never get on," said Nan soberly.

"I have quite enough of them as it is," answered Tom with an air of disgust. "A fellow must lark a bit after dissecting corpuses all day. I can't stand it long at a time, though *some people* seem to enjoy it immensely."

"Then why not leave it, and do what suits you better? I always thought it a foolish thing, you know," said Nan, with a trace of anxiety in the keen eyes that searched for signs of illness in a face as ruddy as a Baldwin apple.

"You know why I chose it, and why I shall stick to it if it kills me. I may not *look* delicate, but I've a deep-seated heart complaint, and it will carry me off sooner or later; for only one doctor in the world can cure it, and she won't."

There was an air of pensive resignation about Tom that was both comic and pathetic; for he was in earnest, and kept on giving hints of this sort, without the least encouragement.

Nan frowned; but she was used to it, and knew how to treat him.

"She *is* curing it in the best and only way; but a more refractory patient never lived. Did you go to that ball, as I directed?"

"I did."

"And devote yourself to pretty Miss West?"

"Danced with her the whole evening."

"No impression made on that susceptible organ of yours?"

"Not the slightest. I gaped in her face once, forgot to feed her, and gave a sigh of relief when I handed her over to her mamma."

"Repeat the dose as often as possible, and note the symptoms. I predict that you'll 'cry for it' by and by."

"Never! I'm sure it doesn't suit my constitution."

"We shall see. Obey orders!" sternly.

"Yes, Doctor," meekly.

Silence reigned for a moment; then, as if the bone of contention was forgotten in the pleasant recollections called up by familiar objects, Nan said suddenly:

"What fun we used to have in that wood! Do you remember how you tumbled out of the big nut-tree and nearly broke your collar-bones?"

"Don't I! and how you steeped me in wormwood till I was a fine mahogany colour, and Aunt Jo wailed over my spoilt jacket," laughed Tom, a boy again in a minute.

"And how you set the house afire?"

"And you ran off for your band-box?"

"Do you ever say 'Thunder-turtles' now?"

"Do people ever call you 'Giddy-gaddy'?"

"Daisy does. Dear thing, I haven't seen her for a week."

"I saw Demi this morning, and he said she was keeping house for Mother Bhaer."

"She always does when Aunt Jo gets into a vortex. Daisy is a model housekeeper; and you couldn't do better than make your bow to her, if you can't go to work and wait till you are grown up before you begin lovering."

"Nat would break his fiddle over my head if I suggested such a thing. No, thank you. Another name is engraved upon my heart as indelibly as the blue anchor on my arm.

'Hope' is my motto, and 'No surrender,' yours; see who will hold out longest."

"You silly boys think we must pair off as we did when children; but we shall do nothing of the kind. How well Parnassus looks from here!" said Nan, abruptly changing the conversation again.

"It is a fine house; but I love old Plum best. Wouldn't Aunt March stare if she could see the changes here?" answered Tom, as they both paused at the great gate to look at the pleasant landscape before them.

A sudden whoop startled them, as a long boy with a wild yellow head came leaping over a hedge like a kangaroo, followed by a slender girl, who stuck in the hawthorn, and sat there laughing like a witch. A pretty little lass she was, with curly dark hair, bright eyes, and a very expressive face. Her hat was at her back, and her skirts a good deal the worse for the brooks she had crossed, the trees she had climbed, and the last leap, which added several fine rents.

"Take me down, Nan, please. Tom, hold Ted; he's got my book, and I *will* have it," called Josie from her perch, not at all daunted by the appearance of her friends.

Tom promptly collared the thief, while Nan picked Josie from among the thorns and set her on her feet without a word of reproof; for having been a romp in her own girlhood, she was very indulgent to like tastes in others. "What's the matter, dear?" she asked, pinning up the longest rip, while Josie examined the scratches on her hands.

"I was studying my part in the willow, and Ted came slyly up and poked the book out of my hands with his rod. It fell in the brook, and before I could scrabble down he was off. You wretch, give it back this moment or I'll box your ears," cried Josie, laughing and scolding in the same breath.

Escaping from Tom, Ted struck a sentimental attitude, and with tender glances at the wet, torn young person before him, delivered Claude Melnotte's famous speech in a lackadaisical way that was irresistibly funny, ending with "Dost like the picture, love?" as he made an object of himself by tying his long legs in a knot and distorting his face horribly.

The sound of applause from the piazza put a stop to these antics, and the young folks went up the avenue together very much in the old style when Tom drove four in hand and Nan was the best horse in the team. Rosy, breathless, and merry, they greeted the ladies and sat down on the steps to rest, Aunt Meg sewing up her daughter's rags while Mrs. Jo smoothed the Lion's mane, and rescued the book. Daisy appeared in a moment to greet her friend, and all began to talk.

"Muffins for tea; better stay and eat 'em; Daisy's never fail," said Ted hospitably.

"He's a judge; he ate nine last time. That's why he's so fat," added Josie, with a withering glance at her cousin, who was as thin as a lath.

"I must go and see Lucy Dove. She has a whitlow, and it's time to lance it. I'll tea at college," answered Nan, feeling in her pocket to be sure she had not forgotten her case of instruments.

"Thanks, I'm going there also. Tom Merryweather has granulated lids, and I promised to touch them up for him. Save a doctor's fee and be good practice for me. I'm clumsy with my thumbs," said Tom, bound to be near his idol while he could.

"Hush! Daisy doesn't like to hear you saw-bones talk of your work. Muffins suit us better"; and Ted grinned sweetly, with a view to future favours in the eating line.

"Any news of the Commodore?" asked Tom.

"He is on his way home, and Dan hopes to come soon. I long to see my boys together, and have begged the wanderers to come to Thanksgiving, if not before," answered Mrs. Jo, beaming at the thought.

"They'll come, every man of them, if they can. Even Jack will risk losing a dollar for the sake of one of our jolly old dinners," laughed Tom.

"There's the turkey fattening for the feast. I never chase him now, but feed him well; and he's 'swellin' wisibly,' bless his drumsticks!" said Ted, pointing out the doomed fowl proudly parading in a neighbouring field.

"If Nat goes the last of the month we shall want a

farewell frolic for him. I suppose the dear old Chirper will come home a second Ole Bull," said Nan to her friend.

A pretty colour came into Daisy's cheek, and the folds of muslin on her breast rose and fell with a quick breath; but she answered placidly: "Uncle Laurie says he has *real* talent, and after the training he will get abroad he can command a good living here, though he may never be famous."

"Young people seldom turn out as one predicts, so it is of little use to expect anything," said Mrs. Meg with a sigh. "If our children are good and useful men and women, we should be satisfied; yet it's very natural to wish them to be brilliant and successful."

"They are like my chickens, mighty uncertain. Now, that fine-looking cockerel of mine is the stupidest one of the lot, and the ugly, long-legged chap is the king of the yard, he's so smart; crows loud enough to wake the Seven Sleepers; but the handsome one croaks, and is no end of a coward. *I* get snubbed; but you wait till I grow up, and then see"; and Ted looked so like his own long-legged pet that everyone laughed at his modest prediction. ·

"I want to see Dan settled somewhere. 'A rolling stone gathers no moss,' and at twenty-five he is still roaming about the world without a tie to hold him, except this"; and Mrs. Meg nodded towards her sister.

"Dan will find his place at last, and experience is his best teacher. He is rough still, but each time he comes home I see a change for the better, and never lose my faith in him. He may never do anything great, or get rich; but if the wild boy makes an honest man, I'm satisfied," said Mrs. Jo, who always defended the black sheep of her flock.

"That's right, mother, stand by Dan! He's worth a dozen Jacks and Neds bragging about money and trying to be swells. You see if he doesn't do something to be proud of and take the wind out of their sails," added Ted, whose love for his "Danny" was now strengthened by a boy's admiration for the bold, adventurous man.

"Hope so, I'm sure. He's just the fellow to do rash things and come to glory—climbing the Matterhorn, taking a 'header' into Niagara, or finding a big nugget.

That's his way of sowing wild oats, and perhaps it's better than ours," said Tom thoughtfully; for he had gained a good deal of experience in that sort of agriculture since he became a medical student.

"Much better!" said Mrs. Jo emphatically. "I'd rather send my boys off to see the world in that way than leave them alone in a city full of temptations, with nothing to do but waste time, money, and health, as so many are left. Dan has to work his way, and that teaches him courage, patience, and self-reliance. I don't worry about him as much as I do about George and Dolly at college, no more fit than two babies to take care of themselves."

"How about John? He's knocking round town as a newspaper man, reporting all sorts of things, from sermons to prize-fights," asked Tom, who thought that sort of life would be much more to his own taste than medical lectures and hospital wards.

"Demi has three safeguards—good principles, refined tastes, and a wise mother. He won't come to harm, and these experiences will be useful to him when he begins to write, as I'm sure he will in time," began Mrs. Jo in her prophetic tone; for she was anxious to have some of her geese turn out swans.

"Speak of Jenkins, and you'll hear the rustling of his paper," cried Tom, as a fresh-faced, brown-eyed young man came up the avenue, waving a newspaper over his head.

"Here's your *Evening Tattler!* Latest Edition! Awful murder! Bank clerk absconded! Powder-mill explosion, and great strike of the Latin School boys!" roared Ted, going to meet his cousin with the graceful gait of a young giraffe.

"The Commodore is in, and will cut his cable and run before the wind as soon as he can get off," called Demi, with "a nice derangement of nautical epitaphs," as he came up smiling over his good news.

Everyone talked together for a moment, and the paper passed from hand to hand that each eye might rest on the pleasant fact that the *Brenda*, from Hamburg, was safe in port.

"He'll come lurching out by tomorrow with his usual

collection of marine monsters and lively yarns. I saw him, jolly and tarry and brown as a coffee-berry. Had a good run, and hopes to be second mate, as the other chap is laid up with a broken leg," added Demi.

"Wish I had the setting of it," said Nan to herself, with a professional twist of her hand.

"How's Franz?" asked Mrs. Jo.

"He's going to be married! There's news for you. The first of the flock, Aunty, so say good-bye to him. Her name is Ludmilla Heldegard Blumenthal; good family, well-off, pretty, and of course an angel. The dear old boy wants Uncle's consent, and then he will settle down to be a happy and an honest burgher. Long life to him!"

"I'm glad to hear it. I do so like to settle my boys with a good wife and a nice little home. Now, if all is right, I shall feel as if Franz was off my mind," said Mrs. Jo, folding her hands contentedly; for she often felt like a distracted hen with a large brood of mixed chickens and ducks upon her hands.

"So do I," sighed Tom, with a sly glance at Nan. "That's what a fellow needs to keep him steady; and it's the duty of nice girls to marry as soon as possible, isn't it, Demi?"

"If there are enough nice fellows to go round. The female population exceeds the male, you know, especially in New England; which accounts for the high state of culture we are in, perhaps," answered John, who was leaning over his mother's chair, telling his day's experiences in a whisper.

"It is a merciful provision, my dears; for it takes three or four women to get each man into, through, and out of the world. You are costly creatures, boys; and it is well that mothers, sisters, wives, and daughters love their duty and do it so well, or you would perish off the face of the earth," said Mrs. Jo solemnly, as she took up a basket filled with dilapidated hose; for the good Professor was still hard on his socks, and his sons resembled him in that respect.

"Such being the case, there is plenty for the 'superfluous women' to do, in taking care of these helpless men and their families. I see that more clearly every day, and am very glad and grateful that my profession will make me a useful, happy, and independent spinster."

Nan's emphasis on the last word caused Tom to groan, and the rest to laugh.

"I take great pride and solid satisfaction in you, Nan, and hope to see you very successful; for we do need just such helpful women in the world. I sometimes feel as if I'd missed my vocation and ought to have remained single; but my duty seemed to point this way, and I don't regret it," said Mrs. Jo, folding a large and very ragged blue sock to her bosom.

"Neither do I. What should I ever have done without my dearest Mum?" added Ted, with a filial hug which caused both to disappear behind the newspaper in which he had been mercifully absorbed for a few minutes.

"My darling boy, if you would wash your hands semi-occasionally, fond caresses would be less disastrous to my collar. Never mind, my precious touslehead, better grass stains and dirt than no cuddlings at all"; and Mrs. Jo emerged from that brief eclipse looking much refreshed, though her back hair was caught in Ted's buttons and her collar under one ear.

Here Josie, who had been studying her part at the other end of the piazza, suddenly burst forth with a smothered shriek, and gave Juliet's speech in the tomb so effectively that the boys applauded, Daisy shivered, and Nan murmured: "Too much cerebral excitement for one of her age."

"I'm afraid you'll have to make up your mind to it, Meg. That child is a born actress. We never did anything so well, not even the *Witch's Curse*," said Mrs. Jo, casting a bouquet of many-coloured socks at the feet of her flushed and panting niece, when she fell gracefully upon the door-mat.

"It is a sort of judgement upon me for my passion for the stage when a girl. Now I know how dear Marmee felt when I begged to be an actress. I never can consent, and yet I may be obliged to give up my wishes, hopes, and plans again."

There was an accent of reproach in his mother's voice,

which made Demi pick up his sister with a gentle shake, and the stern command to "drop that nonsense in public."

"Drop me, Minion, or I'll give you the *Maniac Bride*, with my best *Ha-ha!*" cried Josie, glaring at him like an offended kitten.

Being set on her feet, she made a splendid courtesy, and dramatically proclaiming, "Mrs. Woffington's carriage waits," swept down the steps and round the corner, trailing Daisy's scarlet shawl majestically behind her.

"Isn't she great fun? I couldn't stop in this dull place if I hadn't that child to make it lively for me. If ever she turns prim, I'm off; so mind how you nip her in the bud," said Teddy, frowning at Demi, who was now writing out shorthand notes on the steps.

"You two are a team, and it takes a strong hand to drive you, but I rather like it. Josie ought to have been my child, and Rob yours, Meg. Then your house would have been all peace and mine all Bedlam. Now I must go and tell Laurie the news. Come with me, Meg, a little stroll will do us good"; and sticking Ted's straw hat on her head, Mrs. Jo walked off with her sister, leaving Daisy to attend to the muffins, Ted to appease Josie, and Tom and Nan to give their respective patients a very bad quarter of an hour.

Chapter 2

Parnassus

IT WAS well named; and the Muses seemed to be at home that day, for as the newcomers went up the slope appropriate sights and sounds greeted them. Passing an open window, they looked in upon a library presided over by Clio, Calliope, and Urania; Melpomene and Thalia were disporting themselves in the hall, where some young people were dancing and rehearsing a play; Erato was walking in the garden with her lover, and in the music-room Phoebus himself was drilling a tuneful choir.

A mature Apollo was our old friend Laurie, but comely and genial as ever; for time had ripened the freakish boy into a noble man. Care and sorrow, as well as ease and happiness, had done much for him; and the responsibility of carrying out his grandfather's wishes had been a duty most faithfully performed. Prosperity suits some people, and they blossom best in a glow of sunshine; others need the shade, and are the sweeter for a touch of frost. Laurie was one of the former sort, and Amy was another; so life had been a kind of poem to them since they married—not only harmonious and happy, but earnest, useful, and rich in the beautiful benevolence which can do so much when wealth and wisdom go hand in hand with charity.

Their house was full of unostentatious beauty and comfort, and here the art-loving host and hostess attracted and entertained artists of all kinds. Laurie had music enough now, and was a generous patron to the class he most liked to help. Amy had her protégés among ambitious young painters and sculptors, and found her own art double dear as her daughter grew old enough to share its labours and delights with her; for she was one of those who prove that

women can be faithful wives and mothers without sacrific-
ing the special gift bestowed upon them for their own
development and the good of others.

Her sisters knew where to find her, and Jo went at once
to the studio, where mother and daughter worked together. Bess was busy with the bust of a little child, while
her mother added the last touches to a fine head of her
husband. Time seemed to have stood still with Amy, for
happiness had kept her young and prosperity given her
the culture she needed. A stately, graceful woman, who
showed how elegant simplicity could be made by the taste
with which she chose her dress and the grace with which
she wore it. As someone said: "I never know what Mrs.
Laurence has on, but I always receive the impression that
she is the best-dressed lady in the room."

It was evident that she adored her daughter, and well
she might; for the beauty she had longed for seemed, to
her fond eyes at least, to be impersonated in this younger
self. Bess inherited her mother's Diana-like figure, blue
eyes, fair skin, and golden hair, tied up in the same classic
knot of curls. Also—ah! never-ending source of joy to
Amy—she had her father's handsome nose and mouth,
cast in a feminine mould. The severe simplicity of a long
linen pinafore suited her; and she worked away with the
entire absorption of the true artist, unconscious of the loving eyes upon her, till Aunt Jo came in exclaiming eagerly:
"My dear girls, stop your mud-pies and hear the news!"

Both artists dropped their tools and greeted the irrepressible woman cordially, though genius had been burning splendidly and her coming spoilt a precious hour.
They were in the full tide of gossip when Laurie, who had
been summoned by Meg, arrived, and sitting down between the sisters, with no barricade anywhere, listened
with interest to the news of Franz and Emil.

"The epidemic has broke out, and now it will rage and
ravage your flock. Be prepared for every sort of romance
and rashness for the next ten years, Jo. Your boys are
growing up and will plunge headlong into a sea of worse
scrapes than any you have had yet," said Laurie, enjoying
her look of mingled delight and despair.

"I know it, and I hope I shall be able to pull them

through and land them safely; but it's an awful responsibility, for they *will* come to me and insist that I can make their poor little loves run smoothly. I like it, though, and Meg is such a mush of sentiment she revels in the prospect," answered Jo, feeling pretty easy about her own boys, whose youth made them safe for the present.

"I'm afraid she won't revel when our Nat begins to buzz too near her Daisy. Of course you see what all that means? As musical director I am also his confidante, and would like to know what advice to give," said Laurie soberly.

"Hush! you forget that child," began Jo, nodding towards Bess, who was at work again.

"Bless you! she's in Athens, and doesn't hear a word. She ought to leave off, though, and go out. My darling, put the baby to sleep, and go for a run. Aunt Meg is in the parlour; go and show her the new pictures till we come," added Laurie, looking at his tall girl as Pygmalion might have looked at Galatea; for he considered her the finest statue in the house.

"Yes, papa; but please tell me if it is good"; and Bess obediently put down her tools, with a lingering glance at the bust.

"My cherished daughter, truth compels me to confess that one cheek is plumper than the other; and the curls upon its infant brow are rather too much like horns for perfect grace; otherwise it rivals Raphael's Chanting Cherubs, and I'm proud of it."

Laurie was laughing as he spoke; for these first attempts were so like Amy's early ones, it was impossible to regard them as soberly as the enthusiastic mamma did.

"You can't see beauty in anything but music," answered Bess, shaking the golden head that made the one bright spot in the cool north lights of the great studio.

"Well, I see beauty in you, dear. And if you are not art, what is? I wish to put a little more nature into you, and get you away from this cold clay and marble into the sunshine, to dance and laugh as the others do. I want a flesh-and-blood girl, not a sweet statue in a grey pinafore, who forgets everything but her work."

As he spoke two dusty hands came round his neck, and

Bess said earnestly, punctuating her words with soft touches
of her lips:

"I never forget *you*, papa; but I do want to do something beautiful that you may be proud of me by and by.
Mamma often tells me to stop; but when we get in here
we forget there is any world outside, we are so busy and
so happy. Now I'll go and run and sing, and be a girl to
please you." And throwing away the apron, Bess vanished
from the room, seeming to take all the light with her.

"I'm glad you said that. The dear child *is* too much
absorbed in her artistic dreams for one so young. It is my
fault; but I sympathize so deeply in it all, I forget to be
wise," sighed Amy, carefully covering the baby with a wet
towel.

"I think this power of living in our children is one of the
sweetest things in the world; but I try to remember what
Marmee once said to Meg—that fathers should have their
share in the education of both girls and boys; so I leave
Ted to his father all I can, and Fritz lends me Rob, whose
quiet ways are as restful and good for me as Ted's tem-
pests are for his father. Now I advise you, Amy, to let
Bess drop the mud-pies for a time, and take up music with
Laurie; then she won't be one-sided, and he won't be
jealous."

"Hear, hear! A Daniel—a very Daniel!" cried Laurie,
well pleased. "I thought you'd lend a hand, Jo, and say a
word for me. I *am* a little jealous of Amy, and want more
of a share in my girl. Come, my lady, let me have her this
summer, and next year, when we go to Rome, I'll give her
up to you and high art. Isn't that a fair bargain?"

"I agree; but in trying your hobby, nature, with music
thrown in, don't forget that, though only fifteen, our Bess
is older than most girls of that age, and cannot be treated
like a child. She is so very precious to me, I feel as if I
wanted to keep her always as pure and beautiful as the
marble she loves so well."

Amy spoke regretfully as she looked about the lovely
room where she had spent so many happy hours with this
dear child of hers.

" 'Turn and turn about is fair play,' as we used to say
when we all wanted to ride on Ellen Tree or wear the

russet boots," said Jo briskly; "so you must share your girl between you, and see who will do the most for her."

"We will," answered the fond parents, laughing at the recollections Jo's proverb brought up to them.

"How I did use to enjoy bouncing on the limbs of that old apple-tree! No real horse ever gave me half the pleasure or the exercise," said Amy, looking out of the high window as if she saw the dear old orchard again and the little girls at play there.

"And what fun I had with those blessed boots!" laughed Jo. "I've got the relics now. The boys reduced them to rags; but I love them still, and would enjoy a good theatrical stalk in them if it were possible."

"My fondest memories twine about the warming-pan and the sausage. What larks we had! And how long ago it seems!" said Laurie, staring at the two women before him as if he found it hard to realize that they ever had been little Amy and riotous Jo.

"Don't suggest that we are growing old, my Lord. We have only bloomed; and a very nice bouquet we make with our buds about us," answered Mrs. Amy, shaking out the folds of her rosy muslin with much the air of dainty satisfaction the girl used to show in a new dress.

"Not to mention our thorns and dead leaves," added Jo, with a sigh; for life had never been very easy to her, and even now she had her troubles both within and without.

"Come and have a dish of tea, old dear, and see what the young folks are about. You are tired, and want to be 'stayed with flagons and comforted with apples,'" said Laurie, offering an arm to each sister, and leading them away to afternoon tea, which flowed as freely on Parnassus as the nectar of old.

They found Meg in the summer-parlour, an airy and delightful room, full now of afternoon sunshine and the rustle of trees; for the three long windows opened on the garden. The great music-room was at one end, and at the other, in a deep alcove hung with purple curtains, a little household shrine had been made. Three portraits hung there, two marble busts stood in the corners, and a couch, an oval table, with its urn of flowers, were the only articles of furniture the nook contained. The busts were John

Brooke and Beth—Amy's work—both excellent likenesses, and both full of the placid beauty which always recalls the saying, that "Clay represents life; plaster, death; marble, immortality." On the right, as became the founder of the house, hung the portrait of Mr. Laurence, with its expression of mingled pride and benevolence, as fresh and attractive as when he caught the girl Jo admiring it. Opposite was Aunt March—a legacy to Amy—in an imposing turban, immense sleeves, and long mittens decorously crossed on the front of her plum-coloured satin gown. Time had mellowed the severity of her aspect; and the fixed regard of the handsome old gentleman opposite seemed to account for the amiable simper on lips that had not uttered a sharp word for years.

In the place of honour, with the sunshine warm upon it, and a green garland always round it, was Marmee's beloved face, painted with grateful skill by a great artist whom she had befriended when poor and unknown. So beautifully lifelike was it that it seemed to smile down upon her daughters, saying cheerfully: "Be happy; I am with you still."

The three sisters stood a moment looking up at the beloved picture with eyes full of tender reverence and the longing that never left them; for this noble mother had been so much to them that no one could ever fill her place. Only two years since she had gone away to live and love anew, leaving such a sweet memory behind her that it was both an inspiration and a comforter to all the household. They felt this as they drew closer to one another, and Laurie put it into words as he said earnestly:

"I can ask nothing better for my child than that she may be a woman like our mother. Please God, she shall be, if I can do it; for I owe the best I have to this dear saint."

Just then a fresh voice began to sing "Ave Maria" in the music-room, and Bess unconsciously echoed her father's prayer for her as she dutifully obeyed his wishes. The soft sound of the air Marmee used to sing led the listeners back into the world again from that momentary reaching after the loved and lost, and they sat down together near the open windows enjoying the music, while Laurie brought

them tea, making the little service pleasant by the tender
care he gave to it.

Nat came in with Demi, soon followed by Ted and
Josie, the Professor and his faithful Rob, all anxious to
hear more about "the boys." The rattle of cups and tongues
grew brisk, and the setting sun saw a cheerful company
resting in the bright room after the varied labours of the
day.

Professor Bhaer was grey now, but robust and genial as
ever; for he had the work he loved, and did it so heartily
that the whole college felt his beautiful influence. Rob was
as much like him as it was possible for a boy to be, and
was already called the "young Professor," he so adored
study and closely imitated his honoured father in all ways.

"Well, heart's dearest, we go to have our boys again, all
two, and may rejoice greatly," said Mr. Bhaer, seating
himself beside Jo with a beaming face and a handshake of
congratulation.

"Oh, Fritz, I'm so delighted about Emil, and if you
approve about Franz also. Did you know Ludmilla? Is it a
wise match?" asked Mrs. Jo, handing him her cup of tea
and drawing closer, as if she welcomed her refuge in joy as
well as sorrow.

"It all goes well. I saw the *Mädchen* when I went over
to place Franz. A child then, but most sweet and charming. Blumenthal is satisfied, I think, and the boy will be
happy. He is too German to be content away from
Vaterland, so we shall have him as a link between the new
and the old, and that pleases me much."

"And Emil, he is to be second mate next voyage; isn't
that fine? I'm so happy that both *your* boys have done
well; you gave up so much for them and their mother. You
make light of it, dear, but I never forget it," said Jo, with
her hand in his as sentimentally as if she was a girl again
and her Fritz had come a-wooing.

He laughed his cheery laugh, and whispered behind her
fan: "If I had not come to America for the poor lads, I
never should have found my Jo. The hard times are very
sweet now, and I bless Gott for all I seemed to lose,
because I gained the blessing of my life."

"Spooning! spooning! Here's an awful flirtation on the

sly," cried Teddy, peering over the fan just at that interesting moment, much to his mother's confusion and his
father's amusement; for the Professor never was ashamed
of the fact that he still considered his wife the dearest
woman in the world. Rob promptly ejected his brother
from one window, to see him skip in at the other, while
Mrs. Jo shut her fan and held it ready to rap her unruly
boy's knuckles if he came near her again.

Nat approached in answer to Mr. Bhaer's beckoning
teaspoon, and stood before them with a face full of the
respectful affection he felt for the excellent man who had
done so much for him.

"I have the letters ready for thee, my son. They are two
old friends of mine in Leipzig, who will befriend thee in
that new life. It is well to have them, for thou wilt be
heartbroken with *Heimweh* at the first, Nat, and need
comforting," said the professor, giving him several letters.

"Thanks, sir. Yes, I expect to be pretty lonely till I get
started, then my music and the hope of getting on will
cheer me up," answered Nat, who both longed and dreaded
to leave all these friends behind him and make new ones.

He was a man now; but the blue eyes were as honest as
ever, the mouth still a little weak, in spite of the carefully
cherished moustache over it, and the broad forehead more
plainly than ever betrayed the music-loving nature of the
youth. Modest, affectionate, and dutiful, Nat was considered a pleasant though not a brilliant success by Mrs. Jo.
She loved and trusted him, and was sure he would do his
best, but did not expect that he would be great in any
way, unless the stimulus of foreign training and self-
dependence made him a better artist and a stronger man
than now seemed likely.

"I've marked all your things—or rather, Daisy did—and
as soon as your books are collected, we can see about the
packing," said Mrs. Jo, who was so used to fitting boys off
for all quarters of the globe that a trip to the North Pole
would not have been too much for her.

Nat grew red at mention of that name—or was it the last
glow of sunset on his rather pale cheek?—and his heart
beat happily at the thought of the dear girl working Ns
and Bs on his humble socks and handkerchiefs; for Nat

adored Daisy, and the cherished dream of his life was to earn a place for himself as a musician and win this angel for his wife. This hope did more for him than the Professor's counsels, Mrs. Jo's care, or Mr. Laurie's generous help. For her sake he worked, waited, and hoped, finding courage and patience in the dream of that happy future when Daisy should make a little home for him and he fiddle a fortune into her lap.

Mrs. Jo knew this; and though he was not exactly the man she would have chosen for her niece, she felt that Nat would always need just the wise and loving care Daisy could give him, and that without it there was danger of his being one of the amiable and aimless men who fail for want of the right pilot to steer them safely through the world. Mrs. Meg decidedly frowned upon the poor boy's love, and would not hear of giving her dear girl to any but the best man to be found on the face of the earth. She was very kind, but as firm as such gentle souls can be; and Nat fled for comfort to Mrs. Jo, who always espoused the interests of her boys heartily. A new set of anxieties was beginning now that the aforesaid boys were growing up, and she foresaw no end of worry as well as amusement in the love-affairs already budding in her flock. Mrs. Meg was usually her best ally and adviser, for she loved romances as well now as when a blooming girl herself. But in this case she hardened her heart, and would not hear a word of entreaty. "Nat was not man enough, never would be, no one knew his family, a musician's life was a hard one; Daisy was too young, five or six years hence when time had proved both perhaps. Let us see what absence will do for him." And that was the end of it, for when the maternal Pelican was roused she could be very firm, though for her precious children she would have plucked her last feather and given the last drop of her blood.

Mrs. Jo was thinking of this as she looked at Nat while he talked with her husband about Leipzig, and she resolved to have a clear understanding with him before he went; for she was used to confidences, and talked freely with her boys about the trials and temptations that beset all lives in the beginning, and so often mar them, for want of the right word at the right moment.

This is the first duty of parents, and no false delicacy should keep them from the watchful care, the gentle warning, which makes self-knowledge and self-control the compass and pilot of the young as they leave the safe harbour of home.

"Plato and his disciples approach," announced irreverent Teddy, as Mr. March came in with several young men and women about him; for the wise old man was universally beloved, and ministered so beautifully to his flock that many of them thanked him all their lives for the help given to both hearts and souls.

Bess went to him at once; for since Marmee died, Grandpapa was her special care, and it was sweet to see the golden head bend over the silver one as she rolled out his easy-chair and waited on him with tender alacrity.

"Aesthetic tea always on tap here, sir; will you have a flowing bowl or a bit of ambrosia?" asked Laurie, who was wandering about with a sugar-basin in one hand and a plate of cake in the other; for sweetening cups and feeding the hungry was work he loved.

"Neither, thanks; this child has taken care of me"; and Mr. March turned to Bess, who sat on one arm of his chair, holding a glass of fresh milk.

"Long may she live to do it, sir, and I be here to see this pretty contradiction of the song that 'youth and age cannot live together'!" answered Laurie, smiling at the pair.

" 'Crabbed age,' papa; that makes all the difference in the world," said Bess quickly; for she loved poetry, and read the best.

> "Wouldst thou see fresh roses grow
> In a reverend bed of snow?"

quoted Mr. March, as Josie came and perched on the other arm, looking like a very thorny little rose; for she had been having a hot discussion with Ted, and had got the worst of it.

"Grandpa, must women always obey men and say they are the wisest, just because they are the strongest?" she cried, looking fiercely at her cousin, who came stalking up with a provoking smile on the boyish face that was always very comical atop of that tall figure.

"Well, my dear, that is the old-fashioned belief, and it will take some time to change it. But I think the woman's hour has struck; and it looks to me as if the boys must do their best, for the girls are abreast now, and may reach the goal first," answered Mr. March, surveying with paternal satisfaction the bright faces of the young women, who were among the best students in the college.

"The poor little Atalantas are sadly distracted and delayed by the obstacles thrown in their way—not golden apples, by any means—but I think they will stand a fair chance when they have learned to run better," laughed Uncle Laurie, stroking Josie's breezy hair, which stood up like the fur of an angry kitten.

"Whole barrels of apples won't stop me when *I* start, and a dozen Teds won't trip me up, though they may try. I'll show him that a woman can act as well, if not better, than a man. It *has* been done, and will be again; and I'll never own that *my* brain isn't as good as his, though it may be smaller," cried the excited young person.

"If you shake your head in that violent way you'll addle what brains you have got; and I'd take care of 'em, if I were you," began teasing Ted.

"What started this civil war?" asked Grandpapa, with a gentle emphasis on the adjective, which caused the combatants to calm their ardour a little.

"Why, we were pegging away at the Iliad and came to where Zeus tells Juno not to inquire into his plans or he'll whip her, and Jo was disgusted because Juno meekly hushed up. I said it was all right, and agreed with the old fellow that women didn't know much and ought to obey men," explained Ted, to the great amusement of his hearers.

"Goddesses may do as they like, but those Greek and Trojan women were poor-spirited things if they minded men who couldn't fight their own battles and had to be hustled off by Pallas, and Venus, and Juno, when they were going to get beaten. The idea of two armies stopping and sitting down while a pair of heroes flung stones at one another! I don't think much of your old Homer. Give me Napoleon or Grant for my hero."

Josie's scorn was as funny as it a hummingbird scolded at an ostrich, and everyone laughed as she sniffed at the immortal poet and criticized the gods.

"Napoleon's Juno had a nice time; didn't she? That's just the way girls argue—first one way and then the other," jeered Ted.

"Like Johnson's young lady, who was 'not categorical, but all wiggle-waggle,' " added Uncle Laurie, enjoying the battle immensely.

"I was only speaking of them as soldiers. But if you come to the woman side of it, wasn't Grant a kind husband and Mrs. Grant a happy woman? He didn't threaten to whip her if she asked a natural question; and if Napoleon did do wrong about Josephine, he could fight, and didn't want any Minerva to come fussing over him. They *were* a stupid set, from dandified Paris to Achilles sulking in his ships, and I won't change my opinion for all the Hectors and Agamemnons in Greece," said Josie, still unconquered.

"You can fight like a Trojan, that's evident; and we will be the two obedient armies looking on while you and Ted have it out," began Uncle Laurie, assuming the attitude of a warrior leaning on his spear.

"I fear we must give it up, for Pallas is about to descend and carry off our Hector," said Mr. March, smiling, as Jo came to remind her son that suppertime was near.

"We will fight it out later when there are no goddesses to interfere," said Teddy, as he turned away with unusual alacrity, remembering the treat in store.

"Conquered by a muffin, by Jove!" called Josie after him, exulting in an opportunity to use the classical exclamation forbidden to her sex.

But Ted shot a Parthian arrow as he retired in good order by replying, with a highly virtuous expression: "Obedience is a soldier's first duty."

Bent on her woman's privilege of having the last word, Josie ran after him, but never uttered the scathing speech upon her lips, for a very brown young man in a blue suit came leaping up the steps with a cheery "Ahoy! ahoy! where is everybody?"

"Emil! Emil!" cried Josie, and in a moment Ted was

upon him, and the late enemies ended their fray in a joyful welcome to the newcomer.

Muffins were forgotten, and towing their cousin like two fussy little tugs with a fine merchantman, the children returned to the parlour, where Emil kissed all the women and shook hands with all the men except his uncle; him he embraced in the good old German style, to the great delight of the observers.

"Didn't think I could get off today, but found I could, and steered straight for old Plum. Not a soul there, so I luffed and bore away for Parnassus, and here is every man Jack of you. Bless your hearts, how glad I am to see you all!" exclaimed the sailor boy, beaming at them, as he stood with his legs apart as if he still felt the rocking deck under his feet.

"You ought to 'shiver your timbers,' not 'bless our hearts,' Emil; it's not nautical at all. Oh, how nice and shippy and tarry you do smell!" said Josie, sniffing at him with great enjoyment of the fresh sea odours he brought with him. This was her favourite cousin, and she was his pet; so she knew that the bulging pockets of the blue jacket contained treasures for her at least.

"Avast, my hearty, and let me take soundings before you dive," laughed Emil, understanding her affectionate caresses, and holding her off with one hand while with the other he rummaged out sundry foreign little boxes and parcels marked with different names, and handed them round with appropriate remarks, which caused much laughter; for Emil was a wag.

"There's a hawser that will hold our little cock-boat still about five minutes," he said, throwing a necklace of pretty pink coral over Josie's head; "and here's something the mermaids sent to Undine," he added, handing Bess a string of pearly shells on a silver chain. "I thought Daisy would like a fiddle, and Nat can find her a *beau*," continued the sailor, with a laugh, as he undid a dainty filigree brooch in the shape of a violin.

"I know she will, and I'll take it to her," answered Nat, as he vanished, glad of an errand, and sure that *he* could find Daisy though Emil had missed her.

Emil chuckled, and handed out a quaintly carved bear

whose head opened, showing a capacious ink-stand. This he presented, with a scrape, to Aunt Jo.

"Knowing your fondness for these fine animals, I brought this one to your pen."

"Very good, Commodore! Try again," said Mrs. Jo, much pleased with her gift, which caused the Professor to prophesy "works of Shakespeare" from its depths, so great would be the inspiration of the beloved bruin.

"As Aunt Meg *will* wear caps, in spite of her youth, I got Ludmilla to get me some bits of lace. Hope you'll like 'em"; and out of a soft paper came some filmy things, one of which soon lay like a net of snowflakes on Mrs. Meg's pretty hair.

"I couldn't find anything swell enough for Aunt Amy, because she has everything she wants, so I brought a little picture that always makes me think of her when Bess was a baby"; and he handed her an oval ivory locket, on which was painted a golden-haired Madonna, with a rosy child folded in her blue mantle.

"How lovely!" cried everyone; and Aunt Amy at once hung it about her neck on the blue ribbon from Bess's hair, charmed with her gift; for it recalled the happiest year of her life.

"Now, I flatter myself I've got just the thing for Nan, neat but not gaudy, a sort of sign you see, and very appropriate for a doctor," said Emil, proudly displaying a pair of lava earrings shaped like little skulls.

"Horrid!" And Bess, who hated ugly things, turned her eyes to her own pretty shells.

"She won't wear earrings," said Josie.

"Well, she'll enjoy punching your ears then. She's never so happy as when she's overhauling her fellow creatures and going for 'em with a knife," answered Emil, undisturbed. "I've got a lot of plunder for you fellows in my chest, but I knew I should have no peace till my cargo for the girls was unloaded. Now tell me all the news." And, seated on Amy's best marble-topped table, the sailor swung his legs and talked at the rate of ten knots an hour, till Aunt Jo carried them all off to a grand family tea in honour of the Commodore.

Chapter 3

Jo's Last Scrape

THE MARCH FAMILY had enjoyed a great many surprises in the course of their varied career, but the greatest of all was when the Ugly Duckling turned out to be, not a swan, but a golden goose, whose literary eggs found such an unexpected market that in ten years Jo's wildest and most cherished dream actually came true. How or why it happened she never clearly understood, but all of a sudden she found herself famous in a small way, and, better still, with a snug little fortune in her pocket to clear away the obstacles of the present and assure the future of her boys.

It began during a bad year when everything went wrong at Plumfield; times were hard, the school dwindled, Jo overworked herself and had a long illness; Laurie and Amy were abroad, and the Bhaers too proud to ask help even of those as near and dear as this generous pair. Confined to her room, Jo got desperate over the state of affairs, till she fell back upon the long-disused pen as the only thing she could do to help fill up the gaps in the income. A book for girls being wanted by a certain publisher, she hastily scribbled a little story describing a few scenes and adventures in the lives of herself and sisters—though boys were more in her line—and with very slight hopes of success sent it out to seek its fortune.

Things always went by contraries with Jo. Her first book, laboured over for years, and launched full of the high hopes and ambitious dreams of youth, foundered on its voyage, though the wreck continued to float long afterward, to the profit of the publisher at least. The hastily written story, sent away with no thought beyond the few

dollars it might bring, sailed with a fair wind and a wise
pilot at the helm into public favour, and came home
heavily laden with an unexpected cargo of gold and glory.

A more astonished woman probably never existed than
Josephine Bhaer when her little ship came into port with
flags flying, cannon that had been silent before now boom-
ing gaily, and, better than all, many kind faces rejoicing
with her, many friendly hands grasping hers with cordial
congratulations. After that it was plain sailing, and she
merely had to load her ships and send them off on prosperous trips, to bring home stores of comfort for all she
loved and laboured for.

The fame she never did quite accept; for it takes very
little fire to make a great deal of smoke nowadays, and
notoriety is not real glory. The fortune she could not
doubt, and gratefully received; though it was not half so
large a one as a generous world reported it to be. The tide
having turned continued to rise, and floated the family
comfortably into a snug harbour where the older members
could rest secure from storms, and whence the younger
ones could launch their boats for the voyage of life.

All manner of happiness, peace, and plenty came in
those years to bless the patient waiters, hopeful workers,
and devout believers in the wisdom and justice of Him
who sends disappointment, poverty, and sorrow to try the
love of human hearts and make success the sweeter when
it comes. The world saw the prosperity, and kind souls
rejoiced over the improved fortunes of the family; but the
success Jo valued most, the happiness that nothing could
change or take away, few knew much about.

It was the power of making her mother's last years
happy and serene; to see the burden of care laid down for
ever, the weary hands at rest, the dear face untroubled by
any anxiety, and the tender heart free to pour itself out in
the wise charity which was its delight. As a girl, Jo's
favourite plan had been a room where Marmee could sit in
peace and enjoy herself after her hard, heroic life. Now
the dream had become a happy fact, and Marmee sat in
her pleasant chamber with every comfort and luxury about
her, loving daughters to wait on her as infirmities increased, a faithful mate to lean upon, and grandchildren to

brighten the twilight of life with their dutiful affection. A very precious time to all, for she rejoiced as only mothers can in the good fortunes of their children. She had lived to reap the harvest she sowed; had seen prayers answered, hopes blossom, good gifts bear fruit, peace and prosperity bless the home she had made; and then, like some brave, patient angel, whose work was done, turned her face heavenward, glad to rest.

This was the sweet and sacred side of the change; but it had its droll and thorny one, as all things have in this curious world of ours. After the first surprise, incredulity, and joy, which came to Jo, with the ingratitude of human nature, she soon tired of renown, and began to resent her loss of liberty. For suddenly the admiring public took possession of her and all her affairs, past, present, and to come. Strangers demanded to look at her, question, advise, warn, congratulate, and drive her out of her wits by well-meant but very wearisome attentions. If she declined to open her heart to them, they reproached her; if she refused to endow her pet charities, relieve private wants, or sympathize with every ill and trial known to humanity, she was called hard-hearted, selfish, and haughty; if she found it impossible to answer the piles of letters sent her, she was neglectful of her duty to the admiring public; and if she preferred the privacy of home to the pedestal upon which she was requested to pose, "the airs of literary people" were freely criticized.

She did her best for the children, they being the public for whom she wrote, and laboured stoutly to supply the demand always in the mouths of voracious youth—"More stories; more right away!" Her family objected to this devotion at their expense, and her health suffered; but for a time she gratefully offered herself up on the altar of juvenile literature, feeling that she owed a good deal to the little friends in whose sight she had found favour after twenty years of effort.

But a time came when her patience gave out; and wearying of being a lion, she became a bear in nature as in name, and returning to her den, growled awfully when ordered out. Her family enjoyed the fun, and had small sympathy with her trials, but Jo came to consider it the worse scrape of her life; for liberty had always been her dearest possession, and it seemed to be fast going from her. Living in a lantern soon loses its charm, and she was too old, too tired, and too busy to like it. She felt that she had done all that could reasonably be required of her when autographs, photographs, and autobiographical sketches had been sown broadcast over the land; when artists had taken her home in all its aspects, and reporters had taken her in the grim one she always assumed on these trying occasions; when a series of enthusiastic boarding-schools had ravaged her grounds for trophies, and a steady stream of amiable pilgrims had worn her doorsteps with their respectful feet; when servants left after a week's trial of the bell that rang all day; when her husband was forced to guard her at meals, and the boys to cover her retreat out of back windows on certain occasions when enterprising guests walked in unannounced at unfortunate moments.

A sketch of one day may perhaps explain the state of things, offer some excuse for the unhappy woman, and give a hint to the autograph-fiend now rampant in the land; for it is a true tale.

"There ought to be a law to protect unfortunate authors," said Mrs. Jo one morning soon after Emil's arrival, when the mail brought her an unusually large and varied assortment of letters. "To me it is a more vital subject than international copyright; for time is money, peace is health, and I lose both with no return but less respect for my fellow creatures and a wild desire to fly into the wilderness, since I cannot shut my doors even in free America."

"Lion-hunters are awful when in search of their prey. If they could change places for a while it would do them good; and they'd see what bores they were when they 'do themselves the honour of calling to express their admiration of our charming work,'" quoted Ted, with a bow to his parent, now frowning over twelve requests for autographs.

"I have made up my mind on one point," said Mrs. Jo with great firmness. "I will *not* answer this kind of letter. I've sent at least six to this boy, and he probably sells them. This girl writes from a seminary, and if I send her one all the other girls will at once write for more. All begin by saying they know they intrude, and that I am of course annoyed by these requests; but they venture to ask because I like boys, or they like the books, or it is only one. Emerson and Whittier put these things in the waste-paper-basket; and though only a literary nursery-maid who provides moral pap for the young, I will follow their illustrious example; for I shall have no time to eat or sleep if I try to satisfy these dear unreasonable children"; and Mrs. Jo swept away the entire batch with a sigh of relief.

"I'll open the others and let you eat your breakfast in peace, *liebe Mutter*," said Rob, who often acted as her secretary. "Here's one from the South"; and breaking an imposing seal, he read:

"MADAM. As it has pleased Heaven to bless your efforts with a large fortune, I feel no hesitation in asking you to supply funds to purchase a new communion-service for our church. To whatever denomination you belong, you will of course respond with liberality to such a request,

"Respectfully yours,
"MRS X. Y. ZAVIER"

"Send a civil refusal, dear. All I have to give must go to feed and clothe the poor at my gates. That is my thank-offering for success. Go on," answered his mother, with a grateful glance about her happy home.

"A literary youth of eighteen proposes that you put your name to a novel he has written, and after the first edition your name is to be taken off and his put on. There's a cool proposal for you. I guess you won't agree to that, in spite of your soft-heartedness towards most of the young scribblers."

"Couldn't be done. Tell him so kindly, and don't let him send the manuscript. I have seven on hand now, and barely time to read my own," said Mrs. Jo, pensively fishing a small letter out of the slop-bowl and opening it

with care, because the down-hill address suggested that a
child wrote it.

"I will answer this myself. A little sick girl wants a book,
and she shall have it, but I can't write sequels to all the
rest to please her. I should never come to an end if I tried
to suit these voracious little Oliver Twists, clamouring for
more. What next, Robin?"

"This is short and sweet.

"DEAR MRS. BHAER, I am now going to give you my
opinion of your works. I have read them all many
times, and call them first-rate. Please go ahead.
                              "Your admirer,
                                    "BILLY BABCOCK"

"Now that is what I like. Billy is a man of sense and a
critic worth having, since he had read my works many
times before expressing his opinion. He asks for no answer, so send my thanks and regards."

"Here's a lady in England with seven girls, and she
wishes to know your views upon education. Also what
careers they shall follow—the oldest being twelve. Don't
wonder she's worried," laughed Rob.

"I'll try to answer it. But as I have no girls, my opinion
isn't worth much and will probably shock her, as I shall
tell her to let them run and play and build up good, stout
bodies before she talks about careers. They will soon show
what they want, if they are let alone, and not all run in the
same mould."

"Here's a fellow who wants to know what sort of a girl
he shall marry, and if you know of any like those in your
stories."

"Give him Nan's address, and see what he'll get,"
proposed Ted, privately resolving to do it himself if
possible.

"This is from a lady who wants you to adopt her child
and lend her money to study art abroad for a few years.
Better take it, and try your hand at a girl, mother."

"No, thank you, I will keep to my own line of business.
What is that blotted one? It looks rather awful, to judge by
the ink," asked Mrs. Jo, who beguiled her daily task by

trying to guess from the outside what was inside her many letters. This proved to be a poem from an insane admirer, to judge by its incoherent style.

"TO J.M.B.

"Oh, were I a heliotrope,
   I would play poet,
And blow a breeze of fragrance
   To you; and none should know it.

"Your form like the stately elm
   When Phoebus gilds the morning ray;
Your cheeks like the ocean bed
   That blooms a rose in May.

"Your words are wise and bright,
   I bequeath them to you a legacy given;
And when your spirit takes its flight,
   May it bloom a flower in heaven.

"My tongue in flattering language spoke,
   And sweeter silence never broke
In busiest street or loneliest glen.
   I take you with the flashes of my pen.

"Consider the lilies, how they grow;
   They toil not, yet are fair,
Gems and flowers and Solomon's seal.
   The geranium of the world is J.M. Bhaer.
                        "James"

While the boys shouted over this effusion—which is a true one—their mother read several liberal offers from budding magazines for her to edit them gratis; one long letter from a young girl inconsolable because her favourite hero died, and "would dear Mrs. Bhaer rewrite the tale, and make it end good?" another from an irate boy denied an autograph, who darkly foretold financial ruin and loss of favour if she did not send him and all other fellows who asked autographs, photographs, and autobiographical sketches; a minister wished to know her religion; and an undecided maiden asked which of her two lovers she should marry. These samples will suffice to show a few of the claims made on a busy woman's time, and make my readers pardon Mrs. Jo if she did not carefully reply to all.

"That job is done. Now I will dust a bit, and then go to my work. I'm all behind-hand, and serials can't wait; so deny me to everybody, Mary. I won't see Queen Victoria if she comes today." And Mrs. Bhaer threw down her napkin as if defying all creation.

"I hope the day will go well with thee, my dearest," answered her husband, who had been busy with his own voluminous correspondence. "I will dine at college with Professor Plock, who is to visit us today. The *Jünglings* can lunch on Parnassus; so thou shalt have a quiet time." And smoothing the worried lines out of her forehead with his good-bye kiss, the excellent man marched away, both pockets full of books, an old umbrella in one hand, and a bag of stones for the geology class in the other.

"If all literary women had such thoughtful angels for husbands, they would live longer and write more. Perhaps that wouldn't be a blessing to the world though, as most of us write too much now," said Mrs. Jo, waving her feather duster to her spouse, who responded with flourishes of the umbrella as he went down the avenue.

Rob started for school at the same time, looking so much like him with his books and bag and square shoulders and steady air that his mother laughed as she turned away, saying heartily: "Bless both my dear professors, for better creatures never lived!"

Emil was already gone to his ship in the city; but Ted lingered to steal the address he wanted, ravage the sugar-bowl, and talk with "Mum"; for the two had great larks together.

Mrs. Jo always arranged her own parlour, refilled her vases, and gave the little touches that left it cool and neat for the day. Going to draw down the curtain, she beheld an artist sketching on the lawn, and groaned as she hastily retired to the back window to shake her duster.

At that moment the bell rang and the sound of wheels was heard in the road.

"I'll go; Mary lets 'em in"; and Ted smoothed his hair as he made for the hall.

"Can't see anyone. Give me a chance to fly upstairs," whispered Mrs. Jo, preparing to escape. But before she could do so, a man appeared at the door with a card in his hand. Ted met him with a stern air, and his mother dodged behind the window-curtains to bide her time for escape.

"I am doing a series of articles for the *Saturday Tattler*, and I called to see Mrs. Bhaer the first of all," began the newcomer in the insinuating tone of his tribe, while his quick eyes were taking in all they could, experience having taught him to make the most of his time, as his visits were usually short ones.

"Mrs. Bhaer never sees reporters, sir."

"But a few moments will be all I ask," said the man, edging his way farther in.

"You can't see her, for she is out," replied Teddy, as a backward glance showed him that his unhappy parent had vanished—through the window, he supposed, as she sometimes did when hard bested.

"Very sorry. I'll call again. Is this her study? Charming room!" And the intruder fell back on the parlour, bound to see something and bag a fact if he died in the attempt.

"It is not," said Teddy, gently but firmly backing him down the hall, devoutly hoping that his mother had escaped round the corner of the house.

"If you could tell me Mrs. Bhaer's age and birthplace, date of marriage, and number of children, I should be much obliged," continued the unabashed visitor as he tripped over the door-mat.

"She is about sixty, born in Nova Zembla, married just forty years ago today, and has eleven daughters. Anything else, sir?" And Ted's sober face was such a funny contrast to his ridiculous reply that the reporter owned himself routed, and retired laughing just as a lady followed by three beaming girls came up the steps.

"We are all the way from Oshkosh, and couldn't go home without seein' dear Aunt Jo. My girls just admire her works, and lot on gettin' a sight of her. I know it's early; but we are goin' to see Holmes and Longfeller, and

the rest of the celebrities, so we ran out here fust thing.
Mrs. Erastus Kingsbury Parmalee, of Oshkosh, tell her.
We don't mind waitin'; we can look round a spell if she
ain't ready to see folks yet."

All this was uttered with such rapidity that Ted could
only stand gazing at the buxom damsels, who fixed their
six blue eyes upon him so beseechingly that his native
gallantry made it impossible to deny them a civil reply at
least.

"Mrs. Bhaer is not visible today—out just now, I believe; but you can see the house and grounds if you like,"
he murmured, falling back as the four pressed in gazing
rapturously about them.

"Oh, thank you! Sweet, pretty place I'm sure! That's
where she writes, ain't it? Do tell me if that's her picture!
Looks just as I imagined her!"

With these remarks the ladies paused before a fine
engraving of the Hon. Mrs. Norton, with a pen in her
hand and a rapt expression of countenance, likewise a
diadem and pearl necklace.

Keeping his gravity with an effort, Teddy pointed to a
very bad portrait of Mrs. Jo, which hung behind the door,
and afforded her much amusement, it was so dismal, in
spite of a curious effect of light upon the end of the nose
and cheeks as red as the chair she sat in.

"This was taken for my mother; but it is not very good,"
he said, enjoying the struggles of the girls not to look
dismayed at the sad difference between the real and the
ideal. The youngest, aged twelve, could not conceal her
disappointment, and turned away, feeling as so many of us
have felt when we discover that our idols are very ordi-
nary men and women.

"I thought she'd be about sixteen and have her hair
braided in two tails down her back. I don't care about
seeing her now," said the honest child, walking off to the
hall door, leaving her mother to apologize, and her sisters
to declare that the bad portrait was "perfectly lovely, so
speaking and poetic, you know, 'specially about the brow."

"Come girls, we must be goin', if we want to get through
today. You can leave your albums and have them sent
when Mrs. Bhaer has written a sentiment in 'em. We are

a thousand times obliged. Give our best love to your ma, and tell her we are so sorry not to see her."

Just as Mrs. Erastus Kingsbury Parmalee uttered the words her eye fell upon a middle-aged woman in a large checked apron, with a handkerchief tied over her head, busily dusting an end room which looked like a study.

"One peep at her sanctum since she is out," cried the enthusiastic lady, and swept across the hall with her flock before Teddy could warn his mother, whose retreat had been cut off by the artist in front, the reporter at the back of the house—for he hadn't gone—and the ladies in the hall.

"They've got her!" thought Teddy, in comical dismay. "No use for her to play housemaid since they've seen the portrait."

Mrs. Jo did her best, and being a good actress, would have escaped if the fatal picture had not betrayed her. Mrs. Parmalee paused at the desk, and regardless of the meerschaum that lay there, the man's slippers close by, and a pile of letters directed to "Prof. F. Bhaer," she clasped her hands, exclaiming impressively: "Girls, this is the spot where she wrote those sweet, those moral tales which have thrilled us to the soul! Could I—ah, could I take one morsel of paper, an old pen, a postage stamp even, as a memento of this gifted woman?"

"Yes'm, help yourselves," replied the maid, moving away with a glance at the boy, whose eyes were now full of merriment he could not suppress.

The oldest girl saw it, guessed the truth, and a quick look at the woman in the apron confirmed her suspicion. Touching her mother, she whispered: "Ma, it's Mrs. Bhaer herself. I know it is."

"No? yes? it is! Well, I do declare, how nice that is!" And hastily pursuing the unhappy woman, who was making for the door, Mrs. Parmalee cried eagerly: "Don't mind us! I know you're busy, but just let me take your hand and then we'll go."

Giving herself up for lost, Mrs. Jo turned and presented her hand like a tea-tray, submitting to have it heartily shaken, as the matron said, with somewhat alarming hospitality:

"If ever you come to Oshkosh, your feet won't be allowed to touch the pavement; for you'll be borne in the arms of the populace, we shall be so dreadful glad to see you."

Mentally resolving never to visit that effusive town, Jo responded as cordially as she could; and having written her name in the albums, provided each visitor with a memento, and kissed them all round, they at last departed, to call on "Longfeller, Holmes, and the rest" —who were all out, it is devoutly to be hoped.

"You villain, why didn't you give me a chance to whip away? Oh, my dear, what fibs you told that man! I hope we shall be forgiven our sins in this line, but I don't know what *is* to become of us if we don't dodge. So many against one isn't fair play." And Mrs. Jo hung up her apron in the hall closet, with a groan at the trials of her lot.

"More people coming up the avenue! Better dodge while the coast is clear! I'll head them off!" cried Teddy, looking back from the steps, as he was departing to school.

Mrs. Jo flew upstairs, and having locked her door, calmly viewed a young ladies' seminary camp on the lawn, and being denied the house, proceed to enjoy themselves by picking the flowers, doing up their hair, eating lunch, and freely expressing their opinion of the place and its possessors before they went.

A few hours of quiet followed, and she was just settling down to a long afternoon of hard work, when Rob came home to tell her that the Young Men's Christian Union would visit the college, and two or three of the fellows whom she knew wanted to pay their respects to her on the way.

"It is going to rain, so they won't come, I dare say; but father thought you'd like to be ready, in case they do call. You always see the boys, you know, though you harden your heart to the poor girls," said Rob, who had heard from his brother about the morning visitations.

"Boys don't gush, so I can stand it. The last time I let in a party of girls one fell into my arms and said, 'Darling, love me!' I wanted to shake her," answered Mrs. Jo, wiping her pen with energy.

"You may be sure the fellows won't do it, but they *will*

want autographs, so you'd better be prepared with a few dozen," said Rob, laying out a quire of note-paper, being a hospitable youth and sympathizing with those who admired his mother.

"They can't outdo the girls. At X College I really believe I wrote three hundred during the day I was there, and I left a pile of cards and albums on my table when I came away. It is one of the most absurd and tiresome manias that ever afflicted the world."

Nevertheless Mrs. Jo wrote her name a dozen times, put on her black silk, and resigned herself to the impending call, praying for rain, however, as she returned to her work.

The shower came, and feeling quite secure, she rumpled up her hair, took off her cuffs, and hurried to finish her chapter; for thirty pages a day was her task, and she liked to have it well done before evening. Josie had brought some flowers for the vases, and was just putting the last touches when she saw several umbrellas bobbing down the hill.

"They are coming, Aunty! I see uncle hurrying across the field to receive them," she called at the stair-foot.

"Keep an eye on them, and let me know when they enter the avenue. It will take but a minute to tidy up and run down," answered Mrs. Jo, scribbling away for dear life, because serials wait for no man, not even the whole Christian Union *en masse*.

"There are more than two or three. I see half a dozen at least," called sister Ann from the hall door. "No! a dozen, I do believe; Aunty, look out; they are all coming! What *shall* we do?" And Josie quailed at the idea of facing the black throng rapidly approaching.

"Mercy on us, there are hundreds! Run and put a tub in the back entry for their umbrellas to drip into. Tell them to go down the hall and leave them, and pile their hats on the table; the tree won't hold them all. No use to get mats; my poor carpets!" And down went Mrs. Jo to prepare for the invasion, while Josie and the maids flew about dismayed at the prospect of so many muddy boots.

On they came, a long line of umbrellas, with splashed legs and flushed faces underneath; for the gentlemen had

been having a good time all over the town, undisturbed by
the rain. Professor Bhaer met them at the gate, and was
making a little speech of welcome, when Mrs. Jo, touched
by their bedraggled state, appeared at the door, beckoning them in. Leaving their host to orate bareheaded in the
wet, the young men hastened up the steps, merry, warm,
and eager, clutching off their hats as they came, and
struggling with their umbrellas, as the order was passed to
march in and stack arms.

Tramp, tramp, tramp, down the hall went seventy-five
pairs of boots; soon seventy-five umbrellas dripped socia-
bly in the hospitable tub, while their owners swarmed all
over the lower part of the house; and seventy-five hearty
hands were shaken by the hostess without a murmur,
though some were wet, some very warm, and nearly all
bore trophies of the day's ramble. One impetuous party
flourished a small turtle as he made his compliments;
another had a load of sticks cut from noted spots; and all
begged for some memento of Plumfield. A pile of cards
mysteriously appeared on the table, with a written request
for autographs; and despite her morning vow, Mrs. Jo
wrote everyone, while her husband and boys did the
honours of the house.

Josie fled to the back parlour, but was discovered by
exploring youths, and mortally insulted by one of them,
who innocently inquired if she was Mrs. Bhaer. The reception did not last long, and the end was better than the
beginning; for the rain ceased, and a rainbow shone beautifully over them as the good fellows stood upon the lawn
singing sweetly for a farewell. A happy omen, that bow of
promise arched over the young heads, as if Heaven smiled
upon their union, and showed them that above the muddy
earth and rainy skies the blessed sun still shone for all.

Three cheers, and then away they went, leaving a pleasant recollection of their visit to amuse the family as they
scraped the mud off the carpets with shovels and emptied
the tub half-full of water.

"Nice, honest, hard-working fellows, and I don't be-
grudge my half-hour at all; but I *must* finish, so don't let
anyone disturb me till tea-time," said Mrs. Jo, leaving
Mary to shut up the house; for papa and the boys had

gone off with the guests, and Josie had run home to tell
her mother about the fun at Aunt Jo's.

Peace reigned for an hour, then the bell rang and Mary
came giggling up to say: "A queer kind of a lady wants to
know if she can catch a grasshopper in the garden."

"A what?" cried Mrs. Jo, dropping her pen with a blot;
for of all the odd requests ever made, this was the oddest.

"A grasshopper, ma'am. I said you was busy, and asked
what she wanted, and says she: 'I've got grasshoppers
from the grounds of several famous folks, and I want one
from Plumfield to add to my collection.' Did you ever?"
And Mary giggled again at the idea.

"Tell her to take all there are and welcome. I shall be
glad to get rid of them; always bouncing in my face and
getting in my dress," laughed Mrs. Jo.

Mary retired, to return in a moment nearly speechless
with merriment.

"She's much obliged, ma'am, and she'd like an old gown
or a pair of stockings of yours to put in a rug she's making.
Got a vest of Emerson's, she says, and a pair of Mr.
Holmes's trousers, and a dress of Mrs. Stowe's. She must
be crazy!"

"Give her that old red shawl, then I shall make a gay
show among the great ones in that astonishing rug. Yes,
they are all lunatics, these lion-hunters; but this seems to
be a harmless maniac, for she doesn't take my time, and
gives me a good laugh," said Mrs. Jo, returning to her
work after a glance from the window, which showed her a
tall, thin lady in rusty black, skipping wildly to and fro on
the lawn in pursuit of the lively insect she wanted.

No more interruptions till the light began to fade, then
Mary popped her head in to say a gentleman wished to
see Mrs. Bhaer, and wouldn't take no for an answer.

"He must. I shall *not* go down. This has been an awful
day, and I won't be disturbed again," replied the harassed
authoress, pausing in the midst of the grand finale of her
chapter.

"I told him so, ma'am; but he walked right in as bold as
brass. I guess he's another crazy one, and I declare I'm
'most afraid of him, he's so big and black, and cool as
cucumbers, though I will say he's good-looking," added

Mary, with a simper; for the stranger had evidently found favour in her sight despite his boldness.

"My day has been ruined, and I *will* have this last half-hour to finish. Tell him to go away; I *won't* go down," cried Mrs. Jo, fiercely.

Mary went; and listening, in spite of herself, her mistress heard first a murmur of voices, then a cry from Mary, and remembering the ways of reporters, also that her maid was both pretty and timid, Mrs. Bhaer flung down her pen and went to the rescue. Descending with her most majestic air she demanded in an awe-inspiring voice, as she paused to survey the somewhat brigandish intruder, who seemed to be storming the staircase which Mary was gallantly defending:

"*Who* is this person who insists on remaining when I have declined to see him?"

"I'm sure I don't know, ma'am. He won't give no name, and says you'll be sorry if you don't see him," answered Mary, retiring flushed and indignant from her post.

"Won't you be sorry?" asked the stranger, looking up with a pair of black eyes full of laughter, the flash of white teeth through a long beard, and both hands out as he boldly approached the irate lady.

Mrs. Jo gave one keen look, for the voice was familiar; then completed Mary's bewilderment by throwing both arms round the brigand's neck, exclaiming joyfully: "My dearest boy, where did you come from?"

"California, on purpose to see you, Mother Bhaer. Now won't you be sorry if I go away?" answered Dan, with a hearty kiss.

"To think of my ordering you out of the house when I've been longing to see you for a year," laughed Mrs. Jo, and she went down to have a good talk with her returned wanderer, who enjoyed the joke immensely.

Chapter 4

Dan

MRS. JO often thought that Dan had Indian blood in him, not only because of his love of a wild, wandering life, but his appearance; for as he grew up, this became more striking. At twenty-five he was very tall, with sinewy limbs, a keen, dark face, and the alert look of one whose senses were all alive; rough in manner, full of energy, quick with word and blow, eyes full of the old fire, always watchful as if used to keep guard, and a general air of vigour and freshness very charming to those who knew the dangers and delights of his adventurous life. He was looking his best as he sat talking with "Mother Bhaer," one strong brown hand in hers, and a world of affection in his voice as he said:

"Forget old friends! How could I forget the only home I ever knew? Why, I was in such a hurry to come and tell my good luck that I didn't stop to fix up, you see; though I knew you'd think I looked more like a wild buffalo than ever," with a shake of his shaggy black head, a tug at his beard, and a laugh that made the room ring.

"I like it; I always had a fancy for banditti—and you look just like one. Mary, being a newcomer, was frightened at your looks and manners. Josie won't know you, but Ted will recognize his Danny in spite of the big beard and flowing mane. They will all be here soon to welcome you; so before they come tell me more about yourself. Why, Dan, dear! it's nearly two years since you were here! Has it gone well with you?" asked Mrs. Jo, who had been listening with maternal interest to his account of life in California, and the unexpected success of a small investment he had made.

51

"First-rate! I don't care for the money, you know. I only want a trifle to pay my way—rather earn as I go, and not be bothered with the care of a lot. It's the fun of the thing coming to me, and my being able to give away, that I like. No use to lay up; I shan't live to be old and need it—my sort never do," said Dan, looking as if his little fortune rather oppressed him.

"But if you marry and settle somewhere, as I hope you will, you must have something to begin with, my son. So be prudent and invest your money; don't give it away, for rainy days come to all of us, and dependence would be very hard for you to bear," answered Mrs. Jo with a sage air, though she liked to see that the money-making fever had not seized her lucky boy yet.

Dan shook his head, and glanced about the room as if he already found it rather confined and longed for all out-of-doors again.

"Who would marry a jack-o'-lantern like me? Women like a steady-going man; I shall never be that."

"My dear boy, when I was a girl I liked just such adventurous fellows as you are. Anything fresh and daring, free and romantic, is always attractive to us womenfolk. Don't be discouraged; you'll find an anchor some day, and be content to take shorter voyages and bring home a good cargo."

"What should you say if I brought you an Indian squaw some day?" asked Dan, with a glimmer of mischief in the eyes that rested on a marble bust of Galatea gleaming white and lovely in the corner.

"Welcome her heartily, if she was a good one. Is there a prospect of it?" and Mrs. Jo peered at him with the interest which even literary ladies take in love affairs.

"Not at present, thank you. I'm too busy 'to gallivant,' as Ted calls it. How is the boy?" asked Dan, skilfully turning the conversation, as if he had had enough of sentiment.

Mrs. Jo was off at once, and expatiated upon the talents and virtues of her sons till they came bursting in and fell upon Dan like two affectionate young bears, finding a vent for their joyful emotions in a sort of friendly wrestling-match; in which both got worsted, of course, for the hunter soon settled them. The professor followed, and tongues went like mill-clappers while Mary lighted up and cook devoted herself to an unusually good supper, instinctively divining that this guest was a welcome one.

After tea Dan was walking up and down the long rooms as he talked, with occasional trips into the hall for a fresher breath of air, his lungs seeming to need more than those of civilized people. In one of these trips he saw a white figure framed in the dark doorway, and paused to look at it. Bess paused also, not recognizing her old friend, and quite unconscious of the pretty picture she made standing, tall and slender, against the soft gloom of the summer night, with her golden hair like a halo round her head, and the ends of a white shawl blown out like wings by the cool wind sweeping through the hall.

"Is it Dan?" she asked, coming in with a gracious smile and outstretched hand.

"Looks like it; but I didn't know *you*, Princess. I thought it was a spirit," answered Dan, looking down at her with a curious softness and wonder in his face.

"I've grown very much, but two years have changed you entirely"; and Bess looked up with girlish pleasure at the picturesque figure before her—for it was a decided contrast to the well-dressed people about her.

Before they could say more, Josie rushed in, and, forgetful of the newly acquired dignity of her teens, let Dan catch her up and kiss her like a child. Not till he set her down did he discover she also was changed, and exclaimed in comic dismay:

"Hallo! Why, you are growing up too! What am I going to do, with no young one to play with? Here's Ted going it like a beanstalk, and Bess a young lady, and even you, my mustard-seed, letting down your frocks and putting on airs."

The girls laughed, and Josie blushed as she stared at the tall man, conscious that she had leaped before she looked. They made a pretty contrast, these two young cousins— one as fair as a lily, the other a little wild rose. And Dan gave a nod of satisfaction as he surveyed them; for he had seen many bonny girls in his travels, and was glad that these old friends were blooming so beautifully.

"Here! we can't allow any monopoly of Dan!" called Mrs. Jo. "Bring him back and keep an eye on him, or he will be slipping off for another little run of a year or two before we have half seen him."

Led by these agreeable captors, Dan returned to the parlour to receive a scolding from Josie for getting ahead of all the other boys and looking like a man first.

"Emil is older; but he's only a boy, and dances jigs and sings sailor songs just as he used to. You look about thirty, and as big and black as a villain in a play. Oh, I've got a splendid idea! You are just the thing for Arbaces in *The Last Days of Pompeii*. We want to act it; have the lion and the gladiators and the eruption. Tom and Ted are going to shower bushels of ashes down and roll barrels of stones about. We wanted a dark man for the Egyptian; and you will be gorgeous in red and white shawls. Won't he, Aunt Jo?"

This deluge of words made Dan clap his hands over his ears; and before Mrs. Bhaer could answer her impetuous niece the Laurences, with Meg and her family, arrived, soon followed by Tom and Nan, and all sat down to listen to Dan's adventures—told in brief yet effective manner, as the varying expressions of interest, wonder, merriment, and suspense painted on the circle of faces round him plainly showed. The boys all wanted to start at once for California and make fortunes; the girls could hardly wait for the curious and pretty things he had picked up for them in his travels; while the elders rejoiced heartily over the energy and good prospects of their wild boy.

"Of course you will want to go back for another stroke of luck; and I hope you will have it. But speculation is a dangerous game, and you may lose all you've won," said Mr. Laurie, who had enjoyed the stirring tale as much as any of the boys, and would have liked to rough it with Dan as well as they.

"I've had enough of it, for a while at least; too much like gambling. The excitement is all I care for, and it isn't good for me. I have a notion to try farming out West. It's grand on a large scale; and I feel as if steady work would be rather jolly after loafing round so long. I can make a beginning, and you can send me your black sheep to stock my place with. I tried sheep-farming in Australia, and know something about black ones, any way."

A laugh chased away the sober look in Dan's face as he ended; and those who knew him best guessed that he had learned a lesson there in San Francisco, and dared not try again.

"That is a capital idea, Dan!" cried Mrs. Jo, seeing great hope in this desire to fix himself somewhere and help others. "We shall know where you are, and can go and see you, and not have half the world between us. I'll send my Ted for a visit. He's such a restless spirit, it would do him good. With you he would be safe while he worked off his surplus energies and learned a wholesome business."

"I'll use the 'shubble and de hoe' like a good one, if I get a chance out there; but the Speranza mines sound rather jollier," said Ted, examining the samples of ore Dan had brought for the professor.

"You go and start a new town, and when we are ready to swarm we will come out and settle there. You will want a newspaper very soon, and I like the idea of running one myself much better than grinding away as I do now," observed Demi, panting to distinguish himself in the journalistic line.

"We could easily plant a new college there. These sturdy Westerners are hungry for learning, and very quick to see and choose the best," added ever-young Mr. March, beholding with his prophetic eye many duplicates of their own flourishing establishment springing up in the wide West.

"Go on, Dan. It is a fine plan, and we will back you up. I shouldn't mind investing in a few prairies and cowboys myself," said Mr. Laurie, always ready to help the lads to help themselves, both by his cheery words and ever-open purse.

"A little money sort of ballasts a fellow, and investing it in land anchors him—for a while, at least. I'd like to see what I can do, but I thought I'd consult you before I decided. Have my doubts about it suiting me for many years; but I can cut loose when I'm tired," answered Dan, both touched and pleased at the eager interest of these friends in his plans.

"I know you *won't* like it. After having the whole world to roam over, one farm will seem dreadfully small and stupid," said Josie, who much preferred the romance of the wandering life which brought her thrilling tales and pretty things at each return.

"Is there any art out there?" asked Bess, thinking what a good study in black and white Dan would make as he stood talking, half turned from the light.

"Plenty of nature, dear; and that is better. You will find splendid animals to model, and scenery such as you never saw in Europe to paint. Even prosaic pumpkins are grand out there. You can play *Cinderella* in one of them, Josie, when you open your theatre in Dansville," said Mr. Laurie, anxious that no cold water should be thrown on the new plan.

Stage-struck Josie was caught at once, and being promised all the tragic parts on the yet unbuilt stage, she felt a deep interest in the project and begged Dan to lose no time in beginning his experiment. Bess also confessed that studies from nature would be good for her, and wild scenery improve her taste, which might grow over-nice if only the delicate and beautiful were set before her.

"I speak for the practice of the new town," said Nan, always eager for fresh enterprises. "I shall be ready by the time you get well started—towns grow so fast out there."

"Dan isn't going to allow any woman under forty in his place. He doesn't like them, 'specially young and pretty ones," put in Tom, who was raging with jealousy, because he read admiration for Nan in Dan's eyes.

"That won't affect me, because doctors are exceptions to all rules. There won't be much sickness in Dansville, everyone will lead such active, wholesome lives, and only energetic young people will go there. But accidents will be frequent, owing to wild cattle, fast riding, Indian scrimmages, and the recklessness of Western life. That will just suit me. I long for broken bones, surgery is *so* interesting and I get so little here," answered Nan, yearning to put out her shingle and begin.

"I'll have you, Doctor, and be glad of such a good sample of what we can do in the East. Peg away, and I'll send for you as soon as I have a roof to cover you. I'll scalp

a few red fellows or smash up a dozen or so of cowboys for
your special benefit," laughed Dan, well pleased with the
energy and fine physique which made Nan a conspicuous
figure among other girls.

"Thanks. I'll come. Would you just let me feel your
arm? Splendid biceps! Now, boys, see here: *this* is what I
call muscle." And Nan delivered a short lecture with
Dan's sinewy arm to illustrate it.

Tom retired to the alcove and glowered at the stars,
while he swung his own right arm with a vigour suggestive
of knocking someone down.

"Make Tom sexton; he'll enjoy burying the patients Nan
kills. He's trying to get up the glum expression proper to
the business. Don't forget him, Dan," said Ted, directing
attention to the blighted being in the corner.

But Tom never sulked long, and came out from his brief
eclipse with the cheerful proposition:

"Look here, we'll get the city to ship out to Dansville all
the cases of yellow fever, smallpox, and cholera that arrive; then Nan will be happy and her mistakes won't
matter much with emigrants and convicts."

"I should advise settling near Jacksonville, or some such
city, that you might enjoy the society of cultivated persons. The Plato Club is there, and a most ardent thirst for
philosophy. Everything from the East is welcomed hospitably, and new enterprises would flourish in such kindly
soil," observed Mr. March, mildly offering a suggestion,
as he sat among the elders enjoying the lively scene.

The idea of Dan studying Plato was very funny; but no
one except naughty Ted smiled, and Dan made haste to
unfold another plan seething in that active brain of his.

"I'm not sure the farming will succeed, and have a
strong leaning towards my old friends the Montana Indians. They are a peaceful tribe, and need help awfully;
hundreds have died of starvation because they don't get
their share. The Sioux are fighters, thirty thousand strong,
so Government fears 'em, and gives 'em all they want. I call
that a damned shame!" Dan stopped short as the oath
slipped out, but his eyes flashed, and he went on quickly:
"It *is* just that, and I won't beg pardon. If I'd had any
money when I was there I'd have given every cent to

those poor devils, cheated out of everything, and waiting
patiently, after being driven from their own land to places
where nothing will grow. Now, honest agents could do
much, and I've a feeling that I ought to go and lend a
hand. I know their lingo, and I like 'em. I've got a few
thousands, and I ain't sure I have any right to spend it on
myself and settle down to enjoy it. Hey?"

Dan looked very manly and earnest as he faced his
friends, flushed and excited by the energy of his words;
and all felt that little thrill of sympathy which links hearts
together by the tie of pity for the wronged.

"Do it, do it!" cried Mrs. Jo, fired at once; for misfortune was much more interesting to her than good luck.

"Do it, do it!" echoed Ted, applauding as if at a play,
"and take me along to help. I'm just raging to get among
those fine fellows and hunt."

"Let us hear more and see if it is wise," said Mr.
Laurie, privately resolving to people his as yet unbought
prairies with Montana Indians, and increase his donations
to the society that sent missionaries to this much wronged
people.

Dan plunged at once into the history of what he saw
among the Dakotas, and other tribes in the Northwest,
telling of their wrongs, patience, and courage as if they
were his brothers.

"They called me Dan Fire Cloud, because my rifle was
the best they ever saw. And Black Hawk was as good a
friend as a fellow would want; saved my life more than
once, and taught me just what will be useful if I go back.
They are down on their luck, now, and I'd like to pay my
debts."

By this time everyone was interested, and Dansville
began to lose its charm. But prudent Mr. Bhaer suggested
that one honest agent among many could not do much,
and noble as the effort would be, it was wiser to think over
the matter carefully, get influence and authority from the
right quarters, and meantime look at lands before deciding.

"Well, I will. I'm going to take a run to Kansas and see
how that promises. Met a fellow in 'Frico who'd been
there, and he spoke well of it. The fact is, there's so much
to be done *every* where that I don't know where to catch

on, and half wish I hadn't any money," answered Dan, knitting his brows in the perplexity all kind souls feel when anxious to help at the great task of the world's charity.

"I'll keep it for you till you decide. You are such an impetuous lad you'll give it to the first beggar that gets hold of you. I'll turn it over while you are prospecting, and hand it back when you are ready to invest, shall I?" asked Mr. Laurie, who had learned wisdom since the days of his own extravagant youth.

"Thanky, sir, I'd be glad to get rid of it. You just hold on till I say the word; and if anything happens to me this time, keep it to help some other scamp as you helped me. This is my will, and you all witness it. Now I feel better." And Dan squared his shoulders as if relieved of a burden, after handing over the belt in which he carried his little fortune.

No one dreamed how much was to happen before Dan came to take his money back, nor how nearly that act *was* his last will and testament; and while Mr. Laurie was explaining how he would invest it, a cheery voice was heard singing:

> "Oh, Peggy was a jolly lass,
>   Ye heave ho, boys, ye heave ho!
> She never grudged her Jack a glass,
>   Ye heave ho, boys, ye heave ho!
> And when he sailed the raging main,
> She faithful was unto her swain,
>   Ye heave ho, boys, he yeave ho!"

Emil always announced his arrival in that fashion, and in a moment he came hurrying in with Nat, who had been giving lessons in town all day. It was good to see the latter beam at his friend as he nearly shook his hand off; better still to see how Dan gratefully remembered all he owed Nat, and tried to pay the debt in his rough way; and best of all to hear the two travellers compare notes and reel off yarns to dazzle the landlubbers and homekeepers.

After this addition the house would not contain the gay youngsters, so they migrated to the piazza and settled on the steps, like a flock of night-loving birds. Mr. March and the Professor retired to the study, Meg and Amy went to look after the little refection of fruit and cake which was to come, and Mrs. Jo and Mr. Laurie sat in the long window listening to the chat that went on outside.

"There they are, the flower of our flock!" she said, pointing to the group before them. "The others are dead or scattered, but these seven boys and four girls are my especial comfort and pride. Counting Alice Heath, my dozen is made up, and my hands are full trying to guide these young lives as far as human skill can do it."

"When we remember how different they are, from what some of them came, and the home influences about others, I think we may feel pretty well satisfied so far," answered Mr. Laurie soberly, as his eyes rested on one bright head among the black and brown ones, for the young moon shone alike on all.

"I don't worry about the girls; Meg sees to them, and is so wise and patient and tender they can't help doing well; but my boys are more care every year, and seem to drift farther away from me each time they go," sighed Mrs. Jo. "They *will* grow up, and I can only hold them by one little thread, which may snap at any time, as it has with Jack and Ned. Dolly and George still like to come back, and I can say my word to them; and dear old Franz is too true ever to forget his own. But the three who are soon going out into the world again I can't help worrying about. Emil's good heart will keep him straight, I hope, and—

> *A sweet little cherub sits up aloft,*
> *To look out for the life of poor Jack.*

Nat is to make his first flight, and he's weak in spite of your strengthening influence; and Dan is still untamed. I fear it will take some hard lesson to do that."

"He's a fine fellow, Jo, and I almost regret this farming project. A little polish would make a gentleman of him, and who knows what he might become here among us," answered Mr. Laurie, leaning over Mrs. Bhaer's chair, just as he used to do years ago when they had mischievous secrets together.

"It wouldn't be safe, Teddy. Work and the free life he loves will make a good man of him, and that is better than any amount of polish, with the dangers an easy life in a city would bring him. We can't change his nature—only help it to develop in the right direction. The old impulses are there, and must be controlled, or he will go wrong. I see that; but his love for us is a safeguard, and we must keep a hold on him till he is older or has a stronger tie to help him."

Mrs. Jo spoke earnestly, for, knowing Dan better than anyone else, she saw that her colt was not thoroughly broken yet, and feared while she hoped, knowing that life would always be hard for one like him. She was sure that before he went away again, in some quiet moment he would give her a glimpse of his inner self, and then she could say the word of warning or encouragement that he needed. So she bided her time, studying him meanwhile, glad to see all that was promising, and quick to detect the harm the world was doing him. She was very anxious to make a success of her "firebrand" because others predicted failure; but having learned that people cannot be moulded like clay, she contented herself with the hope that this neglected boy might become a good man, and asked no more. Even that was much to expect, so full was he of wayward impulses, strong passions, and the lawless nature born in him! Nothing held him but the one affection of his life—the memory of Plumfield, the fear of disappointing these faithful friends, the pride, stronger than principle, that made him want to keep the regard of the mates who always had admired and loved him in spite of all his faults.

"Don't fret, old dear; Emil is one of the happy-go-lucky sort who always fall on their legs. I'll see to Nat, and Dan is in a good way now. Let him take a look at Kansas, and if the farm plan loses its charm, he can fall back on poor Lo, and really do good out there. He's unusually fitted for that peculiar task and I hope he'll decide to do it. Fighting oppressors, and befriending the oppressed will keep those dangerous energies of his busy, and the life will suit him better than sheep-folds and wheat-fields."

"I hope so. What is that?" and Mrs. Jo leaned forward

to listen, as exclamations from Ted and Josie caught her ear.

"A mustang! a real, live one; and we can ride it. Dan, you are a first-class trump!" cried the boy.

"A whole Indian dress for me! Now I can play Namioka, if the boys act *Metamora*," added Josie, clapping her hands.

"A buffalo's head for Bess! Good gracious, Dan, why did you bring such a horrid thing as that to her?" asked Nan.

"Thought it would do her good to model something strong and natural. She'll never amount to anything if she keeps on making namby-pamby gods and pet kittens," answered irreverent Dan, remembering that when he was last here Bess was vibrating distractedly between a head of Apollo and her Persian cat as models.

"Thank you; I'll try it, and if I fail we can put the buffalo up in the hall to remind us of you," said Bess, indignant at the insult offered the gods of her idolatry, but too well bred to show it except in her voice, which was as sweet and as cold as ice-cream.

"I suppose you won't come out to see our new settlement when the rest do? Too rough for you?" asked Dan, trying to assume the deferential air all the boys used when addressing their Princess.

"I am going to Rome to study for years. All the beauty and art of the world is there, and a lifetime isn't long enough to enjoy it," answered Bess.

"Rome is a mouldy old tomb compared to the 'Garden of the gods' and my magnificent Rockies. I don't care a hang for art; nature is as much as I can stand, and I guess I could show you things that would knock your old masters higher than kites. Better come, and while Josie rides the horses you can model 'em! If a drove of a hundred or so of wild ones can't show you beauty, I'll give up," cried Dan, waxing enthusiastic over the wild grace and vigour which he could enjoy but had no power to describe.

"I'll come some day with papa, and see if they are better than the horses of St. Mark and those on Capitol Hill. Please don't abuse my gods, and I will try to like yours," said Bess, beginning to think the West might be worth seeing, though no Raphael or Angelo had yet appeared there.

"That's a bargain! I do think people ought to see their own country before they go scooting off to foreign parts, as if the new world wasn't worth discovering," began Dan, ready to bury the hatchet.

"It has some advantages, but not all. The women of England can vote, and we can't. I'm ashamed of America that she isn't ahead in *all* good things," cried Nan, who held advanced views on all reforms, and was anxious about her rights, having had to fight for some of them.

"Oh, please don't begin on that. People always quarrel over that question, and call names, and never agree. Do let us be quiet and happy tonight," pleaded Daisy, who hated discussion as much as Nan loved it.

"You shall vote as much as you like in our new town, Nan; be mayor and aldermen, and run the whole concern. It's going to be as free as air, or I can't live in it," sad Dan, adding, with a laugh, "I see Mrs. Giddy-gaddy and Mrs. Shakespeare Smith don't agree any better than they used to."

"If everyone agreed, we should never get on. Daisy is a dear, but inclined to be an old fogy; so I stir her up; and next fall she will go and vote with me. Demi will escort us to do the one thing we *are* allowed to do as yet."

"Will you take 'em, Deacon?" asked Dan, using the old name as if he liked it. "It works capitally in Wyoming."

"I shall be proud to do it. Mother and the aunts go every year, and Daisy will come with me. She is my better half still; and I don't mean to leave her behind in anything," said Demi, with an arm round his sister of whom he was fonder than ever.

Dan looked at them wistfully, thinking how sweet it must be to have such a tie; and his lonely youth seemed sadder than ever as he recalled its struggles. A gusty sigh from Tom made sentiment impossible, as he said pensively:

"I always wanted to be a twin. It's so sociable and so cosy to have someone glad to lean on a fellow and comfort him, if other girls are cruel."

As Tom's unrequited passion was the standing joke of the family, this allusion produced a laugh, which Nan

increased by whipping out a bottle of *Nux*, saying, with
her professional air:

"I knew you ate too much lobster for tea. Take four
pellets, and your dyspepsia will be all right. Tom always
sighs and is silly when he's overeaten."

"I'll take 'em. These are the only sweet things you ever
give me." And Tom gloomily crunched his dose.

" 'Who can minister to a mind diseased, or pluck out a
rooted sorrow?' " quoted Josie tragically from her perch on
the railing.

"Come with me, Tommy, and I'll make a man of you.
Drop your pills and powders, and cavort round the world
a spell, and you'll soon forget you've got a heart, or a
stomach either," said Dan, offering his one panacea for all
ills.

"Ship with me, Tom. A good fit of seasickness will set
you up, and a stiff north-easter blow your blue-devils
away. Come along as surgeon—easy berth, and no end of
larks."

> *"And if your Nancy frowns, my lad,*
> *And scorns a jacket blue,*
> *Just hoist your sails for other ports,*
> *And find a maid more true."—*

added Emil, who had a fragment of song to cheer every
care and sorrow, and freely offered them to his friends.

"Perhaps I'll think of it when I've got my diploma. I'm
not going to grind three mortal years and have nothing to
show for it. Till then —"

"I'll never desert Mrs. Micawber," interrupted Teddy,
with a gurgling sob.

Tom immediately rolled him off the step into the wet
grass below; and by the time this slight skirmish was over,
the jingle of teaspoons suggested refreshments of a more
agreeable sort. In former times the little girls waited on
the boys, to save confusion; now the young men flew to
serve the ladies, young and old; and that slight fact showed
plainly how the tables were turned by time. And what a
pleasant arrangement it was! Even Josie sat still, and let
Emil bring her berries; enjoying her young ladyhood, till

Ted stole her cake, when she forgot manners, and chastised him with a rap on the knuckles. As guest of honour, Dan was only allowed to wait on Bess, who still held the highest place in this small world. Tom carefully selected the best of everything for Nan, to be crushed by the remark:

"I never eat at this hour; and you will have a nightmare if *you* do."

So, dutifully curbing the pangs of hunger, he gave the plate to Daisy, and chewed rose-leaves for his supper.

When a surprising quantity of wholesome nourishment had been consumed, someone said, "Let's sing!" and a tuneful hour followed. Nat fiddled, Demi piped, Dan strummed the old banjo, and Emil warbled a doleful ballad about the wreck of the *Bounding Betsey*; then everybody joined in the old songs till there was very decidedly "music in the air"; and passers-by said, as they listened smiling: "Old Plum is gay tonight!"

When all had gone Dan lingered on the piazza, enjoying the balmy wind that blew up from the hayfields, and brought the breath of flowers from Parnassus; and as he leaned there romantically in the moonlight, Mrs. Jo came to shut the door.

"Dreaming dreams, Dan?" she asked, thinking the tender moment might have come. Imagine the shock when, instead of some interesting confidence or affectionate word, Dan swung round, saying bluntly:

"I was wishing I could smoke."

Mrs. Jo laughed at the downfall of her hopes, and answered kindly:

"You may, in your room; but don't set the house afire."

Perhaps Dan saw a little disappointment in her face, or the memory of the sequel of that boyish frolic touched his heart; for he stooped and kissed her, saying in a whisper: "Good night, mother." And Mrs. Jo was half satisfied.

Chapter 5

Vacation

EVERYONE WAS GLAD of a holiday next morning, and all lingered over the breakfast-table, till Mrs. Jo suddenly exclaimed:

"Why, there's a dog!" And on the threshold of the door appeared a great deer-hound, standing motionless, with his eyes fixed on Dan.

"Hallo, old boy! Couldn't you wait till I came for you? Have you cut away on the sly? Own up now, and take your whipping like a man," said Dan, rising to meet the dog, who reared on his hind legs to look his master in the face and bark as if uttering an indignant denial of any disobedience.

"All right; Don never lies." And Dan gave the tall beast a hug, adding as he glanced out of the window, where a man and horse were seen approaching:

"I left my plunder at the hotel over night, not knowing how I should find you. Come out and see Octoo, my mustang; she's a beauty." And Dan was off, with the family streaming after him, to welcome the newcomer.

They found her preparing to go up the steps in her eagerness to reach her master, to the great dismay of the man, who was holding her back.

"Let her come," called Dan; "she climbs like a cat and jumps like a deer. Well, my girl, do you want a gallop?" he asked, as the pretty creature clattered up to him and whinnied with pleasure as he rubbed her nose and slapped her glossy flank.

"That's what I call a horse worth having," said Ted, full of admiration and delight; for he was to have the care of her during Dan's absence.

"What intelligent eyes! She looks as if she would speak," said Mrs. Jo.

"She talks like a human in her way. Very little that *she* don't know. Hey, old Lass?" and Dan laid his cheek to hers as if the little black mare was very dear to him.

"What does 'Octoo' mean?" asked Rob.

"Lightning; she deserves it, as you'll see. Black Hawk gave her to me for my rifle, and we've had high times together out yonder. She's saved my life more than once. Do you see that scar?"

Dan pointed to a small one, half hidden by the long mane; and standing with his arm about Octoo's neck, he told the story of it.

"Black Hawk and I were after buffalo one time, but didn't find 'em as soon as we expected; so our food gave out, and there we were a hundred miles from Red Deer River, where our camp was. I thought we were done for, but my brave pal says: 'Now I'll show you how we can live till we find the herds.' We were unsaddling for the night by a little pond; there wasn't a living creature in sight anywhere, not even a bird, and we could see for miles over the prairies. What do you think we did?" And Dan looked into the faces round him.

"Ate worms like the Australian fellows," said Rob.

"Boiled grass or leaves," added Mrs. Jo.

"Perhaps filled the stomach with clay, as we read of savages doing?" suggested Mr. Bhaer.

"Killed one of the horses," cried Ted, eager for bloodshed of some sort.

"No; but we bled one of them. See, just here; filled a tin cup, put some wild sage leaves in it, with water, and heated it over a fire of sticks. It was good, and we slept well."

"I guess Octoo didn't." And Josie patted the animal, with a face full of sympathy.

"Never minded it a bit. Black Hawk said we could live on the horses several days and still travel before they felt it. But by another morning we found the buffalo, and I shot the one whose head is in my box, ready to hang up and scare brats into fits. He's a fierce old fellow, you bet."

"What is this strap for?" asked Ted, who was busily

examining the Indian saddle, the single rein and snaffle, with lariat, and round the neck the leather band he spoke of.

"We hold on to that when we lie along the horse's flank farthest from the enemy, and fire under the neck as we gallop round and round. I'll show you." And springing into the saddle, Dan was off down the steps, tearing over the lawn at a great pace, sometimes on Octoo's back, sometimes half hidden as he hung by stirrup and strap, and sometimes off altogether, running beside her as she loped along, enjoying the fun immensely; while Don raced after, in a canine rapture at being free again and with his mates.

It was a fine sight—the three wild things at play, so full of vigour, grace, and freedom, that for the moment the smooth lawn seemed a prairie; and the spectators felt as if this glimpse of another life made their own seem rather tame and colourless.

"This is better than a circus!" cried Mrs. Jo, wishing she were a girl again, that she might take a gallop on this chained lightning of a horse. "I foresee that Nan will have her hands full setting bones, for Ted will break every one of his trying to rival Dan."

"A few falls will not harm, and this new care and pleasure will be good for him in all ways. But I fear Dan will never follow a plough after riding a Pegasus like that," answered Mr. Bhaer, as the black mare leaped the gate and came flying up the avenue, to stop at a word and stand quivering with excitement, while Dan swung himself off and looked up for applause.

He received plenty of it, and seemed more pleased for his pet's sake than for his own. Ted clamoured for a lesson at once, and was soon at ease in the queer saddle, finding Octoo gentle as a lamb, as he trotted away to show off at college. Bess came hastening down the hill, having seen the race from afar; and all collected on the piazza while Dan "yanked" the cover off the big box the express had "dumped" before the door—to borrow his own words.

Dan usually travelled in light marching order, and hated to have more luggage than he could carry in his well-worn valise. But now that he had a little money of his own, he had cumbered himself with a collection of trophies won by his bow and spear, and brought them home to bestow upon his friends.

"We shall be devoured with moths," thought Mrs. Jo, as the shaggy head appeared, followed by a wolf-skin rug for her feet, a bear-skin ditto for the Professor's study, and Indian garments bedecked with foxes' tails for the boys.

All nice and warm for a July day, but received with delight nevertheless. Ted and Josie immediately "dressed up," learned the war-whoop, and proceeded to astonish their friends by a series of skirmishes about the house and grounds, with tomahawks and bows and arrows, till weariness produced a lull.

Gay birds' wings, plumy pampas grass, strings of wampum, and pretty work in beads, bark, and feathers, pleased the girls. Minerals, arrow-heads, and crude sketches interested the Professor; and when the box was empty, Dan gave Mr. Laurie, as his gift, several plaintive Indian songs written on birch-bark.

"We only want a tent over us to be quite perfect. I feel as if I ought to give you parched corn and dried meat for dinner, my braves. Nobody will want lamb and green peas after this splendid pow-wow," said Mrs. Jo, surveying the picturesque confusion of the long hall, where people lay about on the rugs, all more or less bedecked with feathers, moccasins, or beads.

"Moose noses, buffalo tongues, bear steaks, and roasted marrow-bones would be the thing, but I don't mind a change; so bring on your baa-baa and green meat," answered Dan from the box, where he sat in state like a chief among his tribe, with the great hound at his feet.

The girls began to clear up, but made little headway; for everything they touched had a story, and all were thrilling, comical, or wild; so they found it hard to settle to their work, till Dan was carried off by Mr. Laurie.

This was the beginning of the summer holiday, and it was curious to see what a pleasant little stir Dan's and Emil's coming made in the quiet life of the studious community; for they seemed to bring a fresh breeze with them that enlivened everyone. Many of the collegians remained during vacation; and Plumfield and Parnassus did their best to make these days pleasant for them, since most came from distant States, were poor, and had few opportunities but this for culture or amusement. Emil was hail-fellow-well-met with men and maids, and went rollicking about in true sailor fashion; but Dan stood rather in awe of the "fair girl-graduates," and was silent when among them, eyeing them as an eagle might a flock of doves. He got on better with the young men, and was their hero at once. Their admiration for his manly accomplishments did him good; because he felt his educational defects keenly, and often wondered if he could find anything in books to satisfy him as thoroughly as did the lessons he was learning from Nature's splendidly illustrated volume. In spite of his silence, the girls found out his good qualities, and regarded "the Spaniard," as they named him, with great favour; for his black eyes were more eloquent than his tongue, and the kind creatures tried to show their friendly interests in many charming ways.

He saw this, and endeavoured to be worthy of it—curbing his free speech, toning down his rough manners, and watching the effect of all he said and did, anxious to make a good impression. The social atmosphere warmed his lonely heart, the culture excited him to do his best, and the changes which had taken place during his absence, both in himself and others, made the old home seem like a new world. After the life in California, it was sweet and restful to be here, with these familiar faces round him, helping him to forget much that he regretted, and to resolve to deserve more entirely the confidence of these good fellows, the respect of these innocent girls.

So there was riding, rowing, and picnicking by day, music, dancing, and plays by night; and everyone said there had not been so gay a vacation for years. Bess kept her promise, and let the dust gather on her beloved clay while she went pleasuring with her mates or studied music with her father, who rejoiced over the fresh roses in her cheeks and the laughter which chased away the dreamy look she used to wear. Josie quarrelled less with Ted; for Dan had a way of looking at her which quelled her instantly, and had almost as good an effect upon her rebellious cousin. But Octoo did even more for the lively youth, who found that her charms entirely eclipsed those

of the bicycle which had been his heart's delight before.
Early and late he rode this untiring beast, and began to
gain flesh—to the great joy of his mother, who feared that
her beanstalk was growing too fast for health.

Demi, finding business dull, solaced his leisure by pho-
tographing everybody he could induce to sit or stand to
him, producing some excellent pictures among many failures; for he had a pretty taste in grouping, and endless
patience. He might be said to view the world through the
lens of his camera, and seemed to enjoy himself very
much squinting at his fellow beings from under a bit of
black cambric. Dan was a treasure to him; for he took
well, and willingly posed in his Mexican costume, with
horse and hound, and all wanted copies of these effective
photographs.

Bess, also, was a favourite sitter; and Demi received a
prize at the Amateur Photographic Exhibition for one of
his cousin with all her hair about her face, which rose from
the cloud of white lace draping the shoulders. These were
freely handed round by the proud artist; and one copy had
a tender little history yet to be told.

Nat was snatching every minute he could get with Daisy
before the long parting; and Mrs. Meg relented somewhat, feeling sure that absence would quite cure this
unfortunate fancy. Daisy said little; but her gentle face
was sad when she was alone, and a few quiet tears dropped
on the handkerchiefs she marked so daintily with her own
hair. She was sure Nat would *not* forget her; and life
looked rather forlorn without the dear fellow who had
been her friend since the days of patty-pans and confidences in the willow-tree. She was an old-fashioned daughter, dutiful and docile, with such love and reverence for
her mother that her will was law; and if love was forbidden, friendship must suffice. So she kept her little sorrow
to herself, smiled cheerfully at Nat, and made his last days
of home-life very happy with every comfort and pleasure
she could give, from sensible advice and sweet words to a
well-filled work-bag for his bachelor establishment and a
box of goodies for the voyage.

Tom and Nan took all the time they could spare from
their studies to enjoy high jinks at Plumfield with their

old friends; for Emil's next voyage was to be a long one, Nat's absence was uncertain, and no one ever knew when Dan would turn up again. They all seemed to feel that life was beginning to grow serious; and even while they enjoyed those lovely summer days together they were conscious that they were children no longer, and often in the pauses of their fun talked soberly of their plans and hopes, as if anxious to know and help one another before they drifted farther apart on their different ways.

A few weeks were all they had; then the *Brenda* was ready, Nat was to sail from New York, and Dan went along to see him off; for his own plans fermented in his head, and he was eager to be up and doing. A farewell dance was given on Parnassus in honour of the travellers, and all turned out in their best array and gayest spirits. George and Dolly came with the latest Harvard airs and graces, radiant to behold, in dress-suits and "crushed hats," as Josie called the especial pride and joy of their boyish souls. Jack and Ned sent regrets and best wishes, and no one mourned their absence; for they were among what Mrs. Jo called her failures. Poor Tom got into trouble, as usual, by deluging his head with some highly scented preparation in the vain hope of making his tight curls lie flat and smooth, as was the style. Unhappily, his rebellious crop only kinked the closer, and the odour of many barbers' shops clung to him in spite of his frantic efforts to banish it. Nan wouldn't allow him near her, and flapped her fan vigorously whenever he was in sight; which cut him to the heart, and made him feel like the Peri shut out from Paradise. Of course his mates jeered at him, and nothing but the unquenchable jollity of his nature kept him from despair.

Emil was resplendent in his new uniform, and danced with an abandon which only sailors know. His pumps seemed to be everywhere, and his partners soon lost breath trying to keep up with him; but the girls all declared he steered like an angel, and in spite of his pace no collisions took place; so he was happy, and found no lack of damsels to ship with him.

Having no dress-suit, Dan had been coaxed to wear his Mexican costume, and feeling at ease in the many-buttoned trousers, loose jacket, and gay sash, flung his *serape* over his shoulder with a flourish and looked his best, doing great execution with his long spurs, as he taught Josie strange steps or rolled his black eyes admiringly after certain blonde damsels whom he dared not address.

The mammas sat in the alcove, supplying pins, smiles, and kindly words to all, especially the awkward youths new to such scenes, and the bashful girls conscious of faded muslins and cleaned gloves. It was pleasant to see stately Mrs. Amy promenade on the arm of a tall country boy, with thick boots and a big forehead, or Mrs. Jo dance like a girl with a shy fellow whose arms went like pump-handles, and whose face was scarlet with confusion and pride at the honour of treading on the toes of the president's wife. Mrs. Meg always had room on her sofa for two or three girls, and Mr. Laurie devoted himself to these plain, poorly dressed damsels with a kindly grace that won their hearts and made them happy. The good Professor circulated like refreshments, and his cheerful face shone on all alike, while Mr. March discussed Greek comedy in the study with such serious gentlemen as never unbent their mighty minds to frivolous joys.

The long music-room, parlour, hall, and piazza were full of white-gowned maidens with attendant shadows; the air was full of lively voices, and hearts and feet went lightly together as the home band played vigorously, and the friendly moon did her best to add enchantment to the scene.

"Pin me up, Meg; that dear Dunbar boy has nearly rent me, 'in sunder,' as Mr. Peggotty would say. But didn't he enjoy himself, bumping against his fellow men and swinging me round like a mop. On these occasions I find that I'm not as young as I was, nor as light of foot. In ten years more we shall be meal-bags, sister; so be resigned." And Mrs. Jo subsided into a corner, much dishevelled by her benevolent exertions.

"I know *I* shall be stout; but you won't keep still long enough to get much flesh on your bones, dear; and Amy will always keep her lovely figure. She looks about eighteen tonight, in her white gown and roses," answered Meg, busily pinning up one sister's torn frills, while her eyes fondly followed the other's graceful movements; for Meg still adored Amy in the old fashion.

It was one of the family jokes that Jo was getting fat, and she kept it up, though as yet she had only acquired a matronly outline, which was very becoming. They were laughing over the impending double chins, when Mr. Laurie came off duty for a moment.

"Repairing damages as usual, Jo? You never could take a little gentle exercise without returning in rags. Come and have a quiet stroll with me and cool off before supper. I've a series of pretty tableaux to show you while Meg listens to the raptures of lisping Miss Carr, whom I made happy by giving her Demi for a partner."

As he spoke, Laurie led Jo to the music-room, nearly empty now after a dance which sent the young people into garden and hall. Pausing before the first of the four long windows that opened on a very wide piazza, he pointed to a group outside, saying: "The name of this is 'Jack Ashore'."

A pair of long, blue legs, ending in very neat pumps, hung_from the veranda roof among the vines; and roses, gathered by unseen hands, evidently appertaining to aforesaid legs, were being dropped into the laps of several girls perched like a flock of white birds on the railing below; while a manly voice "fell like a falling star," as it sung this pensive ditty to a most appreciative audience:

MARY'S DREAM

"The moon had climbed the eastern hill
   Which rises o'er the sands of Dee,
And from its highest summit shed
   A silver light on tower and tree,
When Mary laid her down to sleep
   (Her thoughts on Sandy far at sea);
When soft and low a voice was heard,
   Saying, 'Mary, weep no more for me.'

"She from her pillow gently raised
   Her head, to see who there might be,
And saw young Sandy, shivering stand
   With visage pale and hollow e'e.

'Oh Mary dear, cold is my clay;
  It lies beneath the stormy sea;
Far, far from thee, I sleep in death.
  Dear Mary, weep no more for me.

" *'Three stormy nights and stormy days*
  We tossed upon the raging main.
And long we strove our bark to save;
  But all our striving was in vain.
E'en then, when terror chilled my blood,
  My heart was filled with love of thee.
The storm is past, and I'm at rest;
  So, Mary, weep no more for me.

" *'Oh maiden dear, yourself prepare;*
  We soon shall meet upon that shore
Where love is free from doubt and care,
  And you and I shall part no more.'
Loud crew the cock, the shadow fled;
  No more her Sandy did she see;
But soft the passing spirit said,
  'Sweet Mary, weep no more for me.' "

"The constant jollity of that boy is worth a fortune to him. He'll never sink with such a buoyant spirit to keep him afloat through life," said Mrs. Jo, as the roses were tossed back with much applause when the song ended.

"Not he; and it's a blessing to be grateful for, isn't it? We moody people know its worth. Glad you like my first tableau. Come and see number two. Hope it isn't spoilt; it was very pretty just now. This is 'Othello telling his adventures to Desdemona.' "

The second window framed a very picturesque group of three. Mr. March in an arm-chair, with Bess on a cushion at his feet, was listening to Dan, who, leaning against a pillar, was talking with unusual animation. The old man was in shadow, but little Desdemona was looking up with the moonlight full upon her into young Othello's face, quite absorbed in the story he was telling so well. The gay drapery over Dan's shoulder, his dark colouring, and the gesture of his arm made the picture very striking, and both spectators enjoyed it with silent pleasure, till Mrs. Jo said in a quick whisper:

"I'm glad he's going away. He's too picturesque to have here among so many romantic girls. Afraid his 'grand, gloomy, and peculiar' style will be too much for our simple maids."

"No danger; Dan is in the rough as yet, and always will be, I fancy; though he is improving in many ways. How well Queenie looks in that soft light!"

"Dear little Goldilocks looks well everywhere." And with a backward glance full of pride and fondness, Mrs. Jo went on. But that scene returned to her long afterward and her own prophetic words also.

Number three was a tragical tableau at first sight; and Mr. Laurie stifled a laugh as he whispered "The Wounded Knight," pointing to Tom with his head enveloped in a large handkerchief, as he knelt before Nan, who was extracting a thorn or splinter from the palm of his hand with great skill, to judge from the patient's blissful expression of countenance.

"Do I hurt you?" she asked, turning the hand to the moonlight for a better view.

"Not a bit; dig away; I like it," answered Tom, regardless of his aching knees and the damage done to his best trousers.

"I won't keep you long."

"Hours, if you please. Never so happy as here."

Quite unmoved by this tender remark, Nan put on a pair of large, round-eyed glasses, saying in a matter-of-fact tone: "Now I see it. Only a splinter, and there it is."

"My hand is bleeding; won't you bind it up?" asked Tom, wishing to prolong the situation.

"Nonsense; suck it. Only take care of it tomorrow if you dissect. Don't want any more blood-poisoning."

"That was the only time you were kind to me. Wish I'd lost my arm."

"I wish you'd lost your head; it smells more like turpentine and kerosene than ever. Do take a run in the garden and air it."

Fearing to betray themselves by laughter, the watchers went on, leaving the Knight to rush away in despair, and the Lady to bury her nose in the cup of a tall lily for refreshment.

"Poor Tom, his fate is a hard one, and he's wasting his time! Do advise him to quit philandering and go to work, Jo."

"I have, Teddy, often; but it will take some great shock to make that boy wise. I wait with interest to see what it will be. Bless me! what is all this?"

She might well ask; for on a rustic stool stood Ted trying to pose on one foot, with the other extended, and both hands waving in the air. Josie, with several young mates, was watching his contortions with deep interest as they talked about "little wings," "gilded wire twisted," and a "cunning skull-cap."

"This might be called 'Mercury Trying to Fly,' " said Mr. Laurie, as they peeped through the lace curtains.

"Bless the long legs of that boy! how does he expect to manage them? They are planning for the Owlsdark Marbles, and a nice muddle they will make of my gods and goddesses with no one to show them how," answered Mrs. Jo, enjoying this scene immensely.

"Now, he's got it!" "That's perfectly splendid!" "See how long you can keep so!" cried the girls, as Ted managed to maintain his equilibrium a moment by resting one toe on the trellis. Unfortunately this brought all his weight on the other foot; the straw seat of the stool gave way, and the flying Mercury came down with a crash, amid shrieks of laughter from the girls. Being accustomed to ground and lofty tumbling, he quickly recovered himself, and hopped gaily about, with one leg through the stool as he improvised a classic jig.

"Thanks for four nice little pictures. You have given me an idea, and I think some time we will get up regular tableaux of this sort and march our company round a set of dissolving views. New and striking; I'll propose it to our manager and give you all the glory," said Mrs. Jo, as they strolled towards the room whence came the clash of glass and china, and glimpses of agitated black coats.

Let us follow the example of our old friends and stroll about among the young people, eavesdropping, so gathering up various little threads to help in the weaving of the

story. George and Dolly were at supper, and having served
the ladies in their care stood in a corner absorbing nourishment of all kinds with a vain attempt to conceal hearty
appetites under an air of elegant indifference.

"Good spread, this; Laurence does things in style. First-
rate coffee, but no wine, and that's a mistake," said Stuffy,
who still deserved his name, and was a stout youth with a
heavy eye and bilious complexion.

"Bad for boys, he says. Jove! wish he could see us at
some of our wines. Don't we just 'splice the main-brace'
as Emil says," answered Dolly, the dandy, carefully spread-
ing a napkin over the glossy expanse of shirt-front whereon
a diamond stud shone like a lone star. His stutter was
nearly outgrown; but he, as well as George, spoke in the
tone of condescension, which, with the blasé airs they
assumed, made a very funny contrast to their youthful
faces and foolish remarks. Good-hearted little fellows both,
but top-heavy with the pride of being Sophs and the
freedom that college life gave them.

"Little Jo is getting to be a deuced pretty girl, isn't she?"
said George, with a long sigh of satisfaction as his first
mouthful of ice went slowly down his throat.

"H'm—well, fairish. The Princess is rather more to my
taste. I like 'em blonde and queenly and elegant, don't you
know."

"Yes, Jo *is* too lively; might as well dance with a grasshopper. I've tried her, and she's one too many for me.
Miss Perry is a nice, easy-going girl. Got her for the
german."

"You'll never be a dancing man. Too lazy. Now I'll
undertake to steer any girl and dance down any fellow you
please. Dancing's my forte." And Dolly glanced from his
trim feet to his flashing gem with the defiant air of a young
turkey-cock on parade.

"Miss Grey is looking for you. Wants more grub. Just
see if Miss Nelson's plate is empty, there's a good fellow.
Can't eat ice in a hurry." And George remained in his safe
corner, while Dolly struggled through the crowd to do his
duty, coming back in a fume, with a splash of salad dressing
on his coat-cuff.

"Confound these country chaps! they go blundering round

like so many dor-bugs, and make a deuce of a mess. Better
stick to books and not try to be society men. Can't do it.
Beastly stain. Give it a rub, and let me bolt a mouthful,
I'm starved. Never saw girls eat such a lot. It proves that
they ought not to study so much. Never liked co-ed,"
growled Dolly, much ruffled in spirit.

"So they do. 'Tisn't ladylike. Ought to be satisfied with
an ice and a bit of cake, and eat it prettily. Don't like to
see a girl feed. We hard-working men need it, and, by
Jove, I mean to get some more of that meringue if it's not
all gone. Here, waiter! bring along that dish over there,
and be lively," commanded Stuffy, poking a young man in
a rather shabby dress-suit, who was passing with a tray of
glasses.

His order was obeyed promptly; but George's appetite
was taken away the next moment by Dolly's exclaiming, as
he looked up from his damaged coat, with a scandalized
face:

"You've put your foot in it now, old boy! that's Morton,
Mr. Bhaer's crack man. Knows everything, no end of a
'dig,' and bound to carry off all the honours. You won't
hear the last of it in a hurry." And Dolly laughed so
heartily that a spoonful of ice flew upon the head of a lady
sitting below him, and got *him* into a scrape also.

Leaving them to their despair, let us listen to the whispered chat of two girls comfortably seated in a recess
waiting till their escorts were fed.

"I do think the Laurences give lovely parties. Don't you
enjoy them?" asked the younger, looking about her with
the eager air of one unused to this sort of pleasure.

"Very much, only I never feel as if I was dressed right.
My things seemed elegant at home, and I thought I'd be
over over-dressed if anything; but I look countrified and
dowdy here. No time or money to change now, even if I
knew how to do it," answered the other, glancing anxiously at her bright pink silk grown, trimmed with cheap
lace.

"You must get Mrs. Brooke to tell you how to fix your
things. She was very kind to me. I had a green silk, and it
looked so cheap and horrid by the side of the nice dresses
here I felt regularly unhappy about it, and asked her how

much a dress like one Mrs. Laurence had would cost. That
looked so simple and elegant I thought it wouldn't be
costly; but it was India mull and Valenciennes lace, so, of
course, I couldn't have it. Then Mrs. Brooke said: 'Get
some muslin to cover the green silk, and wear hops or
some white flowers, instead of pink, in your hair, and you
will have a pretty suit.' Isn't it lovely and becoming?" And
Miss Burton surveyed herself with girlish satisfaction; for a
little taste had softened the harsh green, and hop-bells
became her red hair better than roses.

"It's sweet: I've been admiring it. I'll do mine so and
ask about my purple one. Mrs. Brooke has helped me to
get rid of my headaches, and Mary Clay's dyspepsia is all
gone since she gave up coffee and hot bread."

"Mrs. Laurence advised me to walk and run and use the
gymnasium to cure my round shoulders and open my
chest, and I'm a much better figure than I was."

"Did you know that Mr. Laurence pays all Amelia Mer-
rill's bills? Her father failed, and she was heartbroken at
having to leave college; but that splendid man just stepped
in and made it all right."

"Yes, and Professor Bhaer has several of the boys down
at his house evenings to help them along so they can keep
up with the rest; and Mrs. Bhaer took care of Charles
Mackey herself when he had a fever last year. I do think
they are the best and kindest people in the world."

"So do I, and my time here will be the happiest and
most useful years of my life."

And both girls forgot their gowns and their suppers for a
moment to look with grateful, affectionate eyes at the
friends who tried to care for bodies and for souls as well as
minds.

Now come to a lively party supping on the stairs, girls
like foam at the top, and a substratum of youths below,
where the heaviest particles always settle. Emil, who never
sat if he could climb or perch, adorned the newel-post;
Tom, Nat, Demi, and Dan were camped on the steps,
eating busily, as their ladies were well served and they
had earned a moment's rest, which they enjoyed with
their eyes fixed on the pleasing prospect above them.

"I'm so sorry the boys are going. It will be dreadfully

dull without them. Now they have stopped teasing and are polite, I really enjoy them," said Nan, who felt unusually gracious tonight as Tom's mishap kept him from annoying her.

"So do I; and Bess was mourning about it today, though as a general thing she doesn't like boys unless they are models of elegance. She has been doing Dan's head, and it is not quite finished. I never saw her so interested in any work, and it's very well done. He is so striking and big he always makes me think of the Dying Gladiator or some of those antique creatures. There's Bess now. Dear child, how sweet she looks tonight!" answered Daisy, waving her hand as the Princess went by with Grandpa on her arm.

"I never thought he would turn out so well. Don't you remember how we used to call him 'the bad boy' and be sure he would become a pirate or something awful because he glared at us and swore sometimes? Now he is the handsomest of all the boys, and very entertaining with his stories and plans. I like him very much; he's so big and strong and independent. I'm tired of molly-coddles and book-worms," said Nan in her decided way.

"Not handsomer than Nat!" cried loyal Daisy, contrasting two faces below, one unusually gay, the other sentimentally sober even in the act of munching cake. "I like Dan, and am glad he is doing well; but he tires me, and I'm still a little afraid of him. Quiet people suit me best."

"Life is a fight, and I like a good soldier. Boys take things too easily, don't see how serious it all is and go to work in earnest. Look at that absurd Tom, wasting his time and making an object of himself just because he can't have what he wants, like a baby crying for the moon. I've no patience with such nonsense," scolded Nan, looking down at the jovial Thomas, who was playfully putting macaroons in Emil's shoes, and trying to beguile his exile as best he could.

"Most girls would be touched by such fidelity. I think it's beautiful," said Daisy behind her fan; for other girls sat just below.

"You are a sentimental goose and not a judge. Nat will be twice the man when he comes back after his trip. I wish Tom was going with him. My idea is that if we girls

have any influence we should use it for the good of these
boys, and not pamper them up, making slaves of ourselves
and tyrants of them. Let them prove what they can do and
be before they ask anything of us, and give us a chance to
do the same. Then we know where we are, and shall not
make mistakes to mourn over all our lives."

"Hear, hear!" cried Alice Heath, who was a girl after
Nan's own heart, and had chosen a career, like a brave
and sensible young woman. "Only give us a chance, and
have patience till we can do our best. Now we are expected to be as wise as men who have had generations of
all the help there is, and we scarcely anything. Let us
have equal opportunities, and in a few generations we will
see what the judgement is. I like justice, and we get very
little of it."

"Still shouting the battle-cry of freedom?" asked Demi,
peering through the banisters at this moment. "Up with
your flag! I'll stand by and lend a hand if you want it. With
you and Nan to lead the van, I think you won't need much
help."

"You are a great comfort, Demi, and I'll call on you in
all emergencies; for you are an honest boy, and don't
forget that you owe much to your mother and your sisters
and your aunts," continued Nan. "I do like men who come
out frankly and own that they are *not* gods. How can *we*
think them so when such awful mistakes are being made
all the time by these great creatures? See them sick, as I
do, then you know them."

"Don't hit us when we are down; be merciful, and set
us up to bless and believe in you evermore," pleaded
Demi from behind the bars.

"We'll be kind to you if you will be just to us. I don't
say generous, only just.·I went to a suffrage debate in the
Legislature last winter; and of all the feeble, vulgar twaddle I ever heard, that was the worst; and those men were
our representatives. I blushed for them, and the wives
and mothers. I want an intelligent man to represent *me*, if
I can't do it myself, not a fool."

"Nan is on the stump. Now we shall catch it," cried
Tom, putting up an umbrella to shield his unhappy head;

for Nan's earnest voice was audible, and her indignant eye
happened to rest on him as she spoke.

"Go on, go on! I'll take notes, and put in 'great applause' liberally," added Demi, producing his ball-book
and pencil, with his Jenkins air.

Daisy pinched his nose through the bars, and the meeting was rather tumultuous for a moment, for Emil called:
"Avast, avast, here's a squall to wind'ard"; Tom applauded
wildly; Dan looked up as if the prospect of a fight, even
with words, pleased him, and Nat went to support Demi,
as his position seemed to be a good one. At this crisis,
when everyone laughed and talked at once, Bess came
floating through the upper hall and looked down like an
angel of peace upon the noisy group below, as she asked,
with wondering eyes and smiling lips:

"What is it?"

"An indignation meeting. Nan and Alice are on the
rampage, and we are at the bar to be tried for our lives.
Will Your Highness preside and judge between us?"
answered Demi, as a lull at once took place; for no one
rioted in the presence of the Princess.

"I'm not wise enough. I'll sit here and listen. Please go
on." And Bess took her place above them all as cool and
calm as a little statue of Justice, with fan and nosegay in
place of sword and scales.

"Now, ladies, free your minds, only spare us till morning; for we've got a german to dance as soon as everyone is
fed, and Parnassus expects every man to do his duty. Mrs.
President Giddy-gaddy has the floor," said Demi, who
liked this sort of fun better than the very mild sort of
flirtation which was allowed at Plumfield, for the simple
reason that it could not be entirely banished, and is a part
of all education, co—or otherwise.

"I have only one thing to say, and it is this," began Nan
soberly, though her eyes sparkled with a mixture of fun
and earnestness. "I want to ask every boy of you what you
really think on this subject. Dan and Emil have seen the
world and ought to know their own minds. Tom and Nat
have had five examples before them for years. Demi is
ours and we are proud of him. So is Rob. Ted is a weath-
ercock, and Dolly and George, of course, are fogies in

spite of the Annex, and girls at Girton going ahead of the men. Commodore, are you ready for the question?"

"Ay, ay, skipper."

"Do you believe in Woman's Suffrage?"

"Bless your pretty figger head! I do, and I'll ship a crew of girls any time you say so. Aren't they worse than a press-gang to carry a fellow out of his moorings? Don't we all need one as pilot to steer us safe to port? and why shouldn't they share our mess afloat and ashore since we are sure to be wrecked without 'em?"

"Good for you, Emil! Nan will take you for first mate after that handsome speech," said Demi, as the girls applauded, and Tom glowered.

"Now, Dan, you love liberty so well yourself, are you willing we should have it?"

"All you can get, and I'll fight any man who's mean enough to say you don't deserve it."

This brief and forcible reply delighted the energetic President, and she beamed upon the member from California, as she said briskly:

"Nat wouldn't dare to say he was on the other side even if he were, but I hope he has made up his mind to pipe for us, at least when we take the field, and not be one of those who wait till the battle is won, and then beat the drums and share the glory."

Mrs. Giddy-gaddy's doubts were most effectually removed, and her sharp speech regretted, as Nat looked up blushing, but with a new sort of manliness in face and manner, saying, in a tone that touched them all:

"I should be the most ungrateful fellow alive if I did not love, honour, and serve women with all my heart and might, for to them I owe everything I am or ever shall be."

Daisy clapped her hands, and Bess threw her bouquet into Nat's lap, while the other girls waved their fans, well pleased; for real feeling made his little speech eloquent.

"Thomas B. Bangs, come into court, and tell the truth, the whole truth, and nothing but the truth, if you can," commanded Nan, with the rap to call the meeting to order.

Tom shut the umbrella, and standing up raised his hand, saying solemnly:

"I believe in suffrage of *all* kinds. I adore *all* women, and will die for them at any moment if it will help the cause."

"Living and working for it is harder, and therefore more honourable. Men are always ready to die for us, but not to make our lives worth having. Cheap sentiment and bad logic. You will pass, Tom, only don't twaddle. Now, having taken the sense of the meeting we will adjourn, as the hour for festive gymnastics has arrived. I am glad to see that old Plum has given six true men to the world, and hope they will continue to be staunch to her and the principles she has taught them, wherever they may go. Now, girls, don't sit in draughts, and, boys, beware of ice-water when you are warm."

With this characteristic close Nan retired from office, and the girls went to enjoy one of the few rights allowed them.

Chapter 6

Last Words

THE NEXT DAY was Sunday, and a goodly troop of young and old set forth to church—some driving, some walking, all enjoying the lovely weather and the happy quietude which comes to refresh us when the work and worry of the week are over. Daisy had a headache; and Aunt Jo remained at home to keep her company, knowing very well that the worst ache was in the tender heart struggling dutifully against the love that grew stronger as the parting drew nearer.

"Daisy knows my wishes, and I trust her. You must keep an eye on Nat, and let him clearly understand that there is to be no 'lovering,' or I shall forbid the letter-writing. I hate to seem cruel, but it is too soon for my dear girl to bind herself in any way," said Mrs. Meg, as she rustled about in her best grey silk, while waiting for Demi, who always escorted his pious mother to church as a peace-offering for crossing her wishes in other things.

"I will, dear; I'm lying in wait for all three boys today, like an old spider; and I will have a good talk with each. They know I understand them, and they always open their hearts sooner or later. You look like a nice, plump little Quakeress, Meg; and no one will believe that big boy is your son," added Mrs. Jo, as Demi came in shining with Sunday neatness, from his well-blacked boots to his smooth brown head.

"You flatter me, to soften my heart toward *your* boy. I know your ways, Jo, and I don't give in. Be firm, and spare me a scene by and by. As for John, as long as he is satisfied with his old mother, I don't care what people think," answered Mrs. Meg, accepting with a smile the

86

little posy of sweet peas and mignonette Demi brought her.

Then, having buttoned her dove-coloured gloves with care, she took her son's arm and went proudly away to the carriage, where Amy and Bess waited, while Jo called after them, just as Marmee used to do:

"Girls, *have* you got nice pocket-handkerchiefs?" They all smiled at the familiar words, and three white banners waved as they drove away, leaving the spider to watch for her first fly. She did not wait long. Daisy was lying down with a wet cheek on the little hymn-book out of which she and Nat used to sing together; so Mrs. Jo strolled about the lawn, looking very like a wandering mushroom with her large buff umbrella.

Dan had gone for a ten-mile stroll; and Nat was supposed to have accompanied him, but presently came sneaking back, unable to tear himself away from the Dovecote or lose a moment of nearness to his idol that last day. Mrs. Jo saw him at once, and beckoned him to a rustic seat under the old elm, where they could have their confidences undisturbed, and both keep an eye on a certain white-curtained window, half hidden in vines.

"Nice and cool here. I'm not up to one of Dan's tramps today—it's so warm, and he goes so like a steam-engine. He headed for the swamp where his pet snakes used to live, and I begged to be excused," said Nat, fanning himself with his straw hat, though the day was not oppressive.

"I'm glad you did. Sit and rest with me, and have one of our good old talks. We've both been so busy lately, I feel as if I didn't half know your plans; and I want to," answered Mrs. Jo, feeling sure that though they might start with Leipzig they would bring up at Plumfield.

"You are very kind, and there's nothing I'd like better. I don't realize I'm going so far—suppose I shan't till I get afloat. It's a splendid start, and I don't know how I can ever thank Mr. Laurie for all he's done, or you either," added Nat, with a break in his voice; for he was a tender-hearted fellow, and never forgot a kindness.

"You can thank us beautifully by being and doing all we hope and expect of you, my dear. In the new life you are going to there will be a thousand trials and temptations, and only your own wit and wisdom to rely on. That will be the time to test the principles we have tried to give you, and see how firm they are. Of course, you will make mistakes—we all do; but don't let go of your conscience and drift along blindly. Watch and pray, dear Nat; and while your hand gains skill, let your head grow wiser, and keep your heart as innocent and warm as it is now."

"I'll try, Mother Bhaer, my very best to be a credit to you. I know I shall improve in my music—can't help it there; but I never shall be very wise, I'm afraid. As for my heart, you know, I leave it behind me in good keeping."

As he spoke, Nat's eyes were fixed on the window with a look of love and longing that made his quiet face both manly and sad—plainly showing how strong a hold this boyish affection had upon him.

"I want to speak of that; and I know you will forgive what seems hard, because I do most heartily sympathize with you," said Mrs. Jo, glad to have her say.

"Yes, do talk about Daisy! I think of nothing but leaving and losing her. I have no hope—I suppose it is too much to ask; only I can't help loving her, wherever I am!" cried Nat, with a mixture of defiance and despair in his face that rather startled Mrs. Jo.

"Listen to me and I'll try to give you both comfort and good advice. We all know that Daisy is fond of you, but her mother objects, and being a good girl she tries to obey. Young people think they never can change, but they do in the most wonderful manner, and very few die of broken hearts." Mrs. Jo smiled as she remembered another boy whom she had once tried to comfort, and then went soberly on while Nat listened as if his fate hung upon her lips.

"One of two things will happen. You will find someone else to love, or, better still, be so busy and happy in your music that you will be willing to wait for time to settle the matter for you both. Daisy will perhaps forget when you are gone, and be glad you are only friends. At any rate it is much wiser to have no promises made; then both are free, and in a year or two may meet to laugh over the little romance nipped in the bud."

"Do you honestly think that?" asked Nat, looking at her so keenly that the truth had to come; for all his heart was in those frank blue eyes of his.

"No, I don't!" answered Mrs. Jo.

"Then if you were in my place, what would you do?" he added, with a tone of command never heard in his gentle voice before.

"Bless me! the boy is in dead earnest, and I shall forget prudence in sympathy I'm afraid," thought Mrs. Jo, surprised and pleased by the unexpected manliness Nat showed.

"I'll tell you what I should do. I'd say to myself: 'I'll prove that my love is strong and faithful, and make Daisy's mother proud to give her to me by being not only a good musician but an excellent man, and so command respect and confidence. This I will try for; and if I fail, I shall be the better for the effort, and find comfort in the thought that I did my best for her sake.' "

"That is what I meant to do. But I wanted a word of hope to give me courage," cried Nat, firing up as if the smouldering spark was set ablaze by a breath of encouragement. "Other fellows, poorer and stupider than I, have done great things and come to honour. Why may not I, though I'm nothing now? I know Mrs. Brooke remembers what I came from, but my father was *honest* though everything went wrong; and I have nothing to be ashamed of though I *was* a charity boy. I never will be ashamed of my people or myself, and I'll make other folks respect me if I can."

"Good! that's the right spirit, Nat. Hold to it and make yourself a man. No one will be quicker to see and admire the brave work than my sister Meg. She does not despise your poverty or your past; but mothers are very tender over their daughters, and we Marches, though we have been poor, *are*, I confess, a little proud of our good family. We don't care for money; but a long line of virtuous ancestors *is* something to desire and to be proud of."

"Well, the Blakes are a good lot. I looked 'em up, and not one was ever in prison, hanged, or disgraced in any way. We used to be rich and honoured years ago, but we've died out and got poor, and father was a street musician rather than beg; and I'll be one again before I'll do the mean things some men do and pass muster."

Nat was so excited that Mrs. Jo indulged in a laugh to calm him, and both went on more quietly.

"I told my sister all that and it pleased her. I am sure if you do well these next few years that she will relent and all be happily settled, unless that wonderful change, which you don't believe possible, should occur. Now, cheer up; don't be lackadaisical and blue. Say good-bye cheerfully and bravely, show a manly front, and leave a pleasant memory behind you. We all wish you well and hope much for you. Write to me every week and I'll send a good, gossipy answer. Be careful what you write to Daisy; don't gush or wail, for sister Meg will see the letters; and you can help your cause very much by sending sensible, cheery accounts of your life to us all."

"I will; I will; it looks brighter and better already, and I won't lose my one comfort by any fault of my own. Thank you so much, Mother Bhaer, for taking my side. I felt so ungrateful and mean and crushed when I thought you all considered me a sneak, who had no business to love such a precious girl as Daisy. No one said anything, but I knew how you felt, and that Mr. Laurie sent me off partly to get me out of the way. Oh dear, life is pretty tough sometimes, isn't it?" And Nat took his head in both hands as if it ached with the confusion of hopes and fears, passions and plans that proved boyhood was past and manhood had begun.

"Very tough, but it is that very struggle with obstacles which does us good. Things have been made easy for you in many ways, but no one can do everything. You must paddle your own canoe now, and learn to avoid the rapids and steer straight to the port you want to reach. I don't know just what your temptations will be, for you have no bad habits and seem to love music so well, nothing can lure you from it. I only hope you won't work too hard."

"I feel as if I *could* work like a horse, I'm so eager to get on; but I'll take care. Can't waste time being sick, and you've given me doses enough to keep me all right, I guess." Nat laughed as he remembered the book of directions Mrs. Jo had written for him to consult on all occasions.

She immediately added some verbal ones on the subject of foreign messes, and having mounted one of her pet hobbies, was in full gallop when Emil was seen strolling about on the roof of the old house, that being his favourite promenade; for there he could fancy himself walking the deck, with only blue sky and fresh air about him.

"I want a word with the Commodore, and up there we shall be nice and quiet. Go and play to Daisy: it will put her to sleep and do you both good. Sit in the porch, so I can keep an eye on you as I promised"; and with a motherly pat on the shoulder Mrs. Jo left Nat to his delightful task and briskly ascended to the house-top, not up the trellis as of old but by means of the stairs inside.

Emerging on the platform she found Emil cutting his initials afresh in the wood-work and singing "Pull for the Shore," like the tuneful mariner he was.

"Come aboard and make yourself at home, Aunty," he said, with a playful salute. "I'm just leaving a P.P.C. in the old place, so when you fly up here for refuge you'll remember me."

"Ah, my dear, I'm not likely to forget you. It doesn't need E.B.H. cut on all the trees and railings to remind me of my sailor boy; and Mrs. Jo took the seat nearest the blue figure astride the balustrade, not quite sure how to begin the little sermon she wanted to preach.

"Well, you don't pipe your eye and look squally when I sheer off as you used to, and that's a comfort. I like to leave port in fair weather and have a jolly send-off all round. Specially this time, for it will be a year or more before we drop anchor here again," answered Emil, pushing his cap back, and glancing about him as if he loved old Plum and would be sorry never to see it any more.

"You have salt water enough without my adding to it. I'm going to be quite a Spartan mother, and send my sons to battle with no wailing, only the command: 'With your shield or on it,' " said Mrs. Jo cheerfully, adding after a pause: "I often wish I could go too, and some day I will, when you are captain and have a ship of your own—as I've no doubt you will before long, with Uncle Herman to push you on."

"When I do I'll christen her the *Jolly Jo* and take you as

first mate. It would be regular larks to have you aboard,
and I'd be a proud man to carry you round the world
you've wanted to see so long and never could," answered
Emil, caught at once by this splendid vision.

"I'll make my first voyage with you and enjoy myself
immensely in spite of seasickness and all the stormy winds
that blow. I've always thought I'd like to see a wreck, a
nice safe one with all saved after great danger and heroic
deeds, while we clung like Mr. Pillicoddy to main-top jibs
and lee scuppers."

"No wrecks yet, ma'am, but we'll try to accommodate
customers. Captain says I'm a lucky dog and bring fair
weather, so we'll save the dirty weather for you if you
want it," laughed Emil, digging at the ship in full sail
which he was adding to his design.

"Thanks, I hope you will. This long voyage will give you
new experiences, and being an officer, you will have new
duties and responsibilities. Are you ready for them? You
take everything so gaily, I've been wondering if you real-
ized that now you will have not only to obey but to
command also, and power is a dangerous thing. Be careful
that you don't abuse it or let it make a tyrant of you."

"Right you are, ma'am. I've seen plenty of that, and
have got my bearings pretty well, I guess. I shan't have
very wide swing with Peters over me, but I'll see that the
boys don't get abused when he's bowsed up his jib. No
right to speak before, but now I won't stand it."

"That sounds mysteriously awful; could I ask what nautical torture 'bowsing jibs' is?" asked Mrs. Jo, in a tone of
deep interest.

"Getting drunk. Peters can hold more grog than any
man I ever saw; he keeps right side up, but is as savage as
a norther, and makes things lively all round. I've seen him
knock a fellow down with a belaying pin, and couldn't lend
a hand. Better luck now, I hope." And Emil frowned as if
he already trod the quarter-deck, lord of all he surveyed.

"Don't get into trouble, for even Uncle Herman's favour
won't cover insubordination, you know. You have proved
yourself a good sailor; now be a good officer, which is a
harder thing, I fancy. It takes a fine character to rule justly
and kindly; you will have to put by your boyish ways and

remember your dignity. That will be excellent training for you, Emil, and sober you down a bit. No more skylarking except here, so mind your ways, and do honour to your buttons," said Mrs. Jo, tapping one of the very bright brass ones that ornamented the new suit Emil was so proud of.

"I'll do my best. I know my time for skirmshander (chaff) is over, and I must steer a straighter course; but don't you fear, Jack ashore is a very different craft from what he is with blue water under his keel. I had a long talk with Uncle last night and got my orders; I won't forget 'em nor all I owe him. As for you, I'll name my first ship as I say, and have your bust for the figurehead, see if I don't; and Emil gave his aunt a hearty kiss to seal the vow, which proceeding much amused Nat, playing softly in the porch of the Dovecote.

"You do me proud, Captain. But, dear, I want to say one thing and then I'm done; for you don't need much advice of mine after my good man has spoken. I read somewhere that every inch of rope used in the British Navy has a strand of red in it, so that wherever a bit of it is found it is known. That is the text of my little sermon to you. Virtue, which means honour, honesty, courage, and all that makes character, is the red thread that marks a good man wherever he is. Keep that always and everywhere, so that even if wrecked by misfortune, that sign shall still be found and recognized. Yours is a rough life, and your mates not all we could wish, but you can be a gentleman in the true sense of the word; and no matter what happens to your body, keep your soul clean, your heart true to those who love you, and do your duty to the end."

As she spoke Emil had risen and stood listening with his cap off and a grave, bright look as if taking orders from a superior officer; when she ended, he answered briefly, but heartily:

"Please God, I will!"

"That's all; I have little fear for you, but one never knows when or how the weak moment may come, and sometimes a chance word helps us, as so many my dear mother spoke come back to me now for my own comfort

and the guidance of my boys," said Mrs. Jo, rising; for the
words had been said and no more were needed.

"I've stored 'em up and know where to find 'em when
wanted. Often and often in my watch I've seen old Plum,
and heard you and Uncle talking so plainly, I'd have sworn
I was here. It *is* a rough life, Aunty, but a wholesome one
if a fellow loves it as I do, and has an anchor to windward
as I have. Don't worry about me, and I'll come home next
year with a chest of tea that will cheer your heart and give
you ideas enough for a dozen novels. Going below? All
right, steady in the gangway! I'll be along by the time
you've got out the cake-box. Last chance for a good old
lunch ashore."

Mrs. Jo descended laughing, and Emil finished his ship
whistling cheerfully, neither dreaming when and where
this little chat on the house-top would return to the memory of one of them.

Dan was harder to catch, and not until evening did a
quiet moment come in that busy family; when, while the
rest were roaming about, Mrs. Jo sat down to read in the
study, and presently Dan looked in at the window.

"Come and rest after your long tramp; you must be
tired," she called, with an inviting nod towards the big
sofa where so many boys had reposed—as much as that
active animal ever does.

"Afraid I shall disturb you"; but Dan looked as if he
wanted to stay his restless feet somewhere.

"Not a bit; I'm always ready to talk, shouldn't be a
woman if I were not," laughed Mrs. Jo, as Dan swung
himself in and sat down with an air of contentment very
pleasant to see.

"Last day is over, yet somehow I don't seem to hanker
to be off. Generally, I'm rather anxious to cut loose after a
short stop. Odd, ain't it?" asked Dan, gravely picking
grass and leaves out of his hair and beard; for he had been
lying on the grass, thinking many thoughts in the quiet
summer night.

"Not at all; you are beginning to get civilized. It's a
good sign, and I'm glad to see it," answered Mrs. Jo
promptly. "You've had your swing, and want a change.
Hope the farming will give it to you, though helping the

Indians pleases me more: it is so much better to work for others than for one's self alone."

"So 'tis," assented Dan heartily. "I seem to want to root somewhere and have folks of my own to take care of. Tired of my own company, I suppose, now I've seen so much better. I'm a rough, ignorant lot, and I've been thinking maybe I've missed it loafing round creation, instead of going in for education as the other chaps did. Hey?"

He looked anxiously at Mrs. Jo; and she tried to hide the surprise this new outburst caused her; for till now Dan had scorned books and gloried in his freedom.

"No; I don't think so in your case. So far I'm sure the free life was best. Now that you are a man you can control that lawless nature better; but as a boy only great activity and much adventure could keep you out of mischief. Time is taming my colt, you see, and I shall yet be proud of him, whether he makes a pack-horse of himself to carry help to the starving or goes to ploughing as Pegasus did."

Dan liked the comparison, and smiled as he lounged in the sofa-corner, with the new thoughtfulness in his eyes.

"Glad you think so. The fact is it's going to take a heap of taming to make me go well in harness anywhere. I want to, and I try now and then, but always kick over the traces and run away. No lives lost yet; but I shouldn't wonder if there was some time, and a general smash-up."

"Why, Dan, did you have any dangerous adventures during this last absence? I fancied so, but didn't ask before, knowing you'd tell me if I could help in any way. Can I?" And Mrs. Jo looked anxiously at him; for a sudden lowering expression had come into his face, and he leaned forward as if to hide it.

"Nothing very bad; but 'Frisco isn't just a heaven on earth, you know, and it's harder to be a saint there than here," he answered slowly; then, as if he had made up his mind to 'fess,' as the children used to say, he sat up, and added rapidly, in a half-defiant, half-shamefaced way, "I tried gambling, and it wasn't good for me."

"Was that how you made your money?"

"Not a penny of it! That's all honest, if speculation isn't a bigger sort of gambling. I won a lot; but I lost or gave it

away, and cut the whole concern before it got the better of
me."

"Thank heaven for that! Don't try it again; it may have
the terrible fascination for you it has for so many. Keep to
your mountains and prairies, and shun cities, if these
things tempt you, Dan. Better lose your life than your
soul, and one such passion leads to worse sins, as you
know better than I."

Dan nodded, and seeing how troubled she was, said, in
a lighter tone, though still the shadow of that past experience remained:

"Don't be scared; I'm all right now; and a burnt dog
dreads the fire. I don't drink, or do the things you dread;
don't care for 'em; but I get excited, and then this devilish
temper of mine is more than I can manage. Fighting a
moose or a buffalo is all right; but when you pitch into a
man, no matter how great a scamp he is, you've got to
look out. I shall kill someone some day; that's all I'm afraid
of. I do hate a sneak!" And Dan brought his fist down on
the table with a blow that made the lamp totter and the
books skip.

"That always was your trial, Dan, and I can sympathize
with you; for I've been trying to govern my own temper
all my life, and haven't learnt yet," said Mrs. Jo, with a
sigh. "For heaven's sake, guard your demon well, and
don't let a moment's fury ruin all your life. As I said to
Nat, watch and pray, my dear boy. There is no other help
or hope for human weakness but God's love and patience."

Tears were in Mrs. Jo's eyes as she spoke; for she felt
this deeply, and knew how hard a task it is to rule these
bosom sins of ours. Dan looked touched, also uncomfort-
able, as he always did when religion of any sort was
mentioned, though he had a simple creed of his own, and
tried to live up to it in his blind way.

"I don't do much praying; don't seem to come handy to
me; but I can watch like a redskin, only it's easier to
mount guard over a lurking grizzly than my own cursed
temper. It's that I'm afraid of, if I settle down. I can get on
with wild beasts first-rate; but men rile me awfully, and I
can't take it out in a free fight, as I can with a bear or a
wolf. Guess I'd better head for the Rockies, and stay there

a spell longer—till I'm tame enough for decent folks, if I ever am." And Dan leaned his rough head on his hands in a despondent attitude.

"Try my sort of help, and don't give up. Read more, study a little, and try to meet a better class of people, who won't 'rile,' but soothe and strengthen you. We don't make you savage, I'm sure; for you have been as meek as a lamb, and made us very happy."

"Glad of it; but I've felt like a hawk in a hen-house all the same, and wanted to pounce and tear more than once. Not so much as I used, though," added Dan, after a short laugh at Mrs. Jo's surprised face. "I'll try your plan, and keep good company this bout if I can; but a man can't pick and choose, knocking about as I do."

"Yes, you can this time; for you are going on a peaceful errand and can keep clear of temptation if you try. Take some books and read; that's an immense help; and books are always good company if you have the right sort. Let me pick out some for you." And Mrs. Jo made a bee-line to the well-laden shelves, which were the joy of her heart and the comfort of her life.

"Give me travels and stories, please; don't want any pious works, can't seem to relish 'em, and won't pretend I do," said Dan, following to look over her head with small favour at the long lines of well-worn volumes.

Mrs. Jo turned short round, and putting a hand on either broad shoulder, looked him in the eye, saying soberly:

"Now, Dan, see here; never sneer at good things or pretend to be worse than you are. Don't let false shame make you neglect the religion without which no man can live. You needn't talk about it if you don't like, but don't shut your heart to it in whatever shape it comes. Nature is your God now; she has done much for you; let her do more, and lead you to know and love a wiser and more tender teacher, friend, and comforter than she can ever be. That is your only hope; don't throw it away, and waste time; for sooner or later you will feel the need of Him, and He will come to you and hold you up when all other help fails."

Dan stood motionless, and let her read in his softened

eyes the dumb desire that lived in his heart, though he
had no words to tell it, and only permitted her to catch a
glimpse of the divine spark which smoulders or burns
clearly in every human soul. He did not speak; and glad to
be spared some answer which should belie his real feelings, Mrs. Jo hastened to say, with her most motherly
smile:

"I saw in your room the little Bible I gave you long ago;
it was well worn *outside*, but fresh within, as if not much
read. Will you promise me to read a little once a week,
dear, for my sake? Sunday is a quiet day everywhere, and
this book is never old nor out of place. Begin with the
stories you used to love when I told them to you boys.
David was your favourite, you remember? Read him again;
he'll suit you even better now, and you'll find his sins and
repentance useful reading till you come to the life and
work of a diviner example than he. You will do it, for love
of mother Bhaer, who always loved her 'firebrand' and
hoped to save him?"

"I will," answered Dan, with a sudden brightening of
face that was like a sunburst through a cloud, full of
promise though so short-lived and rare.

Mrs. Jo turned at once to the books and began to talk of
them, knowing well that Dan would not hear any more
just then. He seemed relieved; for it was always hard for
him to show his inner self, and he took pride in hiding it
as an Indian does in concealing pain or fear.

"Hallo, here's old Sintram! I remember him; used to
like him and his tantrums, and read about 'em to Ted.
There he is riding ahead with Death and the Devil
alongside."

As Dan looked at the little picture of the young man with
horse and hound going bravely up the rocky defile, accompanied by the companions who ride beside most men
through this world, a curious impulse made Mrs. Jo say
quickly:

"That's you, Dan, just you at this time! Danger and sin
are near you in the life you lead; moods and passions
torment you; the bad father left you to fight alone, and the
wild spirit drives you to wander up and down the world
looking for peace and self-control. Even the horse and

hound are there, your Octoo and Don, faithful friends, unscared by the strange mates that go with you. You have not got the armour yet, but I'm trying to show you where to find it. Remember the mother Sintram loved and longed to find, and did find when his battle was bravely fought, his reward well earned? You can recollect *your* mother; and I have always felt that all the good qualities you possess come from her. Act out the beautiful old story in this as in the other parts, and try to give her back a son to be proud of."

Quite carried away by the likeness of the quaint tale to Dan's life and needs, Mrs. Jo went on pointing to the various pictures which illustrated it, and when she looked up was surprised to see how struck and interested he seemed to be. Like all people of his temperament he was very impressionable, and his life among hunters and Indians had made him superstitious; he believed in dreams, liked weird tales, and whatever appealed to the eye or mind, vividly impressed him more than the wisest words. The story of poor, tormented Sintram came back clearly as he looked and listened, symbolizing his secret trials even more truly than Mrs. Jo knew; and just at that moment this had an effect upon him that never was forgotten. But all he said was:

"Small chance of that. I don't take much stock in the idea of meeting folks in heaven. Guess mother won't remember the poor little brat she left so long ago; why should she?"

"Because true mothers never forget their children; and I know *she* was one, from the fact that she ran away from the cruel husband, to save her little son from bad influences. Had she lived, life would have been happier for you, with this tender friend to help and comfort you. Never forget that she risked everything for your sake, and don't let it be in vain."

Mrs. Jo spoke very earnestly, knowing that this was the one sweet memory of Dan's early life, and glad to have recalled it at this moment; for suddenly a great tear splashed down on the page where Sintram kneels at his mother's feet, wounded, but victorious over sin and death. She looked up, well pleased to have touched Dan to the heart's core, as that drop proved; but a sweep of the arm brushed away the tell-tale, and his beard hid the mate to it, as he shut the book, saying with a suppressed quiver in his strong voice:

"I'll keep this, if nobody wants it. I'll read it over, and maybe it will do me good. I'd like to meet her anywhere, but don't believe I ever shall."

"Keep it and welcome. My mother gave it to me; and when you read it try to believe that neither of your mothers will ever forget you."

Mrs. Jo gave the book with a caress; and simply saying: "Thanks; good night," Dan thrust it into his pocket, and walked straight away to the river to recover from this unwonted mood of tenderness and confidence.

Next day the travellers were off. All were in good spirits, and a cloud of handkerchiefs whitened the air as they drove away in the old bus, waving their hats to everyone and kissing their hands, especially to mother Bhaer, who said in her prophetic tone as she wiped her eyes, when the familiar rumble died away:

"I have a feeling that something is going to happen to some of them, and they will never come back to me, or come back changed. Well, I can only say, God be with my boys!"

And He was.

Chapter 7

The Lion and the Lamb

WHEN THE BOYS were gone a lull fell upon Plumfield, and the family scattered to various places for brief outings, as August had come and all felt the need of change. The Professor took Mrs. Jo to the mountains. The Laurences were at the seashore, and there Meg's family and the Bhaer boys took turns to visit, as someone must always be at home to keep things in order.

Mrs. Meg, with Daisy, was in office when the events occurred which we are about to relate. Rob and Ted were just up from Rocky Nook, and Nan was passing a week with her friend as the only relaxation she allowed herself. Demi was off on a run with Tom, so Rob was man of the house, with old Silas as general overseer. The sea air seemed to have gone to Ted's head, for he was unusually freakish, and led his gentle aunt and poor Rob a life of it with his pranks. Octoo was worn out with the wild rides he took, and Don openly rebelled when ordered to leap and show off his accomplishments; while the girls at college were both amused and worried by the ghosts who haunted the grounds at night, the unearthly melodies that disturbed their studious hours, and the hairbreadth escapes of this restless boy by flood and field and fire. Something happened at length which effectually sobered Ted and made a lasting impression on both the boys; for sudden danger and a haunting fear turned the Lion into a lamb and the Lamb into a lion, as far as courage went.

On the first of September—the boys never forgot the date—after a pleasant tramp and good luck with their fishing, the brothers were lounging in the barn; for Daisy had company, and the lads kept out of the way.

"I tell you what it is, Bobby, that dog is sick. He won't play, nor eat, nor drink, and acts queerly. Dan will kill us if anything happens to him," said Ted, looking at Don, who lay near his kennel resting a moment after one of the restless wanderings which kept him vibrating between the door of Dan's room and the shady corner of the yard, where his master had settled him with an old cap to guard till he came back.

"It's the hot weather, perhaps. But I sometimes think he's pining for Dan. Dogs do, you know, and the poor fellow has been low in his mind ever since the boys went. Maybe something has happened to Dan. Don howled last night and can't rest. I've heard of such things," answered Rob thoughtfully.

"Pooh! he can't know. He's cross. I'll stir him up and take him for a run. Always makes me feel better. Hi, boy! wake up and be jolly;" and Ted snapped his fingers at the dog, who only looked at him with grim indifference.

"Better let him alone. If he isn't right tomorrow, we'll take him to Dr. Watkins and see what he says." And Rob went on watching the swallows as he lay in the hay polishing up some Latin verses he had made.

The spirit of perversity entered into Ted, and merely because he was told not to tease Don he went on doing it, pretending that it was for the dog's good. Don took no heed of his pats, commands, reproaches, or insults, till Ted's patience gave out; and seeing a convenient switch near by he could not resist the temptation to conquer the great hound by force, since gentleness failed to win obedience. He had the wisdom to chain Don up first; for a blow from any hand but his master's made him savage, and Ted had more than once tried the experiment, as the dog remembered. This indignity roused Don and he sat up with a growl. Rob heard it, and seeing Ted raise the switch, ran to interfere, exclaiming:

"Don't touch him! Dan forbade it! Leave the poor thing in peace; I won't allow it."

Rob seldom commanded, but when he did Master Ted had to give in. His temper was up, and Rob's masterful tone made it impossible to resist one cut at the rebellious dog before he submitted. Only a single blow, but it was a costly one; for as it fell, the dog sprang at Ted with a snarl, and Rob, rushing between the two, felt the sharp teeth pierce his leg. A word made Don let go and drop remorsefully at Rob's feet, for he loved him and was evidently sorry to have hurt his friend by mistake. With a forgiving pat Rob left him, to limp to the barn followed by Ted, whose wrath was changed to shame and sorrow when he saw the red drops on Rob's sock and the little wounds in his leg.

"I'm awfully sorry. Why *did* you get in the way? Here, wash it up, and I'll get a rag to tie on it," he said quickly filling a sponge with water and pulling out a very demoralized handkerchief.

Rob usually made light of his own mishaps and was over ready to forgive if others were to blame; but now he sat quite still, looking at the purple marks with such a strange expression on his white face that Ted was troubled, though he added with a laugh: "Why, you're not afraid of a little dig like that, are you, Bobby?"

"I am afraid of hydrophobia. But if Don *is* mad I'd rather be the one to have it," answered Rob, with a smile and a shiver.

At that dreadful word Ted turned whiter than his brother, and, dropping sponge and handkerchief, stared at him with a frightened face, whispering in a tone of despair:

"Oh, Rob, don't say it! What shall we do, what *shall* we do?"

"Call Nan; she will know. Don't scare Aunty, or tell a soul but Nan; she's on the back piazza; get her out here as quick as you can. I'll wash it till she comes. Maybe it's nothing; don't look so staggered, Ted. I only thought it might be, as Don is queer."

Rob tried to speak bravely; but Ted's long legs felt strangely weak as he hurried away, and it was lucky he met no one, for his face would have betrayed him. Nan was swinging luxuriously in a hammock, amusing herself with a lively treatise on croup, when an agitated boy suddenly clutched her, whispering, as he nearly pulled her overboard:

"Come to Rob in the barn! Don's mad and he's bitten

him, and we don't know what to do; it's all my fault; no one must know. Oh, do be quick!"

Nan was on her feet at once, startled, but with her wits about her, and both were off without more words as they dodged round the house where unconscious Daisy chatted with her friends in the parlour and Aunt Meg peacefully took her afternoon nap upstairs.

Rob was braced up, and was as calm and steady as ever when they found him in the harness-room, whither he had wisely retired, to escape observation. The story was soon told, and after a look at Don, now in his kennel, sad and surly, Nan said slowly, with her eye on the full water-pan:

"Rob, there is one thing to do for the sake of safety, and it must be done at once. We can't wait to see if Don is— sick—or to go for a doctor. I *can* do it, and I *will*; but it is very painful, and I hate to hurt you, dear."

A most unprofessional quiver got into Nan's voice as she spoke, and her keen eyes dimmed as she looked at the two anxious young faces turned so confidingly to her for help.

"I know, burn it; well, do it, please; I can bear it. But Ted better go away," said Rob, with a firm setting of his lips, and a nod at his afflicted brother.

"I won't stir; I can stand it if he can, only it ought to be me!" cried Ted, with a desperate effort not to cry, so full of grief and fear and shame was he that it seemed as if he couldn't bear it like a man.

"He'd better stay and help; do him good," answered Nan sternly, because her heart was faint within her, knowing as she did all that might be in store for both poor boys. "Keep quiet; I'll be back in a minute," she added, going towards the house, while her quick mind hastily planned what was best to be done.

It was ironing day, and a hot fire still burned in the empty kitchen, for the maids were upstairs resting. Nan put a slender poker to heat, and as she sat waiting for it, covered her face with her hands, asking help in this sudden need—strength, courage, and wisdom; for there was no one else to call upon, and young as she was, she knew what was to be done if she only had the nerve to do it. Any other patient would have been calmly interesting, but dear, good Robin, his father's pride, his mother's comfort, everyone's favourite and friend, that he should be in danger was very terrible; and a few hot tears dropped on the well-scoured table as Nan tried to calm her trouble by remembering how very likely it was to be all a mistake, a natural but vain alarm.

"I must make light of it, or the boys will break down, and then there will be a panic. Why afflict and frighten everyone when all is in doubt? I won't. I'll take Rob to Dr. Morrison at once, and have the dog man see Don. Then, having done all we can, we will either laugh at our scare—if it is one—or be ready for whatever comes. Now for my poor boy."

Armed with the red-hot poker, a pitcher of ice-water, and several handkerchiefs from the clothes-horse, Nan went back to the barn ready to do her best in this her most serious "emergency case". The boys sat like statues, one of despair, the other of resignation; and it took all Nan's boasted nerve to do her work quickly and well.

"Now, Rob, only a minute, then we are safe. Stand by, Ted; he may be a bit faintish."

Rob shut his eyes, clinched his hands, and sat like a hero. Ted knelt beside him, white as a sheet, and as weak as a girl; for the pangs of remorse were rending him, and his heart failed at the thought of all this pain because of his wilfulness. It was all over in a moment, with only one little groan; but when Nan looked to her assistant to hand the water, poor Ted needed it the most, for he had fainted away, and lay on the floor in a pathetic heap of arms and legs.

Rob laughed, and, cheered by that unexpected sound, Nan bound up the wound with hands that never trembled, though great drops stood on her forehead; and she shared the water with patient number one before she turned to patient number two. Ted was much ashamed, and quite broken in spirit, when he found how he had failed at the critical moment, and begged them not to tell, as he really could not help it; then by way of finishing his utter humiliation, a burst of hysterical tears disgraced his manly soul, and did him a world of good.

"Never mind, never mind, we are all right now, and no one need be the wiser," said Nan briskly, as poor Ted hiccoughed on Rob's shoulder, laughing and crying in the most tempestuous manner, while his brother soothed him, and the young doctor fanned both with Silas's old straw hat.

"Now, boys, listen to me and remember what I say. We won't alarm anyone *yet*, for I've made up my mind our scare is all nonsense. Don was out lapping the water as I came by, and I don't believe he's mad any more than I am. Still, to ease our minds and compose our spirits, and get our guilty faces out of sight for a while, I think we had better drive into town to my old friend Dr. Morrison, and let him just take a look at my work, and give us some quieting little dose; for we are all rather shaken by this flurry. Sit still, Rob; and Ted, you harness up while I run and get my hat and tell Aunty to excuse me to Daisy. I don't know those Penniman girls, and she will be glad of our room at tea, and we'll have a cosy bite at my house, and come home as gay as larks."

Nan talked on as a vent for the hidden emotions which professional pride would not allow her to show, and the boys approved her plan at once; for action is always easier than quiet waiting. Ted went staggering away to wash his face at the pump, and rub some colour into his cheeks before he harnessed the horse. Rob lay tranquilly on the hay, looking up at the swallows again as he lived through some very memorable moments. Boy as he was, the thought of death coming suddenly to him, and in this way, might well make him sober; for it is a very solemn thing to be arrested in the midst of busy life by the possibility of the great change. There were no sins to be repented of, few faults, and many happy, dutiful years to remember with infinite comfort. So Rob had no fears to daunt him, no regrets to sadden, and best of all, a very strong and simple piety to sustain and cheer him.

"Mein Vater," was his first thought; for Rob was very near the professor's heart, and the loss of his eldest would have been a bitter blow. These words, whispered with a tremble of the lips that had been so firm when the hot iron burned, recalled that other Father who is always near, always tender and helpful; and, folding his hands, Rob said the heartiest little prayer he ever prayed, there on the hay, to the soft twitter of the brooding birds. It did him good; and wisely laying all his fear and doubt and trouble in God's hand, the boy felt ready for whatever was to come, and from that hour kept steadily before him the one duty that was plain—to be brave and cheerful, keep silent, and hope for the best.

Nan stole her hat, and left a note on Daisy's pincushion, saying she had taken the boys to drive, and all would be out of the way till after tea. Then she hurried back and found her patients much better, the one for work, the other for rest. In they got, and, putting Rob on the back seat with his leg up drove away, looking as gay and carefree as if nothing had happened.

Dr. Morrison made light of the affair, but told Nan she had done right; and as the much-relieved lads went downstairs, he added in a whisper: "Send the dog off for a while, and keep your eye on the boy. Don't let him know it, and report to me if anything seems wrong. One never knows in these cases. No harm to be careful."

Nan nodded, and feeling much relieved now that the responsibility was off her shoulders, took the lads to Dr. Watkins, who promised to come out later and examine Don. A merry tea at Nan's house, which was kept open for her all summer, did them good, and by the time they got home in the cool of the evening no sign of the panic remained but Ted's heavy eyes, and a slight limp when Rob walked. As the guests were still chattering on the front piazza they retired to the back, and Ted soothed his remorseful soul by swinging Rob in the hammock, while Nan told stories till the dog man arrived.

He said Don was a little under the weather, but no more mad than the grey kitten that purred round his legs while the examination went on.

"He wants his master, and feels the heat. Fed too well, perhaps. I'll keep him a few weeks and send him home all right," said Dr. Watkins, as Don laid his great head in his hand, and kept his intelligent eyes on his face, evidently feeling that this man understood his trials, and knew what to do for him.

So Don departed without a murmur, and our three conspirators took counsel together how to spare the family all anxiety, and give Rob the rest his leg demanded. Fortunately, he always spent many hours in his little study, so he could lie on the sofa with a book in his hand as long as he liked, without exciting any remark. Being of a quiet temperament, he did not worry himself or Nan with useless fears, but believed what was told him, and dismissing all dark possibilities, went cheerfully on his way, soon recovering from the shock of what he called "our scare."

But excitable Ted was harder to manage, and it took all Nan's wit and wisdom to keep him from betraying the secret; for it was best to say nothing and spare all discussion of the subject for Rob's sake. Ted's remorse preyed upon him, and having no "Mum" to confide in, he was very miserable. By day he devoted himself to Rob, waiting on him, talking to him, gazing anxiously at him, and worrying the good fellow very much; though he wouldn't own it, since Ted found comfort in it. But at night, when all was quiet, Ted's lively imagination and heavy heart got the better of him, and kept him awake, or set him walking in his sleep. Nan had her eye on him, and more than once administered a little dose to give him a rest, read to him, scolded him, and when she caught him haunting the house in the watches of the night, threatened to lock him up if he did not stay in his bed.

This wore off after a while; but a change came over the freakish boy, and everyone observed it, even before his mother returned to ask what they had done to quench the Lion's spirits. He was gay, but not so heedless; and often when the old wilfulness beset him, he would check it sharply, look at Rob, and give up, or stalk away to have his sulk out alone. He no longer made fun of his brother's old-fashioned ways and bookish tastes, but treated him with a new and very marked respect, which touched and -pleased modest Rob, and much amazed all observers. It seemed as if he felt that he owed him reparation for the foolish act that might have cost him his life; and love being stronger than will, Ted forgot his pride, and paid his debt like an honest boy.

"I don't understand it," said Mrs. Jo, after a week of home life, much impressed by the good behaviour of her

younger son. "Ted is such a saint, I'm afraid we are going
to lose him. Is it Meg's sweet influence, or Daisy's fine
cooking, or the pellets I catch Nan giving him on the sly?
Some witchcraft has been at work during my absence, and
this will-o'-the-wisp is so amiable, quiet, and obedient, I
don't know him."

"He is growing up, heart's-dearest, and being a pre-
cocious plant, he begins to bloom early. I also see a
change in my Robchen. He is more manly and serious
than ever, and is seldom far from me, as if his love for the
old papa was growing with his growth. Our boys will often
surprise us in this way, Jo, and we can only rejoice over
them and leave them to become what Gott pleases."

As the professor spoke, his eyes rested proudly on the
brothers, who came walking up the steps together, Ted's
arm over Rob's shoulder as he listened attentively to some
geological remarks Rob was making on a stone he held.
Usually, Ted made fun of such tastes, and loved to lay
boulders in the student's path, put brickbats under his
pillow, gravel in his shoes, or send parcels of dirt by
express to "Prof. R. M. Bhaer." Lately, he had treated
Rob's hobbies respectfully, and had begun to appreciate
the good qualities of this quiet brother whom he had
always loved but rather undervalued, till his courage under fire won Ted's admiration, and made it impossible to
forget a fault, the consequences of which might have been
so terrible. The leg was still lame, though doing well, and
Ted was always offering an arm as support, gazing anxiously at his brother, and trying to guess his wants; for
regret was still keen in Ted's soul, and Rob's forgiveness
only made it deeper. A fortunate slip on the stairs gave
Rob an excuse for limping, and no one but Nan and Ted
saw the wound; so the secret was safe up to this time.

"We are talking about you, my lads. Come in and tell us
what good fairy has been at work while we were gone. Or
is it because absence sharpens our eyes, that we find such
pleasant changes when we come back?" said Mrs. Jo,
patting the sofa on either side, while the Professor forgot
his piles of letters to admire the pleasing prospect of his
wife in a bower of arms, as the boys sat down beside her,
smiling affectionately, but feeling a little guilty; for till

now "Mum" and "Vater" knew every event in their boyish
lives.

"Oh, it's only because Bobby and I have been alone so
much; we are sort of twins. I stir him up a bit, and he
steadies me a great deal. You and father do the same, you
know. Nice plan. I like it"; and Ted felt that he had settled
the matter capitally.

"Mother won't thank you for comparing yourself to her,
Ted. I'm flattered at being like father in any way. I try to
be," answered Rob, as they laughed at Ted's compliment.

"I do thank him, for it's true; and if you, Robin, do half
as much for your brother as Papa has for me, your life
won't be a failure," said Mrs. Jo heartily. "I'm very glad to
see you helping one another. It's the right way, and we
can't begin too soon to try to understand the needs, virtues, and failings of those nearest us. Love should not
make us blind to faults, nor familiarity make us too ready
to blame the shortcomings we see. So work away, my
sonnies, and give us more surprises of this sort as often as
you like."

"The *liebe Mutter* has said all. I too am well pleased at
the friendly brother-warmth I find. It is good for everyone; long may it last!" and Professor Bhaer nodded at the
boys, who looked gratified, but rather at a loss how to
respond to these flattering remarks.

Rob wisely kept silent, fearing to say too much; but Ted
burst out, finding it impossible to help telling something:

"The fact is I've been finding out what a brave good
chap Bobby is, and I'm trying to make up for all the
bother I've been to him. I knew he was awfully wise, but I
thought him rather soft, because he liked books better
than larks, and was always fussing about his conscience.
But I begin to see that it isn't the fellows who talk the
loudest and show off best that are the manliest. No, sir!
quiet old Bob is a hero and a trump, and I'm proud of
him; so would you be if you knew all about it."

Here a look from Rob brought Ted up with a round
turn; he stopped short, grew red, and clapped his hand on
his mouth in dismay.

"Well, are we not to 'know all about it?' " asked Mrs.
Jo quickly; for her sharp eye saw signs of danger and her

maternal heart felt that something had come between her and her sons. "Boys," she went on solemnly, "I suspect that the change we talk about is not altogether the effect of growing up, as we say. It strikes me that Ted has been in mischief and Rob has got him out of some scrape; hence the lovely mood of my bad boy and the sober one of my conscientious son, who never hides anything from his mother."

Rob was as red as Ted now, but after a moment's hesitation he looked up and answered with an air of relief:

"Yes, mother, that's it; but it's all over and no harm done, and I think we'd better let it be, for a while at least. I did feel guilty to keep anything from you, but now you know so much I shall not worry and you needn't either. Ted's sorry, I don't mind, and it has done us both good."

Mrs. Jo looked at Ted, who winked hard but bore the look like a man; then she turned to Rob, who smiled at her so cheerfully that she felt reassured; but something in his face struck her, and she saw what it was that made him seem older, graver, yet more lovable than ever. It was the look pain of mind, as well as body, brings, and the patience of a sweet submission to some inevitable trial. Like a flash she guessed that some danger had been near her boy, and the glances she had caught between the two lads and Nan confirmed her fears.

"Rob, dear, you have been ill, hurt, or seriously troubled by Ted? Tell me at once; I will not have any secrets now. Boys sometimes suffer all their lives from neglected accidents or carelessness. Fritz, make them speak out!"

Mr. Bhaer put down his papers and came to stand before them, saying in a tone that quieted Mrs. Jo, and gave the boys courage:

"My sons, give us the truth. We can bear it; do not hold it back to spare us. Ted knows we forgive much because we love him, so be frank, all two."

Ted instantly dived among the sofa pillows and kept there, with only a pair of scarlet ears visible, while Rob in a few words told the little story, truthfully, but as gently as he could, hastening to add the comfortable assurance that Don was *not* mad, the wound nearly well, and no danger would ever come of it.

But Mrs. Jo grew so pale he had to put his arms about
her, and his father turned and walked away, exclaiming:
"Ach Himmel!" in a tone of such mingled pain, relief, and
gratitude, that Ted pulled an extra pillow over his head to
smother the sound. They were all right in a minute; but
such news is always a shock, even if the peril is past, and
Mrs. Jo hugged her boy close till his father came and took
him away, saying with a strong shake of both hands and a
quiver in his voice:

"To be in danger of one's life tries a man's mettle, and
you bear it well; but I cannot spare my good boy yet;
thank Gott, we keep him safe!"

A smothered sound, between a choke and a groan, came
from under the pillows, and the writhing of Ted's long legs
so plainly expressed despair that his mother relented
towards him, and burrowing till she found a tousled yellow
head, pulled it out and smoothed it, exclaiming with an
irrepressible laugh, though her cheeks were wet with
tears:

"Come and be forgiven, poor sinner! I know you have
suffered enough, and I won't say a word; only if harm *had*
come to Rob you would have made me more miserable
than yourself. Oh, Teddy, Teddy, do try to cure that
wilful spirit of yours before it is too late!"

"Oh, Mum, I do try! I never can forget this—I hope it's
cured me; if it hasn't, I am afraid I ain't worth saving,"
answered Ted, pulling his own hair as the only way of
expressing his deep remorse.

"Yes, you are, my dear; I felt just so at fifteen when
Amy was nearly drowned, and Marmee helped me as I'll
help you. Come to me, Teddy, when the evil one gets
hold of you, and together we'll rout him. Ah, me! I've had
many a tussle with that old Apollyon, and often got worsted, but not always. Come under my shield, and we'll
fight till we win."

No one spoke for a minute as Ted and his mother
laughed and cried in one handkerchief, and Rob stood
with his father's arm round him so happy that all was told
and forgiven, though never to be forgotten; for such experiences do one good, and knit hearts that love more closely
together.

Presently Ted rose straight up and going to his father, said bravely and humbly:

"I ought to be punished. please do it; but first say you forgive me, as Rob does."

"Always that, *mein Sohn*, seventy time seven, if needs be, else I am not worthy the name you give me. The punishment has come; I can give no greater. Let it not be in vain. It will not with the help of the mother and the All Father. Room here for both, always!"

The good professor opened his arms and embraced his boys like a true German, not ashamed to express by gesture or by word the fatherly emotions an American would have compressed into a slap on the shoulder and a brief "All right."

Mrs. Jo sat and enjoyed the prospect like a romantic soul as she was, and then they had a quiet talk together, saying freely all that was in their hearts, and finding much comfort in the confidence which comes when love casts out fear. It was agreed that nothing be said except to Nan, who was to be thanked and rewarded for her courage, discretion, and fidelity.

"I always knew that girl had the making of a fine woman in her, and this proves it. No panics and shrieks and faintings and fuss, but calm sense and energetic skill. Dear child, what can I give or do to show my gratitude?" said Mrs. Jo enthusiastically.

"Make Tom clear out and leave her in peace," suggested Ted, almost himself again, though a pensive haze still partially obscured his native gaiety.

"Yes, do! he frets her like a mosquito. She forbade him to come out here while she stayed, and packed him off with Demi. I like old Tom, but he is a regular noodle about Nan," added Rob, as he went away to help his father with the accumulated letters.

"I'll do it!" said Mrs. Jo decidedly. "That girl's career shall *not* be hampered by a foolish boy's fancy. In a moment of weariness she may give in, and then it's all over. Wiser women have done so and regretted it all their lives. Nan shall earn her place first, and prove that she can fill it; then she may marry if she likes, and can find a man worthy of her."

But Mrs. Jo's help was not needed; for love and gratitude can work miracles, and when youth, beauty, accident, and photography are added, success is sure; as was proved in the case of the unsuspecting but too susceptible Thomas.

Chapter 8

Josie Plays Mermaid

WHILE THE YOUNG Bhaers were having serious experiences at home, Josie was enjoying herself immensely at Rocky Nook; for the Laurences knew how to make summer idleness both charming and wholesome. Bess was very fond of her little cousin; Mrs. Amy felt that whether her niece was an actress or not she *must* be a gentlewoman, and gave her the social training which marks the well-bred woman everywhere; while Uncle Laurie was never happier than when rowing, riding, playing, or lounging with two gay girls beside him. Josie bloomed like a wild flower in this free life, Bess grew rosy, brisk, and merry, and both were great favourites with the neighbours, whose villas were by the shore or perched on the cliffs along the pretty bay.

One crumpled rose-leaf disturbed Josie's peace, one baffled wish filled her with a longing which became a mania, and kept her as restless and watchful as a detective with a case to "work up." Miss Cameron, the great actress, had hired one of the villas and retired thither to rest and "create" a new part for next season. She saw no one but a friend or two, had a private beach, and was invisible except during her daily drive, or when the opera-glasses of curious gazers were fixed on a blue figure disporting itself in the sea. The Laurences knew her, but respected her privacy, and after a call left her in peace till she expressed a wish for society—a courtesy which she remembered and repaid later, as we shall see.

But Josie was like a thirsty fly buzzing about a sealed honey-pot, for this nearness to her idol was both delightful and maddening. She pined to see, hear, talk with, and study this great and happy woman who could thrill thou-

sands by her art, and win friends by her virtue, benevolence, and beauty. This was the sort of actress the girl
meant to be, and few could object if the gift was really
hers; for the stage needs just such women to purify and
elevate the profession which should teach as well as amuse.
If kindly Miss Cameron had known what passionate love
and longing burned in the bosom of the little girl whom
she idly observed skipping over the rocks, splashing about
the beach, or galloping past her gate on a Shetland pony,
she would have made her happy by a look or a word. But
being tired with her winter's work and busy with her new
part, the lady took no more notice of this young neighbour
than of the sea-gulls in the bay or the daisies dancing in
the fields. Nosegays left on her doorstep, serenades under
her garden-wall, and the fixed stare of admiring eyes were
such familiar things that she scarcely minded them; and
Josie grew desperate when all her little attempts failed.

"I might climb that pine-tree and tumble off on her
piazza roof, or get Sheltie to throw me just at her gate and
be taken in fainting. It's no use to try to drown myself
when she is bathing. I can't sink, and she'd only send a
man to pull me out. What can I do? I *will* see her and tell
her my hopes and make her say I can act some day.
Mamma would believe *her*; and if—oh, if she only *would*
let me study with her, what perfect joy that would be!"

Josie made these remarks one afternoon as she and Bess
prepared for a swim, a fishing party having prevented
their morning bathe.

"You must bide your time, dear, and not be so impatient. Papa promised to give you a chance before the
season is over, and he always manages things nicely. That
will be better than any queer prank of yours," answered
Bess, tying her pretty hair in a white net to match her
suit, while Josie made a little lobster of herself in scarlet.

"I hate to wait; but I suppose I must. Hope she will
bathe this afternoon, though it is low tide. She told Uncle
she should have to go in then because in the morning
people stared so and went on her beach. Come and have a
good dive from the big rock. No one round but nurses and
babies, so we can romp and splash as much as we like."

Away they went to have a fine time; for the little bay

was free from other bathers, and the babies greatly admired their aquatic gymnastics, both being expert swimmers.

As they sat dripping on the big rock Josie suddenly gave a clutch that nearly sent Bess overboard, as she cried excitedly:

"There she is! Look! coming to bathe. How splendid! Oh, if she only would drown a little and let me save her! or even get her toe nipped by a crab; anything so I could go and speak!"

"Don't seem to look; she comes to be quiet and enjoy herself. Pretend we don't see her, that's only civil," answered Bess, affecting to be absorbed in a white-winged yacht going by.

"Let's carelessly float that way as if going for seaweed on the rocks. She can't mind if we are flat on our backs, with only our noses out. Then when we can't help seeing her, we'll swim back as if anxious to retire. That will impress her, and she may call to thank the very polite young ladies who respect her wishes," proposed Josie, whose lively fancy was always planning dramatic situations.

Just as they were going to slip from their rock, as if Fate relented at last, Miss Cameron was seen to beckon wildly as she stood waist-deep in the water, looking down. She called to her maid, who seemed searching along the beach for something, and not finding what she sought, waved a towel towards the girls as if summoning them to help her.

"Run, fly! she wants us, she wants us!" cried Josie, tumbling into the water like a very energetic turtle, and swimming away in her best style towards this long-desired haven of joy. Bess followed more slowly, and both came panting and smiling up to Miss Cameron, who never lifted her eyes, but said in that wonderful voice of hers:

"I've dropped a bracelet. I see it, but can't get it. Will the little boy find me a long stick? I'll keep my eye on it, so the water shall not wash it away."

"I'll dive for it with pleasure; but I'm not a boy," answered Josie, laughing as she shook the curly head which at a distance had deceived the lady.

"I beg your pardon. Dive away, child; the sand is cover-

ing it fast. I value it very much. Never forgot to take it off
before."

"I'll get it!" and down went Josie, to come up with a
handful of pebbles, but no bracelet.

"It's gone; never mind—my fault," said Miss Cameron,
disappointed, but amused at the girl's dismay as she shook
the water out of her eyes and gasped bravely:

"No, it isn't. I'll have it, if I stay down all night!" and
with one long breath Josie dived again, leaving nothing
but a pair of agitated feet to be seen.

"I'm afraid she will hurt herself," said Miss Cameron,
looking at Bess, whom she recognized by her likeness to
her mother.

"Oh, no; Josie is a little fish. She likes it"; and Bess
smiled happily at this wonderful granting of her cousin's
desire.

"You are Mr. Laurence's daughter, I think? How d'ye
do, dear? Tell papa I'm coming to see him soon. Too tired
before. Quite savage. Better now. Ah! here's our pearl of
divers. What luck?" she asked, as the heels went down
and a dripping head came up.

Josie could only choke and splutter at first, being half
strangled; but though her hands had failed again, her
courage had not; and with a resolute shake of her wet hair,
a bright look at the tall lady, and a series of puffs to fill her
lungs, she said calmly:

" 'Never give up' is my motto. I'm going to get it, if I go
to Liverpool for it! Now, then!" and down went the mermaid quite out of sight this time, groping like a real
lobster at the bottom of the sea.

"Plucky little girl! I like that. Who is she?" asked the
lady, sitting down on a half-covered stone to watch her
diver, since the bracelet was lost sight of.

Bess told her, adding, with the persuasive smile of her
father: "Josie longs to be an actress, and has waited for a
month to see you. This is a great happiness for her."

"Bless the child! why didn't she come and call? I'd have
let her in; though usually I avoid stage-struck girls as I do
reporters," laughed Miss Cameron.

There was no time for more; a brown hand, grasping the
bracelet, rose out of the sea, followed by a purple face as

Josie came up so blind and dizzy she could only cling to Bess, half drowned but triumphant.

Miss Cameron drew her to the rock where she sat, and pushing the hair out of her eyes, revived her with a hearty "Bravo! bravo!" which assured the girl that her first act was a hit. Josie had often imagined her meeting with the great actress—the dignity and grace with which she would enter and tell her ambitious hopes, the effective dress she would wear, the witty things she would say, the deep impression her budding genius would make. But never in her wildest moments had she imagined an interview like this; scarlet, sandy, streaming, and speechless she leaned against the illustrious shoulder, looking like a beautiful seal as she blinked and wheezed till she could smile joyfully and exclaim proudly:

"I did get it! I'm so glad!"

"Now get your breath, my dear; then I shall be glad also. It was very nice of you to take all that trouble for me. How shall I thank you?" asked the lady, looking at her with the beautiful eyes that could say so many things without words.

Josie clasped her hands with a wet spat which rather destroyed the effect of the gesture, and answered in a beseeching tone that would have softened a far harder heart than Miss Cameron's:

"Let me come and see you once—only once! I want you to tell me if I can act; you will know. I'll abide by what you say; and if you think I can—by and by, when I've studied very hard—I shall be the happiest girl in the world. May I?"

"Yes; come tomorrow at eleven. We'll have a good talk; you shall show me what you can do, and I'll give you my opinion. But you won't like it."

"I will, no matter if you tell me I'm a fool. I want it settled; so does mamma. I'll take it bravely if you say no; and if you say yes, I'll never give up till I've done my best —as you did."

"Ah, my child, it's a weary road, and there are plenty of thorns among the roses when you've won them. I think you have the courage, and this proves that you have perseverance. Perhaps you'll do. Come, and we'll see."

Miss Cameron touched the bracelet as she spoke, and smiled so kindly that impetuous Josie wanted to kiss her; but wisely refrained, though her eyes were wet with softer water than any in the sea as she thanked her.

"We are keeping Miss Cameron from her bathe, and the tide is going out. Come, Josie," said thoughtful Bess, fearing to outstay their welcome.

"Run over the beach and get warm. Thank you very much, little mermaid. Tell papa to bring his daughter to see me any time. Good-bye"; and with a wave of her hand the tragedy queen dismissed her court, but remained on her weedy throne watching the two lithe figures race over the sand with twinkling feet till they were out of sight. Then, as she calmly bobbed up and down in the water, she said to herself: "The child has a good stage face, vivid, mobile, fine eyes, abandon, pluck, will. Perhaps she'll do. Good stock—talent in the family. We shall see."

Of course Josie never slept a wink, and was in a fever of joyful excitement next day. Uncle Laurie enjoyed the episode very much, and Aunt Amy looked out her most becoming white dress for the grand occasion; Bess lent her most artistic hat, and Josie ranged the wood and marsh for a bouquet of wild roses, sweet white azalea, ferns, and graceful grasses, as the offering of a very grateful heart.

At ten she solemnly arrayed herself, and then sat looking at her neat gloves and buckled shoes till it was time to go, growing pale and sober with the thought that her fate was soon to be decided; for, like all young people she was sure that her whole life could be settled by one human creature, quite forgetting how wonderfully Providence trains us by disappointment, surprises us with unexpected success, and turns our seeming trials into blessings.

"I will go alone: we shall be freer so. Oh, Bess, pray that she may tell me rightly! So much depends on that! Don't laugh, uncle! It *is* a very serious moment for me. Miss Cameron knows that, and will tell you so. Kiss me, Aunt Amy, since mamma isn't here. If you say I look nice, I'm quite satisfied. Good-bye." And with a wave of the hand as much like her model's as she could make it, Josie departed looking very pretty and feeling very tragical.

Sure now of admittance, she boldly rang at the door

which excluded so many, and being ushered into a shady parlour, feasted her eyes upon several fine portraits of great actors while she waited. She had read about most of them, and knew their trials and triumphs so well that she soon forgot herself, and tried to imitate Mrs. Siddons as Lady Macbeth, looking up at the engraving as she held her nosegay like the candle in the sleep-walking scene, and knit her youthful brows distressfully while murmuring the speech of the haunted queen. So busy was she that Miss Cameron watched her for several minutes unseen, then startled her by suddenly sweeping in with the words upon her lips, the look upon her face, which made that one of her greatest scenes.

"I never can do it like that; but I'll keep trying, if you say I may," cried Josie, forgetting her manners in the intense interest of the moment.

"Show me what you *can* do," answered the actress, wisely plunging into the middle of things at once, well knowing that no common chat would satisfy this very earnest little person.

"First let me give you these. I thought you'd like wild things better than hot-house flowers; and I loved to bring them, as I'd no other way to thank you for your great kindness to me," said Josie, offering her nosegay with a simple warmth that was very sweet.

"I do love them best, and keep my room full of the posies some good fairy hangs on my gate. Upon my word, I think I've found the fairy out—these are so like," she added quickly, as her eye went from the flowers in her hand to others that stood near by, arranged with the same taste.

Josie's blush and smile betrayed her before she said, with a look full of girlish adoration and humility:

"I couldn't help it; I admire you so much. I know it was a liberty; but as I couldn't get in myself, I loved to think my posies pleased you."

Something about the child and her little offering touched the woman, and, drawing Josie to her, she said, with no trace of actress in face or voice:

"They did please me, dear, and so do you. I'm tired of

praise; and love is very sweet, when it is simple and
sincere like this."

Josie remembered to have heard, among many other
stories, that Miss Cameron lost her lover years ago, and
since had lived only for art. Now she felt that this might
have been true; and pity for the splendid, lonely life made
her face very eloquent, as well as grateful. Then, as if
anxious to forget the past, her new friend said, in the
commanding way that seemed natural to her:

"Let me see what you can do. Juliet, of course. All
begin with that. Poor soul, how she is murdered!"

Now, Josie *had* intended to begin with Romeo's much-
enduring sweetheart, and follow her up with Bianca, Pau-
line, and several of the favourite idols of stage-struck girls;
but being a shrewd little person, she suddenly saw the
wisdom of Uncle Laurie's advice, and resolved to follow it.
So instead of the rant Miss Cameron expected, Josie gave
poor Ophelia's mad scene, and gave it very well, having
been trained by the college professor of elocution and
done it many times. She was too young, of course, but the
white gown, the loose hair, the real flowers she scattered
over the imaginary grave, added to the illusion; and she
sung the songs sweetly, dropped her pathetic curtsies, and
vanished behind the curtain that divided the rooms with a
backward look that surprised her critical auditor into a
quick gesture of applause. Cheered by that welcome sound,
Josie ran back as a little hoyden in one of the farces she
had often acted, telling a story full of fun and naughtiness
at first, but ending with a sob of repentance and an earnest prayer for pardon.

"Very good! Try again. Better than I expected," called
the voice of the oracle.

Josie tried Portia's speech, and recited very well, giving
due emphasis to each fine sentence. Then, unable to
refrain from what she considered her greatest effort, she
burst into Juliet's balcony scene, ending with the poison
and the tomb. She felt sure that she surpassed herself, and
waited for applause. A ringing laugh made her tingle with
indignation and disappointment, as she went to stand before Miss Cameron, saying in a tone of polite surprise:

"I have been told that I did it *very well*. I'm sorry you don't think so."

"My dear, it's very bad. How can it help being so? What can a child like you know of love and fear and death? Don't try it yet. Leave tragedy alone till you are ready for it."

"But you clapped Ophelia."

"Yes, that was very pretty. Any clever girl can do it effectively. But the real meaning of Shakespeare is far above you yet, child. The comedy bit was best. There you showed real talent. It was both comic and pathetic. That's art. Don't lose it. The Portia was good declamation. Go on with that sort of thing; it trains the voice—teaches shades of expression. You've a good voice and natural grace—great helps both, hard to acquire."

"Well, I'm glad I've got something," sighed Josie, sitting meekly on a stool, much crestfallen, but not daunted yet, and bound to have her say out.

"My dear little girl, I told you that you would not like what I should say to you; yet I must be honest if I would really help you. I've had to do it for many like you; and most of them have never forgiven me, though my words have proved true, and they are what I advised them to be—good wives and happy mothers in quiet homes. A few have kept on, and done fairly well. One you will hear of soon, I think; for she has talent, indomitable patience, and mind as well as beauty. You are too young to show to which class you belong. Geniuses are very rare, and even at fifteen seldom give much promise of future power."

"Oh, I don't think I'm a genius!" cried Josie, growing calm and sober as she listened to the melodious voice and looked into the expressive face that filled her with confidence, so strong, sincere, and kindly was it. "I only want to find out if I have talent enough to go on, and after years of study to be able to act well in any of the good plays people never tire of seeing. I don't expect to be a Mrs. Siddons or a Miss Cameron, much as I long to be; but it *does* seem as if I had something in me which can't come out in any way but this. When I act I'm perfectly happy. I seem to live, to be in my own world, and each new part is a new friend. I love Shakespeare, and am never tired of his splendid people. Of course, I don't understand it all; but it's like being alone at night with the mountains and the stars, solemn and grand, and I try to imagine how it will look when the sun comes up, and all is glorious and clear to me. I can't see, but I feel the beauty, and long to express it."

As she spoke with the most perfect self-forgetfulness Josie was pale with excitement, her eyes shone, her lips trembled, and all her little soul seemed trying to put into words the emotions that filled it to overflowing. Miss Cameron understood, felt that this was something more than a girlish whim; and when she answered there was a new tone of sympathy in her voice, a new interest in her face, though she wisely refrained from saying all she thought, well knowing what splendid dreams young people build upon a word, and how bitter is the pain when the bright bubbles burst.

"If you feel this, I can give you no better advice than to go on loving and studying our great master," she said slowly; but Josie caught the changed tone, and felt, with a thrill of joy, that her new friend was speaking to her now as to a comrade. "It is an education in itself, and a lifetime is not long enough to teach you all his secret. But there is much to do before you can hope to echo his words. Have you the patience, courage, strength, to begin at the beginning, and slowly, painfully, lay the foundation for future work? Fame is a pearl many dive for and only a few bring up. Even when they do, it is not perfect, and they sigh for more, and lose better things in struggling for them."

The last words seemed spoken more to herself than to her hearer, but Josie answered quickly, with a smile and an expressive gesture:

"I got the bracelet in spite of all the bitter water in my eyes."

"You did! I don't forget it. A good omen. We will accept it."

Miss Cameron answered the smile with one that was like sunshine to the girl, and stretched her white hands as if taking some invisible gift. Then added in a different tone, watching the effect of her words on the expressive face before her:

"Now you will be disappointed, for instead of telling you to come and study with me, or go and act in some second-rate theatre at once, I advise you to go back to school and finish your education. That is the first step, for all accomplishments are needed, and a single talent makes a very imperfect character. Cultivate mind and body, heart and soul, and make yourself an intelligent, graceful, beautiful, and healthy girl. Then, at eighteen or twenty, go into training and try your powers. Better start for the battle with your arms in order, and save the hard lesson which comes when we rush on too soon. Now and then genius carries all before it, but not often. We have to climb slowly, with many slips and falls. Can you wait as well as work?"

"I will!"

"We shall see. It would be pleasant to me to know that when I quit the stage I leave behind me a well-trained, faithful, gifted comrade to more than fill my place, and carry on what I have much at heart—the purification of the stage. Perhaps you are she; but remember, mere beauty and rich costumes do not make an actress, nor are the efforts of a clever little girl to play great characters real art. It is all dazzle and sham, and a disgrace and disappointment now. Why will the public be satisfied with opera bouffe, or the trash called society plays when a world of truth and beauty, poetry and pathos lies waiting to be interpreted and enjoyed?"

Miss Cameron had forgotten to whom she spoke, and walked to and fro, full of the noble regret all cultivated people feel at the low state of the stage nowadays.

"That's what Uncle Laurie says; and he and Aunt Jo try to plan plays about true and lovely things—simple domestic scenes that touch people's hearts, and make them laugh and cry and feel better. Uncle says that sort is my style, and I must not think of tragedy. But it's so much nicer to sweep about in crowns and velvet trains than to wear everyday clothes, and just be myself, though it is so easy."

"Yet that is high art, child, and what we need for a time till we are ready for the masters. Cultivate that talent of yours. It is a special gift, this power to bring tears and smiles, and a sweeter task to touch the heart than to freeze the blood or fire the imagination. Tell your uncle he is right, and ask your aunt to try a play for you. I'll come and see it when you are ready."

"Will you? Oh! will you? We are going to have some at Christmas, with a nice part for me. A simple little thing, but I can do it, and should be so proud, so happy to have you there."

Josie rose as she spoke, for a glance at the clock showed her that her call was a long one; and hard as it was to end this momentous interview, she felt that she must go. Catching up her hat she went to Miss Cameron, who stood looking at her so keenly that she felt as transparent as a pane of glass, and coloured prettily as she looked up, saying, with a grateful little tremor in her voice:

"I can never thank you for this hour and all you have told me. I shall do just what you advise, and mamma will be very glad to see me settled at my books again. I can study now with all my heart, because it is to help me on; and I won't hope too much, but work and wait, and try to please you, as the only way to pay my debt."

"That reminds me that I have not paid mine. Little friend, wear this for my sake. It is fit for a mermaid, and will remind you of your first dive. May the next bring up a better jewel, and leave no bitter water on your lips!"

As she spoke, Miss Cameron took from the lace at her throat a pretty pin of aquamarine, and fastened it like an order on Josie's proud bosom; then lifting the happy little face, she kissed it very tenderly, and watched it go smiling away with eyes that seemed to see into a future full of the trials and the triumphs which she knew so well.

Bess expected to see Josie come flying in, all raptures and excitement, or drowned in tears of disappointment, but was surprised at the expression of calm content and resolution which she wore. Pride and satisfaction, and a new feeling of responsibility both sobered and sustained her, and she felt that any amount of dry study and long waiting would be bearable, if in the glorious future she could be an honour to her profession and a comrade to the new friend whom she already adored with girlish ardour.

She told her little story to a deeply interested audience,

and all felt that Miss Cameron's advice was good. Mrs Amy was relieved at the prospect of delay; for she did not want her niece to be an actress and hoped the fancy would die out.

Uncle Laurie was full of charming plans and prophecies and wrote one of his most delightful notes to thank their neighbour for her kindness; while Bess, who loved art of all kinds, fully sympathized with her cousin's ambitious hopes, only wondering why she preferred to act out her visions rather than embody them in marble.

That first interview was not the last; for Miss Cameron was really interested, and had several memorable conversations with the Laurences, while the girls sat by, drinking in every word with the delight all artists feel in their own beautiful world, and learning to see how sacred good gifts are, how powerful, and how faithfully they should be used for high ends, each in its own place helping to educate, refine, and refresh.

Josie wrote reams to her mother; and when the visit ended rejoiced her heart by bringing her a somewhat changed little daughter, who fell to work at the once-detested books with a patient energy which surprised and pleased everyone. The right string had been touched, and even French exercises and piano practice became endurable, since accomplishments would be useful by and by; dress, manners, and habits were all interesting now, because "mind and body, heart and soul, must be cultivated," and while training to become an "intelligent, graceful, healthy girl," little Josie was unconsciously fitting herself to play her part well on whatever stage the great Manager might prepare for her.

Chapter 9

The Worm Turns

Two very superior bicycles went twinkling up the road to Plumfield one September afternoon, bearing two brown and dusty riders evidently returning from a successful run, for though their legs might be a trifle weary, their faces beamed as they surveyed the world from their lofty perches with the air of calm content all wheelmen wear *after* they have learned to ride; before that happy period anguish of mind and body is the chief expression of the manly countenance.

"Go ahead and report, Tom; I'm due here. See you later," said Demi, swinging himself down at the door of the Dovecote.

"Don't peach, there's a good fellow. Let me have it out with Mother Bhaer first," returned Tom, wheeling in at the gate with a heavy sigh.

Demi laughed, and his comrade went slowly up the avenue, devoutly hoping that the coast was clear; for he was the bearer of tidings which would, he thought, convulse the entire family with astonishment and dismay.

To his great joy Mrs. Jo was discovered alone in a grove of proof-sheets, which she dropped, to greet the returning wanderer cordially. But after the first glance she saw that something was the matter, recent events having made her unusually sharp-eyed and suspicious.

"What is it now, Tom?" she asked, as he subsided into an easy-chair with a curious expression of mingled fear, shame, amusement, and distress in his brick-red countenance.

"I'm in an awful scrape, ma'am."

"Of course; I'm always prepared for scrapes when you

appear. What is it? Run over some old lady who is going to law about it?" asked Mrs. Jo cheerfully.

"Worse than that," groaned Tom.

"Not poisoned some trusting soul who asked you to prescribe, I hope?"

"Worse than that."

"You haven't let·Demi catch any horrid thing and left him behind, have you?"

"Worse even than that."

"I give it up. Tell me quick; I hate to wait for bad news."

Having got his listener sufficiently excited, Tom launched his thunderbolt in one brief sentence, and fell back to watch the effect.

"I'm engaged!"

Mrs. Jo's proof-sheets flew wildly about as she clasped her hands, exclaiming in dismay:

"If Nan has yielded, I'll never forgive her!"

"She hasn't; it's another girl."

Tom's face was so funny as he said the words, that it was impossible to help laughing; for he looked both sheepish and pleased, besides very much perplexed and worried.

"I'm glad, *very* glad indeed! Don't care who it is; and I hope you'll be married soon. Now tell me all about it," commanded Mrs. Jo, so much relieved that she felt ready for anything.

"What will Nan say?" demanded Tom, rather taken aback at this view of his predicament.

"She will be rejoiced to get rid of the mosquito who has plagued her so long. Don't worry about Nan. Who is this 'other girl?' "

"Demi hasn't written about her?"

"Only something about your upsetting a Miss West down at Quitno; I thought that was scrape enough."

"That was only the beginning of a series of scrapes. Just my luck! Of course after sousing the poor girl I had to be attentive to her, hadn't I? Everyone seemed to think so, and I couldn't get away, and so I was lost before I knew it. It's all Demi's fault, he *would* stay there and fuss with his old photos, because the views were good and all the girls wanted to be taken. Look at these, will you, ma'am? That's the way we spent our time when we weren't playing tennis"; and Tom pulled a handful of pictures from his pocket, displaying several in which he was conspicuous, either holding a sun-umbrella over a very pretty young lady on the rocks, reposing at her feet in the grass, or perched on a piazza railing with other couples in seaside costumes and effective attitudes.

"This is *she* of course?" asked Mrs. Jo, pointing to the much-ruffled damsel with the jaunty hat, coquettish shoes, and racket in her hand.

"That's Dora. Isn't she lovely?" cried Tom, forgetting his tribulations for a moment and speaking with loverlike ardour.

"Very nice little person to look at. Hope she is not a Dickens Dora? That curly crop looks like it."

"Not a bit; she's very smart; can keep house, and sew, and do lots of things, I assure you, ma'am. All the girls like her, and she's sweet-tempered and jolly, and sings like a bird, and dances beautifully, and loves books. Thinks yours are splendid, and made me talk about you no end."

"That last sentence is to flatter me and win my help to get you out of the scrape. Tell me first how you got in"; and Mrs. Jo settled herself to listen with interest, never tired of boys' affairs.

Tom gave his head a rousing rub all over to clear his wits, and plunged into his story with a will.

"Well, we've met her before, but I didn't know she was there. Demi wanted to see a fellow, so we went, and finding it nice and cool rested over Sunday. Found some pleasant people and went out rowing; I had Dora, and came to grief on a confounded rock. She could swim, no harm done, only the scare and the spoilt gown. She took it well, and we got friendly at once—couldn't help it, scrambling into that beast of a boat while the rest laughed at us. Of course we had to stay another day to see that Dora was all right. Demi wanted to. Alice Heath is down there and two other girls from our college, so we sort of lingered along, and Demi kept taking pictures, and we danced, and got into a tennis tournament; and that was as good exercise as wheeling, we thought. Fact is, tennis is a danger-

ous game, ma'am. A great deal of courting goes on in
those courts, and we fellows find that sort of 'serving'
mighty agreeable, don't you know?"

"Not much tennis in my day, but I understand perfectly," said Mrs. Jo, enjoying it all as much as Tom did.

"Upon my word, I hadn't the least idea of being serious," he continued slowly, as if this part of his tale was
hard to tell; "but everyone else spooned, so I did. Dora
seemed to like it and expect it, and of course I was glad to
be agreeable. *She* thought I amounted to something, though
Nan does not, and it was pleasant to be appreciated after
years of snubbing. Yes, it was right down jolly to have a
sweet girl smile at you all day, and blush prettily when
you said a neat thing to her, and look glad when you
came, sorry when you left, and admire all you did, and
make you feel like a man and act your best. That's the sort
of treatment a fellow enjoys and ought to get if he behaves
himself; not frowns and cold shoulders year in and year
out, and made to look like a fool when he means well, and
is faithful, and has loved a girl ever since he was a boy.
No, by Jove, it's not fair, and I won't stand it!"

Tom waxed warm and eloquent as he thought over his
wrongs, and bounced up to march about the room, wagging his head and trying to feel aggrieved as usual, but
surprised to find that his heart did not ache a bit.

"I wouldn't. Drop the old fancy, for it was nothing
more—and take up the new one, if it is genuine. But how
came you to propose, Tom, as you must have done to be
engaged?" asked Mrs. Jo, impatient for the crisis of the
tale.

"Oh, that was an accident. I didn't mean it at all; the
donkey did it, and I couldn't get out of the scrape without
hurting Dora's feelings, you see," began Tom, seeing that
the fatal moment had come.

"So there were two donkeys in it, were there?" said Mrs.
Jo, foreseeing fun of some sort.

"Don't laugh! It sounds funny, I know; but it might
have been awful," answered Tom darkly, though a twinkle
of the eye showed that his love trails did not quite blind
him to the comic side of the adventure.

"The girls admired our new wheels, and of course we liked to show off. Took 'em to ride, and had larks generally. Well, one day, Dora was on behind, and we were going nicely along a good bit of road, when a ridiculous old donkey got right across the way. I thought he'd move, but he didn't, so I gave him a kick; he kicked back, and over we went in a heap, donkey and all. Such a mess! I thought only of Dora, and she had hysterics; at least, she laughed till she cried, and that beast brayed, and I lost my head. Any fellow would, with a poor girl gasping in the road, and he wiping her tears and begging pardon, not knowing whether her bones were broken or not. I called her my darling, and went on like a fool in my flurry, till she grew calmer, and said, with such a look: 'I forgive you, Tom. Pick me up, and let us go on again.'

"Wasn't that sweet now, after I'd upset her for the second time? It touched me to the heart; and I said I'd like to go on for ever with such an angel to steer for, and—well I don't know *what* I did say; but you might have knocked me down with a feather when she put her arm round my neck and whispered: 'Tom, dear, with you I'm not afraid of any lions in the path.' She might have said *donkeys*; but she was in earnest, and she spared my feelings. Very nice of the dear girl; but there I am with two sweethearts on my hands, and in a deuce of a scrape."

Finding it impossible to contain herself another moment, Mrs. Jo laughed till the tears ran down her cheeks at this characteristic episode; and after one reproachful look, which only added to her merriment, Tom burst into a jolly roar that made the room ring.

"Tommy Bangs! Tommy Bangs! who but you could ever get into such a catastrophe?" said Mrs. Jo, when she recovered her breath.

"Isn't it a muddle all round, and won't everyone chaff me to death about it? I shall have to quit old Plum for a while," answered Tom, as he mopped his face, trying to realize the full danger of his position.

"No, indeed; I'll stand by you, for I think it the best joke of the season. But tell me how things ended. Is it really serious, or only a summer flirtation? I don't approve of them, but boys and girls will play with edged tools and cut their fingers."

"Well, Dora considers herself engaged, and wrote to her people at once. I couldn't say a word when she took it all in solemn earnest and seemed so happy. She's only seventeen, never liked anyone before, and is sure all will be all right; as her father knows mine, and we are both well off. I was so staggered that I said: 'Why, you can't love me *really* when we know so little of one another?' But she answered right out of her tender little heart: 'Yes, I do, dearly, Tom; you are so gay and kind and honest, I couldn't help it.' Now, after that what *could* I do but go ahead and make her happy while I stayed, and trust to luck to straighten the snarl out afterwards?"

"A truly Tomian way of taking things easy. I hope you told your father at once."

"Oh yes, I wrote off and broke it to him in three lines. I said: 'Dear Father, I'm engaged to Dora West, and I hope she will suit the family. She suits me tip-top. Yours ever, Tom.' He was all right, never liked Nan, you know; but Dora will suit him down to the ground." And Tom looked entirely satisfied with his own tact and taste.

"What did Demi say to this rapid and funny lovemaking? Wasn't he scandalized?" asked Mrs. Jo, trying not to laugh again as she thought of the unromantic spectacle of donkey, bicycle, boy, and girl all in the dust together.

"Not a bit. He was immensely interested and very kind; talked to me like a father; said it was a good thing to steady a fellow, only I must be honest with her and myself and not trifle a moment. Demi is a regular Solomon, especially when he is in the same boat," answered Tom, looking wise.

"You don't mean—?" gasped Mrs. Jo, in sudden alarm at the bare idea of more love-affairs just yet.

"Yes, I do, please, ma'am; it's a regular sell all the way through, and I owe Demi one for taking me into temptation blindfold. He *said* he went to Quitno to see Fred Wallace, but he never saw the fellow. How could he, when Wallace was off in his yacht all the time we were there? Alice was the real attraction, and I was left to my fate, while they were maundering round with that old

camera. There were three donkeys in this affair, and I'm
not the worst one, though I shall have to bear the laugh.
Demi will look innocent and sober, and no one will say a
word to him."

"The midsummer madness has broken out, and no one
knows who will be stricken next. Well, leave Demi to his
mother, and let us see what you are going to do, Tom."

"I don't know exactly; it's awkward to be in love with
two girls at once. What do you advise?"

"A common-sense view of the case, by all means. Dora
loves you and thinks you love her. Nan does not care for
you, and you only care for her as a friend, though you
have tried to do more. It is my opinion, Tom, that you
love Dora, or are on the way to it; for in all these years
I've never seen you look or speak about Nan as you do
about Dora. Opposition has made you obstinately cling to
her till accident has shown you a more attractive girl.
Now, I think you had better take the old love for a friend,
the new one for a sweetheart, and in due time, if the
sentiment is genuine, marry her."

If Mrs. Jo had any doubts about the matter, Tom's face
would have proved the truth of her opinion; for his eyes
shone, his lips smiled, and in spite of dust and sunburn a
new expression of happiness quite glorified him as he
stood silent for a moment, trying to understand the beautiful miracle which real love works when it comes to a
young man's heart.

"The fact is I meant to make Nan jealous, for she knows
Dora, and I was sure would hear of our doings. I was tired
of being walked on, and I thought I'd try to break away
and not be a bore and a laughing-stock any more," he said
slowly, as if it relieved him to pour out his doubts and
woes and hopes and joys to his old friend. "I was regularly
astonished to find it so easy and so pleasant. I didn't mean
to do any harm, but drifted along beautifully, and told
Demi to mention things in his letters to Daisy, so Nan
might know. Then I forgot Nan altogether, and saw, heard,
felt, cared for no one but Dora, till the donkey—bless his
old heart!—pitched her into my arms and I found she
loved me. Upon my soul, I don't see why she should! I'm
not half good enough."

"Every honest man feels that when an innocent girl puts her hand in his. Make yourself worthy of her, for she isn't an angel, but a woman with faults of her own for you to bear, and forgive, and you must help one another," said Mrs. Jo, trying to realize that this sober youth was her scapegrace Tommy.

"What troubles me is that I didn't mean it when I began, and was going to use the dear girl as an instrument of torture for Nan. It wasn't right, and I don't deserve to be so happy. If all my scrapes ended as well as this, what a state of bliss I should be in!" and Tom beamed again at the rapturous prospect.

"My dear boy, it is not a scrape, but a very sweet experience suddenly dawning upon you," answered Mrs. Jo, speaking very soberly; for she saw he was in earnest. "Enjoy it wisely and be worthy of it, for it is a serious thing to accept a girl's love and trust, and let her look up to you for tenderness and truth in return. Don't let little Dora look in vain, but be a man in all things for her sake, and make this affection a blessing to you both."

"I'll try. Yes, I do love her, only I can't believe it just yet. Wish you knew her. Dear little soul, I long to see her already! She cried when we parted last night and I hated to go." Tom's hand went to his cheek as if he still felt the rosy little seal Dora had set upon his promise not to forget her, and for the first time in his happy-go-lucky life Tommy Bangs understood the difference between sentiment and sentimentality. The feeling recalled Nan, for he had never known that tender thrill when thinking of her, and the old friendship seemed rather a prosaic affair beside this delightful mingling of romance, surprise, love, and fun.

"I declare, I feel as if a weight was off me, but what the dickens *will* Nan say when she knows it!" he exclaimed with a chuckle.

"Knows what?" asked a clear voice that made both start and turn, for there was Nan calmly surveying them from the doorway.

Anxious to put Tom out of suspense and see how Nan would take the news, Mrs. Jo answered quickly:

"Tom's engagement to Dora West."

"Really?" and Nan looked so surprised that Mrs. Jo was

afraid she might be fonder of her old playmate than she knew; but her next words set the fear at rest, and made everything comfortable and merry at once.

"I knew my prescription would work wonders if he only took it long enough. Dear old Tom, I'm so glad. Bless you! bless you!" And she shook both his hands with hearty affection.

"It was an accident, Nan. I didn't mean to, but I'm always getting into messes, and I couldn't seem to get out of this any other way. Mother Bhaer will tell you all about it. I must go and make myself tidy. Going to tea with Demi. See you later."

Stammering, blushing, and looking both sheepish and gratified, Tom suddenly bolted, leaving the elder lady to enlighten the younger at length, and have another laugh over this new sort of courtship, which might well be called accidental. Nan was deeply interested, for she knew Dora, thought her a nice little thing, and predicted that in time she would make Tom an excellent wife, since she admired and "appreciated" him so much.

"I shall miss him of course, but it will be a relief to me and better for him; dangling is so bad for a boy. Now he will go into business with his father and do well, and everyone be happy. I shall give Dora an elegant family medicine-chest for a wedding-present, and teach her how to use it. Tom can't be trusted, and is no more fit for the profession than Silas."

The latter part of this speech relieved Mrs. Jo's mind, for Nan had looked about her as if she had lost something valuable when she began; but the medicine-chest seemed to cheer her, and the thought of Tom in a *safe* profession was evidently a great comfort.

"The worm has turned at last, Nan, and your bondman is free. Let him go, and give your whole mind to your work; for *you* are fitted for the profession, and will be an honour to it by and by," she said approvingly.

"I hope so. That reminds me—measles are in the village, and you had better tell the girls not to call where there are children. It would be bad to have a run of them just as term begins. Now I'm off to Daisy. Wonder what she will say to Tom. Isn't he great fun?" And Nan departed, laughing over the joke with such genuine satisfaction that it was evident no sentimental regrets disturbed her "maiden meditation, fancy-free."

"I shall have my eye on Demi, but won't say a word. Meg likes to manage her children in her own way, and a very good way it is. But the dear Pelican will be somewhat ruffled if her boy has caught the epidemic which seems to have broken out among us this summer."

Mrs. Jo did not mean the measles, but that more serious malady called love, which is apt to ravage communities, spring and autumn, when winter gaiety and summer idleness produce whole bouquets of engagements, and set young people to pairing off like the birds. Franz began it, Nat was a chronic and Tom a sudden case; Demi seemed to have the symptoms; and worst of all, her own Ted had only the day before calmly said to her: "Mum, I think I should be happier if I had a sweetheart, like the other boys." If her cherished son had asked her for dynamite to play with, she would hardly have been more startled, or have more decidedly refused the absurd request.

"Well, Barry Morgan said I ought to have one and offered to pick me out a nice one among our set. I asked Josie first, and she hooted at the idea, so I thought I'd let Barry look round. You say it steadies a fellow, and I want to be steady," explained Ted in a serious tone, which would have convulsed his parent at any other time.

"Good lack! What are we coming to in this fast age when babes and boys make such demands and want to play with one of the most sacred things in life?" exclaimed Mrs. Jo, and having in a few words set the matter in its true light, sent her son away to wholesome baseball and Octoo for a safe sweetheart.

Now, here was Tom's bomb-shell to explode in their midst, carrying widespread destruction, perhaps; for though one swallow does not make a summer, one engagement is apt to make several, and her boys were, most of them, at the inflammable age when a spark ignites the flame, which soon flickers and dies out, or burns warm and clear for life. Nothing could be done about it but to help them make wise choices, and be worthy of good mates. But of all the lessons Mrs. Jo had tried to teach her boys, this

great one was the hardest; for love is apt to make lunatics
of even saints and sages, so young people cannot be expected to escape the delusions, disappointments, and mistakes, as well as the delights, of this sweet madness.

"I suppose it is inevitable, since we live in America, so I
won't borrow trouble, but hope that some of the new ideas
of education will produce a few hearty, happy, capable,
and intelligent girls for my lads. Lucky for me that I
haven't the whole twelve on my hands, I should lose my
wits if I had, for I foresee complications and troubles
ahead worse than Tom's boats, bicycles, donkeys, and
Doras," meditated Mrs. Jo, as she went back to her neglected proof-sheets.

Tom was quite satisfied with the tremendous effect his
engagement produced in the little community at Plumfield. "It was paralysing," as Demi said; and astonishment
left most of Tom's mates little breath for chaff. That he,
the faithful one, should turn from the idol to strange
goddesses, was a shock to the romantic and a warning to
the susceptible. It was comical to see the airs our Thomas
put on; for the most ludicrous parts of the affair were
kindly buried in oblivion by the few who knew them, and
Tom burst forth as a full-blown hero who had rescued the
maiden from a watery grave, and won her gratitude and
love by his daring deed. Dora kept the secret, and enjoyed the fun when she came to see Mother Bhaer and
pay her respects to the family generally. Everyone liked
her at once, for she was a gay and winning little soul;
fresh, frank, and so happy, it was beautiful to see her
innocent pride in Tom, who was a new boy, or man
rather; for with this change in his life a great change took
place in him. Jolly he would always be, and impulsive, but
he tried to become all that Dora believed him, and his
best side came uppermost for everyday wear. It was surprising to see how many good traits Tom had; and his
efforts to preserve the manly dignity belonging to his
proud position as an engaged man was very comical. So
was the entire change from his former abasement and
devotion to Nan to a somewhat lordly air with his little
betrothed; for Dora made an idol of him, and resented the
idea of a fault or a flaw in her Tom. This new state of

things suited both, and the once blighted being bloomed finely in the warm atmosphere of appreciation, love, and confidence. He was very fond of the dear girl, but meant to be a slave no longer, and enjoyed his freedom immensely, quite unconscious that the great tyrant of the world had got hold of him for life.

To his father's satisfaction he gave up his medical studies, and prepared to go into business with the old gentleman, who was a flourishing merchant, ready now to make the way smooth and smile upon his marriage with Mr. West's well-endowed daughter. The only thorn in Tom's bed of roses was Nan's placid interest in his affairs, and evident relief at his disloyalty. He did not want her to suffer, but a decent amount of regret at the loss of such a lover would have gratified him; a slight melancholy, a word of reproach, a glance of envy as he passed with adoring Dora on his arm, seemed but the fitting tribute to such years of faithful service and sincere affection. But Nan regarded him with a maternal sort of air that nettled him very much, and patted Dora's curly head with a worldly-wise air worthy of the withered spinster, Julia Mills, in *David Copperfield*.

It took some time to get the old and the new emotions comfortably adjusted, but Mrs. Jo helped him, and Mr. Laurie gave him some wise advice upon the astonishing gymnastic feats the human heart can perform, and be all the better for it if it only held fast to the balancing-pole of truth and common sense. At last our Tommy got his bearings, and as autumn came on Plumfield saw but little of him; for his new lodestar was in the city, and business kept him hard at work. He was evidently in his right place now, and soon throve finely, to his father's great contentment; for his jovial presence pervaded the once quiet office like a gale of fresh wind, and his lively wits found managing men and affairs much more congenial employment than studying disease, or playing unseemly pranks with skeletons.

Here we will leave him for a time and turn to the more serious adventures of his mates, though this engagement, so merrily made, was the anchor which kept our mercurial Tom happy, and made a man of him.

Chapter 10

Demi Settles

MOTHER, can I have a little serious conversation with you?" asked Demi one evening, as they sat together enjoying the first fire of the season, while Daisy wrote letters upstairs and Josie was studying in the little library close by.

"Certainly, dear. No bad news, I hope?" and Mrs. Meg looked up from her sewing with a mixture of pleasure and anxiety on her motherly face; for she dearly loved a good talk with her son, and knew that he always had something worth telling.

"It will be good news for you, I think," answered Demi, smiling as he threw away his paper and went to sit beside her on the little sofa which just held two.

"Let me hear it, then, at once."

"I know you don't like the reporting, and will be glad to hear that I have given it up."

"I am very glad! It is too uncertain a business, and there is no prospect of getting on for a long time. I want you settled in some good place where you can stay, and in time make money. I wish you liked a profession; but as you don't, any clean, well-established business will do."

"What do you say to a railroad office?"

"I don't like it. A noisy, hurried kind of place, I know, with all sorts of rough men about. I hope it isn't that, dear?"

"I could have it; but does book-keeping in a wholesale leather business please you better?"

"No; you'll get round-shouldered writing at a tall desk; and they say, once a book-keeper always a book-keeper."

"How does a travelling agent suit your views?"

"Not at all; with all those dreadful accidents, and the exposure and bad food as you go from place to place, you are sure to get killed or lose your health."

"I could be private secretary to a literary man; but the salary is small, and may end any time."

"That would be better, and more what I want. It isn't that I object to honest work of any kind; but I don't want my son to spend his best years grubbing for a little money in a dark office, or be knocked about in a rough-and-tumble scramble to get on. I want to see you in some business where your tastes and talents can be developed and made useful; where you can go on rising, and in time put in your little fortune and be a partner; so that your years of apprenticeship will not be wasted, but fit you to take your place among the honourable men who make their lives and work useful and respected. I talked it all over with your dear father when you were a child; and if he had lived he would have shown you what I mean, and helped you to be what he was."

Mrs. Meg wiped away a quiet tear as she spoke; for the memory of her husband was a very tender one, and the education of his children had been a sacred task to which she gave all her heart and life, and so far she had done wonderfully well—as her good son and loving daughters tried to prove. Demi's arm was round her now, as he said, in a voice so like his father's that it was the sweetest music to her ear:

"Mother dear, I think I have got just what you want for me; and it shall not be my fault if I don't become the man you hope to see me. Let me tell you all about it. I didn't say anything till it was sure, because it would only worry you; but Aunt Jo and I have been on the look-out for it some time, and now it has come. You know her publisher, Mr. Tiber, is one of the most successful men in the business; also generous, kind, and the soul of honour—as his treatment of Aunty proves. Well, I've rather hankered for that place; for I love books, and as I can't make them I'd like to publish them. That needs some literary taste and judgement, it brings you in contact with fine people, and is an education in itself. Whenever I go into that large, handsome room to see Mr. Tiber for Aunt Jo, I always want to stay; for it's lined with books and pictures, famous men and women come and go, and Mr. Tiber sits at his desk like a sort of king, receiving his subjects; for the greatest authors are humble to him, and wait his Yes or No with anxiety. Of course I've nothing to do with all that, and may never have; but I like to see it, and the atmosphere is so different from the dark offices and hurly-burly of many other trades, where nothing but money is talked about, that it seems another world, and I feel at home in it. Yes, I'd rather beat the door-mats and make fires there than be head clerk in the great hide and leather store at a big salary." Here Demi paused for breath; and Mrs. Meg, whose face had been growing brighter and brighter, exclaimed eagerly:

"Just what I should like! Have you got it? Oh, my dear boy! your fortune is made if you go to that well-established and flourishing place, with those good men to help you along!"

"I think I have, but we mustn't be too sure of anything yet. I may not suit; I'm only on trial, and must begin at the beginning and work my way up faithfully. Mr. Tiber was very kind, and will push me on as fast as is fair to the other fellows, and as I prove myself fit to go up. I'm to begin the first of next month in the book-room, filing orders; and I go round and get orders, and do various other things of the sort. I like it. I am ready to do anything about books, if it's only to dust them," laughed Demi, well pleased with his prospects, for, after trying various things, he seemed at last to have found the sort of work he liked, and a prospect that was very inviting to him.

"You inherit that love of books from grandpa; he can't live without them. I'm glad of it. Tastes of that kind show a refined nature, and are both a comfort and a help all one's life. I am truly glad and grateful, John, that at last you want to settle, and have got such an entirely satisfactory place. Most boys begin much earlier; but I don't believe in sending them out to face the world so young, just when body and soul need home care and watchfulness. Now you are a man, and must begin your life for yourself. Do your best, and be as honest, useful, and happy as your father, and I won't care about making a fortune."

"I'll try, mother. Couldn't have a better chance; for Tiber & Co. treat their people like gentlemen, and pay generously for faithful work. Things are done in a businesslike way there, and that suits me. I hate promises that are not kept, and shiftless or tyrannical ways anywhere. Mr. Tiber said: 'This is only to teach you the ropes, Brooke; I shall have other work for you by and by.' Aunty told him I had done book notices, and had rather a fancy for literature; so though I can't produce any 'works of Shakespeare,' as she says, I may get up some little things later. If I don't, I think it a very honourable and noble profession to select and give good books to the world; and I'm satisfied to be a humble helper in the work."

"I'm glad you feel so. It adds so much to one's happiness to love the task one does. I used to hate teaching; but housekeeping for my own family was always sweet, though much harder in many ways. Isn't Aunt Jo pleased about all this?" asked Mrs. Meg, already seeing in her mind's eye a splendid sign with "Tiber, Brooke & Co." over the door of a famous publishing house.

"So pleased that I could hardly keep her from letting the cat out of the bag too soon. I've had so many plans, and disappointed you so often, I wanted to be very sure this time. I had to bribe Rob and Ted to keep her at home tonight till I'd told my news, she was eager to rush down and tell you herself. The castles that dear woman has built for me would fill all Spain, and have kept us jolly while we waited to know our fate. Mr. Tiber doesn't do things in a hurry; but when he makes up his mind, you are all right; and I feel that I am fairly launched."

"Bless you, dear, I hope so! It is a happy day for me, because I've been so anxious lest, with all my care, I have been too easy and indulgent, and my boy, with his many good gifts, might fritter his time away in harmless but unsatisfactory things. Now I am at ease about you. If only Daisy can be happy, and Josie give up her dream, I shall be quite contented."

Demi let his mother enjoy herself for a few minutes, while he smiled over a certain little dream of his own, not ready yet for the telling; then he said, in the paternal tone which he unconsciously used when speaking of his sisters:

"I'll see to the girls; but I begin to think grandpa is right in saying we must each be what God and nature makes us. We can't change it much—only help to develop the good and control the bad elements in us. I have fumbled my way into my right place at last, I hope. Let Daisy be happy in her way, since it is a good and womanly one. If Nat comes home all right, I'd say: 'Bless you, my children,' and give them a nest of their own. Then you and I will help little Jo to find out if it is to be 'All the world's a stage' or 'Home, sweet home', for her."

"I suppose we must, John; but I can't help making plans, and hoping they will come to pass. I see that Daisy is bound up in Nat; and if he is worthy of her I shall let them be happy in their own way, as my parents let me. But Josie will be a trial, I foresee; and much as I love the stage, and always did, I don't see how I can ever let my little girl be an actress, though she certainly has great talent for it."

"Whose fault is that?" asked Demi, smiling, as he remembered his mother's early triumphs and unquenchable interest in the dramatic efforts of the young people round her.

"Mine, I know. How could it be otherwise when I acted *Babes in the Wood* with you and Daisy before you could speak, and taught Josie to declaim *Mother Goose* in her cradle. Ah, me! the tastes of the mother come out in her children, and she must atone for them by letting them have their own way, I suppose." And Mrs. Meg laughed, even while she shook her head over the undeniable fact that the Marches were a theatrical family.

"Why not have a great actress of our name, as well as an authoress, a minister, and an eminent publisher? We don't choose our talents, but we needn't hide them in a napkin because they are not just what we want. I say, let Jo have her way, and do what she can. Here am I to take care of her; and you can't deny you'd enjoy fixing her furbelows, and seeing her shine before the footlights, where you used to long to be. Come, mother, better face the music and march gaily, since your wilful children will 'gang their ain gait.' "

"I don't see but I must, and 'leave the consequences to the Lord,' as Marmee used to say when she had to decide, and only saw a step of the road. I *should* enjoy it immensely, if I could only feel that the life would not hurt my girl, and leave her unsatisfied when it was too late to change; for nothing is harder to give up than the excitements of that profession. I know something of it; and if your blessed father had not come along, I'm afraid I should have been an actress in spite of Aunt March and all our honoured ancestors."

"Let Josie add new honour to the name, and work out the family talent in its proper place. I'll play dragon to her, and you play nurse, and no harm can come to our little Juliet, no matter how many Romeos spoon under her balcony. Really, ma'am, opposition comes badly from an old lady who is going to wring the hearts of our audience in the heroine's part in Aunty's play next Christmas. It's the most pathetic thing I ever saw, mother; and I'm sorry you didn't become an actress, though we should be nowhere if you had."

Demi was on his legs now, with his back to the fire, in the lordly attitude men like to assume when things go well with them, or they want to lay down the law on any subject.

Mrs. Meg actually blushed at her son's hearty praise, and could not deny that the sound of applause was as sweet now as when she played the *Witch's Curse* and *The Moorish Maiden's Vow* long years ago.

"It's perfectly absurd for me to do it, but I couldn't resist when Jo and Laurie made the part for me, and you children were to act in it. The minute I get on the old mother's dress I forget myself and feel the same thrill at the sound of the bell that I used to feel when we got up plays in the garret. If Daisy would only take the daughter's part it would be so complete; for with you and Josie I am hardly acting, it is all so real."

"Especially the hospital scene, where you find the wounded son. Why, mother, do you know when we did that at last rehearsal my face was wet with real tears as you cried over me. It will bring down the house; but don't forget to wipe 'em off, or I shall sneeze," said Demi, laughing at the recollection of his mother's hit.

"I won't; but it almost broke my heart to see you so pale and dreadful. I hope there will never be another war in my time, for I should have to let you go; and I never want to live through the same experience we had with father."

"Don't you think Alice does the part better than Daisy would? Daisy hasn't a bit of the actress in her, and Alice puts life into the dullest words she speaks. I think the Marquise is just perfect in our piece," said Demi, strolling about the room as if the warmth of the fire sent a sudden colour to his face.

"So do I. She is a dear girl, and I'm proud and fond of her. Where is she tonight?"

"Pegging away at her Greek, I suppose. She usually is in the evening. More's the pity," added Demi, in a low tone, as he stared intently at the book-case, though he couldn't read a title.

"Now, there is a girl after my own heart. Pretty, well-bred, well-educated, and yet domestic, a real companion as well as help-meet for some good and intelligent man. I hope she will find one."

"So do I," muttered Demi.

Mrs. Meg had taken up her work again, and was surveying a half-finished buttonhole with so much interest that her son's face escaped her eye. He shed a beaming smile upon the rows of poets, as if even in their glass prison they could sympathize and rejoice with him at the first rosy dawn of the great passion which they knew so well. But Demi was a wise youth, and never leaped before looking carefully. He hardly knew his own heart yet, and was contented to wait till the sentiment, the fluttering of those folded wings he began to feel, should escape from the chrysalis and be ready to soar away in the sunshine to seek and claim its lovely mate. He had said nothing; but the brown eyes were eloquent, and there was an unconscious underplot to all the little plays he and Alice Heath acted so well together. She was busy with her books, bound to graduate with high honours, and he was trying to do the same in that larger college open to all, and where each man has his own prize to win or lose. Demi had nothing but himself to offer and, being a modest youth, considered that a poor gift till he had proved his power to earn his living, and the right to take a woman's happiness into his keeping.

No one guessed that he had caught the fever except sharp-eyed Josie, and she, having a wholesome fear of her brother—who could be rather awful when she went too far—wisely contented herself with watching him like a little cat, ready to pounce on the first visible sign of weakness. Demi had taken to playing pensively upon his flute after he was in his room for the night, making this melodious friend his confidante, and breathing into it all the tender hopes and fears that filled his heart. Mrs. Meg, absorbed in domestic affairs, and Daisy, who cared for no music but Nat's violin, paid no heed to these chamber concerts, but Josie always murmured to herself, with a naughty chuckle, "Dick Swiveller is thinking of his Sophy Wackles," and bided her time to revenge certain wrongs inflicted upon her by Demi, who always took Daisy's side when she tried to curb the spirits of her unruly little sister.

This evening she got her chance, and made the most of it. Mrs. Meg was just rounding off her buttonhole, and Demi still strolling restlessly about the room, when a book was heard to slam in the study, followed by an audible yawn and the appearance of the student looking as if sleep and a desire for mischief were struggling which should be master.

"I heard my name; have you been saying anything bad about me?" she demanded, perching on the arm of an easychair.

Her mother told the good news, over which Josie duly rejoiced, and Demi received her congratulations with a benignant air which made her feel that too much satisfaction was not good for him, and incited her to put a thorn into his bed of roses at once.

"I caught something about the play just now, and I want to tell you that I'm going to introduce a song into my part to liven it up a bit. How would this do?" and seating herself at the piano she began to sing to these words the air of "Kathleen Mavourneen";

> *"Sweetest of maidens, oh, how can I tell*
> *The love that transfigures the whole earth to me?*
> *The longing that causes my bosom to swell,*
> *When I dream of a life all devoted to thee?"*

She got no further, for Demi, red with wrath, made a rush at her, and the next moment a very agile young person was seen dodging round tables and chairs with the future partner of Tiber & Co. in hot pursuit. "You monkey, how dare you meddle with my papers?" cried the irate poet, making futile grabs at the saucy girl, who skipped to and fro, waving a bit of paper tantalizingly before him.

"Didn't; found it in the big 'Dic.' Serves you right if you leave your rubbish about. Don't you like my song? It's very pretty."

"I'll teach you one that you won't like if you don't give me my property."

"Come and get it if you can;" and Josie vanished into the study to have out her squabble in peace, for Mrs. Meg was already saying:

"Children, children! don't quarrel."

The paper was in the fire by the time Demi arrived and he at once calmed down, seeing that the bone of contention was out of the way.

"I'm glad it's burnt; I don't care for it, only some verse I was trying to set to music for one of the girls. But I'll trouble you to let my papers alone, or I shall take back the advice I gave mother tonight about allowing you to act as much as you like."

Josie was sobered at once by this dire threat, and in her most wheedling tone begged to know what he had said. By way of heaping coals of fire on her head he told her, and this diplomatic performance secured him an ally on the spot.

"You dear old boy! I'll never tease you again though you moon and spoon both day and night. If you stand by me, I'll stand by you and never say a word. See here! I've got a note for you from Alice. Won't that be a peace-offering and soothe your little feelings?"

Demi's eyes sparkled as Josie held up a paper cocked hat, but as he knew what was probably in it, he took the wind out of Josie's sails, and filled her with blank astonishment by saying carelessly:

"That's nothing; it's only to say whether she will go to the concert with us tomorrow night. You can read it if you like."

With the natural perversity of her sex Josie ceased to be curious the moment she was told to read it, and meekly handed it over; but she watched Demi as he calmly read the two lines it contained and then threw it into the fire.

"Why, Jack, I thought you'd treasure every scrap the 'sweetest maid' touched. Don't you care for her?"

"Very much; we all do; but 'mooning and spooning,' as you elegantly express it, is not in my line. My dear little girl, your plays make you romantic, and because Alice and I act lovers sometimes you take it into your silly head that we are really so. Don't waste time hunting mares' nests, but attend to your own affairs and leave me to mine. I forgive you, but don't do it again; it's bad taste, and tragedy queens don't romp."

The last cut finished Josie; she humbly begged pardon and went off to bed, while Demi soon followed, feeling that he had not only settled himself but his too inquisitive little sister also. But if he had seen her face as she listened to the soft wailing of his flute he would not have been so sure, for she looked as cunning as a magpie as she said, with a scornful sniff: "Pooh, you can't deceive me; I *know* Dick is serenading Sophy Wackles."

Chapter 11

Emil's Thanksgiving

THE *Brenda* was scudding along with all sail set to catch the rising wind, and everyone on board was rejoicing, for the long voyage was drawing towards an end.

"Four weeks more, Mrs. Hardy, and we'll give you a cup of tea such as you never had before," said second mate Hoffmann, as he paused beside two ladies sitting in a sheltered corner of the deck.

"I shall be glad to get it, and still gladder to put my feet on solid ground," answered the elder lady, smiling; for our friend Emil was a favourite, as well he might be, since he devoted himself to the captain's wife and daughter, who were the only passengers on board.

"So shall I, even if I have to wear a pair of shoes like Chinese junks. I've tramped up and down the deck so much, I shall be barefooted if we don't arrive soon," laughed Mary, the daughter, showing two shabby little boots as she glanced up at the companion of these tramps, remembering gratefully how pleasant he had made them.

"Don't think there are any small enough in China," answered Emil, with a sailor's ready gallantry, privately resolving to hunt up the handsomest shoes he could find the moment he landed.

"I don't know what you would have done for exercise, dear, if Mr. Hoffmann had not made you walk every day. This lazy life is bad for young people, though it suits an old body like me well enough in calm weather. Is this likely to be a gale, think ye?" added Mrs. Hardy, with an anxious glance at the west, where the sun was setting redly.

"Only a capful of wind, ma'am, just enough to send us

along lively," answered Emil, with a comprehensive glance aloft and alow.

"Please sing, Mr. Hoffmann, it's so pleasant to have music at this time. We shall miss it very much when we get ashore," said Mary, in a persuasive tone which would have won melody from a shark, if such a thing were possible.

Emil had often blessed his one accomplishment during these months, for it cheered the long days, and made the twilight hour his happiest time, wind and weather permitting. So now he gladly tuned his pipe, and leaning on the taffrail near the girl, watched the brown locks blowing in the wind as he sang her favourite song:

> *"Give me freshening breeze, my boys,*
> *A white and swelling sail,*
> *A ship that cuts the dashing waves,*
> *And weathers every gale.*
> *What life is like a sailor's life,*
> *So free, so bold, so brave?*
> *His home the ocean's wide expanse,*
> *A coral bed his grave."*

Just as the last notes of the clear, strong voice died away, Mrs. Hardy suddenly exclaimed: "What's that?"

Emil's quick eye saw at once the little puff of smoke coming up a hatchway where no smoke should be, and his heart seemed to stand still for an instant as the dread word "Fire!" flashed through his mind. Then he was quite steady, and strolled away saying quietly:

"Smoking not allowed there, I'll go and stop it." But the instant he was out of sight his face changed, and he leaped down the hatchway, thinking, with a queer smile on his lips: "If we are afire, shouldn't wonder if I did make a coral bed my grave!"

He was gone a few minutes, and when he came up, half stifled with smoke, he was as white as a very brown man could be, but calm and cool as he went to report to the captain.

"Fire in the hold, sir."

"Don't frighten the women," was Captain Hardy's first

order; then both bestirred themselves to discover how strong the treacherous enemy was, and to rout it if possible.

The *Brenda's* cargo was a very combustible one, and in spite of the streams of water poured into the hold it was soon evident that the ship was doomed. Smoke began to ooze up between the planks everywhere, and the rising gale soon fanned the smouldering fire to flames that began to break out here and there, telling the dreadful truth too plainly for anyone to hide. Mrs. Hardy and Mary bore the shock bravely when told to be ready to quit the ship at a minute's notice; the boats were hastily prepared, and the men worked with a will to batten down every loophole whence the fire might escape. Soon the poor *Brenda* was a floating furnace, and the order to "Take to the boats!" came for all. The women first, of course, and it was fortunate that, being a merchantman, there were no more passengers on board, so there was no panic, and one after the other the boats pushed off. That in which the women were lingered near, for the brave captain would be the last to leave his ship.

Emil stayed by him till ordered away, and reluctantly obeyed; but it was well for him he went, for just as he had regained the boat, rocking far below, half hidden by a cloud of smoke, a mast, undermined by the fire now raging in the bowels of the ship, fell with a crash, knocking Captain Hardy overboard. The boat soon reached him as he floated out from the wreck, and Emil sprung into the sea to rescue him, for he was wounded and senseless. This accident made it necessary for the young man to take command, and he at once ordered the men to pull for their lives, as an explosion might occur at any moment.

The other boats were out of danger and all lingered to watch the splendid yet awesome spectacle of the burning ship alone on the wide sea, reddening the night and casting a lurid glare upon the water, where floated the frail boats filled with pale faces, all turned for a last look at the fated *Brenda*, slowly settling to her watery grave. No one saw the end, however, for the gale soon swept the watchers far away and separated them, some never to meet again till the sea gives up its dead.

The boat whose fortunes we must follow was alone

when dawn came up, showing these survivors all the dangers of their situation. Food and water had been put in, and such provision for comfort and safety as time allowed; but it was evident that with a badly wounded man, two women, and seven sailors, their supply would not last long, and help was sorely needed. Their only hope was in meeting a ship, although the gale, which had raged all night, had blown them out of their course. To this hope all clung, and wiled away the weary hours, watching the horizon and cheering one another with prophecies of speedy rescue.

Second mate Hoffmann was very brave and helpful, though his unexpected responsibility weighed heavily on his shoulders; for the captain's state seemed desperate, the poor wife's grief wrung his heart, and the blind confidence of the young girl in his power to save them made him feel that no sign of doubt or fear must lessen it. The men did their part readily now, but Emil knew that if starvation and despair made brutes of them, his task might be a terrible one. So he clutched his courage with both hands, kept up a manly front, and spoke so cheerily of their good chances, that all instinctively turned to him for guidance and support.

The first day and night passed in comparative comfort, but when the third came, things looked dark and hope began to fail. The wounded man was delirious, the wife worn out with anxiety and suspense, the girl weak for want of food, having put away half her biscuit for her mother, and given her share of water to wet her father's feverish lips. The sailors ceased rowing and sat grimly waiting, openly reproaching their leader for not following their advice, others demanding more food, all waxing dangerous as privation and pain brought out the animal instincts lurking in them. Emil did his best, but mortal man was helpless there, and he could only turn his haggard face from the pitiless sky, that dropped no rain for their thirst, to the boundless sea where no sail appeared to gladden their longing eyes. All day he tried to cheer and comfort them, while hunger gnawed, thirst parched, and growing fear lay heavy at his heart. He told stories to the men, implored them to bear up for the helpless women's sake, and promised rewards if they would pull while they had strength to regain the lost route, as nearly as he could make it out, and increase their chance of rescue. He rigged an awning of sailcloth over the suffering man and tended him like a son, comforted the wife, and tried to make the pale girl forget herself, by singing every song he knew or recounting his adventures by land and sea, till she smiled and took heart; for all ended well.

The fourth day came and the supply of food and water was nearly gone. Emil proposed to keep it for the sick man and the women, but two of the men rebelled, demanding their share. Emil gave up his as an example, and several of the good fellows followed it, with the quiet heroism which so often crops up in rough but manly natures. This shamed the others, and for another day an ominous peace reigned in that little world of suffering and suspense. But during the night, while Emil, worn out with fatigue, left the watch to the most trustworthy sailor, that he might snatch an hour's rest, these two men got at the stores and stole the last of the bread and water, and the one bottle of brandy, which was carefully hoarded to keep up their strength and make the brackish water drinkable. Half mad with thirst, they drank greedily and by morning one was in a stupor, from which he never woke; the other so crazed by the strong stimulant, that when Emil tried to control him, he leaped overboard and was lost. Horror-stricken by this terrible scene, the other men were submissive henceforth, and the boat floated on and on with its sad freight of suffering souls and bodies.

Another trial came to them that left all more despairing than before. A sail appeared, and for a time a frenzy of joy prevailed, to be turned to bitterest disappointment when it passed by, too far away to see the signals waved to them or hear the frantic cries for help that rang across the sea. Emil's heart sank then, for the captain seemed dying, and the women could not hold out much longer. He kept up till night came; then in the darkness, broken only by the feeble murmuring of the sick man, the whispered prayers of the poor wife, the ceaseless swash of waves, Emil hid his face, and had an hour of silent agony that aged him more than years of happy life could have done. It was not the physical hardship that daunted him, though want and weakness tortured him; it was his dreadful powerlessness to conquer the cruel fate that seemed hanging over them. The men he cared little for, since these perils were but a part of the life they chose; but the master he loved, the good woman who had been so kind to him, the sweet girl whose winsome presence had made the long voyage so pleasant for them all—if he could only save these dear and innocent creatures from a cruel death, he felt that he could willingly give his life for them.

As he sat there with his head in his hands, bowed down by the first great trial of his young life, the starless sky overhead, the restless sea beneath, and all around him suffering, for which he had no help, a soft sound broke the silence, and he listened like one in a dream. It was Mary singing to her mother, who lay sobbing in her arms, spent with this long anguish. A very faint and broken voice it was, for the poor girl's lips were parched with thirst; but the loving heart turned instinctively to the great Helper in this hour of despair, and He heard her feeble cry. It was a sweet old hymn often sung at Plumfield; and as he listened, all the happy past came back so clearly that Emil forgot the bitter present, and was at home again. His talk on the housetop with Aunt Jo seemed but yesterday, and, with a pang of self-reproach, he thought:

"The scarlet strand! I must remember it, and do my duty to the end. Steer straight, old boy; and if you can't come into port, go down with all sail set."

Then, as the soft voice crooned on to lull the weary woman to a fitful sleep, Emil for a little while forgot his burden in a dream of Plumfield. He saw them all, heard the familiar voices, felt the grip of welcoming hands, and seemed to say to himself: "Well, they shall not be ashamed of me if I never see them any more."

A sudden shout startled him from that brief rest, and a drop on his forehead told him that the blessed rain had come at last, bringing salvation with it; for thirst is harder to bear than hunger, heat, or cold. Welcomed by cries of joy, all lifted up their parched lips, held out their hands, and spread their garments to catch the great drops that soon came pouring down to cool the sick man's fever,

quench the agony of thirst, and bring refreshment to
every weary body in the boat. All night it fell, all night the
castaways revelled in the saving shower, and took heart
again, like dying plants revived by heaven's dew. The
clouds broke away at dawn, and Emil sprung up, wonderfully braced and cheered by those hours of silent gratitude for this answer to their cry for help. But this was not
all; as his eye swept the horizon, clear against the rosy sky
shone the white sails of a ship, so near that they could see
the pennon at her mast-head and black figures moving on
the deck.

One cry broke from all those eager throats, and rang
across the sea, as every man waved hat or handkerchief
and the women stretched imploring hands towards this
great white angel of deliverance coming down upon them
as if the fresh wind filled every sail to help her on.

No disappointment now; answering signals assured them
of help; and in the rapture of that moment the happy
women fell on Emil's neck, giving him his reward in tears
and blessings as their grateful hearts overflowed. He always said that was the proudest moment of his life, as he
stood there holding Mary in his arms; for the brave girl,
who had kept up so long, broke down then, and clung to
him half fainting; while her mother busied herself about
the invalid, who seemed to feel the joyful stir, and gave an
order, as if again on the deck of his lost ship.

It was soon over; and then all were safely aboard the
good *Urania*, homeward bound. Emil saw his friends in
tender hands, his men among their mates, and told the
story of the wreck before he thought of himself. The
savoury odour of the soup, carried by to the cabin for the
ladies, reminded him that he was starving, and a sudden
stagger betrayed his weakness. He was instantly borne
away, to be half killed by kindness, and being fed, clothed,
and comforted, was left to rest. Just as the surgeon left the
state-room, he asked in his broken voice: "What day is
this? My head is so confused, I've lost my reckoning."

"Thanksgiving Day, man! And we'll give you a regular
New England dinner, if you'll eat it," answered the surgeon heartily.

But Emil was too spent to do anything, except lie still and give thanks, more fervently and gratefully than ever before, for the blessed gift of life, which was the sweeter for a sense of duty faithfully performed.

Chapter 12

Dan's Christmas

WHERE WAS Dan? In prison. Alas for Mrs. Jo! how her heart would have ached if she had known that while old Plum shone with Christmas cheer her boy sat alone in his cell, trying to read the little book she gave him, with eyes dimmed now and then by the hot tears no physical suffering had ever wrung from him, and longing with a homesick heart for all that he had lost.

Yes, Dan was in prison; but no cry for help from him as he faced the terrible strait he was in with the dumb despair of an Indian at the stake; for his own bosom sin had brought him there, and this was to be the bitter lesson that tamed the lawless spirit and taught him self-control.

The story of his downfall is soon told; for it came, as so often happens, just when he felt unusually full of high hopes, good resolutions, and dreams of a better life. On his journey he met a pleasant young fellow, and naturally felt an interest in him, as Blair was on his way to join his elder brothers on a ranch in Kansas. Card-playing was going on in the smoking-car, and the lad—for he was barely twenty—tired with the long journey, beguiled the way with such partners as appeared, being full of spirits, and a little intoxicated with the freedom of the West. Dan, true to his promise, would not join, but watched with intense interest the games that went on, and soon made up his mind that two of the men were sharpers anxious to fleece the boy, who had imprudently displayed a well-filled pocket-book. Dan always had a soft spot in his heart for any younger, weaker creature whom he met, and something about the lad reminded him of Teddy; so he kept an eye on Blair, and warned him against his new friends.

Vainly, of course; for when all stopped overnight in one of the great cities, Dan missed the boy from the hotel whither he had taken him for safe-keeping; and learning who had come for him, went to find him, calling himself a fool for his pains, yet unable to leave the confiding boy to the dangers that surrounded him.

He found him gambling in a low place with the men, who were bound to have his money; and by the look of relief on Blair's anxious face when he saw him Dan knew without words that things were going badly with him, and he saw the peril too late.

"I can't come yet—I've lost; it's not my money; I must get it back, or I dare not face my brothers," whispered the poor lad, when Dan begged him to get away without further loss. Shame and fear made him desperate; and he played on, sure that he could recover the money confided to his care. Seeing Dan's resolute face, keen eye, and travelled air, the sharpers were wary, played fair, and let the boy win a little; but they had no mind to give up their prey, and finding that Dan stood sentinel at the boy's back, an ominous glance was exchanged between them, which meant: "We must get this fellow out of the way."

Dan saw it, and was on his guard; for he and Blair were strangers, evil deeds are easily done in such places, and no tales told. But he would not desert the boy, and still kept watch of every card till he plainly detected false play, and boldly said so. High words passed, Dan's indignation overcame his prudence; and when the cheat refused to restore his plunder with insulting words and drawn pistol, Dan's hot temper flashed out, and he knocked the man down with a blow that sent him crashing head first against a stove, to roll senseless and bleeding to the floor. A wild scene followed, but in the midst of it Dan whispered to the boy: "Get away, and hold your tongue. Don't mind me."

Frightened and bewildered, Blair quitted the city at once, leaving Dan to pass the night in the lock-up, and a few days later to stand in court charged with manslaughter; for the man was dead. Dan had no friends, and having

once briefly told the story, held his peace, anxious to keep
all knowledge of this sad affair from those at home. He
even concealed his name—giving that of David Kent, as
he had done several times before in emergencies. It was
all over very soon; but as there were extenuating circum-
stances his sentence was a year in prison, with hard labour.

Dazed by the rapidity with which this horrible change
in his life came upon him, Dan did not fully realize it till
the iron door clanged behind him and he sat alone in a cell
as narrow, cold, and silent as a tomb. He knew that a
word would bring Mr. Laurie to help and comfort him;
but he could not bear to tell of this disgrace, or see the
sorrow and the shame it would cause the friends who
hoped so much for him.

"No," he said, clenching his fist, "I'll let them think me
dead first. I shall be if I am kept here long;" and he sprang
up to pace the stone floor like a caged lion, with a turmoil
of wrath and grief, rebellion and remorse, seething in
heart and brain, till he felt as if he should go mad and beat
upon the walls that shut him away from the liberty which
was his life. For days he suffered terribly, then worn out,
sank into a black melancholy sadder to see than his
excitement.

The warden of this prison was a rough man who had
won the ill will of all by unnecessary harshness, but the
chaplain was full of sympathy, and did his hard duty
faithfully and tenderly. He laboured with poor Dan, but
seemed to make no impression, and was forced to wait till
work had soothed the excited nerves and captivity famed
the proud spirit that would suffer but not complain.

Dan was put in the brush-shop, and feeling that activity
was his only salvation, worked with a feverish energy that
soon won the approval of the master and the envy of less
skilful mates. Day after day he sat in his place, watched by
an armed overseer, forbidden any but necessary words, no
intercourse with the men beside him, no change but from
cell to shop, no exercise but the dreary marches to and
fro, each man's hand on the other's shoulder keeping step
with the dreary tramp so different from the ringing tread
of soldiers. Silent, gaunt, and grim, Dan did his daily task,
ate his bitter bread, and obeyed commands with a rebel-

lious flash of the eye, that made the warden say: "That's a dangerous man. Watch him. He'll break out some day."

There were others more dangerous than he, because older in crime and ready for any desperate outbreak to change the monotony of long sentences. These men soon divined Dan's mood, and in the mysterious way convicts invent, managed to convey to him before a month was over that plans were being made for a mutiny at the first opportunity. Thanksgiving Day was one of the few chances for them to speak together as they enjoyed an hour of freedom in the prison yard. Then all would be settled and the rash attempt made if possible, probably to end in bloodshed and defeat for most, but liberty for a few. Dan had already planned his own escape and bided his time, growing more and more moody, fierce, and rebellious, as loss of liberty wore upon soul and body; for this sudden change from his free, healthy life to such a narrow, gloomy, and miserable one, could not but have a terrible effect upon one of Dan's temperament and age.

He brooded over his ruined life, gave up all his happy hopes and plans, felt that he could never face dear old Plumfield again, or touch those friendly hands, with the stain of blood upon his own. He did not care for the wretched man whom he had killed, for such a life was better ended, he thought; but the disgrace of prison would never be wiped out of his memory, though the cropped hair would grow again, the grey suit easily be replaced, and the bolts and bars left far behind.

"It's all over with me; I've spoilt my life, now let it go. I'll give up the fight and get what pleasure I can any-where, anyhow. They shall think me dead and so still care for me, but never know what I am. Poor Mother Bhaer! she tried to help me, but it's no use; the firebrand can't be saved."

And dropping his head in his hands as he sat on his low bed, Dan would mourn over all he had lost in tearless misery, till merciful sleep would comfort him with dreams of the happy days when the boys played together, or those still later and happier ones when all smiled on him, and Plumfield seemed to have gained a new and curious charm.

There was one poor fellow in Dan's shop whose fate was harder than his, for his sentence expired in the spring, but there was little hope of his living till that time; and the coldest-hearted man pitied poor Mason as he sat coughing his life away in that close place and counting the weary days yet to pass before he could see his wife and little child again. There was some hope that he might be pardoned out, but he had no friends to bestir themselves in the matter, and it was evident that the great Judge's pardon would soon end his patient pain for ever.

Dan pitied him more than he dared to show, and this one tender emotion in that dark time was like the little flower that sprung up between the stones of the prison yard and saved the captive from despair, in the beautiful old story. Dan helped Mason with his work when he was too feeble to finish his task, and the grateful look that thanked him was a ray of sunshine to cheer his cell when he was alone. Mason envied the splendid health of his neighbour, and mourned to see it wasting there. He was a peaceful soul and tried, as far as a whispered word or warning glance could do it, to deter Dan from joining the "bad lot," as the rebels were called. But having turned his face from the light, Dan found the downward way easy, and took a grim satisfaction in the prospect of a general outbreak during which he might revenge himself upon the tyrannical warden, and strike a blow for his own liberty, feeling that an hour of insurrection would be a welcome vent for the pent-up passions that tormented him. He had tamed many a wild animal, but his own lawless spirit was too much for him, till he found the curb that made him master of himself.

The Sunday before Thanksgiving, as he sat in chapel, Dan observed several guests in the seats reserved for them, and looked anxiously to see if any familiar face was there; for he had a mortal fear that someone from home would suddenly confront him. No, all were strangers, and he soon forgot them in listening to the chaplain's cheerful words, and the sad singing of many heavy hearts. People often spoke to the convicts, so it caused no surprise when, on being invited to address them, one of the ladies rose and said she would tell them a little story; which announcement caused the younger listeners to prick up their ears, and even the older ones to look interested; for any change in their monotonous life was welcome.

The speaker was a middle-aged woman in black, with a sympathetic face, eyes full of compassion, and a voice that seemed to warm the heart, because of certain motherly tones in it. She reminded Dan of Mrs. Jo, and he listened intently to every word, feeling that each was meant for him, because by chance, they came at the moment when he needed a softening memory to break up the ice of despair which was blighting all the good impulses of his nature.

It was a very simple little story, but it caught the men's attention at once, being about two soldiers in a hospital during the late war, both badly wounded in the right arm, and both anxious to save these breadwinners and go home unmaimed. One was patient, docile, and cheerfully obeyed orders, even when told that the arm must go. He submitted and after much suffering recovered, grateful for life, though he could fight no more. The other rebelled, would listen to no advice, and having delayed too long, died a lingering death, bitterly regretting his folly when it was too late. "Now, as all stories should have a little moral, let me tell you mine," added the lady, with a smile, as she looked at the row of young men before her, sadly wondering what brought them there.

"This is a hospital for soldiers wounded in life's battle; here are sick souls, weak wills, insane passions, blind consciences, all the ills that come from broken laws, bringing their inevitable pain and punishment with them. There is hope and help for every one, for God's mercy is infinite and man's charity is great; but penitence and submission must come before the cure is possible. Pay the forfeit manfully, for it is just; but from the suffering and shame wring new strength for a nobler life. The scar will remain, but it is better for a man to lose both arms than his soul; and these hard years, instead of being lost, may be made the most precious of your lives, if they teach you to rule yourselves. O friends, try to outlive the bitter past, to wash the sin away, and begin anew. If not for your own sakes, for that of the dear mothers, wives, and children, who wait and hope so patiently for you. Remember them, and do not let them love and long in vain. And if there be any here so forlorn that they have no friend to care for them, never forget the Father whose arms are always open to receive, forgive, and comfort His prodigal sons, even at the eleventh hour."

There the little sermon ended; but the preacher of it felt that her few hearty words had not been uttered in vain, for one boy's head was down, and several faces wore the softened look which told that a tender memory was touched. Dan was forced to set his lips to keep them steady, and drop his eyes to hide the sudden dew that dimmed them when waiting, hoping friends were spoken of. He was glad to be alone in his cell again, and sat thinking deeply, instead of trying to forget himself in sleep. It seemed as if those words were just what he needed to show him where he stood and how fateful the next few days might be to him. Should he join the "bad lot," and perhaps add another crime to the one already committed, lengthen the sentence already so terrible to bear, deliberately turn his back on all that was good, and mar the future that might yet be redeemed? Or should he, like the wiser man in the story, submit, bear the just punishment, try to be better for it; and though the scar would remain, it might serve as a reminder of a battle not wholly lost, since he had saved his soul though innocence was gone? Then he would dare go home, perhaps, confess, and find fresh strength in the pity and consolation of those who never gave him up.

Good and evil fought for Dan that night as did the angel and the devil for Sintram, and it was hard to tell whether lawless nature or loving heart would conquer. Remorse and resentment, shame and sorrow, pride and passion, made a battle-field of that narrow cell, and the poor fellow felt as if he had fiercer enemies to fight now than any he had met in all his wanderings. A little thing turned the scale, as it so often does in these mysterious hearts of ours, and a touch of sympathy helped Dan decide the course which would bless or ban his life.

In the dark hour before the dawn, as he lay wakeful on his bed, a ray of light shone through the bars, the bolts turned softly, and a man came in. It was the good chaplain, led by the same instinct that brings a mother to her sick child's pillow; for long experience as nurse of souls had taught him to see the signs of hope in the hard faces about him, and to know when the moment came for a helpful word and the cordial of sincere prayer that brings such comfort and healing to tried and troubled hearts. He had been to Dan before at unexpected hours, but always found him sullen, indifferent, or rebellious, and had gone away to patiently bide his time. Now it had come; a look of relief was in the prisoner's face as the light shone on it, and the sound of a human voice was strangely comfortable after listening to the whispers of the passions, doubts, and fears which had haunted the cell for hours, dismaying Dan by their power, and showing him how much he needed help to fight the good fight, since he had no armour of his own.

"Kent, poor Mason has gone. He left a message for you, and I felt impelled to come and give it now, because I think you were touched by what we heard today, and in need of the help Mason tried to give you," said the chaplain, taking the one seat and fixing his kind eyes on the grim figure in the bed.

"Thank you, sir, I'd like to hear it," was all Dan's answer; but he forgot himself in pity for the poor fellow dead in prison, with no last look at wife or child.

"He went suddenly, but remembered you, and begged me to say these words: 'Tell him *not to do it*, but to hold on, do his best, and when his time is out go right to Mary, and she'll make him welcome for my sake. He's got no friends in these parts and will feel lonesome, but a woman's always safe and comfortable when a fellow's down on his luck. Give him my love and good-bye for he was kind to me, and God will bless him for it.' Then he died quietly, and tomorrow will go home with God's pardon, since man's came too late."

Dan said nothing, but laid his arm across his face and lay quite still. Seeing that the pathetic little message had done its work even better than he hoped, the chaplain went on, unconscious how soothing his paternal voice was

to the poor prisoner who longed to "go home," but felt he
had forfeited the right.

"I hope you won't disappoint this humble friend whose
last thought was for you. I know that there is trouble
brewing, and fear that you may be tempted to lend a hand
on the wrong side. Don't do it, for the plot will not
succeed—it never does—and it would be a pity to spoil
your record which is fair so far. Keep up your courage, my
son, and go out at the year's end better, not worse, for this
hard experience. Remember a grateful woman waits to
welcome and thank you if you have no friends of your
own; if you have, do your best for their sake, and let us
ask God to help you as He only can."

Then waiting for no answer the good man prayed heartily, and Dan listened as he never had before; for the
lonely hour, the dying message, the sudden uprising of his
better self, made it seem as if some kind angel had come
to save and comfort him.

After that night there was a change in Dan, though no
one knew it but the chaplain; for to all the rest he was the
same silent, stern, unsocial fellow as before, and turning
his back on the bad and the good alike, found his only
pleasure in the books his friend brought him. Slowly, as
the steadfast drop wears away the rock, the patient kindness of this man won Dan's confidence, and led by him he
began to climb out of the Valley of Humiliation towards
the mountains, whence, through the clouds, one can catch
glimpses of the Celestial City whither all true pilgrims
sooner or later turn their wistful eyes and stumbling feet.
There were many back-slidings, many struggles with Giant
Despair and fiery Apollyon, many heavy hours when life
did not seem worth living and Mason's escape the only
hope. But through all, the grasp of a friendly hand, the
sound of a brother's voice, the unquenchable desire to
atone for the past by a better future, and win the right to
see home again, kept poor Dan to his great task as the old
year drew to its end, and the new waited to turn another
leaf in the book whose hardest lesson he was learning
now.

At Christmas he yearned so for Plumfield that he devised a way to send a word of greeting to cheer their

anxious hearts, and comfort his own. He wrote to Mary Mason, who lived in another State, asking her to mail the letter he enclosed. In it he merely said he was well and busy, had given up the farm, and had other plans which he would tell later; would not be home before autumn probably, nor write often, but was all right, and sent love and merry Christmas to everyone.

Then he took up his solitary life again, and tried to pay his forfeit manfully.

Chapter 13

Nat's New Year

"I DON'T EXEPECT to hear from Emil yet, and Nat writes regularly, but where is Dan? Only two or three postals since he went. Such an energetic fellow as he is could buy up all the farms in Kansas by this time," said Mrs. Jo one morning when the mail came in and no card or envelope bore Dan's dashing hand.

"He never writes often, you know, but does his work and then comes home. Months and years seem to mean little to him, and he is probably prospecting in the wilderness, forgetful of time," answered Mr. Bhaer, deep in one of Nat's long letters from Leipzig.

"But he promised he would let me know how he got on, and Dan keeps his word if he can. I'm afraid something has happened to him"; and Mrs. Jo comforted herself by patting Don's head, as he came at the sound of his master's name to look at her with eyes almost human in their wistful intelligence.

"Don't worry, Mum dear, nothing ever happens to the old fellow. He'll turn up all right, and come stalking in some day with a gold-mine in one pocket and a prairie in the other, as jolly as a grig," said Ted, who was in no haste to deliver Octoo to her rightful owner.

"Perhaps he has gone to Montana and given up the farm plan. He seemed to like Indians best, I thought"; and Rob went to help his mother with her pile of letters and his cheerful suggestions.

"I hope so, it would suit him best. But I am sure he would have told us his change of plan and sent for some money to work with. No, I feel in my prophetic bones that something is wrong," said Mrs. Jo, looking as solemn as Fate in a breakfast-cap.

"Then we shall hear; ill news always travels fast. Don't borrow trouble, Jo, but hear how well Nat is getting on. I'd no idea the boy would care for anything but music. My good friend Baumgarten has launched him well, and it will do him good if he lose not his head. A good lad, but new to the world, and Leipzig is full of snares for the unwary. Gott be with him!"

The professor read Nat's enthusiastic account of certain literary and musical parties he had been to, the splendours of the opera, the kindness of his new friends, the delight of studying under such a master as Bergmann, his hopes of rapid gain, and his great gratitude to those who had opened this enchanted world to him.

"That, now, is satisfactory and comfortable. I felt that Nat had unsuspected power in him before he went away; he was so manly and full of excellent plans," said Mrs. Jo, in a satisfied tone.

"We shall see. He will doubtless get his lesson and be the better for it. That comes to us all in our young days. I hope it will not be too hard for our good *Jüngling*," answered the Professor, with a wise smile, remembering his own student life in Germany.

He was right; and Nat was already getting his lesson in life with a rapidity which would have astonished his friends at home. The manliness over which Mrs. Jo rejoiced was developing in unexpected ways, and quiet Nat had plunged into the more harmless dissipations of the gay city with all the ardour of an inexperienced youth taking his first sip of pleasure. The entire freedom and sense of independence was delicious, for many benefits began to burden him, and he longed to stand on his own legs and make his own way. No one knew his past here; and with a well-stocked wardrobe, a handsome sum at his banker's, and the best teacher in Leipzig, he made his début as a musical young gentleman, presented by the much-respected Professor Bhaer and the wealthy Mr. Laurence, who had many friends glad to throw open their houses to his protégé. Thanks to these introductions, his fluent German, modest manners, and undeniable talent, the stranger was cordially welcomed, and launched at once into a circle which many an ambitious young man strove in vain to enter.

All this rather turned Nat's head; and as he sat in the brilliant opera-house, chatted among the ladies at some select coffee-party, or whisked an eminent professor's amiable daughter down the room, trying to imagine she was Daisy, he often asked himself if this gay fellow could be the poor homeless little street musician who once stood waiting in the rain at the gates of Plumfield. His heart was true, his impulses good, and his ambitions high; but the weak side of his nature came uppermost here; vanity led him astray, pleasure intoxicated him, and for a time he forgot everything but the delights of this new and charming life. Without meaning to deceive, he allowed people to imagine him a youth of good family and prospects; he boasted a little of Mr. Laurie's wealth and influence, of Professor Bhaer's eminence, and the flourishing college at which he himself had been educated. Mrs. Jo was introduced to the sentimental *Fräuleins* who read her books, and the charms and virtues of his own dear *Mädchen* confided to sympathetic mammas. All these boyish boastings and innocent vanities were duly circulated among the gossips, and his importance much increased thereby, to his surprise and gratification, as well as some shame.

But they bore fruit that was bitter in the end; for, finding that he was considered one of the upper class, it very soon became impossible for him to live in the humble quarters he had chosen, or to lead the studious, quiet life planned for him. He met other students, young officers, and gay fellows of all sorts, and was flattered at being welcomed among them; though it was a costly pleasure, and often left a thorn of regret to vex his honest conscience. He was tempted to take better rooms in a more fashionable street, leaving good Frau Tetzel to lament his loss, and his artist neighbour, Fräulein Vogelstein, to shake her grey ringlets and predict his return, a sadder and a wiser man.

The sum placed at his disposal for expenses and such simple pleasures as his busy life could command seemed a fortune to Nat, though it was smaller than generous Mr. Laurie first proposed. Professor Bhaer wisely counselled prudence, as Nat was unused to the care of money, and the good man knew the temptations that a well-filled purse makes possible at this pleasure-loving age. So Nat enjoyed his handsome little apartment immensely, and insensibly let many unaccustomed luxuries creep in. He loved his music and never missed a lesson; but the hours he should have spent in patient practice were too often wasted at theatre, ball, beer-garden, or club—doing no harm beyond that waste of precious time, and money not his own; for he had no vices, and took his recreation like a gentleman, so far. But slowly a change for the worse was beginning to show itself, and he felt it. These first steps along the flowery road were downward, not upward; and the constant sense of disloyalty which soon began to haunt him made Nat feel, in the few quiet hours he gave himself, that all was not well with him, spite of the happy whirl in which he lived.

"Another month, and then I will be steady," he said more than once, trying to excuse the delay by the fact that all was new to him, that his friends at home wished him to be happy, and that society was giving him the polish he needed. But as each month slipped away it grew harder to escape; he was inevitably drawn on, and it was so easy to drift with the tide that he deferred the evil day as long as possible. Winter festivities followed the more wholesome summer pleasures, and Nat found them more costly; for the hospitable ladies expected some return from the stranger; and carriages, bouquets, theatre tickets, and all the little expenses a young man cannot escape at such times, told heavily on the purse which seemed bottomless at first. Taking Mr. Laurie for his model, Nat became quite a gallant, and was universally liked; for through all the newly acquired airs and graces the genuine honesty and simplicity of his character plainly shone, winning confidence and affection from all who knew him.

Among these was a certain amiable old lady with a musical daughter—well-born but poor, and very anxious to marry the aforesaid daughter to some wealthy man. Nat's little fictions concerning his prospects and friends charmed the *gnädige Frau* as much as his music and devoted manners did the sentimental Minna. Their quiet

parlour seemed homelike and restful to Nat, when tired of
gayer scenes; and the motherly interest of the elder lady
was sweet and comfortable to him; while the tender blue
eyes of the pretty girl were always so full of welcome
when he came, of regret when he left, and of admiration
when he played to her, that he found it impossible to keep
away from this attractive spot. He meant no harm, and
feared no danger, having confided to the Frau Mamma
that he was betrothed; so he continued to call, little dreaming what ambitious hopes the old lady cherished, nor the
peril there was in receiving the adoration of a romantic
German girl, till it was too late to spare her pain and
himself great regret.

Of course some inkling of these new and agreeable
experiences got into the voluminous letters he never was
too gay, too busy, or too tired to write each week; and
while Daisy rejoiced over his happiness and success, and
the boys laughed at the idea of "old Chirper coming out as
a society man," the elders looked sober, and said among
themselves:

"He is going too fast; he must have a word of warning,
or trouble may come."

But Mr. Laurie said: "Oh, let him have his fling; he's
been dependent and repressed long enough. He can't go
far with the money he has, and I've no fear of his getting
into debt. He's too timid and too honest to be reckless. It
is his first taste of freedom; let him enjoy it, and he'll work
the better by and by; I know—and I'm sure I'm right."

So the warnings were very gentle, and the good people
waited anxiously to hear more of hard study, and less of
"splendid times." Daisy sometimes wondered, with a pang
of her faithful heart, if one of the charming Minnas, Hilde-
gardes, and Lottchens mentioned were not stealing her
Nat away from her; but she never asked, always wrote
calmly and cheerfully, and looked in vain for any hint of
change in the letters that were worn out with much reading.

Month after month slipped away, till the holidays came
with gifts, good wishes, and brilliant festivities. Nat expected to enjoy himself very much, and did at first; for a
German Christmas is a spectacle worth seeing. But he
paid dearly for the abandon with which he threw himself

into the gaieties of that memorable week; and on New Year's Day the reckoning came. It seemed as if some malicious fairy had prepared the surprises that arrived, so unwelcome were they, so magical the change they wrought, turning his happy world into a scene of desolation and despair as suddenly as a transformation at the pantomime.

The first came in the morning when, duly armed with costly bouquets and bon-bons, he went to thank Minna and her mother for the braces embroidered with forget-me-nots and the silk socks knit by the old lady's nimble fingers, which he had found upon his table that day. The Frau Mamma received him graciously; but when he asked for the daughter the good lady frankly demanded what his intentions were, adding that certain gossip which had reached her ear made it necessary for him to declare himself or come no more, as Minna's peace must not be compromised.

A more panic-stricken youth was seldom seen than Nat as he received this unexpected demand. He saw too late that his American style of gallantry had deceived the artless girl, and might be used with terrible effect by the artful mother, if she chose to do it. Nothing but the truth could save him, and he had the honour and honesty to tell it faithfully. A sad scene followed; for Nat was obliged to strip off his fictitious splendour, confess himself only a poor student, and humbly ask pardon for the thoughtless freedom with which he had enjoyed their too confiding hospitality. If he had any doubts of Frau Schomburg's motives and desires, they were speedily set at rest by the frankness with which she showed her disappointment, the vigour with which she scolded him, and the scorn with which she cast him off when her splendid castles in the air collapsed.

The sincerity of Nat's penitence softened her a little and she consented to a farewell word with Minna, who had listened at the keyhole, and was produced drenched in tears, to fall on Nat's bosom, crying: "Ah, thou dear one, never can I forget thee, though my heart is broken!"

This was worse than the scolding; for the stout lady also wept, and it was only after much German gush and twaddle that he escaped, feeling like another Werther; while the deserted Lotte consoled herself with the bonbons, her mother with the more valuable gifts.

The second surprise arrived as he dined with Professor Baumgarten. His appetite had been effectually taken away by the scene of the morning, and his spirits received another damper when a fellow student cheerfully informed him that he was about to go to America, and should make it his agreeable duty to call on the "lieber Herr Professor Bhaer," to tell him how gaily his protégé was disporting himself at Leipzig. Nat's heart died within him as he imagined the effect these glowing tales would have at Plumfield—not that he had wilfully deceived them, but in his letters many things were left untold; and when Carlsen added, with a friendly wink, that he would merely hint at the coming betrothal of the fair Minna and his "heart's friend," Nat found himself devoutly hoping that this other inconvenient heart's friend might go to the bottom of the sea before he reached Plumfield to blast all his hopes by these tales of a misspent winter. Collecting his wits, he cautioned Carlsen with what he flattered himself was Mephisto-phelian art, and gave him such confused directions that it would be a miracle if he ever found Professor Bhaer. But the dinner was spoilt for Nat, and he got away as soon as possible, to wander disconsolately about the streets, with no heart for the theatre or the supper he was to share with some gay comrades afterwards. He com-forted himself a little by giving alms to sundry beggars, making two children happy with gilded gingerbread, and drinking a lonely glass of beer, in which he toasted his Daisy and wished himself a better year than the last had been.

Going home at length, he found a third surprise await-ing him in the shower of bills which had descended upon him like a snowstorm, burying him in an avalanche of remorse, despair, and self-disgust. These bills were so many and so large that he was startled and dismayed; for, as Mr. Bhaer wisely predicted, he knew little about the value of money. It would take every dollar at the bankers to pay them all at once, and leave him penniless for the next six months, unless he wrote home for more. He would rather starve than do that; and his first impulse was

to seek help at the gaming-table, whither his new friends
had often tempted him. But he had promised Mr. Bhaer to
resist what then had seemed an impossible temptation;
and now he would not add another fault to the list already
so long. Borrow he would not, nor beg. What could he
do? For these appalling bills must be paid, and the lessons
go on; or his journey was an ignominious failure. But he
must live meantime. And how? Bowed down with remorse
for the folly of these months, he saw too late whither he
was drifting, and for hours paced up and down his pretty
rooms, floundering in a Slough of Despond, with no helping hand to pull him out—at least he thought so till letters
were brought in, and among fresh bills lay one well-worn
envelope with an American stamp in the corner.

Ah, how welcome it was! how eagerly he read the long
pages full of affectionate wishes from all at home! For
everyone had sent a line, and as each familiar name appeared, his eyes grew dimmer and dimmer till, as he read
the last—"God bless my boy! Mother Bhaer" —he broke
down; and laying his head on his arms, blistered the paper
with a rain of tears that eased his heart and washed away
the boyish sins that now lay so heavy on his conscience.

"Dear people, how they love and trust me! And how
bitterly they would be disappointed if they knew what a
fool I've been! I'll fiddle in the streets again before I'll ask
for help from them!" cried Nat, brushing away the tears of
which he was ashamed, although he felt the good they had
done.

Now he seemed to see more clearly what to do; for the
helping hand had been stretched across the sea, and Love,
the dear Evangelist, had lifted him out of the slough and
shown him the narrow gate, beyond which deliverance
lay. When the letter had been re-read, and one corner
where a daisy was painted, passionately kissed, Nat felt
strong enough to face the worst and conquer it. Every bill
should be paid, every salable thing of his own sold, these
costly rooms given up; and once back with thrifty Frau
Tetzel, he would find work of some sort by which to
support himself, as many another student did. He must
give up the new friends, turn his back on the gay life,
cease to be a butterfly, and take his place among the

grubs. It was the only honest thing to do, but very hard for the poor fellow to crush his little vanities, renounce the delights so dear to the young, own his folly, and step down from his pedestal to be pitied, laughed at, and forgotten.

It took all Nat's pride and courage to do this, for his was a sensitive nature; esteem was very precious to him, failure very bitter, and nothing but the inborn contempt for meanness and deceit kept him from asking help or trying to hide his need by some dishonest device. As he sat alone that night, Mr. Bhaer's words came back to him with curious clearness, and he saw himself a boy again at Plumfield, punishing his teacher as a lesson to himself, when timidity had made him lie.

"He shall not suffer for me again, and I won't be a sneak if I am a fool. I'll go and tell Professor Baumgarten all about it and ask his advice. I'd rather face a loaded cannon; but it must be done. Then I'll sell out, pay my debts, and go back where I belong. Better be an honest pauper than a jackdaw among peacocks"; and Nat smiled in the midst of his trouble, as he looked about him at the little elegancies of his room, remembering what he came from.

He kept his word manfully, and was much comforted to find that his experience was an old story to the professor, who approved his plan, thinking wisely that the discipline would be good for him, and was very kind in offering help and promising to keep the secret of his folly from his friend Bhaer till Nat had redeemed himself.

The first week of the new year was spent by our prodigal in carrying out his plan with penitent dispatch, and his birthday found him alone in the little room high up at Frau Tetzel's, with nothing of his former splendour, but sundry unsalable keepsakes from the buxom maidens, who mourned his absence deeply. His male friends had ridiculed, pitied, and soon left him alone, with one or two exceptions, who offered their purses generously and promised to stand by him. He was lonely and heavy-hearted, and sat brooding over his small fire as he remembered the last New Year's Day at Plumfield, when at this hour he was dancing with his Daisy.

A tap at the door roused him, and with a careless

"Herein," he waited to see who had climbed so far for his sake. It was the good Frau proudly bearing a tray, on which stood a bottle of wine and an astonishing cake bedecked with sugar-plums of every hue, and crowned with candles. Fräulein Vogelstein followed, embracing a blooming rose-tree, above which her grey curls waved and her friendly face beamed joyfully as she cried:

"Dear Herr Blak, we bring you greetings and a little gift or two in honour of this ever-to-be-remembered day. Best wishes! and may the new year bloom for you as beautifully as we your heart-warm friends desire."

"Yes, yes, in truth we do, dear Herr," added Frau Tetzel. "Eat of this with-joy-made Kuchen, and drink to the health of the far-away beloved ones in the good wine."

Amused, yet touched by the kindness of the good souls, Nat thanked them both, and made them stay to enjoy the humble feast with him. This they gladly did, being motherly women full of pity for the dear youth, whose straits they knew, and having substantial help to offer, as well as kind words and creature comforts.

Frau Tetzel, with some hesitation, mentioned a friend of hers who, forced by illness to leave his place in the orchestra of a second-rate theatre, would gladly offer it to Nat, if he could accept so humble a position. Blushing and toying with the roses like a shy girl, good old Vogelstein asked if in his leisure moments he could give English lessons in the young ladies' school where she taught painting, adding that a small but certain salary would be paid him.

Gratefully Nat accepted both offers, finding it less humiliating to be helped by women than by friends of his own sex. This work would support him in a frugal way, and certain musical drudgery promised by his master assured his own teaching. Delighted with the success of their little plot, these friendly neighbours left him with cheery words, warm hand-grasps, and faces beaming with feminine satisfaction at the hearty kiss Nat put on each faded cheek, as the only return he could make for all their helpful kindness.

It was strange how much brighter the world looked after that; for hope was a better cordial than the wine, and good resolutions bloomed as freshly as the little rose-tree that filled the room with fragrance, as Nat woke the echoes with the dear old airs, finding now as always his best comforter in music, to whom henceforth he swore to be a more loyal subject.

Chapter 14

Plays at Plumfield

As IT IS as impossible for the humble historian of the March family to write a story without theatricals in it as for our dear Miss Yonge to get on with less than twelve or fourteen children in her interesting tales, we will accept the fact, and at once cheer ourselves after the last afflicting events, by proceeding to the Christmas plays at Plumfield; for they influence the fate of several of our characters, and cannot well be skipped.

When the college was built Mr. Laurie added a charming little theatre which not only served for plays, but declamations, lectures, and concerts. The drop-curtain displayed Apollo with the Muses grouped about him; and as a compliment to the donor of the hall the artist had given the god a decided resemblance to our friend, which was considered a superb joke by everyone else. Home talent furnished stars, stock company, orchestra, and scene painter; and astonishing performances were given on this pretty little stage.

Mrs. Jo had been trying for some time to produce a play which should be an improvement upon the adaptations from the French then in vogue, curious mixtures of fine toilettes, false sentiment, and feeble wit, with no touch of nature to redeem them. It was easy to plan plays full of noble speeches and thrilling situations, but very hard to write them; so she contented herself with a few scenes of humble life in which the comic and pathetic were mingled; and as she fitted her characters to her actors, she hoped the little venture would prove that truth and simplicity had not entirely lost their power to charm. Mr. Laurie helped her, and they called themselves Beaumont

179

and Fletcher, enjoying their joint labour very much; for Beaumont's knowledge of dramatic art was of great use in curbing Fletcher's too-aspiring pen, and they flattered themselves that they had produced a neat and effective bit of work as an experiment.

All was ready now; and Christmas Day was much enlivened by last rehearsals, the panics of timid actors, the scramble for forgotten properties, and the decoration of the theatre. Evergreen and holly from the woods, blooming plants from the hothouse on Parnassus, and flags of all nations made it very gay that night in honour of the guests who were coming, chief among them, Miss Cameron, who kept her promise faithfully. The orchestra tuned their instruments with unusual care, the scene-shifters set their stage with lavish elegance, the prompter heroically took his seat in the stifling nook provided for him, and the actors dressed with trembling hands that dropped the pins, and perspiring brows whereon the powder wouldn't stick. Beaumont and Fletcher were everywhere, feeling that their literary reputation was at stake; for sundry friendly critics were invited, and reporters, like mosquitoes, cannot be excluded from any earthly scene, be it a great man's death-bed or a dime museum.

"Has she come?" was the question asked by every tongue behind the curtain; and when Tom, who played an old man, endangered his respectable legs among the footlights to peep, announced that he saw Miss Cameron's handsome head in the place of honour, a thrill pervaded the entire company, and Josie declared with an excited gasp that she was going to have stage fright for the first time in her life.

"I'll shake you if you do," said Mrs. Jo, who was in such a wild state of dishevelment with her varied labours that she might have gone on as Madge Wildfire, without an additional rag or crazy elf-lock.

"You'll have time to get your wits together while we do our piece. We are old stagers and calm as clocks," answered Demi, with a nod towards Alice, ready in her pretty dress and all her properties at hand.

But both clocks were going rather faster than usual, as heightened colour, brilliant eyes, and a certain flutter

under the laces and velvet coat betrayed. They were to
open the entertainment with a gay little piece which they
had played before and did remarkably well. Alice was a
tall girl, with dark hair and eyes, and a face which intelligence, health, and a happy heart made beautiful. She was
looking her best now, for the brocades, plumes, and powder of the Marquise became her stately figure; and Demi
in his court suit, with sword, three-cornered hat, and
white wig, made as gallant a Baron as one would wish to
see. Josie was the maid, and looked her part to the life,
being as pretty, pert, and inquisitive as any French soubrette. These three were all the characters; and the success of the piece depended on the spirit and skill with
which the quickly changing moods of the quarrelsome
lovers were given, their witty speeches made to tell, and
by-play suited to the courtly period in which the scene
was laid.

Few would have recognized sober John and studious
Alice in the dashing gentleman and coquettish lady, who
kept the audience laughing at their caprices; while they
enjoyed the brilliant costumes, and admired the ease and
grace of the young actors. Josie was a prominent figure in
the plot, as she listened at keyholes, peeped into notes,
and popped in and out at all the most inopportune moments, with her nose in the air, her hands in her apron-
pockets, and curiosity pervading her little figure from the
topmost bow of her jaunty cap to the red heels of her
slippers. All went smoothly; and the capricious Marquise,
after tormenting the devoted Baron to her heart's content,
owned herself conquered in the war of wits, and was just
offering the hand he had fairly won, when a crash startled
them, and a heavily decorated side-scene swayed forward,
ready to fall upon Alice. Demi saw it and sprung before
her to catch and hold it up, standing like a modern Sam-
son with the wall of a house on his back. The danger was
over in a moment, and he was about to utter his last
speech, when the excited young scene-shifter, who had
flown up a ladder to repair the damage, leaned over to
whisper "All right," and release Demi from his spread-
eagle attitude: as he did so, a hammer slipped out of his
pocket, to fall upon the upturned face below, inflicting a

smart blow and literally knocking the Baron's part out of his head.

"A quick curtain," robbed the audience of a pretty little scene not down on the bill; for the Marquise flew to staunch the blood with a cry of alarm: "Oh! John, you are hurt! Lean on me"—which John gladly did for a moment, being a trifle dazed yet quite able to enjoy the tender touch of the hands busied about him and the anxiety of the face so near his own; for both told him something which he would have considered cheaply won by a rain of hammers and the fall of the whole college on his head.

Nan was on the spot in a moment with the case that never left her pocket; and the wound was neatly plastered up by the time Mrs. Jo arrived, demanding tragically:

"Is he too much hurt to go on again? If he is, my play is lost!"

"I'm all the fitter for it, Aunty; for here's a real instead of a painted wound. I'll be ready; don't worry about me." And catching up his wig, Demi was off, with only a very eloquent look of thanks to the Marquise, who had spoilt her gloves for his sake, but did not seem to mind it at all, though they reached above her elbows, and were most expensive.

"How are your nerves, Fletcher?" asked Mr. Laurie as they stood together during the breathless minute before the last bell rings.

"About as calm as yours, Beaumont," answered Mrs. Jo, gesticulating wildly to Mrs. Meg to set her cap straight.

"Bear up, partner! I'll stand by you whatever comes!"

"I feel that it ought to go; for, though it's a mere trifle, a good deal of honest work and truth have gone into it. Doesn't Meg look the picture of a dear old country woman?"

She certainly did, as she sat in the farmhouse kitchen by a cheery fire, rocking a cradle and darning stockings, as if she had done nothing else all her life. Grey hair, skilfully drawn lines on the forehead, and a plain gown, with cap, little shawl, and check apron, changed her into a comfortable, motherly creature who found favour the moment the curtain went up and discovered her rocking, darning, and crooning an old song. In a short soliloquy about Sam, her boy, who wanted to enlist; Dolly, her discontented little daughter, who longed for city ease and pleasures; and poor "Elizy," who had married badly, and came home to die, bequeathing her baby to her mother, lest its bad father should claim it, the little story was very simply opened, and made effective by the real boiling of the kettle on the crane, the ticking of a tall clock, and the appearance of a pair of blue worsted shoes which waved fitfully in the air to the soft babble of a baby's voice. Those shapeless little shoes won the first applause; and Mr. Laurie, forgetting elegance in satisfaction, whispered to his coadjutor:

"I thought the baby would fetch them!"

"If the dear thing won't squall in the wrong place, we are saved. But it is risky. Be ready to catch it if all Meg's cuddlings prove in vain," answered Mrs. Jo, adding, with a clutch at Mr. Laurie's arm as a haggard face appeared at the window:

"Here's Demi! I hope no one will recognize him when he comes on as the son. I'll never forgive you for not doing the villain yourself."

"Can't run the thing and act too. He's capitally made up, and likes a bit of melodrama."

"This scene ought to have come later; but I wanted to show that the mother was the heroine as soon as possible. I'm tired of love-sick girls and runaway wives. We'll prove that there's romance in old women also. Now he's coming!"

And in slouched a degraded-looking man, shabby, unshaven, and evil-eyed, trying to assume a masterful air as he dismayed the tranquil old woman by demanding his child. A powerful scene followed; and Mrs. Meg surprised even those who knew her best by the homely dignity with which she at first met the man she dreaded; then, as he brutally pressed his claim, she pleaded with trembling voice and hands to keep the little creature she had promised the dying mother to protect; and when he turned to take it by force, quite a thrill went through the house as the old woman sprung to snatch it from the cradle, and holding it close, defied him in God's name to tear it from that sacred refuge. It was really well done; and the round of applause that greeted the fine tableau of the indignant old woman, the rosy, blinking baby clinging to her neck,

and the daunted man who dared not execute his evil
purpose with such a defender for helpless innocence, told
the excited authors that their first scene was a hit.

The second was quieter, and introduced Josie as a bonny
country lass setting the supper-table in a bad humour. The
pettish way in which she slapped down the plates, hustled
the cups, and cut the big brown loaf, as she related her
girlish trials and ambitions, was capital. Mrs. Jo kept her
eye on Miss Cameron, and saw her nod approval several
times at some natural tone or gesture, some good bit of
by-play or a quick change of expression in the young face,
which was as variable as an April day. Her struggle with
the toasting-fork made much merriment; so did her contempt for the brown sugar, and the relish with which she
sweetened her irksome duties by eating it; and when she
sat, like Cinderella, on the hearth, tearfully watching the
flames dance on the homely room, a girlish voice was
heard to exclaim impulsively:

"Poor little thing! she ought to have *some* fun!"

The old woman enters; and mother and daughter have a
pretty scene, in which the latter coaxes and threatens,
kisses and cries, till she wins the reluctant consent of the
former to visit a rich relation in the city; and from being a
little thunder-cloud Dolly becomes bewitchingly gay and
good, as soon as her wilful wish is granted. The poor old
soul has hardly recovered from this trial when the son
enters, in army blue, tells he has enlisted and must go.
That is a hard blow; but the patriotic mother bears it well,
and not till the thoughtless young folks have hastened
away to tell their good news elsewhere does she break
down. Then the country kitchen becomes pathetic as the
old mother sits alone mourning over her children, till the
grey head is hidden in the hands as she kneels down by
the cradle to weep and pray, with only Baby to comfort
her fond and faithful heart.

Sniffs were audible all through the latter part of this
scene; and when the curtain fell, people were so busy
wiping their eyes that for a moment they forgot to ap-
plaud. That silent moment was more flattering than noise;
and as Mrs. Jo wiped the real tears off her sister's face, she

said as solemnly as an unconscious dab of rouge on her nose permitted:

"Meg, you have saved my play! Oh, why aren't you a real actress, and I a real playwright?"

"Don't gush now, dear, but help me dress Josie; she's in such a quiver of excitement, I can't manage her, and this is her best scene, you know."

So it was; for her aunt had written it especially for her, and little Jo was happy in a gorgeous dress, with a train long enough to satisfy her wildest dreams. The rich relation's parlour was in festival array, and the country cousin sails in, looking back at her sweeping flounces with such artless rapture that no one had the heart to laugh at the pretty jay in borrowed plumes. She has confidences with herself in the mirror, from which it is made evident that she had discovered all is not gold that glitters, and has found greater temptations than those a girlish love of pleasure, luxury, and flattery bring her. She is sought by a rich lover; but her honest heart resists the allurements he offers, and in its innocent perplexity wishes "mother" was there to comfort and counsel.

A gay little dance, in which Dora, Nan, Bess, and several of the boys took part, made a good background for the humble figure of the old woman in her widow's bonnet, rusty shawl, big umbrella, and basket. Her naïve astonishment, as she surveys the spectacle, feels the curtains, and smooths her old gloves during the moment she remains unseen, was very good; but Josie's unaffected start when she sees her, and the cry: "Why, there's mother!" was such a hearty little bit of nature, it hardly needed the impatient tripping over her train as she ran into the arms that seemed now to be her nearest refuge.

The lover plays his part; and ripples of merriment greeted the old woman's searching questions and blunt answers during the interview which shows the girl how shallow his love is, and how near she had been to ruining her life as bitterly as poor "Elizy" did. She gives her answer frankly, and when they are alone, looks from her own bedizened self to the shabby dress, work-worn hands, and tender face, crying with a repentant sob and kiss: "Take me

home, mother, and keep me safe. I've had enough of
this!"

"That will do you good, Maria; don't forget it," said one
lady to her daughter as the curtain went down; and the
girl answered: "Well, I'm sure I don't see why it's touching; but it is," as she spread her lace handkerchief to dry.

Tom and Nan came out strong in the next scene; for it
was a ward in an army hospital, and surgeon and nurse
went from bed to bed, feeling pulses, administering doses,
and hearing complaints with an energy and gravity which
convulsed the audience. The tragic element, never far
from the comic at such times and places, came in when,
while they bandaged an arm, the doctor told the nurse
about an old woman who was searching through the hospital for her son, after days and nights on battlefields, through
ambulances, and among scenes which would have killed
most women.

"She will be here directly, and I dread her coming; for
I'm afraid the poor lad who has just gone is her boy. I'd
rather face a cannon than these brave women, with their
hope and courage and great sorrow," says the surgeon.

"Ah, these poor mothers break my heart!" adds the
nurse, wiping her eyes on her big apron; and with the
words Mrs. Meg came in.

There was the same dress, the basket and umbrella, the
rustic speech, the simple manners; but all were made
pathetic by the terrible experience which had changed the
tranquil old woman to that haggard figure with wild eyes,
dusty feet, trembling hands, and an expression of mingled
anguish, resolution, and despair which gave the homely
figure a tragic dignity and power that touched all hearts. A
few broken words told the story of her vain search, and
then the sad quest began again. People held their breath
as, led by the nurse, she went from bed to bed, showing
in her face the alternations of hope, dread, and bitter
disappointment as each was passed. On a narrow cot was a
long figure covered with a sheet, and here she paused to
lay one hand on her heart and one on her eyes, as if to
gather courage to look at the nameless dead. Then she
drew down the sheet, gave a long shivering sigh of relief,
saying softly:

"Not my son, thank God! but some mother's boy." And stooping down, she kissed the cold forehead tenderly.

Somebody sobbed there, and Miss Cameron shook two tears out of her eyes, anxious to lose no look or gesture as the poor soul, nearly spent with the long strain, struggled on down the long line. But her search was happily ended; for, as if her voice had roused him from his feverish sleep, a gaunt, wild-eyed man sat up in his bed, and stretching his arms to her, cried in a voice that echoed through the room:

"Mother, mother! I knew you'd come to me!"

She did go to him, with a cry of love and joy that thrilled every listener, as she gathered him in her arms with the tears and prayers and blessing such as only a fond and faithful old mother could give.

The last scene was a cheerful contrast to this; for the country kitchen was bright with Christmas cheer, the wounded hero, with black patch and crutches well displayed, sat by the fire in the old chair whose familiar creak was soothing to his ear; pretty Dolly was stirring about, gaily trimming dresser, settle, high chimneypiece, and old-fashioned cradle with mistletoe and holly; while the mother rested beside her son, with that blessed baby on her knee. Refreshed by a nap and nourishment, this young actor now covered himself with glory by his ecstatic prancings, incoherent remarks to the audience, and vain attempts to get to the footlights, as he blinked approvingly at these brilliant toys. It was good to see Mrs. Meg pat him on the back, cuddle the fat legs out of sight, and appease his vain longings with a lump of sugar, till Baby embraced her with a grateful ardour that brought him a round of applause all for his little self.

A sound of singing outside disturbs the happy family, and, after a carol in the snowy moonlight, a flock of neighbours troop in with Christmas gifts and greetings. Much by-play made this a lively picture; for Sam's sweetheart hovered round him with a tenderness the Marquise did not show the Baron; and Dolly had a pretty bit under the mistletoe with her rustic adorer, who looked so like Ham Peggotty in his cowhide boots, rough jacket, and dark beard and wig, that no one would have recognized

Ted but for the long legs, which no extent of leather could disguise. It ended with a homely feast, brought by the guests; and as they sat round the table covered with doughnuts and cheese, pumpkin-pie, and other delicacies, Sam rises on his crutches to propose the first toast, and holding up his mug of cider, says, with a salute, and a choke in his voice: "Mother, God bless her!" All drink it standing, Dolly with her arm round the old woman's neck, as she hides her happy tears on her daughter's breast; while the irrepressible baby beat rapturously on the table with a spoon, and crowed audibly as the curtain went down.

They had it up again in a jiffy to get a last look at the group about that central figure, which was showered with bouquets, to the great delight of the infant Roscius; till a fat rosebud hit him on the nose, and produced the much-dreaded squall, which, fortunately, only added to the fun at that moment.

"Well, that will do for a beginning," said Beaumont, with a sigh of relief, as the curtain descended for the last time, and the actors scattered to dress for the closing piece.

"As an experiment, it is a success. Now we can venture to begin our great American drama," answered Mrs. Jo, full of satisfaction and grand ideas for the famous play—which, we may add, she did not write that year, owing to various dramatic events in her own family.

The Owlsdark Marbles closed the entertainment, and, being something new, proved amusing to this very indulgent audience. The gods and goddesses on Parnassus were displayed in full conclave; and, thanks to Mrs. Amy's skill in draping and posing, the white wigs and cotton-flannel robes were classically correct and graceful, though sundry modern additions somewhat marred the effect, while adding point to the showman's learned remarks. Mr. Laurie was Professor Owlsdark in cap and gown; and, after a high-flown introduction, he proceeded to exhibit and explain his marbles. The first figure was a stately Minerva; but a second glance produced a laugh, for the words "Women's Rights" adorned her shield, a scroll bearing the motto "Vote early and often" hung from the beak of the owl perched on her lance, and a tiny pestle and mortar ornamented her helmet. Attention was drawn to the firm mouth, the piercing eye, the awe-inspiring brow, of the strong-minded woman of antiquity, and some scathing remarks made upon the degeneracy of her modern sisters who failed to do their duty. Mercury came next, and was very fine in his airy attitude, though the winged legs quivered as if it was difficult to keep the lively god in his place. His restless nature was dilated upon, his mischievous freaks alluded to, and a very bad character given to the immortal messenger-boy; which delighted his friends and caused the marble nose of the victim to curl visibly with scorn when derisive applause greeted a particularly hard hit. A charming little Hebe stood next, pouring nectar from a silver teapot into a blue china tea-cup. She also pointed a moral; for the Professor explained that the nectar of old was the beverage which cheers but does not inebriate, and regretted that the excessive devotion of American women to this classic brew proved so harmful, owing to the great development of brain their culture produced. A touch at modern servants, in contrast to this accomplished table-girl, made the statue's cheeks glow under the chalk, and brought her a hearty round as the audience recognized Dolly and the smart soubrette.

Jove in all his majesty followed, as he and his wife occupied the central pedestals in the half-circle of immortals. A splendid Jupiter, with hair well set up off the fine brow, ambrosial beard, silver thunderbolts in one hand, and a well-worn ferule in the other. A large stuffed eagle from the museum stood at his feet; and the benign expression of his august countenance showed that he was in a good humour—as well he might be, for he was paid some handsome compliments upon his wise rule, the peaceful state of his kingdom, and the brood of all-accomplished Pallases that yearly issued from his mighty brain. Cheers greeted this and other pleasant words, and caused the thunderer to bow his thanks; for "Jove nods," as everyone knows, and flattery wins the heart of gods and men.

Mrs. Juno, with her peacocks, darning-needle, pen, and cooking-spoon, did not get off so easily; for the Professor was down on her with all manner of mirth-provoking accusations, criticisms, and insults even. He alluded to her domestic infelicity, her meddlesome disposition, sharp tongue, bad temper, and jealousy, closing, however, with a tribute to her skill in caring for the wounds and settling the quarrels of belligerent heroes, as well as her love for youths in Olympus and on earth. Gales of laughter greeted these hits, varied by hisses from some indignant boys, who would not bear, even in joke, any disrespect to dear Mother Bhaer, who, however, enjoyed it all immensely, as the twinkle in her eye and the irrepressible pucker of her lips betrayed.

A jolly Bacchus astride of his cask took Vulcan's place, and appeared to be very comfortable with a beer-mug in one hand, a champagne bottle in the other, and a garland of grapes on his curly head. He was the text of a short temperance lecture, aimed directly at a row of smart young gentlemen who lined the walls of the auditorium. George Cole was seen to dodge behind a pillar at one point, Dolly nudged his neighbour at another, and there was laughter all along the line as the Professor glared at them through his big glasses, and dragged their bacchanalian orgies to the light and held them up to scorn.

Seeing the execution he had done, the learned man turned to the lovely Diana, who stood as white and still as the plaster stag beside her, with sandals, bow, and crescent; quite perfect, and altogether the best piece of statuary in the show. She was very tenderly treated by the paternal critic who, merely alluding to her confirmed spinsterhood, fondness for athletic sports, and oracular powers, gave a graceful little exposition of true art and passed on to the last figure.

This was Apollo in full fig, his curls skilfully arranged to hide a well-whitened patch over the eye, his handsome legs correctly poised, and his gifted fingers about to draw divine music from the silvered gridiron which was his lyre. His divine attributes were described, as well as his little follies and failings, among which were his weakness for photography and flute-playing, his attempts to run a newspaper, and his fondness for the society of the Muses; which latter slap produced giggles and blushes among the girl-graduates, and much mirth among the stricken youths;

for misery loves company, and after this they began to rally.

Then, with a ridiculous conclusion, the Professor bowed his thanks; and after several recalls the curtain fell, but not quickly enough to conceal Mercury, wildly waving his liberated legs, Hebe dropping her teapot, Bacchus taking a lovely roll on his barrel, and Mrs. Juno rapping the impertinent Owlsdark on the head with Jove's ruler.

While the audience filed out to supper in the hall, the stage was a scene of dire confusion as gods and goddesses, farmers and barons, maids and carpenters, congratulated one another on the success of their labours. Assuming various costumes, actors and actresses soon joined their guests, to sip bounteous draughts of praise with their coffee, and cool their modest blushes with ice-cream. Mrs. Meg was a proud and happy woman when Miss Cameron came to her as she sat by Josie, with Demi serving both, and said, so cordially that it was impossible to doubt the sincerity of her welcome words:

"'Mrs. Brooke, I no longer wonder where your children get their talent. I make my compliments to the Baron and next summer you must let me have little 'Dolly' as a pupil when we are at the beach."

One can easily imagine how this offer was received, as well as the friendly commendation bestowed by the same kind critic on the work of Beaumont and Fletcher, who hastened to explain that this trifle was only an attempt to make nature and art go hand in hand, with little help from fine writing or imposing scenery. Everybody was in the happiest mood, especially "little Dolly," who danced like a will-o'-the-wisp with light-footed Mercury and Apollo as he promenaded with the Marquise on his arm, who seemed to have left her coquetry in the green room with her rouge.

When all was over, Mrs. Juno said to Jove, to whose arm she clung as they trudged home along the snowy paths: "Fritz dear, Christmas is a good time for new resolutions, and I've made one never to be impatient or fretful with my beloved husband again. I know I am, though you won't own it; but Laurie's fun had some truth in it, and I felt hit in a tender spot. Henceforth I am a model wife, else I don't deserve the dearest, best man ever born"; and being in a dramatic mood, Mrs. Juno tenderly embraced her excellent Jove in the moonlight, to the great amusement of sundry lingerers behind them.

So all three plays might be considered successes, and that merry Christmas night a memorable one in the March family; for Demi got an unspoken question answered, Josie's fondest wish was granted, and, thanks to Professor Owlsdark's jest, Mrs. Jo made Professor Bhaer's busy life quite a bed of roses by the keeping of her resolution. A few days later she had her reward for this burst of virtue in Dan's letter, which set her fears at rest and made her very happy, though she was unable to tell him so, because he sent her no address.

Chapter 15

Waiting

"My wife, I have bad news for thee," said Professor Bhaer, coming in one day early in January.

"Please tell it at once. I can't bear to wait, Fritz," cried Mrs. Jo, dropping her work and standing up as if to take the shot bravely.

"But we *must* wait and hope, heart's-dearest. Come and let us bear it together. Emil's ship is lost, and as yet no news of him."

It was well Mr. Bhaer had taken his wife into his strong arms, for she looked ready to drop, but bore up after a moment, and sitting by her good man, heard all that there was to tell. Tidings had been sent to the shipowners at Hamburg by some of the survivors, and telegraphed at once by Franz to his uncle. As one boat-load was safe, there was hope that others might also escape, though the gale had sent two to the bottom. A swift-sailing steamer had brought these scanty news, and happier ones might come at any hour; but kind Franz had not added that the sailors reported the captain's boat as undoubtedly wrecked by the falling mast, since the smoke hid its escape, and the gale soon drove all far asunder. But this sad rumour reached Plumfield in time; and deep was the mourning for the happy-hearted Commodore, never to come singing home again.

Mrs. Jo refused to believe it, stoutly insisting that Emil would outlive any storm and yet turn up safe and gay. It was well she clung to this hopeful view, for poor Mr. Bhaer was much afflicted by the loss of his boy, because his sister's sons had been his so long he scarcely knew a different love for his very own. Now was a chance for Mrs.

193

Juno to keep her word; and she did, speaking cheerily of
Emil, even when hope waxed faint and her heart was
heavy. If anything could comfort the Bhaers for the loss of
one boy, it would have been the affection and sorrow
shown by all the rest. Franz kept the cable busy with his
varying messages, Nat sent loving letters from Leipzig,
and Tom harassed the shipping agents for news. Even
busy Jack wrote them with unusual warmth; Dolly and
George came often, bearing the loveliest flowers and the
daintiest bon-bons to cheer Mrs. Bhaer and sweeten Josie's
grief; while good-hearted Ned travelled all the way from
Chicago to press their hands and say, with a tear in his
eye: "I was so anxious to hear all about the dear old boy, I
couldn't keep away."

"That's right comfortable, and shows me that if I didn't
teach my boys anything else, I did give them the brotherly
love that will make them stand by one another all their
lives," said Mrs. Jo, when he had gone.

Rob answered reams of sympathizing letters, which
showed how many friends they had; and the kindly praises
of the lost man would have made Emil a hero and a saint,
had they all been true. The elders bore it quietly, having
learned submission in life's hard school; but the younger
people rebelled; some hoped against hope and kept up,
others despaired at once, and little Josie, Emil's pet cousin
and playmate, was so broken-hearted nothing could comfort her. Nan dosed in vain, Daisy's cheerful words went
by like the wind, and Bess's devices to amuse her all failed
utterly. To cry in mother's arms and talk about the wreck,
which haunted her even in her sleep, was all she cared to
do; and Mrs. Meg was getting anxious when Miss Cameron sent Josie a kind note bidding her learn bravely her
first lesson in real tragedy, and *be* like the self-sacrificing
heroines she loved to *act*. That did the little girl good, and
she made an effort in which Teddy and Octoo helped her
much; for the boy was deeply impressed by this sudden
eclipse of the firefly whose light and life all missed when
they were gone, and lured her out every day for long
drives behind the black mare, who shook her silvery bells
till they made such merry music Josie could not help
listening to it, and whisked her over the snowy roads at a

pace which set the blood dancing in her veins and sent her home strengthened and comforted by sunshine, fresh air, and congenial society—three aids young sufferers seldom can resist.

As Emil was helping nurse Captain Hardy, safe and well, aboard the ship, all this sorrow would seem wasted; but it was not, for it drew many hearts more closely together by a common grief, taught some patience, some sympathy, some regret for faults that lie heavy on the conscience when the one sinned against is gone, and all of them the solemn lesson to be ready when the summons comes. A hush lay over Plumfield for weeks, and the studious faces on the hill reflected the sadness of those in the valley. Sacred music sounded from Parnassus to comfort all who heard; the brown cottage was beseiged with gifts for the little mourner, and Emil's flag hung at half-mast on the roof where he last sat with Mrs. Jo.

So the weeks went heavily by till suddenly, like a thunderbolt out of a clear sky, came the news, "All safe, letters on the way." Then up went the flag, out rang the college bells, bang went Teddy's long-unused cannon, and a chorus of happy voices cried "Thank God," as people went about, laughing, crying, and embracing one another in a rapture of delight. By and by the longed-for letters came, and all the story of the wreck was told; briefly by Emil, eloquently by Mrs. Hardy, gratefully by the captain, while Mary added a few tender words that went straight to their hearts and seemed the sweetest of all. Never were letters so read, passed round, admired, and cried over as these; for Mrs. Jo carried them in *her* pocket when Mr. Bhaer did not have them in his, and both took a look at them when they said their prayers at night. Now the Professor was heard humming like a big bee again as he went to his classes, and the lines smoothed out of Mother Bhaer's forehead, while she wrote this real story to anxious friends and let her romances wait. Now messages of congratulation flowed in, and beaming faces showed everywhere. Rob amazed his parents by producing a poem which was remarkably good for one of his years, and Demi set it to music that it might be sung when the sailor boy returned. Teddy stood on his head literally, and tore about the

neighbourhood on Octoo, like a second Paul Revere—only
his tidings were good. But best of all, little Josie lifted up
her head as the snowdrops did, and began to bloom again,
growing tall and quiet, with the shadow of past sorrow to
tone down her former vivacity and show that she *had*
learned a lesson in trying to act well her part on the real
stage, where all have to take their share in the great
drama of life.

Now another sort of waiting began; for the travellers
were on their way to Hamburg, and would stay there
awhile before coming home, as Uncle Hermann owned
the *Brenda,* and the captain must report to him. Emil
must remain to Franz's wedding, deferred till now because of the season of mourning, so happily ended. These
plans were doubly welcome and pleasant after the trou-
blous times which went before, and no spring ever seemed
so beautiful as this one; for, as Teddy put it:

> *"Now is the winter of our discontent*
> *Made glorious by these sons of Bhaer!"*

Franz and Emil being regarded in the light of elder brothers by the real "sons of Bhaer."

There was great scrubbing and dusting among the ma-
trons as they set their houses in order not only for Class
Day, but to receive the bride and groom, who were to
come to them for the honeymoon trip. Great plans were
made, gifts prepared, and much joy felt at the prospect of
seeing Franz again; though Emil, who was to accompany
them, would be the greater hero. Little did the dear souls
dream what a surprise was in store for them, as they
innocently laid their plans and wished all the boys could
be there to welcome home their eldest and their Casabianca.

While they wait and work so happily, let us see how our
other absent boys are faring as they too wait and work and
hope for better days. Nat was toiling steadily along the
path he had wisely chosen, though it was by no means
strewn with flowers—quite thorny was it, in fact, and hard
to travel, after the taste of ease and pleasure he had got
when nibbling at forbidden fruit. But his crop of wild oats
was a light one, and he resolutely reaped what he had

sowed, finding some good wheat among the tares. He taught by day; he fiddled night after night in the dingy little theatre, and he studied so diligently that his master was well pleased, and kept him in mind as one to whom preferment was due, if any chance occurred. Gay friends forgot him; but the old ones stood fast, and cheered him up when *Heimweh* and weariness made him sad. As spring came on things mended—expenses grew less, work pleasanter, and life more bearable than when wintry storms beat on his thinly clad back, and frost pinched the toes that patiently trudged in old boots. No debts burdened him; the year of absence was nearly over; and if he chose to stay, Herr Bergmann had hopes for him that would bring independence for a time at least. So he walked under the lindens with a lighter heart, and in the May evenings went about the city with a band of strolling students, making music before houses where he used to sit as guest. No one recognized him in the darkness, though old friends often listened to the band; and once Minna threw him money, which he humbly received as part of his penance, being morbid on the subject of his sins.

His reward came sooner than he expected, and was greater than he deserved, he thought, though his heart leaped with joy when his master one day informed him that he was chosen, with several other of his most promising pupils, to join the musical society which was to take part in the great festival in London the next July. Here was not only honour for the violinist but happiness for the man, as it brought him nearer home, and would open a chance of further promotion and profit in his chosen profession.

"Make thyself useful to Bachmeister there in London. with thy English, and if all goes well with him, he will be glad to take thee to America, whither he goes in the early autumn for winter concerts. Thou hast done well these last months, and I have hopes of thee."

As the great Bergmann seldom praised his pupils, these words filled Nat's soul with pride and joy, and he worked yet more diligently than before to fulfil his master's prophecy. He thought the trip to England happiness enough, but found room for more when, early in June, Franz and Emil paid him a flying visit, bringing all sorts of good news, kind wishes, and comfortable gifts for the lonely fellow, who could have fallen on their necks and cried like a girl at seeing his old mates again. How glad he was to be found in his little room busy at his proper work, not living like an idle gentleman on borrowed money! How proud he was to tell his plans, assure them that he had no debts, and receive their praises for his improvement in music, their respect for his economy and steadfastness in well-doing! How relieved when, having honestly confessed his shortcomings, they only laughed, and owned that they also had known like experiences, and were the wiser for them. He was to go to the wedding late in June, and join his comrades in London. As best man, he could not refuse the new suit Franz insisted on ordering for him; and a cheque from home about that time made him feel like a millionaire—and a happy one; for this was accompanied by such kind letters full of delight in his success, he felt that he had earned it, and waited for his joyful holiday with the impatience of a boy.

Dan meantime was also counting the weeks till August, when he would be free. But neither marriage-bells nor festival music awaited him; no friends would greet him as he left the prison; no hopeful prospect lay before him; no happy home-going was to be his. Yet his success was far greater than Nat's, though only God and one good man saw it. It was a hard-won battle; but he would never have to fight so terrible a one again; for though enemies would still assail from within and from without, he had found the little guide-book that Christian carried in his bosom, and Love, Penitence, and Prayer, the three sweet sisters, had given him the armour which would keep him safe. He had not learned to wear it yet, and chafed against it, though he felt its value, thanks to the faithful friend who had stood by him all that bitter year.

Soon he was to be free again, worn and scarred in the fray, but out among men in the blessed sun and air. When he thought of it Dan felt as if he could not wait, but must burst that narrow cell and fly away, as the caddisworms he used to watch by the brookside shed their stony coffins, to climb the ferns and soar into the sky. Night after night he lulled himself to sleep with planning how, when he had seen Mary Mason according to his promise, he would steer straight for his old friends, the Indians, and in the wilderness hide his disgrace and heal his wounds. Working to save the many would atone for the sin of killing one, he thought; and the old free life would keep him safe from the temptations that beset him in cities.

"By and by, when I'm all right again, and have something to tell that I'm not ashamed of, I'll go home," he said, with a quicker beat of the impetuous heart that longed to be there so intensely, he found it as hard to curb as one of his unbroken horses on the plains. "Not yet. I must get over this first. They'd see and smell and feel the prison taint on me, if I went now, and I couldn't look them in the face and hide the truth. I *can't* lose Ted's love, Mother Bhaer's confidence, and the respect of—of—the girls—for they did respect my strength, anyway; but now they wouldn't touch me." And poor Dan looked with a shudder at the brown fist he clenched involuntarily as he remembered what it had done since a certain little white hand had laid in it confidingly. "I'll make 'em proud of me yet; and no one shall ever know of this awful year. I *can* wipe it out, and I will, so help me God!" And the clenched hand was held up as if to take a solemn oath that this lost year should yet be made good, if resolution and repentance could work the miracle.

Chapter 16

In The Tennis-court

ATHLETIC SPORTS were in high favour at Plumfield; and the river where the old punt used to wabble about with a cargo of small boys, or echo to the shrill screams of little girls trying to get lilies, now was alive with boats of all kinds, from the slender wherry to the trim pleasure-craft, gay with cushions, awnings, and fluttering pennons. Everyone rowed, and the girls as well as the youths had their races, and developed their muscles in the most scientific manner. The large, level meadow near the old willow was now the college playground, and here baseball battles raged with fury, varied by football, leaping, and kindred sports fitted to split the fingers, break the ribs, and strain the backs of the too ambitious participants. The gentler pastimes of the damsels were at a safe distance from this Champ de Mars; croquet mallets clicked under the elms that fringed the field, rackets rose and fell energetically in several tennis-courts, and gates of different heights were handy to practise the graceful bound by which every girl expected to save her life some day when the mad bull, which was always coming but never seemed to arrive, should be bellowing at her heels.

One of these tennis grounds was called "Jo's Court," and here the little lady ruled like a queen; for she was fond of the game, and being bent on developing her small self to the highest degree of perfection, she was to be found at every leisure moment with some victim hard at it. On a certain pleasant Saturday afternoon she had been playing with Bess and beating her; for, though more graceful, the Princess was less active than her cousin, and cultivated her roses by quieter methods.

200

"Oh dear! you are tired, and every blessed boy is at that stupid baseball match. What shall I do?" sighed Josie, pushing back the great red hat she wore, and gazing sadly round her for more worlds to conquer.

"I'll play presently, when I'm a little cooler. But it is dull work for me, as I never win," answered Bess, fanning herself with a large leaf.

Josie was about to sit down beside her on the rustic seat and wait, when her quick eye saw afar off two manly forms arrayed in white flannel; their blue legs seemed bearing them towards the battle going on in the distance; but they never reached the fray; for with a cry of joy, Jo raced away to meet them, bent on securing this heaven-sent reinforcement. Both paused as she came flying up, and both raised their hats; but oh, the difference there was in the salutes! The stout youth pulled his off lazily and put it on again at once, as if glad to get the duty over; the slender being, with the crimson tie, lifted his with a graceful bend, and held it aloft while he accosted the rosy, breathless maid, thus permitting her to see his raven locks smoothly parted, with one little curl upon the brow. Dolly prided himself upon that bow, and practised it before his glass, but did not bestow it upon all alike, regarding it as a work of art, fit only for the fairest and most favoured of his female admirers; for he was a pretty youth, and fancied himself an Adonis.

Eager Josie evidently did not appreciate the honour he did her, for with a nod she begged them both to "come along and play tennis, not go and get all hot and dirty with the boys." These two adjectives won the day; for Stuffy was already warmer than he liked to be, and Dolly had on a new suit which he desired to keep immaculate as long as possible, conscious that it was very becoming.

"Charmed to oblige," answered the polite one, with another bend.

"You play, I'll rest," added the fat boy, yearning for repose and gentle converse with the Princess in the cooling shade.

"Well, you can comfort Bess, for I've beaten her all to bits and she needs amusing. I know you've got something nice in your pocket, George; give her some, and 'Dolphus can have her racket. Now then, fly round"; and driving her prey before her, Josie returned in triumph to the court.

Casting himself ponderously upon the bench, which creaked under his weight, Stuffy—as we will continue to call him, though no one else dared to use the old name now—promptly produced the box of confectionery, without which he never travelled far, and regaled Bess with candied violets and other dainties, while Dolly worked hard to hold his own against a most accomplished antagonist. He would have beaten her if an unlucky stumble, which produced an unsightly stain upon the knee of those new shorts, had not distracted his mind and made him careless. Much elated at her victory, Josie permitted him to rest, and offered ironical consolation for the mishap which evidently weighed upon his mind.

"Don't be an old Betty; it can be cleaned. You must have been a cat in some former state, you are so troubled about dirt; or a tailor, and lived for clothes."

"Come now, don't hit a fellow when he is down," responded Dolly from the grass where he and Stuffy now lay to make room for both girls on the seat. One handkerchief was spread under him, and his elbow leaned upon another, while his eyes were sadly fixed upon the green and brown spot which afflicted him. "I like to be neat; don't think it civil to cut about in old shoes and grey flannel shirts before ladies. *Our* fellows are gentlemen, and dress as such," he added, rather nettled at the word "tailor"; for he owed one of those too attractive persons an uncomfortably big bill.

"So are ours; but good clothes alone don't make a gentleman *here*. We require a good deal more," flashed Josie, in arms at once to defend her college. "You will hear of some of the men in 'old boots and grey flannel' when you and your fine gentlemen are twiddling your ties and scenting your hair in obscurity. I *like* old boots and wear them, and I hate dandies; don't you, Bess?"

"Not when they are kind to me, and belong to our old set," answered Bess, with a nod of thanks to Dolly, who was carefully removing an inquisitive caterpillar from one of her little russet shoes.

"*I* like a lady who is always polite, and doesn't snap a man's head off if he has a mind of his own; don't you, George?" asked Dolly, with his best smile for Bess and a Harvard stare of disapprobation for Josie.

A tranquil snore was Stuffy's sole reply, and a general laugh restored peace for the moment. But Josie loved to harass the lords of creation who asserted themselves too much, and bided her time for another attack till she had secured more tennis. She got another game; for Dolly was a sworn knight of dames, so he obeyed her call, leaving Bess to sketch George as he lay upon his back, his stout legs crossed, and his round red face partially eclipsed by his hat. Josie got beaten this time and came back rather cross, so she woke the peaceful sleeper by tickling his nose with a straw till he sneezed himself into a sitting posture, and looked wrathfully about for "that confounded fly."

"Come, sit up and let us have a little elegant conversation; you 'howling swells' ought to improve our minds and manners, 'for we are only poor country girls in dowdy gowns and hats,'" began the gad-fly, opening the battle with a sly quotation from one of Dolly's unfortunate speeches about certain studious damsels who cared more for books than finery.

"I didn't mean you! Your gowns are all right, and those hats the latest thing out," began poor 'Dolphus, convicting himself by the incautious exclamation.

"Caught you that time; I thought you fellows were all *gentlemen*, civil as well as nice. But you are always sneering at girls who don't dress well and that is a very unmanly thing to do; my mother said so"; and Josie felt that she had dealt a shrewd blow at the elegant youth who bowed at many shrines if they were well-decorated ones.

"Got you there, old boy, and she's right. You never hear *me* talk about clothes and such twaddle," said Stuffy, suppressing a yawn, and feeling for another bon-bon wherewith to refresh himself.

"You talk about eating, and that is even worse for a man. You will marry a cook and keep a restaurant some day," laughed Josie, down on him at once.

This fearful prediction kept him silent for several moments; but Dolly rallied, and wisely changing the subject, carried war into the enemy's camp.

"As you wanted us to improve your manners, allow me to say that young ladies in good society don't make personal remarks or deliver lectures. Little girls who are not out do it, and think it witty; but I assure you it's not good form."

Josie paused a moment to recover from the shock of being called "a little girl," when all the honours of her fourteenth birthday were fresh upon her; and Bess said, in the lofty tone which was infinitely more crushing than Jo's impertinence:

"That is true; but we have lived all our lives with superior people, so we have no society talk like your young ladies. We are so accustomed to sensible conversation, and helping one another by telling our faults, that we have no gossip to offer you."

When the Princess reproved, the boys seldom resented it; so Dolly held his peace, and Josie burst out, following her cousin's lead, which she thought a happy one:

"*Our* boys like to have us talk with them, and take kindly any hints we give. *They* don't think they know everything and are quite perfect at eighteen, as I've observed the Harvard men do, especially the *very young* ones."

Josie took immense satisfaction in that return shot; and Dolly showed that he was hit, by the nettled tone in which he answered, with a supercilious glance at the hot, dusty, and noisy crowd on the baseball ground:

"The class of fellows you have here need all the polish and culture you can give them; and I'm glad they get it. Our men are largely from the best families all over the country, so we don't need girls to teach us anything."

"It's a pity you don't have more of such 'fellows' as ours. They value and use well what college gives them, and aren't satisfied to slip through, getting all the fun they can and shirking the work. Oh, I've heard you 'men' talk, and heard your fathers say they wish they hadn't wasted time and money just that you might say you'd been through college. As for the girls, you'll be much better off

in all ways when they do get in, and keep you lazy things
up to the mark, as we do here."

"If you have such a poor opinion of us, why do you wear
our colour?" asked Dolly, painfully conscious that he was
not improving the advantages his Alma Mater offered him,
but bound to defend her.

"I don't; my hat is scarlet, not crimson. Much you know
about a colour," scoffed Josie.

"I know that a cross cow would soon set you scamper-
ing, if you flaunted that red tile under her nose," retorted
Dolly.

"I'm ready for her. Can your fine young ladies do this?
or you either?" and burning to display her latest accomplishment, Josie ran to the nearest gate, put one hand on
the top rail, and vaulted over as lightly as a bird.

Bess shook her head, and Stuffy languidly applauded;
but Dolly scorning to be braved by a girl, took a flying
leap and landed on his feet beside Josie, saying calmly:
"Can you do that?"

"Not yet; but I will by and by."

As his foe looked a little crestfallen, Dolly relented, and
affably added sundry feats of a like nature, quite unconscious that he had fallen into a dreadful snare; for the dull
red paint on the gate, not being used to such vigorous
handling, came off in streaks upon his shoulders when he
turned a backward swing and came up smiling, to be
rewarded with the aggravating remark:

"If you want to know what crimson is, look at your back;
it's nicely stamped on and won't wash out, I think."

"The deuce it won't!" cried Dolly, trying to get an
impossible view, and giving it up in great disgust.

"I guess we'd better be going, Dolf," said peaceable
Stuffy, feeling that it would be wise to retreat before
another skirmish took place, as his side seemed to be
getting the worst of it.

"Don't hurry, I beg; stay and rest; you must need it
after the tremendous amount of brain work you've done
this week. It is time for our Greek. Come, Bess. Good
afternoon, *gentlemen*." And, with a sweeping courtesy,
Josie led the way, with her hat belligerently cocked up,
and her racket borne like a triumphal banner over one

shoulder; for having had the last word, she felt that she could retire with the honours of war.

Dolly gave Bess his best bow, with the chill on; and Stuffy subsided luxuriously, with his legs in the air, murmuring in a dreamy tone:

"Little Jo is as cross as two sticks today. I'm going in for another nap: too hot to play anything."

"So it is. Wonder if Spitfire was right about these beastly spots?" And Dolly sat down to try dry cleansing with one of his handkerchiefs. "Asleep?" he asked, after a few moments of this cheerful occupation, fearing that his chum might be too comfortable when he was in a fume himself.

"No. I was thinking that Jo wasn't far wrong about shirking. 'Tis a shame to get so little done, when we ought to be grinding like Morton and Torry and that lot. I never wanted to go to college; but my governor made me. Much good it will do either of us!" answered Stuffy, with a groan; for he hated work, and saw two more long years of it before him.

"Gives a man prestige, you know. No need to dig. I mean to have a gay old time, and be a 'howling swell,' if I choose. Between you and me though, it *would* be no end jolly to have the girls along. Study be hanged! But if we've got to turn the grindstone, it would be mighty nice to have some of the little dears to lend a hand. Wouldn't it now?"

"I'd like three this minute—one to fan me, one to kiss me, and one to give me some iced lemonade!" sighed Stuffy, with a yearning glance towards the house, whence no succour appeared.

"How would root-beer do?" asked a voice behind them, which made Dolly spring to his feet and Stuffy roll over like a startled porpoise.

Sitting on the stile that crossed the wall near by was Mrs. Jo, with two jugs slung over her shoulder by a strap, several tin mugs in her hand, and an old-fashioned sunbonnet on her head.

"I knew the boys would be killing themselves with ice-water; so I strolled down with some of my good, wholesome beer. They drank like fishes. But Silas was with me; so my cruse still holds out. Have some?"

"Yes, thanks, very much. Let us pour it." And Dolly held the cup while Stuffy joyfully filled it; both very grateful, but rather afraid she had heard what went before the wish she fulfilled.

She proved that she had by saying, as they stood drinking her health, while she sat between them, looking like a middle-aged *vivandière*, with her jugs and mugs:

"I was glad to hear you say you would like to have girls at your college; but I hope you will learn to speak more respectfully of them before they come; for that will be the first lesson they will teach you."

"Really, ma'am, I was only joking," began Stuffy, gulping down his beer in a hurry.

"So was I. I'm sure I—I'm devoted to 'em," stuttered Dolly, panic-stricken; for he saw that he was in for a lecture of some sort.

"Not in the right way. Frivolous girls may like to be called 'little dears' and things of that sort; but the girls who love study wish to be treated like reasonable beings, not dolls to flirt with. Yes, I'm going to preach; that's my business; so stand up and take it like men."

Mrs. Jo laughed; but she was in earnest; for by various hints and signs during the past winter she knew that the boys were beginning to "see life" in the way she especially disapproved. Both were far from home, had money enough to waste, and were as inexperienced, curious, and credulous as most lads of their age. Not fond of books, therefore without the safeguard which keeps many studious fellows out of harm; one self-indulgent, indolent, and so used to luxury that pampering of the senses was an easy thing; the other vain, as all comely boys are, full of conceit, and so eager to find favour in the eyes of his comrades that he was ready for anything which would secure it. These traits and foibles made both peculiarly liable to the temptations which assail pleasure-loving and weak-willed boys. Mrs. Jo knew them well, and had dropped many a warning word since they went to college; but till lately they seemed not to understand some of her friendly hints; now she was sure they would, and meant to speak out: for long experience with boys made her both bold and skilful in handling

some of the dangers usually left to silence, till it is too late
for anything but pity and reproach.

"I'm going to talk to you like a mother, because yours
are far away; and there are things that mothers can manage best, if they do their duty," she solemnly began from
the depths of the sunbonnet.

"Great Scott! We're in for it now!" thought Dolly, in
secret dismay; while Stuffy got the first blow by trying to
sustain himself with another mug of beer.

"That won't hurt you; but I must warn you about drinking other things, George. Overeating is an old story; and a
few more fits of illness will teach you to be wise. But
drinking is a more serious thing, and leads to worse harm
than any that can afflict your body alone. I hear you talk
about wines as if you knew them and cared more for them
than a boy should; and several times I've heard jokes that
meant mischief. For heaven's sake, don't begin to play
with this dangerous taste 'for fun,' as you say, or because it's the fashion, and the other fellows do. Stop at
once, and learn that temperance in all things is the only
safe rule."

"Upon my honour, I only take wine and iron. I need a
tonic, mother says, to repair the waste of brain-tissue
while I'm studying," protested Stuffy, putting down the
mug as if it burnt his fingers.

"Good beef and oatmeal will repair your tissues much
better than any tonic of that sort. Work and plain fare are
what you want; and I wish I had you here for a few months
out of harm's way. I'd Banting you, and fit you to run
without puffing, and get on without four or five meals a
day. What an absurd hand that is for a man! You ought to
be ashamed of it!" And Mrs. Jo caught up the plump fist,
with deep dimples at each knuckle, which was fumbling
distressfully at the buckle of the belt girt about a waist far
too large for a youth of his age.

"I can't help it—we all grow fat; it's in the family," said
Stuffy in self-defence.

"All the more reason you should live carefully. Do you
want to die early, or be an invalid all your life?"

"No, ma'am!"

Stuffy looked so scared that Mrs. Jo could not be hard

upon his budding sins, for they lay at his over-indulgent
mother's door line in a great measure; so she softened the
tone of her voice, and added, with a little slap on the fat
hand, as she used to do when it was small enough to pilfer
lumps of sugar from her bowl:

"Then be careful; for a man writes his character in his
face; and you don't want gluttony and intemperance in
yours, I know."

"I'm sure I don't! Please make out a wholesome bill of
fare, and I'll stick to it, if I can. I *am* getting stout, and I
don't like it; and my liver's torpid, and I have palpitations
and headache. Overwork, mother says; but it may be
overeating." And Stuffy gave a sigh of mingled regret for
the good things he renounced, and relief as he finished
loosening his belt as soon as his hand was free.

"I will; follow it, and in a year you'll be a man and not a
meal-bag. Now, Dolly"; and Mrs. Jo turned to the other
culprit, who shook in his shoes and wished he hadn't
come.

"Are you studying French as industriously as you were
last winter?"

"No ma'am; I don't care for it—that is, I—I'm busy with
G-Greek just now," answered Dolly, beginning bravely,
quite in the dark as to what that odd question meant till a
sudden memory made him stutter and look at his shoes
with deep interest.

"Oh, he doesn't study it; only reads French novels and
goes to the theatre when the opera bouffe is here," said
Stuffy, innocently confirming Mrs. Jo's suspicions.

"So I understood; and that is what I want to speak
about. Ted had a sudden desire to learn French in that
way, from something you said, Dolly; so I went myself,
and was quite satisfied that it was no place for a decent
boy. Your men were out in full force, and I was glad to see
that some of the younger ones looked as ashamed as I felt.
The older fellows enjoyed it, and when we came out were
waiting to take those painted girls to supper. Did you ever
go with them?"

"Once."

"Did you like it?"

"No'm; I—I came away early," stammered Dolly, with a face as red as his splendid tie.

"I'm glad you have not lost the grace of blushing yet; but you will soon, if you keep up this sort of study and forget to be ashamed. The society of such women will unfit you for that of good ones, and lead you into trouble and sin and shame. Oh, why don't the city fathers stop that evil thing, when they know the harm it does? It made my heart ache to see those boys, who ought to be at home and in their beds, going off for a night of riot which would help to ruin some of them for ever."

The youths looked scared at Mrs. Jo's energetic protest against one of the fashionable pleasures of the day, and waited in conscience-stricken silence—Stuffy glad that he never went to those gay suppers, and Dolly deeply grateful that he "came away early." With a hand on either shoulder, and all the terrors smoothed from her brow, Mrs. Jo went on in her most motherly tone, anxious to do for them what no other woman would, and do it kindly:

"My dear boys, if I didn't love you, I would not say these things. I know they are not pleasant; but my conscience won't let me hold my peace when a word may keep you from two of the great sins that curse the world and send so many young men to destruction. You are just beginning to feel the allurement of them, and soon it will be hard to turn away. Stop now, I beg of you, and not only save yourselves but help others by a brave example. Come to me if things worry you; don't be afraid or ashamed; I have heard many sadder confessions than any you are ever likely to bring me, and been able to comfort many poor fellows, gone wrong for want of a word in time. Do this, and you will be able to kiss your mothers with clean lips, and by and by have the right to ask innocent girls to love you."

"Yes'm, thank you. I suppose you're right; but it's pretty hard work to toe the mark when ladies give you wine and gentlemen take their daughters to see Aimée," said Dolly, foreseeing tribulations ahead though he knew it was time to "pull up."

"So it is; but all the more honour to those who are brave and wise enough to resist public opinion, and the easy-

going morals of bad or careless men and women. Think of
the persons whom you respect most, and in imitating
them you will secure the respect of those who look up to
you. I'd rather my boys should be laughed at and cold-
shouldered by a hundred foolish fellows than lose what,
once gone, no power can give them back—innocence and
self-respect. I don't wonder you find it 'hard to toe the
mark,' when books, pictures, ball-rooms, theatres, and
streets offer temptations; yet you *can* resist, if you try.
Last winter Mrs. Brooke used to worry about John's being
out so late reporting; but when she spoke to him about
the things he must see and hear on his way to and fro from
the office at midnight, he said in his sober way, 'I know
what you mean, mother; but no fellow need to go wrong
unless he *wants* to.'"

"That's like the Deacon!" exclaimed Stuffy, with an
approving smile on his fat face.

"I'm glad you told me that. He's right; and it's because
he doesn't want to go wrong we all respect him so," added
Dolly, looking up now with an expression which assured
his Mentor that the right string had been touched, and a
spirit of emulation roused, more helpful, perhaps, than
any words of hers. Seeing this, she was satisfied, and said,
as she prepared to leave the bar before which her culprits
had been tried and found guilty, but recommended to
mercy:

"Then be to others what John is to you—a good example. Forgive me for troubling you, my dear lads, and
remember my little preachment. I think it will do you
good, though I may never know it. Chance words spoken
in kindness often help amazingly; and that's what old
people are here for—else their experience is of little use.
Now, come and find the young folk. I hope I shall never
have to shut the gates of Plumfield upon *you*, as I have on
some of your 'gentlemen.' I mean to keep my boys and
girls safe if I can, and this a wholesome place where the
good old-fashioned virtues are lived and taught."

Much impressed by that dire threat, Dolly helped her
from her perch with deep respect; and Stuffy relieved her
of her empty jugs, solemnly vowing to abstain from all
fermented beverages except root-beer, as long as feeble

flesh could hold out. Of course they made light of "Mother Bhaer's lecture" when they were alone—that was to be expected of "men of our class" but in their secret souls they thanked her for giving their boyish consciences a jog, and more than once afterward had cause to remember gratefully that half-hour in the tennis-court.

Chapter 17

Among the Maids

ALTHOUGH THIS STORY is about Jo's boys, her girls cannot be neglected, because they held a high place in this little republic, and especial care was taken to fit them to play their parts worthily in the great republic which offered them wider opportunities and more serious duties. To many the social influence was the better part of the training they received; for education is not confined to books, and the finest characters often graduate from no college, but make experience their master, and life their book. Others cared only for the mental culture, and were in danger of over-studying, under the delusion which pervades New England that learning must be had at all costs, forgetting that health and real wisdom are better. A third class of ambitious girls hardly knew what they wanted, but were hungry for whatever could fit them to face the world and earn a living, being driven by necessity, the urgency of some half-conscious talent, or the restlessness of strong young natures to break away from the narrow life which no longer satisfied.

At Plumfield all found something to help them; for the growing institution had not yet made its rules as fixed as the laws of the Medes and Persians, and believed so heartily in the right of all sexes, colours, creeds, and ranks to education, that there was room for everyone who knocked, and a welcome to the shabby youths from up country, the eager girls from the West, the awkward freedman or woman from the South, or the well-born student whose poverty made this college a possibility when other doors were barred. There still was prejudice, ridicule, neglect in high places, and prophecies of failure to contend against; but the Faculty was composed of cheerful, hopeful men and women who had seen greater reforms spring from smaller roots, and after stormy seasons blossom beautifully, to add prosperity and honour to the nation. So they worked on steadily and bided their time, full of increasing faith in their attempt as year after year their numbers grew, their plans succeeded, and the sense of usefulness in this most vital of all professions blessed them with its sweet rewards.

Among the various customs which had very naturally sprung up was one especially useful and interesting to "the girls," as the young women liked to be called. It all grew out of the old sewing hour still kept up by the three sisters long after the little work-boxes had expanded into big baskets full of household mending. They were busy women, yet on Saturdays they tried to meet in one of the three sewing-rooms; for even classic Parnassus had its nook where Mrs. Amy often sat among her servants, teaching them to make and mend, thereby giving them a respect for economy, since the rich lady did not scorn to darn her hose, and sew on buttons. In these household retreats, with books and work, and their daughters by them, they read and sewed and talked in the sweet privacy that domestic women love, and can make so helpful by a wise mixture of cooks and chemistry, table linen and theology, prosaic duties and good poetry.

Mrs. Meg was the first to propose enlarging this little circle; for as she went her motherly rounds among the young women she found a sad lack of order, skill, and industry in this branch of education. Latin, Greek, the higher mathematics, and science of all sorts prospered finely; but the dust gathered on the work-baskets, frayed elbows went unheeded, and some of the blue stockings sadly needed mending. Anxious lest the usual sneer at learned women should apply to "our girls," she gently lured two or three of the most untidy to her house, and made the hour so pleasant, the lesson so kindly, that they took the hint, were grateful for the favour, and asked to come again. Others soon begged to make the detested weekly duty lighter by joining the party, and soon it was a privilege so much desired that the old museum was refitted with sewing-machines, tables, rocking-chair, and a cheerful fireplace, so that, rain or shine, the needles might go on undisturbed.

Here Mrs. Meg was in her glory, and stood wielding her big shears like a queen as she cut out white work, fitted dresses, and directed Daisy, her special *aide*, about the trimming of hats, and completing the lace and ribbon trifles which add grace to the simplest costume and save poor or busy girls so much money and time. Mrs. Amy contributed taste, and decided the great question of colours and complexions; for few women, even the most learned, are without that desire to look well which makes many a plain face comely, as well as many a pretty one ugly for want of skill and knowledge of the fitness of things. She also took her turn to provide books for the readings, and as art was her forte she gave them selections from Ruskin, Hamerton, and Mrs. Jameson, who is never old. Bess read these aloud as her contribution, and Josie took her turn at the romances, poetry, and plays her uncles recommended. Mrs. Jo gave little lectures on health, religion, politics, and the various questions in which all should be interested, with copious extracts from Miss Cobbe's *Duties of Women*, Miss Brackett's *Education of American Girls*, Mrs. Duffy's *No Sex in Education*, Mrs. Woolson's *Dress Reform*, and many of the other excellent books wise women write for their sisters, now that they are waking up and asking: "What shall we do?"

It was curious to see the prejudices melt away as ignorance was enlightened, indifference change to interest, and intelligent minds set thinking, while quick wits and lively tongues added spice to the discussions which inevitably followed. So the feet that wore the neatly mended hose carried wiser heads than before, the pretty gowns covered hearts warmed with higher purposes, and the hands that dropped the thimbles for pens, lexicons, and celestial globes, were better fitted for life's work, whether to rock cradles, tend the sick, or help on the great work of the world.

One day a brisk discussion arose concerning careers for women. Mrs. Jo had read something on the subject and asked each of the dozen girls sitting about the room, what she intended to do on leaving college. The answers were as usual: "I shall teach, help mother, study medicine, art," etc.; but nearly all ended with: "Till I marry."

"But if you don't marry, what then?" asked Mrs. Jo, feeling like a girl again as she listened to the answers, and watched the thoughtful, gay, or eager faces.

"Be old maids, I suppose. Horrid, but inevitable, since there are so many superfluous women," answered a lively lass, too pretty to fear single blessedness unless she chose it.

"It is well to consider that fact, and fit yourselves to be useful, not superfluous women. That class, by the way, is largely made up of widows, I find; so don't consider it a slur on maidenhood."

"That's a comfort! Old maids aren't sneered at half as much as they used to be, since some of them have grown famous and proved that woman isn't a half but a whole human being, and can stand alone."

"Don't like it all the same. We can't all be like Miss Cobbe, Miss Nightingale, Miss Phelps, and the rest. So what can we do but sit in a corner and look on?" asked a plain girl with a dissatisfied expression.

"Cultivate cheerfulness and content, if nothing else. But there are so many little odd jobs waiting to be done that nobody need 'sit idle and look on,' unless she chooses," said Mrs. Meg, with a smile, laying on the girl's head the new hat she had just trimmed.

"Thank you very much. Yes, Mrs. Brooke, I see; it's a little job, but it makes me neat and happy—and grateful," she added, looking up with brighter eyes as she accepted the labour of love and the lesson as sweetly as they were given.

"One of the best and most beloved women I know has been doing odd jobs for the Lord for years, and will keep at it till her dear hands are folded in her coffin. All sorts of things she does—picks up neglected children and puts them in safe homes, saves lost girls, nurses poor women in trouble, sews, knits, trots, begs, works for the poor day after day with no reward but the thanks of the needy, the love and honour of the rich who make Saint Matilda their almoner. That's a life worth living; and I think that quiet little woman will get a higher seat in Heaven than many of those of whom the world has heard."

"I know it's lovely, Mrs. Bhaer; but it's dull for young folks. We do want a little fun before we buckle to," said a Western girl with a wide-awake face.

"Have your fun, my dear; but if you must earn your bread, try to make it sweet with cheerfulness, not bitter with the daily regret that it isn't cake. I used to think mine was a very hard fate because I had to amuse a somewhat fretful old lady; but the books I read in that lonely library have been of immense use to me since, and the dear old soul bequeathed me Plumfield for my 'cheerful service and affectionate care.' I didn't deserve it, but I did use to try to be jolly and kind, and get as much honey out of duty as I could, thanks to my dear mother's help and advice."

"Gracious! if I could earn a place like this, I'd sing all day and be an angel; but you have to take your chance, and get nothing for your pains, perhaps. I never do," said the Westerner, who had a hard time with small means and large aspirations.

"Don't do it for the reward; but be sure it will come, though not in the shape you expect. I worked hard for fame and money one winter; but I got neither, and was much disappointed. A year afterwards I found I had earned two prizes: skill with my pen, and—Professor Bhaer."

Mrs. Jo's laugh was echoed blithely by the girls, who liked to have these conversations enlivened by illustrations from life.

"You are a very lucky woman," began the discontented damsel, whose soul soared above new hats, welcome as they were, but did not quite know where to steer.

"Yet her name used to be 'Luckless Jo,' and she never had what she wanted till she had given up hoping for it," said Mrs. Meg.

"I'll give up hoping, then, right away, and see if my wishes will come. I only want to help my folks, and get a good school."

"Take this proverb for your guide: 'Get the distaff ready, and the Lord will send the flax,'" answered Mrs. Jo.

"We'd better all do that, if we are to be spinsters," said

the pretty one, adding gaily, "I think I should like it, on the whole—they are so independent. My Aunt Jenny can do just what she likes, and ask no one's leave; but Ma has to consult Pa about everything. Yes, I'll give you my chance, Sally, and be a 'superfluum,' as Mr. Plock says."

"You'll be one of the first to go into bondage, see if you aren't. Much obliged, all the same."

"Well, I'll get my distaff ready, and take whatever flax the Fates send—single, or double-twisted, as the powers please."

"That is the right spirit, Nelly. Keep it up, and see how happy life will be with a brave heart, a willing hand, and plenty to do."

"No one objects to plenty of domestic work or fashionable pleasure, I find; but the minute we begin to study, people tell us we can't bear it, and warn us to be very careful. I've tried the other things, and got so tired I came to college; though my people predict nervous exhaustion and an early death. Do you think there is any danger?" asked a stately girl, with an anxious glance at the blooming face reflected in the mirror opposite.

"Are you stronger or weaker than when you came two years ago, Miss Winthrop?"

"Stronger in body, and much happier in mind. I think I was dying of ennui; but the doctors called it inherited delicacy of constitution. That is why mamma is so anxious, and I wish not to go too fast."

"Don't worry, my dear; that active brain of yours was starving for good food; it has plenty now, and plain living suits you better than luxury and dissipation. It is all nonsense about girls not being able to study as well as boys. Neither can bear cramming; but with proper care both are better for it; so enjoy the life your instinct led you to, and we will prove that wise headwork is a better cure for that sort of delicacy than tonics, and novels on the sofa, where far too many of our girls go to wreck nowadays. They burn the candle at both ends; and when they break down they blame the books, not the balls."

"Dr. Nan was telling me about a patient of hers who thought she had heart-complaint, till Nan made her take off her corsets, stopped her coffee and dancing all night, and made her eat, sleep, walk, and live regularly for a time; and now she's a brilliant cure. Common sense versus custom, Nan said."

"I've had no headaches since I came here, and can do twice as much studying as I did at home. It's the air, I think, and the fun of going ahead of the boys," said another girl, tapping her big forehead with her thimble, as if the lively brain inside was in good working order and enjoyed the daily gymnastics she gave it.

"Quality, not quantity, wins the day, you know. Our brains may be smaller, but I don't see that they fall short of what is required of them; and if I'm not mistaken, the largest-headed man in our class is the dullest," said Nelly, with a solemn air which produced a gale of merriment; for all knew that the young Goliath she mentioned had been metaphorically slain by this quick-witted David on many a battle-field, to the great disgust of himself and his mates.

"Mrs. Brooke, do I gauge on the right or the wrong side?" asked the best Greek scholar of her class, eyeing a black silk apron with a lost expression.

"The right, Miss Pierson; and leave a space between the tucks; it looks prettier so."

"I'll never make another; but it will save my dresses from ink-stains, so I'm glad I've got it"; and the erudite Miss Pierson laboured on, finding it a harder task than any Greek root she ever dug up.

"We paper-stainers must learn how to make shields, or we are lost. I'll give you a pattern of the pinafore I used to wear in my 'blood-and-thunder days,' as we call them," said Mrs. Jo, trying to remember what became of the old tin-kitchen which used to hold her works.

"Speaking of writers reminds me that my ambition is to be a George Eliot, and thrill the world! It must be so splendid to know that one has such power, and to hear people own that one possesses a 'masculine intellect!' I don't care for most women's novels, but hers are immense; don't you think so, Mrs. Bhaer?" asked the girl with the big forehead, and torn braid on her skirt.

"Yes; but they don't thrill me as little Charlotte Brontë's books do. The brain is there, but the heart seems left out.

I admire, but I don't love, George Eliot; and her life is far sadder to me than Miss Brontë's, because, in spite of the genius, love, and fame, she missed the light without which no soul is truly great, good, or happy."

"Yes'm, I know; but still it's so romantic and sort of new and mysterious, and she *was* great in one sense. Her nerves and dyspepsia do rather destroy the illusion; but I adore famous people and mean to go and see all I can scare up in London some day."

"You will find some of the best of them busy about just the work I recommend to you; and if you want to see a great lady, I'll tell you that Mrs. Laurence means to bring one here today. Lady Abercrombie is lunching with her, and after seeing the college is to call on us. She especially wanted to see our sewing-school, as she is interested in things of this sort, and gets them up at home."

"Bless me! I always imagined lords and ladies did nothing but ride round in a coach and six, go to balls, and be presented to the Queen in cocked hats, and trains and feathers," exclaimed an artless young person from the wilds of Maine, whither an illustrated paper occasionally wandered.

"Not at all; Lord Abercrombie is over here studying up our American prison system, and my lady is busy with the schools—both very high-born, but the simplest and most sensible people I've met this long time. They are neither of them young nor handsome, and dress plainly; so don't expect anything splendid. Mr. Laurence was telling me last night about a friend of his who met my lord in the hall, and owing to a rough greatcoat and a red face, mistook him for a coachman, and said: 'Now, my man, what do you want here?' Lord Abercrombie mildly mentioned who he was, and that he had come to dinner. And the poor host was much afflicted, saying afterward: 'Why didn't he wear his stars and garters? then a fellow would know he was a lord.' "

The girls laughed again, and a general rustle betrayed that each was prinking a bit before the titled guest arrived. Even Mrs. Jo settled her collar, and Mrs. Meg felt if her cap was right, while Bess shook out her curls and

Josie boldly consulted the glass; for they were women, in spite of philosophy and philanthropy.

"Shall we all rise?" asked one girl, deeply impressed by the impending honour.

"It would be courteous."

"Shall we shake hands?"

"No, I'll present you *en masse*, and your pleasant faces will be introduction enough."

"I wish I'd worn my best dress. Ought to have told us," whispered Sally.

"Won't my folks be surprised when I tell them we have had a real lady to call on us?" said another.

"Don't look as if you'd never seen a gentlewoman before, Milly. We are not all fresh from the wilderness," added the stately damsel who, having *Mayflower* ancestors, felt that she was the equal of all the crowned heads of Europe.

"Hush, she's coming! Oh, my heart, what a bonnet!" cried the gay girl in a stage whisper; and every eye was demurely fixed upon the busy hands as the door opened to admit Mrs. Laurence and her guest.

It *was* rather a shock to find, after the general introduction was over, that this daughter of a hundred earls was a stout lady in a plain gown, and a rather weather-beaten bonnet, with a bag of papers in one hand and a note-book in the other. But the face was full of benevolence, the sonorous voice very kind, the genial manners very winning, and about the whole person an indescribable air of high breeding which made beauty of no consequence, costume soon forgotten, and the moment memorable to the keen-eyed girls whom nothing escaped.

A little chat about the rise, growth, and success of this particular class, and then Mrs. Jo led the conversation to the English lady's work, anxious to show her pupils how rank dignifies labour, and charity blesses wealth.

It was good for these girls to hear of the evening-schools supported and taught by women whom they knew and honoured; of Miss Cobbe's eloquent protest winning the protection of the law for abused wives; Mrs. Butler saving the lost; Mrs. Taylor, who devoted one room in her historic house to a library for the servants; Lord Shaftesbury, busy with his new tenement-houses in the slums of London; of prison reforms; and all the brave work being done in God's name by the rich and great for the humble and the poor. It impressed them more than many quiet home lectures would have done, and roused an ambition to help when their time should come, well knowing that even in glorious America there is still plenty to be done before she is what she should be—truly just, and free, and great. They were also quick to see that Lady Abercrombie treated all there as her equals, from stately Mrs. Laurence, to little Josie, taking notes of everything and privately resolving to have some thick-soled English boots as soon as possible. No one would have guessed that she had a big house in London, a castle in Wales, and a grand country seat in Scotland, as she spoke of Parnassus with admiration, Plumfield as a "dear old home," and the college as an honour to all concerned in it. At that, of course, every head went up a little, and when my lady left, every hand was ready for the hearty shake the noble Englishwoman gave them, with words they long remembered:

"I am very pleased to see this much-neglected branch of a woman's education so well conducted here, and I have to thank my friend Mrs. Laurence for one of the most charming pictures I've seen in America—Penelope among her maids."

A group of smiling faces watched the stout boots trudge away, respectful glances followed the shabby bonnet till it was out of sight, and the girls felt a truer respect for their titled guest than if she had come in the coach and six, with all her diamonds on.

"I feel better about the 'odd jobs' now. I only wish I could do them as well as Lady Abercrombie does," said one.

"I thanked my stars my buttonholes were nice, for she looked at them and said: 'Quite workmanlike, upon my word,'" added another, feeling that her gingham gown had come to honour.

"Her manners were as sweet and kind as Mrs. Brooke's. Not a bit stiff or condescending, as I expected. I see now what you meant, Mrs. Bhaer, when you said once that well-bred people were the same all the world over."

Mrs. Meg bowed her thanks for the compliment, and Mrs. Bhaer said:

"I know them when I see them, but never shall be a model of deportment myself. I'm glad you enjoyed the little visit. Now, if you young people don't want England to get ahead of us in many ways, you must bestir yourselves and keep abreast; for our sisters are in earnest, you see, and don't waste time worrying about their sphere, but make it wherever duty calls them."

"We will do our best, ma'am," answered the girls heartily, and trooped away with their work-baskets, feeling that though they might never be Harriet Martineaus, Elizabeth Brownings, or George Eliots, they might become noble, useful, and independent women, and earn for themselves some sweet title from the grateful lips of the poor, better than any a queen could bestow.

Chapter 18

Class Day

THE CLERK of the weather evidently has a regard for young people, and sends sunshine for class days as often as he can. An especially lovely one shone over Plumfield as this interesting anniversary came round, bringing the usual accompaniments of roses, strawberries, white-gowned girls, beaming youths, proud friends, and stately dignitaries full of well-earned satisfaction with the yearly harvest. As Laurence College was a mixed one, the presence of young women as students gave to the occasion a grace and animation entirely wanting where the picturesque half of creation appear merely as spectators. The hands that turned the pages of wise books also possessed the skill to decorate the hall with flowers; eyes tired with study shone with hospitable warmth on the assembling guests; and under the white muslins beat hearts as full of ambition, hope, and courage as those agitating the broadcloth of the ruling sex.

College Hill, Parnassus, and old Plum swarmed with cheery faces, as guests, students, and professors hurried to and fro in the pleasant excitement of arriving and receiving. Everyone was welcomed cordially, whether he rolled up in a fine carriage, or trudged afoot to see the good son or daughter come to honour on the happy day that rewarded many a mutual sacrifice. Mr. Laurie and his wife were on the reception committee, and their lovely house was overflowing. Mrs. Meg, with Daisy and Jo as *aides*, was in demand among the girls, helping on belated toilettes, giving an eye to spreads, and directing the decorations. Mrs. Jo had her hands full as President's

224

lady, and the mother of Ted; for it took all the power and skill of that energetic woman to get her son into his Sunday best.

Not that he objected to be well arrayed; far from it; he adored good clothes, and owing to his great height already revelled in a dress-suit, bequeathed him by a dandy friend. The effect was very funny; but he would wear it in spite of the jeers of his mates, and sighed vainly for a beaver, because his stern parent drew the line there. He pleaded that English lads of ten wore them and were "no end nobby"; but his mother only answered, with a consoling pat of the yellow mane:

"My child, you are absurd enough now; if I let you add a tall hat, Plumfield wouldn't hold either of us, such would be the scorn and derision of all beholders. Content yourself with looking like the ghost of a waiter, and don't ask for the most ridiculous head-gear in the known world."

Denied this noble badge of manhood, Ted soothed his wounded soul by appearing in collars of an amazing height and stiffness, and ties which were the wonder of all female eyes. This freak was a sort of vengeance on his hard-hearted mother; for the collars drove the laundress to despair, never being just right, and the ties required such art in the tying that three women sometimes laboured long before—like Beau Brummel—he turned from a heap of "failures" with the welcome words: "That will do." Rob was devoted on these trying occasions, his own toilet being distinguished only by its speed, simplicity, and neatness. Ted was usually in a frenzy before he was suited, and roars, whistles, commands, and groans were heard from the den wherein the Lion raged and the Lamb patiently toiled. Mrs. Jo bore it till boots were hurled and a rain of hair-brushes set in, then, fearing for the safety of her eldest, she would go to the rescue, and by a wise mixture of fun and authority finally succeed in persuading Ted that he was "a thing of beauty," if not "a joy for ever." At last he would stalk majestically forth, imprisoned in collars compared to which those worn by Dickens's afflicted Biler were trifles not worth mentioning. The dresscoat was a little loose in the shoulders, but allowed a noble expanse of glossy bosom to be seen, and with a delicate handkerchief negligently drooping at the proper angle, had a truly fine effect. Boots that shone, and likewise pinched, appeared at one end of the "long, black clothespin"—as Josie called him—and a youthful but solemn face at the other, carried at an angle which, if long continued, would have resulted in spinal curvature. Light gloves, a cane, and—oh, bitter drop in the cup of joy!—an ignominious straw hat, not to mention a choice floweret in the button-hole, and a festoon of watchguard below, finished off this impressive boy.

"How's that for style?" he asked, appearing to his mother and cousins whom he was to escort to the hall on this particular occasion.

A shout of laughter greeted him, followed by exclamations of horror; for he had artfully added the little blond moustache he often wore when acting. It was very becoming, and seemed the only balm to heal the wound made by the loss of the beloved hat.

"Take it off this moment, you audacious boy! What *would* your father say to such a prank on this day when we must all behave our best?" said Mrs. Jo, trying to frown, but privately thinking that among the many youths about her none were so beautiful and original as her long son.

"Let him wear it, Aunty; it's so becoming. No one will ever guess he isn't eighteen at least," cried Josie, to whom disguise of any sort was always charming.

"Father won't observe it; he'll be absorbed in his bigwigs and the girls. No matter if he does, he'll enjoy the joke and introduce me as his oldest son. Rob is nowhere when I'm in full fig"; and Ted took the stage with a tragic stalk, like Hamlet in a tail-coat and choker.

"My son, obey me!" and when Mrs. Jo spoke in that tone her word was law. Later, however, the moustache appeared, and many strangers firmly believed that there were three young Bhaers. So Ted found one ray of joy to light his gloom.

*   *   *

Mr. Bhaer was a proud and happy man when, at the appointed hour, he looked down upon the parterre of youthful faces before him, thinking of the "little gardens" in which he had hopefully and faithfully sowed good seed years ago, and from which this beautiful harvest seemed to have sprung. Mr. March's fine old face shone with the serenest satisfaction, for this was the dream of his life fulfilled after patient waiting; and the love and reverence in the countenances of the eager young men and women looking up at him plainly showed that the reward he coveted was his in fullest measure. Laurie always effaced himself on these occasions as much as courtesy would permit; for everyone spoke gratefully in ode, poem, and oration of the founder of the college and noble dispenser of his beneficence. The three sisters beamed with pride as they sat among the ladies, enjoying, as only women can, the honour done the men they loved; while "the original Plums," as the younger ones called themselves, regarded the whole affair as their work, receiving the curious, admiring, or envious glances of strangers with a mixture of dignity and delight rather comical to behold.

The music was excellent, and well it might be when Apollo waved the baton. The poems were—as usual on such occasions—of varied excellence, as the youthful speakers tried to put old truths into new words, and made them forceful by the enthusiasm of their earnest faces and fresh voices. It was beautiful to see the eager interest with which the girls listened to some brilliant brother-student, and applauded him with a rustle as of wind over a bed of flowers. It was still more significant and pleasant to watch the young men's faces when a slender white figure stood out against the background of black-coated dignitaries, and with cheeks that flushed and paled, and lips that trembled till earnest purpose conquered maiden fear, spoke to them straight out of a woman's heart and brain concerning the hopes and doubts, the aspirations and rewards all must know, desire, and labour for. This clear, sweet voice seemed to reach and rouse all that was noblest in the souls of these youths, and to set a seal upon the years of comradeship which made them sacred and memorable for ever.

Alice Heath's oration was unanimously pronounced the success of the day; for without being flowery or sentimental, as is too apt to be the case with these first efforts of youthful orators, it was earnest, sensible, and so inspiring that she left the stage in a storm of applause, the good fellows being as much fired by her stirring appeal to "march shoulder to shoulder," as if she had chanted the "Marseillaise" then and there. One young man was so excited that he nearly rushed out of his seat to receive her as she hastened to hide herself among her mates, who welcomed her with faces full of tender pride and tearful eye. A prudent sister detained him, however, and in a moment he was able to listen with composure to the President's remarks.

They were worth listening to, for Mr. Bhaer spoke like a father to the children whom he was dismissing to the battle of life; and his tender, wise, and helpful words lingered in their hearts long after the praise was forgotten. Then came other exercises peculiar to Plumfield, and the end. Why the roof did not fly off when the sturdy lungs of the excited young men pealed out the closing hymn will for ever be a mystery; but it remained firm, and only the fading garlands vibrated as the waves of music rolled up and died away, leaving sweet echoes to haunt the place for another year.

Dinners and spreads consumed the afternoon, and at sunset came a slight lull as everyone sought some brief repose before the festivities of the evening began. The President's reception was one of the enjoyable things in store, also dancing on Parnassus, and as much strolling, singing, and flirting, as could be compressed into a few hours by youths and maidens just out of school.

Carriages were rolling about, and gay groups on piazzas, lawns, and window-seats idly speculated as to who the distinguished guests might be. The appearance of a very dusty vehicle loaded with trunks at Mr. Bhaer's hospitably open door caused much curious comment among the loungers, especially as two rather foreign-looking gentlemen sprang out, followed by two young ladies, all four being greeted with cries of joy and much embracing by the Bhaers. Then they all disappeared into the house, the luggage followed, and the watchers were left to wonder who the mysterious strangers were, till a fair collegian declared that they must be the Professor's nephews, one of whom was expected on his wedding journey.

She was right; Franz proudly presented his blonde and buxom bride, and she was hardly kissed and blessed when Emil led up his bonny English Mary, with the rapturous announcement:

"Uncle, Aunt, Jo, here's another daughter! Have you room for *my* wife, too?"

There could be no doubt of that; and Mary was with difficulty rescued from the glad embraces of her new relatives, who, remembering all the young pair had suffered together, felt that this was the natural and happy ending of the long voyage so perilously begun.

"But why not tell us, and let us be ready for two brides instead of one?" asked Mrs. Jo, looking as usual rather demoralizing in a wrapper and crimping-pins, having rushed down from her chamber, where she was preparing for the labours of the evening.

"Well, I remembered what a good joke you all considered Uncle Laurie's marriage, and I thought I'd give you another nice little surprise," laughed Emil. "I'm off duty, and it seemed best to take advantage of wind and tide, and come along as convoy to the old boy here. We hoped to get in last night, but couldn't fetch it, so here we are in time for the end of the jollification, anyway."

"Ah, my sons, it is too feeling-full to see you both so happy and again in the old home. I have no words to outpour my gratitude, and can only ask of the dear Gott in Himmel to bless and keep you all," cried Professor Bhaer, trying to gather all four into his arms at once, while tears rolled down his cheeks, and his English failed him.

An April shower cleared the air and relieved the full hearts of the happy family; then of course everyone began to talk—Franz and Ludmilla in German with uncle, Emil and Mary with the aunts; and round this group gathered the young folk, clamouring to hear all about the wreck, and the rescue, and the homeward voyage. It was a very

different story from the written one; and as they listened
to Emil's graphic words, with Mary's soft voice breaking in
now and then to add some fact that brought out the
courage, patience, and self-sacrifice he so lightly touched
upon, it became a solemn and pathetic thing to see and
hear these happy creatures tell of that great danger and
deliverance.

"I never hear the patter of rain now that I don't want to
say my prayers; and as for women, I'd like to take my hat
off to every one of 'em, for they are braver than any man I
ever saw," said Emil, with the new gravity that was as
becoming to him as the new gentleness with which he
treated everyone.

"If women are brave, some men are as tender and
self-sacrificing as women. I know one who in the night
slipped his share of food into a girl's pocket, though starving himself, and sat for hours rocking a sick man in his
arms that he might get a little sleep. No, love, I will tell,
and you must let me!" cried Mary, holding in both her
own the hand he laid on her lips to silence her.

"Only did my duty. If that torment had lasted much
longer I might have been as bad as poor Barry and the
boatswain. Wasn't that an awful night?" And Emil shud-
dered as he recalled it.

"Don't think of it, dear. Tell about the happy days on
the *Urania*, when papa grew better and we were all safe
and homeward bound," said Mary, with the trusting look
and comforting touch which seemed to banish the dark
and recall the bright side of that terrible experience.

Emil cheered up at once, and sitting with his arm
about his "dear lass," in true sailor fashion told the happy
ending of the tale.

"Such a jolly old time as we had at Hamburg! Uncle
Hermann couldn't do enough for the captain, and while
mamma took care of him, Mary looked after me. I had to
go into dock for repairs; fire hurt my eyes, and watching
for a sail and want of sleep made 'em as hazy as a London
fog. She was pilot and brought me in all right, you see,
only I couldn't part company, so she came aboard as first
mate, and I'm bound straight for glory now."

"Hush! that's silly, dear," whispered Mary, trying in her turn to stop him, with English shyness about tender topics. But he took the soft hand in his, and proudly surveying the one ring it wore, went on with the air of an admiral aboard his flagship.

"The captain proposed waiting a spell; but I told him we weren't like to see any rougher weather than we'd pulled through together, and if we didn't know one another after such a year as this, we never should. I was sure I shouldn't be worth my pay without this hand on the wheel; so I had my way, and my brave little woman has shipped for the long voyage. God bless her!"

"Shall you really sail with him?" asked Daisy, admiring her courage, but shrinking with cat-like horror from the water.

"I'm not afraid," answered Mary, with a loyal smile. "I've proved my captain in fair weather and in foul, and if he is ever wrecked again, I'd rather be with him than waiting and watching ashore."

"A true woman, and a born sailor's wife! You are a happy man, Emil, and I'm sure *this* trip will be a prosperous one," cried Mrs. Jo, delighted with the briny flavour of this courtship. "Oh, my dear boy, I always felt you'd come back, and when everyone else despaired I never gave up, but insisted that you were clinging to the maintop jib somewhere on that dreadful sea"; and Mrs. Jo illustrated her faith by grasping Emil with a truly Pillycoddian gesture.

"Of course I was!" answered Emil heartily; "and my 'maintop jib' in this case was the thought of what you and Uncle said to me. That kept me up; and among the million thoughts that came to me during those long nights none was clearer than the idea of the red strand, you remember—English navy, and all that. I liked the notion, and resolved that if a bit of my cable was left afloat, the red stripe should be there."

"And it was, my dear, it was! Captain Hardy testifies to that, and here is your reward"; and Mrs. Jo kissed Mary with a maternal tenderness which betrayed that she liked the English rose better than the blue-eyed German *Korn-blumen*, sweet and modest though it was.

Emil surveyed the little ceremony with complacency, saying, as he looked about the room which he never thought to see again: "Odd, isn't it, how clearly trifles come back to one in times of danger? As we floated there, half-starved, and in despair, I used to think I heard the bells ringing here, and Ted tramping downstairs, and you calling, 'Boys, boys, it's time to get up!' I actually smelt the coffee we used to have, and one night I nearly cried when I woke from a dream of Asia's ginger cookies. I declare, it was one of the bitterest disappointments of my life to face hunger with that spicy smell in my nostrils. If you've got any, do give me one!"

A pitiful murmur broke from all the aunts and cousins, and Emil was at once borne away to feast on the desired cookies, a supply always being on hand. Mrs. Jo and her sister joined the other group, glad to hear what Franz was saying about Nat.

"The minute I saw how thin and shabby he was, I knew that something was wrong; but he made light of it, and was so happy over our visit and news that I let him off with a brief confession, and went to Professor Baumgarten and Bergmann. From them I learned the whole story of his spending more money than he ought and trying to atone for it by unnecessary work and sacrifice. Baumgarten thought it would do him good, so kept his secret till I came. It did him good, and he's paid his debts and earned his bread by the sweat of his brow, like an honest fellow."

"I like that much in Nat. It is, as I said, a lesson, and he learns it well. He proves himself a man, and has deserved the place Bergmann offers him," said Mr. Bhaer, looking well pleased as Franz added some facts already recorded.

"I told you, Meg, that he had good stuff in him, and love for Daisy would keep him straight. Dear lad, I wish I had him here this moment!" cried Mrs. Jo, forgetting in delight the doubts and anxieties which had troubled her for months past.

"I am very glad, and suppose I shall give in as I always do, especially now that the epidemic rages so among us. You and Emil have set all their heads in a ferment, and Josie will be demanding a lover before I can turn round," answered Mrs. Meg, in a tone of despair.

But her sister saw that she was touched by Nat's trials, and hastened to add the triumphs, that the victory might be complete, for success is always charming.

"This offer of Herr Bergmann is a good one, isn't it?" she asked, though Mr. Laurie had already satisfied her on that point when Nat's letter brought the news.

"Very fine in every way. Nat will get capital drill in Bachmeister's orchestra, see London in a delightful way, and if he suits come home with them, well started among the violins. No great honour, but a sure thing and a step up. I congratulated him, and he was very jolly over it, saying, like the true lover he is: 'Tell Daisy; be sure and tell her all about it.' I'll leave that to you, Aunt Meg, and you can also break it gently to her that the old boy had a fine blond beard. Very becoming; hides his weak mouth, and gives a noble air to his big eyes and 'Mendelssohnian brow,' as a gushing girl called it. Ludmilla has a photo of it for you."

This amused them; and they listened to many other interesting bits of news which kind Franz, even in his own happiness, had not forgotten to remember for his friend's sake. He talked so well, and painted Nat's patient and pathetic shifts so vividly, that Mrs. Meg was half won; though if she had learned of the Minna episode and the fiddling in beer-gardens and streets, she might not have relented so soon. She stored up all she heard, however, and, womanlike, promised herself a delicious talk with Daisy, in which she would allow herself to melt by degrees, and perhaps change the doubtful "We shall see" to a cordial "He has done well; be happy, dear."

In the midst of this agreeable chat the sudden striking of a clock recalled Mrs. Jo from romance to reality, and she exclaimed, with a clutch at her crimping-pins:

"My blessed people, you must eat and rest; and I must dress, or receive in this disgraceful rig. Meg, will you take

Ludmilla and Mary upstairs and see to them? Franz knows the way to the dining-room. Fritz, come with me and be made tidy, for what with heat and emotion, we are both perfect wrecks."

Chapter 19

White Roses

WHILE THE travellers refreshed, and Mrs. President struggled into her best gown, Josie ran into the garden to gather flowers for the brides. The sudden arrival of these interesting beings had quite enchanted the romantic girl, and her head was full of heroic rescues, tender admiration, dramatic situations, and feminine wonder as to whether the lovely creatures would wear their veils or not. She was standing before a great bush of white roses, culling the most perfect for the bouquets which she meant to tie with the ribbon festooned over her arm, and lay on the toilette tables of the new cousins, as a delicate attention. A step startled her, and looking up she saw her brother coming down the path with folded arms, bent head, and the absent air of one absorbed in deep thought.

"Sophy Wackles," said the sharp child, with a superior smile, as she sucked her thumb just pricked by a too eager pull at the thorny branches.

"What are you at here, Mischief?" asked Demi, with an Irvingesque start, as he felt rather than saw a disturbing influence in his day-dream.

"Getting flowers for 'our brides'. Don't you wish you had one?" answered Josie, to whom the word "mischief" suggested her favourite amusement.

"A bride or a flower?" asked Demi calmly, though he eyed the blooming bush as if it had a sudden and unusual interest for him.

"Both; you get the one, and I'll give you the other."

"Wish I could!" and Demi picked a little bud, with a sigh that went to Josie's warm heart.

"Why don't you, then? It's lovely to see people so

235

happy. Now's a good time to do it if you ever mean to. *She* will be going away for ever soon."

"Who?" and Demi pulled a half-opened bud, with a sudden colour in his own face; which sign of confusion delighted little Jo.

"Don't be a hypocrite. You know I mean Alice. Now, Jack, I'm fond of you, and want to help; it's so interesting— all these lovers and weddings and things, and we ought to have our share. So you take my advice and speak up like a man, and make sure of Alice before she goes."

Demi laughed at the seriousness of the small girl's advice; but he liked it, and showed that it suited him by saying blandly, instead of snubbing her as usual:

"You are very kind, child. Since you are so wise, could you give me a hint how I'd better 'speak up,' as you elegantly express it?"

"Oh, well, there are various ways, you know. In plays the lovers go down on their knees; but that's awkward when they have long legs. Ted never does it well, though I drill him for hours. You could say, 'Be mine, be mine!' like the old man who threw cucumbers over the wall to Mrs. Nickleby, if you want to be gay and easy; or you could write a poetical pop. You've tried it, I dare say."

"But seriously, Jo, I do love Alice, and I think she knows it. I want to tell her so; but I lose my head when I try, and don't care to make a fool of myself. Thought you might suggest some pretty way; you read so much poetry and are so romantic."

Demi tried to express himself clearly, but forgot his dignity and his usual reserve in the sweet perplexity of his love, and asked his little sister to teach him how to put the question which a single word can answer. The arrival of his happy cousins had scattered all his wise plans and brave resolutions to wait still longer. The Christmas play had given him courage to hope, and the oration today had filled him with tender pride; but the sight of those blooming brides and beaming grooms was too much for him, and he panted to secure his Alice without an hour's delay. Daisy was his confidante in all things but this; a brotherly feeling of sympathy had kept him from telling her his hopes, because her own were forbidden. His mother was rather jealous of any girl he admired; but knowing that she liked Alice, he loved on and enjoyed his secret alone, meaning soon to tell her all about it.

Now suddenly Josie and the rose-bush seemed to suggest a speedy end to his tender perplexities; and he was moved to accept her aid as the netted lion did that of the mouse.

"I think I'll write," he was slowly beginning, after a pause during which both were trying to strike out a new and brilliant idea.

"I've got it! perfectly lovely! just suit her, and you too, being a poet!" cried Josie, with a skip.

"What is it? Don't be ridiculous, please," begged the bashful lover, eager, but afraid of this sharp-tongued bit of womanhood.

"I read in one of Miss Edgeworth's stories about a man who offers three roses to his lady—a bud, a half-blown, and a full-blown rose. I don't remember which she took; but it's a pretty way; and Alice knows about it because she was there when we read it. Here are all kinds; you've got the two buds, pick the sweetest rose you can find, and I'll tie them up and put them in her room. She is coming to dress with Daisy, so I can do it nicely."

Demi mused a moment with his eyes on the bridal bush, and a smile came over his face so unlike any it had ever worn before, that Josie was touched, and looked away as if she had no right to see the dawn of the great passion which, while it lasts, makes a young man as happy as a god.

"Do it," was all he said, and gathered a full-blown rose to finish his floral love-message.

Charmed to have a finger in this romantic pie, Josie tied a graceful bow of ribbon about the stems, and finished her last nosegay with much content, while Demi wrote upon a card:

Dear Alice, You know what the flowers mean. Will you wear one, or all tonight, and make me still prouder, fonder, and happier than I am?
                                        Yours entirely,
                                                        John

Offering this to his sister, he said in a tone that made
her feel the deep importance of her mission:

"I trust you, Jo. This means everything to me. No jokes,
dear, if you love me."

Josie's answer was a kiss that promised all things; and
then she ran away to do her "gentle spiriting," like Ariel,
leaving Demi to dream among the roses like Ferdinand.

Mary and Ludmilla were charmed with their bouquets;
and the giver had the delight of putting some of the flowers
into the dark hair and the light as she played maid at the
toilettes of "our brides," which consoled her for a disappointment in the matter of veils.

No one helped Alice dress; for Daisy was in the next
room with her mother; and not even their loving eyes saw
the welcome which the little posy received, nor the tears
and smiles and blushes that came and went as she read the
note and pondered what answer she should give. There
was no doubt about the one she *wished* to give; but duty
held her back; for at home there was an invalid mother
and an old father. She was needed there, with all the help
she could now bring by the acquirements four years of
faithful study had given her. Love looked very sweet, and
a home of her own with John a little heaven on earth; but
not yet. And she slowly laid away the full-blown rose as
she sat before the mirror, thinking over the great question
of her life.

Was it wise and kind to ask him to wait, to bind him by
any promise, or even to put into words the love and
honour she felt for him? No; it would be more generous to
make the sacrifice alone, and spare him the pain of hope
deferred. He was young; he would forget; and she would
do her duty better, perhaps, if no impatient lover waited
for her. With eyes that saw but dimly, and a hand that
lingered on the stem he had stripped of thorns, she laid
the half-blown flower by the rose, and asked herself if
even the little bud might be worn. It looked very poor and
pale beside the others; yet being in the self-sacrificing
mood which real love brings, she felt that even a small
hope was too much to give, if she could not follow it up
with more.

As she sat looking sadly down on the symbols of an

affection that grew dearer every moment, she listened half
unconsciously to the murmur of voices in the adjoining
room. Open windows, thin partitions, and the stillness of
summer twilight made it impossible to help hearing, and
in a few moments more she could not refrain; for they
were talking of John.

"So nice of Ludmilla to bring us all bottles of real
German cologne! Just what we need after this tiring day!
Be sure John has his! He likes it so!"

"Yes, mother. Did you see him jump up when Alice
ended her oration? He'd have gone to her if I hadn't held
him back. I don't wonder he was pleased and proud. I
spoilt my gloves clapping, and quite forgot my dislike of
seeing women on platforms, she was so earnest and unconscious and sweet after the first moment."

"Has he said anything to you, dear?"

"No; and I guess why. The kind boy thinks it would
make me unhappy. It wouldn't. But I know his ways; so I
wait, and hope all will go well with him."

"It must. No girl in her senses would refuse our John,
though he isn't rich, and never will be. Daisy, I've been
longing to tell you what he did with his money. He told
me last night, and I've had no time since to tell you. He
sent poor young Barton to the hospital, and kept him
there till his eyes were saved—a costly thing to do. But
the man can work now and care for his old parents. He
was in despair, sick and poor, and too proud to beg; and
our dear boy found it out, and took every penny he had,
and never told even his mother till she made him."

Alice did not hear what Daisy answered, for she was
busy with her own emotions—happy ones now, to judge
from the smile that shone in her eyes and the decided
gesture with which she put the little bud in her bosom, as
if she said: "He deserves some reward for that good deed,
and he shall have it."

Mrs. Meg was speaking, and still of John, when she
could hear again:

"Some people would call it unwise and reckless, when
John has so little; but *I* think his first investment a safe
and good one, for 'he who giveth to the poor lendeth to

the Lord'; and I was so pleased and proud, I wouldn't
spoil it by offering him a penny."

"It is his having nothing to offer that keeps him silent, I
think. He is so honest, he won't ask till he has much to
give. But he forgets that love is everything. I know he's
rich in that; I see and feel it; and any woman should be
glad to get it."

"Right, dear. I felt just so, and was willing to work and
wait with and for *my* John."

"So she will be, and I hope they will find it out. But she
is so dutiful and good, I'm afraid she won't let herself be
happy. You would like it, mother?"

"Heartily; for a better, nobler girl doesn't live. She is
all I want for my son; and I don't mean to lose the dear,
brave creature if I can help it. Her heart is big enough for
both love and duty; and they can wait more happily if they
do it together—for wait they must, of course."

"I'm so glad *his* choice suits you, mother, and *he* is
spared the saddest sort of disappointment."

Daisy's voice broke there; and a sudden rustle, followed
by a soft murmur, seemed to tell that she was in her
mother's arms, seeking and finding comfort there.

Alice heard no more, and shut her window with a guilty
feeling but a shining face; for the proverb about listeners
failed here, and she had learned more than she dared to
hope. Things seemed to change suddenly; she felt that her
heart *was* large enough for both love and duty; she knew
now that she would be welcomed by mother and sister;
and the memory of Daisy's less happy fate, Nat's weary
probation, the long delay, and possible separation for
ever—all came before her so vividly that prudence seemed
cruelty; self-sacrifice, sentimental folly; and anything but
the whole truth, disloyalty to her lover. As she thought
thus, the half-blown rose went to join the bud; and then,
after a pause, she slowly kissed the perfect rose, and
added it to the tell-tale group, saying to herself with a sort
of sweet solemnity, as if the words were a vow:

"I'll love and work and wait with and for my John."

It was well for her that Demi was absent when she stole
down to join the guests who soon began to flow through
the house in a steady stream. The new brightness which

touched her usually thoughtful face was easily explained
by the congratulations she received as orator, and the
slight agitation observable, when a fresh batch of gentlemen approached soon passed, as none of them noticed the
flowers she wore over a very happy heart.

Demi meantime was escorting certain venerable per-
sonages about the college, and helping his grandfather
entertain them with discussion of the Socratic method of
instruction, Pythagoras, Pestalozzi, Froebel, and the rest,
whom he devoutly wished at the bottom of the Red Sea,
and no wonder, for his head and his heart were full of love
and roses, hopes and fears. He piloted the "potent, grave,
and reverend seigniors" safely down to Plumfield at last,
and landed them before his uncle and aunt Bhaer, who
were receiving in state, the one full of genuine delight in
all men and things, the other suffering martyrdom with a
smile, as she stood shaking hand after hand, and affecting
utter unconsciousness of the sad fact that ponderous Professor Plock had camped upon the train of her state and
festival velvet gown.

With a long sigh of relief Demi glanced about him for
the beloved girl. Most persons would have looked some
time before any particular angel could be discovered among
the white-robed throng in parlours, hall, and study; but
his eye went—like the needle to the pole—to the corner
where a smooth dark head, with its braided crown, rose
like a queen's, he thought, above the crowd which surrounded her. Yes, she has a flower at her throat; one, two,
oh, blessed sight! he saw it all across the room, and gave a
rapturous sigh which caused Miss Perry's frizzled crop to
wave with a sudden gust. He did *not* see the rose, for it
was hidden by a fold of lace; and it was well, perhaps, that
bliss came by instalments, or he might have electrified the
assembled multitude by flying to his idol, there being no
Daisy to clutch him by the coat-tail. A stout lady, thirsting
for information, seized him at that thrilling moment, and
he was forced to point out celebrities with a saintly patience which deserved a better reward than it received;
for a certain absence of mind and incoherence of speech at
times caused the ungrateful dowager to whisper to the
first friend she met after he had escaped:

"I saw no wine at any of the spreads; but it is plain that young Brooke has had too much. Quite gentlemanly, but evidently a trifle intoxicated, my dear."

Ah, so he was! but with a diviner wine than any that ever sparkled at a class-day lunch, though many collegians know the taste of it; and when the old lady was disposed of, he gladly turned to find the young one, bent on having a single word. He saw her standing by the piano now, idly turning over music as she talked with several gentlemen. Hiding his impatience under an air of scholastic repose, Demi hovered near, ready to advance when the happy moment came, wondering meantime why elderly persons persisted in absorbing young ones instead of sensibly sitting in corners with their contemporaries. The elderly persons in question retired at length, but only to be replaced by two impetuous youths who begged Miss Heath to accompany them to Parnassus and join the dance. Demi thirsted for their blood, but was appeased by hearing George and Dolly say, as they lingered a moment after her refusal:

"Really, you know, I'm quite converted to co-education and almost wish I'd remained here. It gives a grace to study, a sort of relish even to Greek to see charming girls at it," said Stuffy, who found the feast of learning so dry, any sauce was welcome; and he felt as if he had discovered a new one.

"Yes, by Jove! we fellows will have to look out or you'll carry off all the honours. You were superb today, and held us all like magic, though it was so hot there, I really think I couldn't have stood it for anyone else," added Dolly, labouring to be gallant and really offering a touching proof of devotion; for the heat melted his collar, took the curl out of his hair, and ruined his gloves.

"There is room for all; and if you will leave us the books, we will cheerfully yield the baseball, boating, dancing, and flirting, which seem to be the branches you prefer," answered Alice sweetly.

"Ah, now you are too hard upon us! We can't grind all the time and you ladies don't seem to mind taking a turn at the two latter 'branches' you mention," returned

Dolly, with a glance at George which plainly said, "I had her there."

"Some of us do in our first years. Later we give up childish things, you see. Don't let me keep you from Parnassus"; and a smiling nod dismissed them, smarting under the bitter consciousness of youth.

"You got it there, Doll. Better not try to fence with these superior girls. Sure to be routed, horse, foot, and dragoons," said Stuffy, lumbering away, somewhat cross with too many spreads.

"So deuced sarcastic! Don't believe she's much older than we are. Girls grow up quicker, so she needn't put on airs and talk like a grandmother," muttered Dolly, feeling that he had sacrificed his kids upon the altar of an ungrateful Pallas.

"Come along and let's find something to eat. I'm faint with so much talking. Old Plock cornered me and made my head spin with Kant and Hegel and that lot."

"I promised Dora West I'd give her a turn. Must look her up; she's a jolly little thing, and doesn't bother about anything but keeping in step."

And arm in arm the boys strolled away, leaving Alice to read music as diligently as if society had indeed no charms for her. As she bent to turn a page, the eager young man behind the piano saw the rose and was struck speechless with delight. A moment he gazed, then hastened to seize the coveted place before a new detachment of bores arrived.

"Alice, I can't believe it—did you understand—how shall I ever thank you?" murmured Demi, bending as if he, too, read the song, not a note or word of which did he see, however.

"Hush! not now. I understood—I don't deserve it—we are too young, we must wait, but—I'm very proud and happy, John!"

What would have happened after that tender whisper I tremble to think, if Tom Bangs had not come bustling up, with the cheerful remark:

"Music? just the thing. People are thinning out, and we all want a little refreshment. My brain fairly reels with the 'ologies and 'isms I've heard discussed tonight. Yes, give us this; sweet thing! Scotch songs are always charming."

Demi glowered; but the obtuse boy never saw it, and
Alice, feeling that this would be a safe vent for sundry
unruly emotions, sat down at once, and sang the song
which gave her answer better than she could have done:

BIDE A WEE

"The puir auld folk at home, ye mind,
   Are frail and failing sair;
And weel I ken they'd miss me, lad,
   Gin I come hame nae mair.
The grist is out, the times are hard,
   The kine are only three;
I canna leave the auld folk now.
   We'd better bide a wee.

"I fear me sair they're failing baith;
   For when I sit apart,
They talk o' Heaven so earnestly,
   It wellnigh breaks my heart.
So, laddie, dinna urge me now,
   It surely winna be;
I canna leave the auld folk yet.
   We'd better bide a wee."

The room was very still before the first verse ended;
and Alice skipped the next, fearing she could not get
through; for John's eyes were on her, showing that he
knew she sang for him and let the plaintive little ballad
tell what her reply must be. He took it as she meant it,
and smiled at her so happily that her heart got the better
of her voice, and she rose abruptly, saying something
about the heat.

"Yes, you are tired; come out and rest, my dearest"; and
with a masterful air Demi took her into the starlight,
leaving Tom to stare after them winking as if a sky-rocket
had suddenly gone off under his nose.

"Bless my soul! the Deacon really meant business last
summer and never told me. Won't Dora laugh?" And Tom
departed in hot haste to impart and exult over his discovery.

What was said in the garden was never exactly known;

but the Brooke family sat up very late that night, and any curious eye at the window would have seen Demi receiving the homage of his womankind as he told his little romance. Josie took great credit to herself in the matter, insisting that she had made the match; Daisy was full of the sweetest sympathy and joy, and Mrs. Meg so happy that when Jo had gone to dream of bridal veils, and Demi sat in his room blissfully playing the air of "Bide a Wee," she had her talk about Nat, ending with her arms round her dutiful daughter and these welcome words as her reward:

"Wait till Nat comes home, and then my good girl shall wear white roses too."

Chapter 20

Life For Life

THE SUMMER DAYS that followed were full of rest and pleasure for young and old, as they did the honours of Plumfield to their happy guests. While Franz and Emil were busy with the affairs of Uncle Hermann and Captain Hardy, Mary and Ludmilla made friends everywhere; for, though very unlike, both were excellent and charming girls. Mrs. Meg and Daisy found the German bride a *Hausfrau* after their own hearts, and had delightful times learning new dishes, hearing about the semi-yearly washes and the splendid linen-room at Hamburg, or discussing domestic life in all its branches. Ludmilla not only taught, but learned, many things, and went home with many new and useful ideas in her blonde head.

Mary had seen so much of the world that she was unusually lively for an English girl; while her various accomplishments made her a most agreeable companion. Much good sense gave her ballast; and the late experiences of danger and happiness added a sweet gravity at times, which contrasted well with her natural gaiety. Mrs. Jo was quite satisfied with Emil's choice, and felt sure this true and tender pilot would bring him safe to port through fair or stormy weather. She had feared that Franz would settle down into a comfortable, moneymaking burgher, and be content with that; but she soon saw that his love of music and his placid Ludmilla put much poetry into his busy life, and kept it from being too prosaic. So she felt at rest about these boys, and enjoyed their visit with real, maternal satisfaction; parting with them in September most regretfully, yet hopefully, as they sailed away to the new life that lay before them.

Demi's engagement was confided to the immediate family only, as both were pronounced too young to do anything but love and wait. They were so happy that time seemed to stand still for them, and after a blissful week they parted bravely—Alice to home duties, with a hope that sustained and cheered her through many trials; and John to his business, full of a new ardour which made all things possible when such a reward was offered.

Daisy rejoiced over them, and was never tired of hearing her brother's plans for the future. Her own hope soon made her what she used to be—a cheery, busy creature, with a smile, kind word, and helping hand for all; and as she went singing about the house again, her mother felt that the right remedy for past sadness had been found. The dear Pelican still had doubts and fears, but kept them wisely to herself, preparing sundry searching tests to be applied when Nat came home, and keeping a sharp eye on the letters from London; for some mysterious hint had flown across the sea, and Daisy's content seemed reflected in Nat's present cheerful state of mind.

Having passed through the Werther period, and tried a little Faust—of which experience he spoke to his Marguerite as if it had included an acquaintance with Mephistopheles, Blocksburg, and Auerbach's winecellar—he now felt that he was a Wilhelm Meister, serving his apprenticeship to the great masters of life. As she knew the truth of his small sins and honest repentance, Daisy only smiled at the mixture of love and philosophy he sent her, knowing that it was impossible for a young man to live in Germany without catching the German spirit.

"His heart is all right; and his head will soon grow clear when he gets out of the fog of tobacco, beer, and metaphysics he's been living in. England will wake up his common sense, and good salt air blow his little follies all away," said Mrs. Jo, much pleased with the good prospects of her violinist—whose return was delayed till spring, to his private regret, but professional advancement.

Josie had a month with Miss Cameron at the seaside, and threw herself so heartily into the lesson given her that her energy, promise, and patience laid the foundation of a friendship which was of infinite value to her in the busy,

brilliant years to come; for little Jo's instincts were right;
and the dramatic talent of the Marches was to blossom by
and by into an actress, virtuous, and beloved.

Tom and his Dora were peacefully ambling altarward;
for Bangs senior was so afraid his son would change his
mind again and try a third profession, that he gladly
consented to an early marriage, as a sort of anchor to hold
the mercurial Thomas fast. Aforesaid Thomas could not
complain of cold shoulders now; for Dora was a most
devoted and adoring little mate, and made life so pleasant
to him that his gift for getting into scrapes seemed lost,
and he bade fair to become a thriving man, with undeniable talent for the business he had chosen.

"We shall be married in the autumn, and live with my
father for a while. The governor is getting on, you know,
and my wife and I must look after him. Later we shall
have an establishment of our own," was a favourite speech
of his about this time, and usually received with smiles;
for the idea of Tommy Bangs at the head of an "establishment" was irresistibly funny to all who knew him.

Things were in this flourishing condition, and Mrs. Jo
was beginning to think her trials were over for that year,
when a new excitement came. Several postal cards had
arrived at long intervals from Dan, who gave them "Care
of M. Mason, etc.," as his address. By this means he was
able to gratify his longing for home news, and to send
brief messages to quiet their surprise at his delay in settling. The last one, which came in September, was dated
"Montana," and simply said:

Here at last, trying mining again; but not going to
stay long. All sorts of luck. Gave up the farm idea.
Tell plans soon. Well, busy, and *very happy*. D. K.

If they had known what the heavy dash under "happy"
meant, that postal would have been a very eloquent bit of
pasteboard; for Dan was free, and had gone straight away
to the liberty he panted for. Meeting an old friend by
accident, he obliged him at a pinch by acting as overseer
for a time, finding the society even of rough miners very
sweet, and something in the muscular work wonderfully

pleasant, after being cooped up in the brush-shop so long.
He loved to take a pick and wrestle with rock and earth till
he was weary—which was very soon; for that year of
captivity had told upon his splendid physique. He longed
to go home, but waited week after week to get the prison
taint off him and the haggard look out of his face. Meanwhile he made friends of masters and men; and as no one
knew his story, he took his place again in the world
gratefully and gladly—with little pride now, and no plans
but to do some good somewhere, and efface the past.

Mrs. Jo was having a grand clearing-out of her desk one
October day, while the rain poured outside, and peace
reigned in her mansion. Coming across the postals, she
pondered over them, and then put them carefully away in
the drawer labelled "Boys' Letters," saying to herself, as
she bundled eleven requests for autographs into the waste-
paper basket:

"It is quite time for another card, unless he is coming to
tell his plans. I'm really curious to know what he has been
about all this year, and how he's getting on now."

That last wish was granted within an hour; for Ted came
rushing in, with a newspaper in one hand, a collapsed
umbrella in the other, and a face full of excitement, an-
nouncing, all in one breathless jumble:

"Mine caved in—twenty men shut up—no way out—wives
crying—water rising—Dan knew the old shaft—risked his
life—got 'em out—most killed—papers full of it—I knew
he'd be a hero—hurray for old Dan!"

"What? Where? When? Who? Stop roaring, and let me
read!" commanded his mother, entirely bewildered.

Relinquishing the paper, Ted allowed her to read for
herself, with frequent interruptions from him—and Rob,
who soon followed, eager for the tale. It was nothing new;
but courage and devotion always stir generous hearts, and
win admiration; so the account was both graphic and enthusiastic; and the name of Daniel Kean, the brave man
who saved the lives of others at the risk of his own, was on
many lips that day. Very proud were the faces of these
friends as they read how their Dan was the only one who,
in the first panic of the accident, remembered the old
shaft that led into the mine—walled up, but the only hope

of escape, if the men could be got out before the rising
water drowned them; how he was lowered down alone,
telling the others to keep back till he saw if it was safe;
how he heard the poor fellows picking desperately for
their lives on the other side, and by knocks and calls
guided them to the right spot; then headed the rescue
party, and working like a hero, got the men out in time.
On being drawn up last of all, the worn rope broke, and
he had a terrible fall, being much hurt, but was still alive.
How the grateful women kissed his blackened face and
bloody hands, as the men bore him away in triumph, and
the owners of the mine promised a handsome reward, if
he lived to receive it!

"He must live; he *shall*, and come home to be nursed as
soon as he can stir, if I go and bring him myself! I always
knew he'd do something fine and brave, if he didn't get
shot or hung for some wild prank instead," cried Mrs. Jo,
much excited.

"Do go, and take me with you, Mum. I ought to be the
one, Dan's so fond of me and I of him," began Ted, feeling
that this would be an expedition after his own heart.

Before his mother could reply, Mr. Laurie came in, with
almost as much noise and flurry as Teddy the second,
exclaiming as he waved the evening paper:

"Seen the news, Jo? What do you think? Shall I go off at
once, and see after that brave boy?"

"I wish you would. But the thing may not be all true—
rumour lies so. Perhaps a few hours will bring an entirely
new version of the story."

'I've telephoned to Demi for all he can find out; and if
it's true, I'll go at once. Should like the trip. If he's able,
I'll bring him home; if not, I'll stay and see to him. He'll
pull through. Dan will never die of a fall on his head. He's
got nine lives, and not lost half of them yet."

"If you go, uncle, mayn't I go with you? I'm just spoiling
for a journey; and it would be such larks to go out there
with you, and see the mines and Dan, and hear all about
it, and help. I can nurse. Can't I, Rob?" cried Teddy, in his
most wheedlesome tones.

"Pretty well. But if mother can't spare you, I'm ready if

uncle needs anyone," answered Rob, in his quiet way, looking much fitter for the trip than excitable Ted.

"I can't spare either of you. My boys get into trouble, unless I keep them close at home. I've no right to hold the others; but I won't let you out of my sight, or something will happen. Never saw such a year, with wrecks and weddings and floods and engagements, and every sort of catastrophe!" exclaimed Mrs. Jo.

"If you deal in girls and boys, you must expect this sort of thing, ma'am. The worst is over, I hope, till these lads begin to go off. Then I'll stand by you; for you'll need every kind of support and comfort, specially if Ted bolts early," laughed Mr. Laurie, enjoying her lamentations.

"I don't think anything can surprise me now; but I am anxious about Dan, and feel that someone had better go to him. It's a rough place out there, and he may need careful nursing. Poor lad, he seems to get a good many hard knocks! But perhaps he needs them as 'a mellerin' process,' as Hannah used to say."

"We shall hear from Demi before long, and then I'll be off." With which cheerful promise Mr. Laurie departed; and Ted, finding his mother firm, soon followed, to coax his uncle to take him.

Further inquiry confirmed and added interest to the news. Mr. Laurie was off at once; and Ted went into town with him, still vainly imploring to be taken to his Dan. He was absent all day; but his mother said, calmly:

"Only a fit of the sulks because he is thwarted. He's safe with Tom or Demi, and will come home hungry and meek at night. I know him."

But she soon found that she *could* still be surprised; for evening brought no Ted, and no one had seen him. Mr. Bhaer was just setting off to find his lost son, when a telegram arrived, dated at one of the way-stations on Mr. Laurie's route:

Found Ted in the cars. Take him along. Write tomorrow.

T. LAURENCE

"Ted bolted sooner than you expected, mother. Never mind—uncle will take good care of him, and Dan be very glad to see him," said Rob, as Mrs Jo sat, trying to realize that her youngest was actually on his way to the wild West.

"Disobedient boy! He shall be severely punished, if I ever get him again. Laurie winked at this prank; I know he did. Just like him. Won't the two rascals have a splendid time? Wish I was with them! Don't believe that crazy boy took even a night-gown with him, or an overcoat. Well, there will be two patients for us to nurse when they get back, if they ever do. Those reckless express trains always go down precipices, and burn up, or telescope. Oh! my Ted, my precious boy, how can I let him go so far away from me?"

And mother-like, Mrs. Jo forgot the threatened chastisement in tender lamentations over the happy scapegrace, now whizzing across the continent in high feather at the success of his first revolt. Mr. Laurie was much amused at his insisting that those words, "when Ted bolts," put the idea into his head; and therefore the responsibility rested upon his shoulders. He assumed it kindly from the moment he came upon the runaway asleep in a car, with no visible luggage but a bottle of wine for Dan and a blacking-brush for himself; and as Mrs. Jo suspected, the "two rascals" did have a splendid time. Penitent letters arrived in due season, and the irate parents soon forgot to chide in their anxiety about Dan, who was very ill, and did not know his friends for several days. Then he began to mend; and everyone forgave the bad boy when he proudly reported that the first conscious words Dan said were: "Hallo, Ted!" with a smile of pleasure at seeing a familiar face bent over him.

"Glad he went, and I won't scold any more. Now, what shall we put in the box for Dan?" And Mrs. Jo worked off her impatience to get hold of the invalid by sending comforts enough for a hospital.

Cheering accounts soon began to come, and at length Dan was pronounced able to travel, but seemed in no haste to go home, though never tired of hearing his nurses talk of it.

"Dan is strangely altered," wrote Laurie to Jo; "not by this illness alone, but by something which has evidently gone before. I don't know what, and leave you to ask; but from his ravings when delirious I fear he has been in some serious trouble the past year. He seems ten years older, but improved, quieter, and so grateful to us. It is pathetic to see the hunger in his eyes as they rest on Ted, as if he couldn't see enough of him. He says Kansas was a failure, but can't talk much; so I bide my time. The people here love him very much, and he cares for that sort of thing now; used to scorn any show of emotion, you know; now he wants everyone to think well of him, and can't do enough to win affection and respect. I may be all wrong. You will soon find out. Ted is in clover, and the trip has done him a world of good. Let me take him to Europe when we go? Apron-strings don't agree with him any better than they did with me when I proposed to run away to Washington with you some century ago. Aren't you sorry you didn't?"

This private letter set Mrs. Jo's lively fancy in a ferment, and she imagined every known crime, affliction, and complication which could possibly have befallen Dan. He was too feeble to be worried with questions now, but she promised herself most interesting revelations when she got him safe at home; for the "firebrand" was her most interesting boy. She begged him to come, and spent more time in composing a letter that should bring him, than she did over the most thrilling episodes in her "works."

No one but Dan saw the letter; but it did bring him, and one November day Mr. Laurie helped a feeble man out of a carriage at the door of Plumfield, and Mother Bhaer received the wanderer like a recovered son; while Ted, in a disreputable-looking hat and an astonishing pair of boots, performed a sort of war-dance round the interesting group.

"Right upstairs and rest; I'm nurse now, and this ghost must eat before he talks to anyone," commanded Mrs. Jo, trying not to show how shocked she was at this shorn and shaven, gaunt and pallid shadow of the stalwart man she parted with.

He was quite content to obey, and lay on the long

lounge in the room prepared for him, looking about as tranquilly as a sick child restored to its own nursery and mother's arms, while his new nurse fed and refreshed him, bravely controlling the questions that burned upon her tongue. Being weak and weary, he soon fell asleep; and then she stole away to enjoy the society of the "rascals," whom she scolded and petted, pumped and praised, to her heart's content.

"Jo, I think Dan has committed some crime and suffered for it," said Mr. Laurie, when Ted had departed to show his boots and tell glowing tales of the dangers and delights of the miners' life to his mates. "Some terrible experience has come to the lad, and broken his spirit. He was quite out of his head when we arrived, and I took the watching, so I heard more of those sad wanderings than anyone else. He talked of the 'warden,' some trail, a dead man, and Blair and Mason, and would keep offering me his hand, asking me if I would take it and forgive him. Once, when he was very wild, I held his arms, and he quieted in a moment, imploring me not to 'put the handcuffs on.' I declare, it was quite awful sometimes to hear him in the night talk of old Plum and you, and beg to be let out and go home to die."

"He isn't going to die, but live to repent of anything he may have done; so don't harrow me up with these dark hints, Teddy. I don't care if he's broken the Ten Commandments, I'll stand by him, and so will you, and we'll set him on his feet and make a good man of him yet. I know he's not spoilt, by the look in his poor face. Don't say a word to anyone, and I'll have the truth before long," answered Mrs. Jo, still loyal to her bad boy, though much afflicted by what she had heard.

For some days Dan rested, and saw few people; then good care, cheerful surroundings, and the comfort of being at home began to tell, and he seemed more like himself, though still very silent as to his late experiences, pleading the doctor's orders not to talk much. Everyone wanted to see him; but he shrank from any but old friends, and "wouldn't lionize worth a cent," Ted said, much disappointed that he could not show off his brave Dan.

"Wasn't a man there who wouldn't have done the same,

so why make a row over me?" asked the hero, feeling more
ashamed than proud of the broken arm, which looked so
interesting in a sling.

"But isn't it pleasant to think that you saved twenty
lives, Dan, and gave husbands, sons, and fathers back to
the women who loved them?" asked Mrs. Jo one evening as
they were alone together after several callers had been
sent away.

"Pleasant! it's all that kept me alive, I do believe; yes,
I'd rather have done it than be made president or any
other big bug in the world. No one knows what a comfort
it is to think I've saved twenty men to more than pay
for—" There Dan stopped short, having evidently spoken
out of some strong emotion to which his hearer had no
key.

"I thought you'd feel so. It is a splendid thing to save life
at the risk of one's own, as you did, and nearly lose it,"
began Mrs. Jo, wishing he had gone on with that impulsive
speech which was so like his old manner.

" 'He that loseth his life shall gain it,' " muttered Dan,
staring at the cheerful fire which lighted the room, and
shone on his thin face with a ruddy glow.

Mrs. Jo was so startled at hearing such words from his
lips that she exclaimed joyfully:

"Then you *did* read the little book I gave you, and kept
your promise?"

"I read it a good deal after a while. I don't know much
yet, but I'm ready to learn; and that's something."

"It's everything. Oh, my dear, tell me about it! I know
something lies heavy on your heart; let me help you bear
it, and so make the burden lighter."

"I know it would; I want to tell; but some things even
you couldn't forgive; and if *you* let go of me, I'm afraid I
can't keep afloat."

"Mothers can forgive *anything*! Tell me all, and be sure
that I will *never* let you go, though the whole world
should turn from you."

Mrs. Jo took one of the big wasted hands in both of hers
and held it fast, waiting silently till that sustaining touch
warmed poor Dan's heart, and gave him courage to speak.
Sitting in his old attitude, with his head in his hands, he

slowly told it all, never once looking up till the last words
left his lips.

"Now you know; can you forgive a murderer, and keep
a jail-bird in your house?"

Her only answer was to put her arms about him, and lay
the shorn head on her breast, with eyes so full of tears
they could but dimly see the hope and fear that made his
own so tragical.

That was better than any words; and poor Dan clung to
her in speechless gratitude, feeling the blessedness of
mother love—that divine gift which comforts, purifies,
and strengthens all who seek it. Two or three great, bitter
drops were hidden in the little woollen shawl where Dan's
cheek rested, and no one ever knew how soft and comfortable it felt to him after the hard pillows he had known so
long. Suffering of both mind and body had broken will and
pride, and the lifted burden brought such a sense of relief
that he paused a moment to enjoy it in dumb delight.

"My poor boy, how you have suffered all this year, when
we thought you free as air! Why didn't you tell us, Dan,
and let us help you? Did you doubt your friends?" asked
Mrs. Jo, forgetting all other emotions in sympathy, as she
lifted up the hidden face, and looked reproachfully into
the great hollow eyes that met her own frankly now.

"I was ashamed. I tried to bear it alone rather than
shock and disappoint you, as I know I have, though you
try not to show it. Don't mind; I must get used to it"; and
Dan's eyes dropped again as if they could not bear to see
the trouble and dismay his confession painted on his best
friend's face.

"I am shocked and disappointed by the sin, but I am also
very glad and proud and grateful that my sinner has repented, atoned, and is ready to profit by the bitter lesson.
No one but Fritz and Laurie need ever know the truth; we
owe it to them, and they will feel as I do," answered Mrs.
Jo, wisely thinking that entire frankness would be a better
tonic than too much sympathy.

"No, they won't; men never forgive like women. But it's
right. Please tell 'em for me, and get it over. Mr. Laurence
knows it, I guess. I blabbed when my wits were gone; but
he was very kind all the same. I can bear their knowing;

but oh, not Ted and the girls!" Dan clutched her arm with such an imploring face that she hastened to assure him no one should know except the two old friends, and he calmed down as if ashamed of his sudden panic.

"It wasn't murder, mind you, it was in self-defence; he drew first, and I had to hit him. Didn't mean to kill him; but it doesn't worry me as much as it ought, I'm afraid. I've more than paid for it, and such a rascal is better out of the world than in it, showing boys the way to hell. Yes, I know you think that's awful in me; but I can't help it. I hate a scamp as I do a skulking coyote, and always want to get a shot at 'em. Perhaps it would have been better if he had killed me; my life is spoilt."

All the old prison gloom seemed to settle like a black cloud on Dan's face as he spoke, and Mrs. Jo was frightened at the glimpse it gave her of the fire through which he had passed to come out alive, but scarred for life. Hoping to turn his mind to happier things, she said cheerfully: -

"No, it isn't; you have learned to value it more and use it better for this trial. It is not a lost year, but one that may prove the most helpful of any you ever know. Try to think so, and begin again; we will help, and have all the more confidence in you for this failure. We all do the same and struggle on."

"I never can be what I was. I feel about sixty, and don't care for anything now I've got here. Let me stay till I'm on my legs, then I'll clear out and never trouble you any more," said Dan despondently.

"You are weak and low in your mind; that will pass, and by and by you will go to your missionary work among the Indians with all the old energy and the new patience, self-control, and knowledge you have gained. Tell me more about that good chaplain and Mary Mason and the lady whose chance word helped you so much. I want to know all about the trials of my poor boy."

Won by her tender interest, Dan brightened up and talked on till he had poured out all the story of that bitter year, and felt better for the load he lifted off.

If he had known how it weighed upon his hearer's heart, he would have held his peace; but she hid her

sorrow till she had sent him to bed, comforted and calm;
then she cried her heart out, to the great dismay of Fritz
and Laurie, till they heard the tale and could mourn with
her; after which they all cheered up and took counsel
together how best to help this worst of all the "catas-
trophes" the year had brought them.

Chapter 21

Aslauga's Knight

IT WAS CURIOUS to see the change which came over Dan after that talk. A weight seemed off his mind; and though the old impetuous spirit flashed out at times, he seemed intent on trying to show his gratitude and love and honour to these true friends by a new humility and confidence very sweet to them, very helpful to him. After hearing the story from Mrs. Jo, the Professor and Mr. Laurie made no allusion to it beyond the hearty handgrasp, the look of compassion, the brief word of good cheer in which men convey sympathy, and a redoubled kindness which left no doubt of pardon. Mr. Laurie began at once to interest influential persons in Dan's mission, and set in motion the machinery which needs so much oiling before anything can be done where Government is concerned. Mr. Bhaer, with the skill of a true teacher, gave Dan's hungry mind something to do, and helped him understand himself by carrying on the good chaplain's task so paternally that the poor fellow often said he felt as if he had found a father. The boys took him to drive, and amused him with their pranks and plans; while the women, old and young, nursed and petted him till he felt like a sultan with a crowd of devoted slaves, obedient to his lightest wish.

A very little of this was enough for Dan, who had a masculine horror of "molly-coddling," and so brief an ac-quaintance with illness that he rebelled against the doctor's orders to keep quiet; and it took all Mrs. Jo's authority and the girls' ingenuity to keep him from leaving his sofa long before strained back and wounded head were well. Daisy cooked for him; Nan attended to his medicines; Josie read aloud to while away the long hours of inaction that hung so heavily on his hands; while Bess brought all her pictures and casts to amuse him, and, at his special desire, set up a modelling-stand in his parlour and began to mould the buffalo head he gave her. Those afternoons seemed the pleasantest part of his day; and Mrs. Jo, busy in her study close by, could see the friendly trio and enjoy the pretty pictures they made. The girls were much flattered by the success of their efforts, and exerted themselves to be very entertaining, consulting Dan's moods with the feminine tact most women creatures learn before they are out of pinafores. When he was gay, the room rang with laughter; when gloomy, they read or worked in respectful silence till their sweet patience cheered him up again; and when in pain they hovered over him like "a couple of angels," as he said. He often called Josie "little mother," but Bess was always "Princess"; and his manner to the two cousins was quite different. Josie sometimes fretted him with her fussy ways, the long plays she liked to read, and the maternal scoldings she administered when he broke the rules; for having a lord of creation in her power was so delightful to her that she would have ruled him with a rod of iron if he had submitted. To Bess, in her gentler ministrations, he never showed either impatience or weariness, but obeyed her least word, exerted himself to seem well in her presence, and took such interest in her work that he lay looking at her with unwearied eyes; while Josie read to him in her best style unheeded.

Mrs. Jo observed this, and called them "Una and the Lion," which suited them very well, though the lion's mane was shorn, and Una never tried to bridle him. The elder ladies did their part in providing delicacies and supplying all his wants; but Mrs. Meg was busy at home, Mrs. Amy preparing for the trip to Europe in the spring, and Mrs. Jo hovering on the brink of a "vortex"—for the forthcoming book had been sadly delayed by the late domestic events. As she sat at her desk, settling papers or meditatively nibbling her pen while waiting for the divine afflatus to descend upon her, she often forgot her fictitious heroes and heroines in studying the live models before her, and thus by chance looks, words, and gestures discovered a little romance unsuspected by anyone else.

The *portière* between the rooms was usually drawn aside, giving a view of the group in the large bay-window —Bess at one side, in her grey blouse, busy with her tools; Josie at the other side with her book; and between, on the long couch, propped with many cushions, lay Dan in a many-hued eastern dressing-gown presented by Mr. Laurie and worn to please the girls, though the invalid much preferred an old jacket "with no confounded tail to bother over." He faced Mrs. Jo's room, but never seemed to see her, for his eyes were on the slender figure before him, with the pale winter sunshine touching her golden head, and the delicate hands that shaped the clay so deftly. Josie was just visible, rocking violently in a little chair at the head of the couch, and the steady murmur of her girlish voice was usually the only sound that broke the quiet of the room, unless a sudden discussion arose about the book or the buffalo.

Something in the big eyes, bigger and blacker than ever in the thin white face, fixed, so steadily on one object, had a sort of fascination for Mrs. Jo after a time, and she watched the changes in them curiously; for Dan's mind was evidently not on the story, and he often forgot to laugh or exclaim at the comic or exciting crises. Sometimes they were soft and wistful, and the watcher was very glad that neither damsel caught that dangerous look for when they spoke it vanished; sometimes it was full of eager fire, and the colour came and went rebelliously, in spite of his attempt to hide it with an impatient gesture of hand or head; but oftenest it was dark, and sad, and stern, as if those gloomy eyes looked out of captivity at some forbidden light or joy. This expression came so often that it worried Mrs. Jo, and she longed to go and ask him what bitter memory overshadowed those quiet hours. She knew that his crime and its punishment must lie heavy on his mind; but youth, and time, and new hopes would bring comfort, and help to wear away the first sharpness of the prison brand. It lifted at other times, and seemed almost forgotten when he joked with the boys, talked with old friends, or enjoyed the first snows as he drove out every fair day. Why should the shadow always fall so darkly on him in the society of these innocent and friendly girls?

They never seemed to see it, and if either looked or spoke, a quick smile came like a sun-burst through the clouds to answer them. So Mrs. Jo went on watching, wondering, and discovering, till accident confirmed her fears.

Josie was called away one day, and Bess, tired of working, offered to take her place if he cared for more reading.

"I do; your reading suits me better than Jo's. She goes so fast my stupid head gets in a muddle and soon begins to ache. Don't tell her; she's a dear little soul, and so good to sit here with a bear like me."

The smile was ready as Bess went to the table for a new book, the last story being finished.

"You are not a bear, but very good and patient, we think. It is always hard for a man to be shut up, mamma says, and must be terrible for you, who have always been so free."

If Bess had not been reading titles she would have seen Dan shrink as if her last words hurt him. He made no answer; but other eyes saw and understood why he looked as if he would have liked to spring up and rush away for one of his long races up the hill, as he used to do when the longing for liberty grew uncontrollable. Moved by a sudden impulse, Mrs. Jo caught up her work-basket and went to join her neighbours, feeling that a nonconductor might be needed; for Dan looked like a thundercloud full of electricity.

"What shall we read, Aunty? Dan doesn't seem to care. You know his taste; tell me something quiet and pleasant and short. Josie will be back soon," said Bess, still turning over the books piled on the centre-table.

Before Mrs. Jo could answer, Dan pulled a shabby little volume from under his pillow, and handing it to her said: "Please read the third one; it's short and pretty—I'm fond of it."

The book opened at the right place, as if the third story had been often read, and Bess smiled as she saw the name.

"Why, Dan, I shouldn't think you'd care for this romantic German tale. There is fighting in it; but it is very sentimental, if I remember rightly."

"I know it; but I've read so few stories, I like the simple ones best. Had nothing else to read sometimes; I guess I know it all by heart, and never seem to be tired of those fighting fellows, and the fiends and angels and lovely ladies. You read 'Aslauga's Knight,' and see if you don't like it. Edwald was rather too soft for my fancy; but Froda was first-rate and the spirit with the golden hair always reminded me of you."

As Dan spoke Mrs. Jo settled herself where she could watch him in the glass, and Bess took a large chair facing him, saying, as she put up her hands to retie the ribbon that held the cluster of thick, soft curls at the back of her head:

"I hope Aslauga's hair wasn't as troublesome as mine, for it's always tumbling down. I'll be ready in a minute."

"Don't tie it up; please let it hang. I love to see it shine that way. It will rest your head, and be just right for the story, Goldilocks," pleaded Dan, using the childish name and looking more like his boyish self than he had done for many a day.

Bess laughed, shook down her pretty hair, and began to read, glad to hide her face a little; for compliments made her shy, no matter who paid them. Dan listened intently on; and Mrs. Jo, with eyes that went often from her needle to the glass, could see, without turning, how he enjoyed every word as if it had more meaning for him than for the other listeners. His face brightened wonderfully, and soon wore the look that came when anything brave or beautiful inspired and touched his better self. It was Fouqué's charming story of the knight Froda, and the fair daughter of Sigurd, who was a sort of spirit, appearing to her lover in hours of danger and trial, as well as triumph and joy, till she became his guide and guard, inspiring him with courage, nobleness, and truth, leading him to great deeds in the field, sacrifices for those he loved, and victories over himself by the gleaming of her golden hair, which shone on him in battle, dreams, and perils by day and night, till after death he finds the lovely spirit waiting to receive and to reward him.

Of all the stories in the book this was the last one would have supposed Dan would like best, and even Mrs. Jo was

surprised at his perceiving the moral of the tale through
the delicate imagery and romantic language by which it
was illustrated. But as she looked and listened she remembered the streak of sentiment and refinement which
lay concealed in Dan like the gold vein in a rock, making
him quick to feel and to enjoy fine colour in a flower,
grace in an animal, sweetness in women, heroism in men,
and all the tender ties that bind heart to heart; though he
was slow to show it, having no words to express the tastes
and instincts which he inherited from his mother. Suffering of soul and body had tamed his stronger passions, and
the atmosphere of love and pity now surrounding him
purified and warmed his heart till it began to hunger for
the food neglected or denied so long. This was plainly
written in his too expressive face, as, fancying it unseen,
he let it tell the longing after beauty, peace, and happiness embodied for him in the innocent fair girl before
him.

The conviction of this sad yet natural fact came to Mrs.
Jo with a pang, for she felt how utterly hopeless such a
longing was; since light and darkness were not farther
apart than snow-white Bess and sin-stained Dan. No dream
of such a thing disturbed the young girl, as her entire
unconsciousness plainly showed. But how long would it be
before the eloquent eyes betrayed the truth? And then
what disappointment for Dan, what dismay for Bess, who
was as cool and high and pure as her own marbles, and
shunned all thought of love with maidenly reserve.

"How hard everything is made for my poor boy! How
can I spoil his little dream, and take away the spirit of
good he is beginning to love and long for? When my own
dear lads are safely settled I'll never try another, for these
things are heart-breaking, and I can't manage any more,"
thought Mrs. Jo, as she put the lining into Teddy's coat-
sleeve upside down, so perplexed and grieved was she at
this new catastrophe.

The story was soon done, and as Bess shook back her
hair, Dan asked as eagerly as a boy:

"Don't you like it?"

"Yes, it's very pretty, and I see the meaning of it; but
Undine was always my favourite."

"Of course, that's like you—lilies and pearls and souls and pure water. Sintram used to be mine; but I took a fancy to this when I was—ahem—rather down on my luck one time, and it did me good, it was so cheerful and sort of spiritual in its meaning, you know."

Bess opened her blue eyes in wonder at this fancy of Dan's for anything "spiritual"; but she only nodded, saying: "Some of the little songs are sweet and might be set to music."

Dan laughed; "I used to sing the last one to a tune of my own sometimes at sunset:

> *Listening to celestial lays,*
> *Bending thy unclouded gaze*
> *On the pure and living light,*
> *Thou art blest, Aslauga's Knight!*

And I was," he added, under his breath, as he glanced towards the sunshine dancing on the wall.

"This one suits you better now"; and glad to please him by her interest, Bess read in her soft voice:

> *"Heal fast, heal fast, ye hero wounds;*
> *O knight, be quickly strong!*
> *Beloved strife*
> *For fame and life,*
> *Oh, tarry not too long!"*

"I'm no hero, never can be, and 'fame and life' can't do much for me. Never mind, read me that paper, please. This knock on the head has made a regular fool of me."

Dan's voice was gentle; but the light was gone out of his face now, and he moved restlessly as if the silken pillows were full of thorns. Seeing that his mood had changed, Bess quietly put down the book, took up the paper, and glanced along the columns for something to suit him.

"You don't care for the money market, I know, nor musical news. Here's a murder; you used to like those; shall I read it? One man kills another—"

"No!"

Only a word, but it gave Mrs. Jo a thrill, and for a

moment she dared not glance at the tell-tale mirror. When she did Dan lay motionless with one hand over his eyes, and Bess was happily reading the art news to ears that never heard a word. Feeling like a thief who has stolen something very precious, Mrs. Jo slipped away to her study, and before long Bess followed to report that Dan was fast asleep.

Sending her home, with the firm resolve to keep her there as much as possible, Mother Bhaer had an hour of serious thought all alone in the red sunset; and when a sound in the next room led her there, she found that the feigned sleep had become real repose; for Dan lay breathing heavily, with a scarlet spot on either cheek, and one hand clinched on his broad breast. Yearning over him with a deeper pity than ever before, she sat in the little chair beside him, trying to see her way out of this tangle, till his hand slipped down, and in doing so snapped a cord he wore about his neck and let a small case drop to the floor.

Mrs. Jo picked it up, and as he did not wake, sat looking at it, idly wondering what charm it held; for the case was of Indian workmanship and the broken cord, of closely woven grass, sweet scented and pale yellow.

"I won't pry into any more of the poor fellow's secrets. I'll mend and put it back, and never let him know I've seen his talisman."

As she spoke she turned the little wallet to examine the fracture, and a card fell into her lap. It was a photograph, cut to fit its covering, and two words were written underneath the face, "My Aslauga." For an instant Mrs. Jo fancied that it might be one of herself, for all the boys had them; but as the thin paper fell away, she saw the picture Demi took of Bess that happy summer day. There was no doubt now, and with a sigh she put it back, and was about to slip it into Dan's bosom so that not even a stitch should betray her knowledge, when as she leaned towards him, she saw that he was looking straight at her with an expression that surprised her more than any of the strange ones she had ever seen in that changeful face before.

"Your hand slipped down; it fell; I was putting it back," explained Mrs. Jo, feeling like a naughty child caught in mischief.

"You saw the picture?"

"Yes."

"And know what a fool I am?"

"Yes, Dan, and am so grieved—"

"Don't worry about me. I'm all right—glad you know, though I never meant to tell you. Of course it is only a crazy fancy of mine, and nothing can ever come of it. Never thought there would. Good Lord! what could that little angel ever be to me but what she is—a sort of dream of all that's sweet and good?"

More afflicted by the quiet resignation of his look and tone than by the most passionate ardour, Mrs. Jo could only say, with a face full of sympathy:

"It is very hard, dear, but there is no other way to look at it. You are wise and brave enough to see that, and to let the secret be ours alone."

"I swear I will! not a word nor a look if I can help it. No one guesses, and if it troubles no one, is there any harm in my keeping this, and taking comfort in the pretty fancy that kept me sane in that cursed place?"

Dan's face was eager now, and he hid away the little worn case as if defying any hand to take it from him. Anxious to know everything before giving counsel or comfort, Mrs. Jo said quietly:

"Keep it, and tell me all about the 'fancy.' Since I have stumbled on your secret, let me know how it came, and how I can help to make it lighter to bear."

"You'll laugh; but I don't mind. You always did find out our secrets and give us a lift. Well, I never cared much for books, you know; but down yonder when the devil tormented me I had to do something or go stark mad, so I read both the books you gave me. One was beyond me, till that good old man showed me how to read it; but the other, this one, was a comfort, I tell you. It amused me, and was as pretty as poetry. I liked 'em all, and most wore out Sintram. See how used up he is! Then I came to this, and it sort of fitted that other happy part of my life, last summer—here."

Dan stopped a moment as the words lingered on his lips; then, with a long breath, went on, as if it was hard to lay bare the foolish little romance he had woven about a

girl, a picture, and a child's story there in the darkness of
the place which was as terrible to him as Dante's Inferno,
till he found his Beatrice.

"I couldn't sleep, and *had* to think about something, so
I used to fancy I was Folko, and see the shining of Aslauga's
hair in the sunset on the wall, the glim of the watchman's
lamp, and the light that came in at dawn. My cell was
high. I could see a bit of sky; sometimes there was a star
in it, and that was most as good as a face. I set great store
by that patch of blue, and when a white cloud went by, I
thought it was the prettiest thing in all this world. I guess
I was pretty near a fool; but those thoughts and things
helped me through, so they are all solemn true to me, and
I can't let them go. The dear shiny head, the white gown,
the eyes like stars, and sweet, calm ways that set her as
high above me as the moon in heaven. Don't take it away!
it's only a fancy, but a man must love something, and I'd
better love a spirit like her than any of the poor common
girls who would care for me."

The quiet despair in Dan's voice pierced Mrs. Jo to the
heart; but there was no hope and she gave none. Yet she
felt that he was right, and that his hapless affection might
do more to uplift and purify him than any other he might
know. Few women would care to marry Dan now, except
such as would hinder, not help, him in the struggle which
life would always be to him; and it was better to go solitary
to his grave than become what she suspected his father
had been—a handsome, unprincipled, and dangerous man,
with more than one broken heart to answer for.

"Yes, Dan, it *is* wise to keep this innocent fancy, if it
helps and comforts you, till something more real and
possible comes to make you happier. I wish I could give
you any hope; but we both know that the dear child is the
apple of her father's eye, the pride of her mother's heart,
and that the most perfect lover they can find will hardly
seem to them worthy of their precious daughter. Let her
remain for you the high, bright star that leads you up and
makes you believe in heaven."

Mrs. Jo broke down there; it seemed so cruel to destroy
the faint hope Dan's eyes betrayed, that she could not
moralize when she thought of his hard life and lonely

future. Perhaps it was the wisest thing she could have done, for in her hearty sympathy he found comfort for his own loss, and very soon was able to speak again in the manly tone of resignation to the inevitable that showed how honest was his effort to give up everything but the pale shadow of what, for another, might have been a happy possibility.

They talked long and earnestly in the twilight; and this second secret bound them closer than the first; for in it there was neither sin nor shame—only the tender pain and patience which has made saints and heroes of far worse men than our poor Dan. When at length they rose at the summons of a bell, all the sunset glory had departed, and in the wintry sky there hung one star, large, soft, and clear, above a snowy world. Pausing at the window before she dropped the curtains, Mrs. Jo said cheerfully:

"Come and see how beautiful the evening star is, since you love it so." And as he stood behind her, tall and pale, like the ghost of his former self, she added softly: "And remember, dear, if the sweet girl is denied you, the old friend is always here to love and trust and pray for you."

This time she was not disappointed; and had she asked any reward for many anxieties and cares, she received it when Dan's strong arm came round her, as he said, in a voice which showed her that she had not laboured in vain to pluck her firebrand from the burning:

"I never can forget that; for she's helped to save my soul, and make me dare to look up there and say: 'God bless her!'"

Chapter 22

Positively Last Appearance

"Upon my word, I feel as if I lived in a powder-magazine, and don't know which barrel will explode next, and send me flying," said Mrs. Jo to herself next day, as she trudged up to Parnassus to suggest to her sister that perhaps the most charming of the young nurses had better return to her marble gods before she unconsciously added another wound to those already won by the human hero. She told no secrets; but a hint was sufficient; for Mrs. Amy guarded her daughter as a pearl of great price, and at once devised a very simple means of escape from danger. Mr. Laurie was going to Washington on Dan's behalf, and was delighted to take his family with him when the idea was carelessly suggested. So the conspiracy succeeded finely; and Mrs. Jo went home, feeling more like a traitor than ever. She expected an explosion; but Dan took the news so quietly, it was plain that he cherished no hope; and Mrs. Amy was sure her romantic sister had been mistaken. If she had seen Dan's face when Bess went to say good-bye, her maternal eye would have discovered far more than the unconscious girl did. Mrs. Jo trembled lest he should betray himself; but he had learned self-control in a stern school, and would have got through the hard moment bravely, only, when he took both hands, saying heartily: "Good-bye, Princess. If we don't meet again, remember your old friend Dan sometimes," she, touched by his late danger and the wistful look he wore, answered with unusual warmth: "How can I help it, when you make us all so proud of you? God bless your mission, and bring you safely home to us again!"

As she looked up at him with a face full of frank affection

and sweet regret, all that he was losing rose so vividly before him that Dan could not resist the impulse to take the "dear goldy head" between his hands and kiss it, with a broken "Good-bye"; then hurried back to his room, feeling as if it were the prison-cell again, with no glimpse of heaven's blue to comfort him.

This abrupt caress and departure rather startled Bess; for she felt with a girl's quick instinct that there was something in that kiss unknown before, and looked after him with sudden colour in her cheeks and new trouble in her eyes. Mrs. Jo saw it, and fearing a very natural question answered it before it was put.

"Forgive him, Bess. He has had a great trouble, and it makes him tender at parting with old friends; for you know he may never come back from the wild world he is going to."

"You mean the fall and danger of death?" asked Bess, innocently.

"No, dear; a greater trouble than that. But I cannot tell you any more—except that he has come through it bravely; so you may trust and respect him, as I do."

"He has lost someone he loved. Poor Dan! We must be very kind to him."

Bess did not ask the question, but seemed content with her solution of the mystery—which was so true that Mrs. Jo confirmed it by a nod, and let her go away believing that some tender loss and sorrow wrought the great change all saw in Dan, and made him so slow to speak concerning the past year.

But Ted was less easily satisfied, and this unusual reticence goaded him to desperation. His mother had warned him not to trouble Dan with questions till he was quite well; but this prospect of approaching departure made him resolve to have a full, clear, and satisfactory account of the adventures which he felt sure must have been thrilling, from stray words Dan let fall in his fever. So one day when the coast was clear, Master Ted volunteered to amuse the invalid, and did so in the following manner:

"Look here, old boy, if you don't want me to read, you've got to talk, and tell me all about Kansas, and the farms, and that part. The Montana business I know, but

you seem to forget what went before. Brace up, and let's
have it," he began, with an abruptness which roused Dan
from a brown study most effectually.

"No, I don't forget; it isn't interesting to anyone but
myself. I didn't see any farms—gave it up," he said slowly.

"Why?"

"Other things to do."

"What?"

"Well, brush-making for one thing."

"Don't chaff a fellow. Tell true."

"I truly did."

"What for?"

"To keep out of mischief, as much as anything."

"Well, of all the queer things—and you've done a lot—
that's the queerest," cried Ted, taken aback at this disappointing discovery. But he didn't mean to give up yet,
and began again.

"What mischief, Dan?"

"Never you mind. Boys shouldn't bother."

"But I do want to know, awfully, because I'm your pal,
and care for you no end. Always did. Come, now, tell me
a good yarn. I love scrapes. I'll be mum as an oyster if you
don't want it known."

"Will you?" and Dan looked at him, wondering how the
boyish face would change if the truth were suddenly told
him.

"I'll swear it on locked fists, if you like. I know it was
jolly, and I'm aching to hear."

"You are as curious as a girl. More than some—Josie
and—and Bess never asked a question."

"They don't care about rows and things; they liked the
mine business, heroes, and that sort. So do I, and I'm as
proud as Punch over it; but I see by your eyes that there
was something else before that, and I'm bound to find out
who Blair and Mason are, and who was hit and who ran
away, and all the rest of it."

"What!" cried Dan, in a tone that made Ted jump.

"Well, you used to mutter about 'em in your sleep, and
Uncle Laurie wondered. So did I; but don't mind, if you
can't remember, or would rather not."

"What else did I say? Queer, what stuff a man will talk when his wits are gone."

"That's all I heard; but it seemed interesting, and I just mentioned it, thinking it might refresh your memory a bit," said Teddy, very politely; for Dan's frown was heavy at that moment.

It cleared off at this reply, and after a look at the boy squirming with suppressed impatience in his chair, Dan made up his mind to amuse him with a game of cross-purposes and half-truths, hoping to quench his curiosity, and so get peace.

"Let me see; Blair was a lad I met in the cars, and Mason a poor fellow who was in a—well, a sort of hospital where I happened to be. Blair ran off to his brothers, and I suppose I might say Mason was hit, because he died there. Does that suit you?"

"No, it doesn't. Why did Blair run? and who hit the other fellow? I'm sure there was a fight somewhere, wasn't there?"

"Yes."

"I guess I know what it was about."

"The devil, you do! Let's hear you guess. Must be amusing," said Dan, affecting an ease he did not feel.

Charmed to be allowed to free his mind, Ted at once unfolded the boyish solution of the mystery which he had been cherishing, for he felt that there was one somewhere.

"You needn't say yes, if I guess right and you are under oath to keep silent. I shall know by your face, and never tell. Now see if I'm not right. Out there they have wild doings, and it's my belief you were in some of 'em. I don't mean robbing mails, and Klu-Kluxing, and that sort of thing; but defending the settlers, or hanging some scamp, or even shooting a few, as a fellow must sometimes, in self-defence. Ah, ha! I've hit it, I see. Needn't speak; I know the flash of your old eye, and the clench of your big fist." And Ted pranced with satisfaction.

"Drive on, smart boy, and don't lose the trail," said Dan, finding a curious sense of comfort in some of these random words, and longing, but not daring, to confirm the true ones. He might have confessed the crime, but not the punishment that followed, the sense of its disgrace was still so strong upon him.

"I knew I should get it; can't deceive me long," began Ted, with such an air of pride Dan could not help a short laugh.

"It's a relief, isn't it, to have it off your mind? Now, just confide in me and it's all safe, unless you've sworn not to tell."

"I have."

"Oh, well, then don't"; and Ted's face fell, but he was himself again in a moment and said, with the air of a man of the world: "It's all right—I understand—honour binds—silence to death, etc. Glad you stood by your mate in the hospital. How many did you kill?"

"Only one."

"Bad lot, of course?"

"A damned rascal."

"Well, don't look so fierce; I've no objection. Wouldn't mind popping at some of those bloodthirsty blackguards myself. Had to dodge and keep quiet after it, I suppose."

"Pretty quiet for a long spell."

"Got off all right in the end, and headed for your mines and did that jolly brave thing. Now, I call that decidedly interesting and capital. I'm glad to know it; but I won't blab."

"Mind you don't. Look here. Ted, if you'd killed a man, would it trouble you—a bad one, I mean?"

The lad opened his mouth to say, "Not a bit," but checked that answer as if something in Dan's face made him change his mind. "Well, if it was my duty in war or self-defence, I suppose I shouldn't; but if I'd pitched into him in a rage, I guess I should be very sorry. Shouldn't wonder if he sort of haunted me, and remorse gnawed me as it did Aram and those fellows. You don't mind, do you? It was a fair fight, wasn't it?"

"Yes, I was in the right; but I wish I'd been out of it. Women don't see it that way, and look horrified at such things. Makes it hard; but it don't matter."

"Don't tell 'em; then they can't worry," said Ted, with the nod of one versed in the management of the sex.

"Don't intend to. Mind you keep your notions to yourself, for some of 'em are wide of the mark. Now you may read if you like"; and there the talk ended; but Ted took great comfort in it, and looked as wise as an owl afterwards.

A few quiet weeks followed, during which Dan chafed at the delay; and when at length word came that his credentials were ready, he was eager to be off, to forget a vain love in hard work, and live for others, since he might not for himself.

So one wild March morning our Sintram rode away, with horse and hound, to face again the enemies who would have conquered him, but for Heaven's help and human pity.

"Ah, me! it does seem as if life was made of partings, and they get harder as we go on," sighed Mrs. Jo, a week later, as she sat in the long parlour at Parnassus one evening, whither the family had gone to welcome the travellers back.

"And meetings too, dear; for here we are, and Nat is on his way at last. Look for the silver lining, as Marmee used to say, and be comforted," answered Mrs. Amy, glad to be at home and find no wolves prowling near her sheepfold.

"I've been so worried lately, I can't help croaking. I wonder what Dan thought at not seeing you again? It was wise; but he would have enjoyed another look at home faces before he went into the wilderness," said Mrs. Jo regretfully.

"Much better so. We left notes and all we could think of that he might need, and slipped away before he came. Bess really seemed relieved; I'm sure I was"; and Mrs. Amy smoothed an anxious line out of her white forehead, as she smiled at her daughter, laughing happily among her cousins.

Mrs. Jo shook her head as if the silver lining of that cloud was hard to find; but she had no time to croak again, for just then Mr. Laurie came in looking well pleased at something.

"A new picture has arrived; face towards the music-room, good people, and tell me how you like it. I call it 'Only a fiddler', after Andersen's story. What name will you give it?"

As he spoke he threw open the wide doors, and just beyond they saw a young man standing, with a beaming

face, and a violin in his hand. There was no doubt about
the name to this picture, and with the cry "Nat! Nat!"
there was a general uprising. But Daisy reached him first,
and seemed to have lost her usual composure somewhere
on the way, for she clung to him, sobbing with the shock
of a surprise and joy too great for her to bear quietly.
Everything was settled by that tearful and tender em-
brace, for, though Mrs. Meg speedily detached her daughter, it was only to take her place; while Demi shook Nat's
hand with brotherly warmth, and Josie danced round them
like Macbeth's three witches in one, chanting in her most
tragic tones:

"Chirper thou wast; second violin thou art; first thou
shalt be. Hail, all hail!"

This caused a laugh, and made things gay and comfortable at once. Then the usual fire of questions and answers
began, to be kept up briskly while the boys admired Nat's
blond beard and foreign clothes, the girls his improved
appearance—for he was ruddy with good English beef and
beer, and fresh with the sea-breezes which had blown him
swiftly home—and the older folk rejoiced over his prospects. Of course all wanted to hear him play; and when
tongues tired, he gladly did his best for them, surprising
the most critical by his progress in music even more than
by the energy and self-possession which made a new man
of bashful Nat. By and by when the violin—that most
human of all instruments—had sung to them the loveliest
songs without words, he said, looking about him at these
old friends with what Mr. Bhaer called a "feeling-full"
expression of happiness and content:

"Now let me play something that you will all remember
though you won't love it as I do"; and standing in the
attitude which Ole Bull has immortalized, he played the
street melody he gave them the first night he came to
Plumfield. They remembered it, and joined in the plaintive chorus, which fitly expressed his own emotions:

> "Oh my heart is sad and weary
> Everywhere I roam,
> Longing for the old plantation
> And for the old folks at home."

"Now I feel better," said Mrs. Jo, as they all trooped down the hill soon after. "Some of our boys are failures, but I think this one is going to be a success, and patient Daisy a happy girl at last. Nat is your work, Fritz, and I congratulate you heartily."

"Ach, we can but sow the seed and trust that it falls on good ground. I planted, perhaps, but you watched that the fowls of the air did not devour it, and brother Laurie watered generously; so we will share the harvest among us, and be glad even for a small one, heart's-dearest."

"I thought the seed had fallen on very stony ground with my poor Dan; but I shall not be surprised if he surpasses all the rest in the real success of life, since there is more rejoicing over one repentant sinner than many saints," answered Mrs. Jo, still clinging fast to her black sheep although a whole flock of white ones trotted happily before her.

It is a strong temptation to the weary historian to close the present tale with an earthquake which should engulf Plumfield and its environs so deeply in the bowels of the earth that no youthful Schliemann could ever find a vestige of it. But as that somewhat melodramatic conclusion might shock my gentle readers, I will refrain, and forestall the usual question, "How did they end?" by briefly stating that all the marriages turned out well. The boys prospered in their various callings; so did the girls, for Bess and Josie won honours in their artistic careers, and in the course of time found worthy mates. Nan remained a busy, cheerful, independent spinster, and dedicated her life to her suffering sisters and their children, in which true woman's work she found abiding happiness. Dan never married, but lived, bravely and usefully, among his chosen people till he was shot defending them, and at last lay quietly asleep in the green wilderness he loved so well, with a lock of golden hair upon his breast, and a smile on his face which seemed to say that Aslauga's Knight had fought his last fight and was at peace. Stuffy became an alderman, and died suddenly of apoplexy after a public dinner. Dolly was a society man of mark till he lost his money, when he found congenial employment in a fashionable tailoring es-

tablishment. Demi became a partner, and lived to see his
name above the door, and Rob was a professor at Laurence College; but Teddy eclipsed them all by becoming
an eloquent and famous clergyman, to the great delight of
his astonished mother. And now, having endeavoured to
suit everyone by many weddings, few deaths, and as much
prosperity as the eternal fitness of things will permit, let
the music stop, the lights die out, and the curtain fall for
ever on the March family.

Afterword

by
Madeleine B. Stern

It was in a matter of months that Louisa May Alcott wrote *Little Women*, the book that converted a struggling, experimenting, compulsive writer into America's best-loved author of juveniles. Still less time was needed for the creation of the sequel *Little Men* which, begun in January 1871, was in proof by May. The sequel to that sequel— *Jo's Boys*—the book that completed the trilogy, was, unlike its famous predecessors, years in the making. Begun in 1882, it was not published until 1886, two years before the author's death. Indeed it is one of the few works in the Alcott canon that preoccupied her, however sporadically, for so long a time.

The reasons for this disparity in Alcott's approach to her work are illuminating, for they elucidate the changes in the life behind the books as well as in the life that became part of the books. Although the cast of characters remained more or less steadfast, the Louisa Alcott who wrote *Jo's Boys* was not the Louisa Alcott who wrote *Little Women* and *Little Men*. Diminished in some ways, enlarged in others, the author who ended this trilogy had learned much and lost much since she began it.

There was much of Jo March in the thirty-six-year-old woman who wrote *Little Women*. The heroine's independent spirit—"the one young woman in 19th-century fiction . . . who gives up no part of her autonomy as payment for being born a woman"—was still manifest in Louisa Alcott when the book was begun in 1868. In a sense she had spent the first three decades of her life in preparation for the creation of her masterpiece. She had been born in Germantown, Pennsylvania, in 1832, the second of four

279

daughters of the Transcendental philosopher and educator
Bronson Alcott and his progressive, stalwart and long-
suffering wife Abba May. Her education, mostly at the
hands of her father whose pedagogical views were innovative and nonconformist, had been informal, leading her,
as she put it in her journal, to have "a pleasant time with
my mind." She had been exposed to the rigors of Fruitlands,
the consociate society modeled by Bronson Alcott and his
friends after Eden but, in its insistence upon linen rai-
ment, cold water and vegetarian diet, more closely resem-
bling purgatory. She had been exposed, too, to family
poverty. But above all she had, by the time the Alcotts had
settled in Concord, Massachusetts, learned to revel in the
joys of skating in winter and berry picking in summer, of
growing up with three sisters as playmates, of writing and
acting melodramas for friends and neighbors. And what
illustrious neighbors she had—Henry David Thoreau, who
introduced her to the secrets of tanagers and cardinal
flowers; Ralph Waldo Emerson, whose library was at her
disposal; Nathaniel Hawthorne, who seemed to her a shadow
in a house of shadows. Reading Dickens, sewing, attend-
ing to household chores, imagining wild melodramas, Louisa had not only taken stage center but had also sat in a
corner, the observer taking notes. The domestic novel she
would write in 1868 unfolded in her own life during the
1840s. By the time the next decade had rolled round, the
potential writer determined to "make a battering-ram" of
her head "and make a way through this rough-and-tumble
world." She tried everything that would earn money for
the family, since Bronson, however elevated his thoughts
and progressive his projects, had but little ability for making a livelihood. Louisa sewed, tutored, went out to domestic service, and wrote.

   She wrote whatever would earn her a $5 or $10 reward—
stories of sweetness and light for the *Saturday Evening
Gazette,* fables for children, poems. By the 1860s, with
the outbreak of the Civil War, she found richer sources for
her pen. In December 1862 she volunteered as army
nurse at the Union Hotel Hospital in Georgetown, Dis-
trict of Columbia, and her short but catastrophic experience there culminated in severe illness as well as in a

book—*Hospital Sketches*—by far the most realistic work she had yet tried. As far as literary genres were concerned, she tried almost anything during those struggling sixties, especially Gothic thrillers which she indited for Frank Leslie's sensational magazines and for the equally gaudy and gruesome *Flag of Our Union* published by Elliott, Thomes and Talbot of Boston. Those narratives, with their undaunted, almost militant heroines and with props that included swords and daggers, opium and hashish, were issued either anonymously or pseudonymously under the pen name of A. M. Barnard. By 1868, when she sat down to write *Little Women*, Alcott's literary experiments had covered a wide spectrum, and her life had ranged from personal Sloughs of Despond to transcendent family joys. She was ready to incorporate all of this into the domestic novel that would become her masterpiece.

A famous line in the journal that Alcott kept for most of her life is dated September 1867: "Niles, partner of Roberts, asked me to write a girls' book. Said I'd try." In Boston's Hayward Place, while her sister May busied herself with drawing classes, Louisa edited a children's magazine, *Merry's Museum*, wrote stories, and began the book that would be entitled *Little Women*. By July of 1868 she had finished it, and after its publication she was requested to supply a second part. This she began in November and in April 1869 it was published. The domestic novel she had created, reanimating the Alcott family as the March family, became a perennial bestseller; thereafter the royalties from *Little Women* would seldom fail to provide Alcott with financial support.

The enormous success of her first book about the Marches was coupled with an enormous obligation to keep her readership supplied with a ceaseless flow of books. In 1871 she added to her oeuvre a sequel to *Little Women*, *Little Men: Life at Plumfield with Jo's Boys*. Written after the death of her beloved brother-in-law while she herself was enjoying a grand tour abroad, the now famous author plumbed her childhood days and her father's pedagogical experiments for the episodes in *Little Men*. The tempestuous Jo March of *Little Women* had become the more or less sedate wife of Professor Bhaer in *Little Men*. As for the author, the wild aspirations of her youth had been tempered. She had been metamorphosed into a successful professional author, admired and lionized, with coteries of worshipers. Even Bronson Alcott, lecturing across country, was now introduced as the Father of Little Women.

In the course of the fifteen years that would pass before the appearance of the final volume in the trilogy, Louisa Alcott underwent still greater changes. Some of them were occasioned merely by the passing of time and the declining health caused by a lifetime of overwork. Some were the results of the tragedies in the life of the family she had immortalized. In 1877 her mother, the unforgettable Marmee of Little Women, died. In 1879 her sister May, the primping, elegant, artistic Amy of Little Women, died in Paris after giving birth to a child. The child, named after Louisa, was bequeathed to her, and Alcott's later years were burdened with the bittersweet joy of caring for young Lulu Nieriker.

Throughout those later years, Louisa Alcott continued to feel the onerous responsibility of spinning stories for her ever increasing audience—an unceasing labor that led to a variety of ills from writer's cramp to vertigo. And throughout those years, too, the threads of various reforms were interwoven into her life. To her early advocacy of anti-slavery and temperance she added co-education, dress reform and especially women's rights. Indeed, the championship of these reforms was part of the fabric not only of her life but of her work. The fifty-year-old woman who in 1882 journeyed from Concord to Boston's Bellevue Hotel to write the sequel to a sequel that would end her March trilogy had come a long way since she had agreed to write a girls' story for Thomas Niles of Roberts Brothers. In many ways the book would be faithful to the dreams and standards of the earlier volumes. But in many ways it would reflect the changes of later years.

The four years during which Jo's Boys had "simmered," as she liked to put it, were years almost totally different from those that had preceded the writing of Little Women and of Little Men. On October 24, 1882, no sooner than she had begun her writing at the Bellevue, a telegram informed her that her father had had a paralytic stroke.

"Home at once," she recorded in her journal, "and found him stricken down. Anxious days; little hope." Bronson Alcott would not die for another six years, and his exodus from life would precede his daughter's by a matter of days. During those six years he remained the care and responsibility of Louisa and her older sister Anna. In addition, May's daughter Lulu Nieriker, who had arrived in Boston in September 1880, was now three years old and required constant attention. Between her helpless, feeble father, her bouncing, boisterous niece and the management of a large household, Louisa was consumed with anxieties. The freedom she had earned was rarely if ever hers. "Freedom," she wrote to a young friend, "was always my longing, but I have never had it." Her health was declining, and she suffered from a variety of ills, from bronchial catarrh to dyspepsia, and tried a variety of treatments, from homeopathy to mind cure. "I 'trudge in harness,'" she wrote, "& find my burdens heavy & various."

There was little time or energy for the reform movements in which she believed. By the 1880s, in her roster of causes, the place of anti-slavery had been taken by "emancipation of the white slaves of America"—the women. Alcott regarded woman suffrage as "this most vital question of the age," and though she could not work actively for it, she could weave it into the book that her public demanded of her.

Through the years when *Jo's Boys* was taking shape in her mind, Louisa continued to feel the urgency to supply her readership with the Alcott bestsellers to which they were accustomed. Mary Mapes Dodge, editor of *St. Nicholas*, "begged me to consider myself mortgaged to her for tales," while Thomas Niles demanded Alcott books for the Roberts Brothers imprint. By gathering together narratives for *Spinning Wheel Stories* and planning a volume of *Lulu's Library* from the tales she told her niece, she tried to appease her editors. But a book like *Jo's Boys* that would ring down the curtain on the March family was another thing altogether. In addition to her poor health and her domestic cares, Louisa Alcott was kept from completing her trilogy by a deep-seated reluctance to bring the saga of the Marches to an end.

The reluctance and the excuses, as well as the publisher's demands, recur in her correspondence and tell the history of a book so long in the making. On August 25, 1883, Thomas Niles wrote to his star author: "I am very glad you are going to work though I wish it might be on 'Jo's Boys.' That book I am sure is needed to keep up the enthusiasm & renew the demand for 'Little Men' & 'Little Women.' " A month later he queried "Dear Miss Alcott Will you allow me to append to an advertisement of 'Little Men' that a sequel is in preparation." Having arranged with the *Youth's Companion* to supply *Little Men* as a premium, Niles wanted *Jo's Boys* advertised on a premium list that would reach 300,000. "Please telegragh your answer, on receipt, because they are waiting to make up the 'copy' for the paper."

The advertisement of a sequel proved premature. As Louisa explained to Mrs. Dodge, who of course wished to run the new novel as a serial in *St. Nicholas,* "About 'Jo's Boys,' I can only say that it is not written, & I see no prospect of its being done for some time. A few chapters were started, but I made my boys *too old* so must begin anew. Niles urged the advertising when I thought I could go at it, but other duties prevented so I am a perjured woman."

Meanwhile the promise of a new Alcott book had been carried by *The New York Times,* and Louisa's English publishers Sampson Low were hot on its trail. "We learn from the New York Times," they wrote to Roberts Brothers, "that it is the intention of Miss Louisa M. Alcott to publish a new story entitled 'Joe's [sic] Boys and How They Turned Out,' being a Sequel to her 'Little Men.' Having held for many years the English copyright of the latter book we are very desirous of Securing the same for 'Joe's Boys.' Will you therefore kindly mail us as soon as possible a Set of sheets that we may be Enabled to have the new work reprinted for the English market."

The market was certainly there—publishers clamored for the work. Niles especially persisted with his demands, reminding the author that since the publication of *Jack and Jill* in 1880, "we have not had a *new* book by you. . . . All we want now to make an additional *furore* is 'Jo's Boys.'

The time is ripe for it." The time was ripe, but the author was still reluctant, still ambivalent. "The prospect of 'Jo's Boys,' " she told Mrs. Dodge, "is a very uncertain one." To Niles she wrote in July 1884: "I wish I might be inspired to do those dreadful boys; but rest is more needed than money. Perhaps during August, my month at home, I may take a grind at the old mill." As the year ended she "Began again on 'Jo's Boys,' . . . Wrote two hours for three days, then had a violent attack of vertigo, and was ill for a week. . . . Put away papers, and tried to dawdle and go about as other people do." Vertigo has many causes, some physical, some emotional. As far as *Jo's Boys* was concerned Alcott's vertigo probably stemmed from both.

By the following summer she reminded Niles, "I ache to fall on some of the ideas that are simmering in my head, but dare not, as my one attempt since the last 'Jo's Boys' break-down cost me a week or two of woe and $30 for the doctor." In January 1886 she reiterated to him: "I heartily wish I could 'swamp the book-room with 'Jo's Boys," . . . and hope to do it by and by when head and hand can safely obey the desire of the heart." In March, however, after another attack of vertigo, she was "ill for a week; sleepless nights. Head worked like a steam-engine; would not stop. Planned 'Jo's Boys' to the end, and longed to get up and write it. Told Dr. W[esselhoeft]. that he had better let me get the ideas *out*, then I could rest. He very wisely agreed."

Allowed at first to work only one half hour a day, Alcott began again and "had some pleasant hours when I forgot my body and lived in my mind." In April she could go on writing "one or two hours a day." By June 1886 almost fifteen chapters were written. "I long to go on and finish 'Jo's Boys' by July 1st," she informed her publisher. "I planned twenty chapters and am on the fifteenth. . . . I have little doubt it will be done early in July, but things are so contrary with me I can never be sure of carrying out a plan, and I don't want to fail again; so far I feel as if I could, without harm, finish off these dreadful boys." Regarding illustrations, she commented: "Why have any . . . ? The book is not a child's book, as the lads are nearly all over twenty, and pretty pictures are not needed. . . . I

shall be at home in a week or two, . . . I can touch up
proofs and confer about the book. Sha'n't we be glad when
it is done?"

Niles' reaction was ecstatic. On June 19 he wrote: "The
news is almost too good to be true—'15 chapters of Jos
Boys done.' Will you send me some of the opening chapters and let me begin putting it in type? A few pages in
print, to enable me to make up a dummy for a sample will
be almost as good as the complete work and 'Gene' [Eugene
Hardy] can start with it in July, a happy man, on his
western trip for orders." Two days later, having received
six chapters, Niles reported: "I have read the first two . . .
and find them in the same happy vein as of old. . . . Do it
as the spirit moves & so 'con amore.' "

In July 1886, nearly four years after she had begun
her story, Louisa recorded in her journal: "Finish 'Jo's
Boys,' and take it to T.N. Much rejoicing over a new
book. Fifty thousand to be the first edition; orders coming
in fast. Not good—too great intervals between the parts,
as it was begun long ago; but the children will be happy,
and my promise kept. Two new chapters were needed, so
I wrote them, and gladly corked my inkstand."

What was the nature of the book that had "simmered"
so long in Alcott's mind and now marked the finale for the
March family? The curtain of *Jo's Boys* rises on the wholesome progressive school of Plumfield ten years after it had
fallen in *Little Men*. Plumfield has become the seat of
Laurence College, donated by and named after the Laurie
of *Little Women*, now a philanthropic pillar of society
married to Jo's artistic sister Amy. Plumfield is a Parnassus
of sorts, a "mixed"—that is, co-educational—college with
many scholars, rich and poor, hailing from distant states.
"At Plumfield all found something to help them; for the
growing institution had not yet made its rules as fixed as
the laws of the Medes and Persians, and believed so
heartily in the right of all sexes, colors, creeds, and ranks
to education that there was room for everyone who
knocked," including "eager girls from the West, the awkward freedman or woman from the South, or the wellborn

student whose poverty made this college a possibility when other doors were barred."

Although the redoubtable Marmee of *Little Women* has died, Mr. March, remaining ever young, with prophetic eyes, is chaplain of the institution which fulfills the dream of his life. However, as in *Little Women*, Mr. March is seldom heard from. Jo's husband, Professor Bhaer, is president. The professor, who combines lofty ethical standards with German sentimentality, and frequently lapses into his native language, exerts a pervasive influence at Plumfield. His innovative pedagogical principles are modeled to some extent upon those of Bronson Alcott, and he sheds an aura of sweetness and light wherever he goes. His liberal-minded faculty includes a professor of elocution (the only discipline named in the book), but academic pursuits seldom interfere with the basic business at hand— the inculcation of "health and real wisdom." Education, we are reminded, as we are in *Little Men*, "is not confined to books." Athletic sports are in high favor, both girls and boys developing their muscles "in the most scientific manner." And there is of course a "charming little theater" where "Plays at Plumfield" written by Frau Professor Jo March Bhaer are enacted by the students.

Private theatricals form only one of many components reminiscent of *Little Women* and *Little Men*. As the author puts it, "As it is . . . impossible for the humble historian of the March family to write a story without theatricals in it . . . we will accept the fact . . . by proceeding to the Christmas plays at Plumfield." The *Owlsdark Marbles* and the *Witch's Curse*, tableaux and dissolving views all find a place in *Jo's Boys*, recalling to readers the melodramas performed by Louisa Alcott as well as by her alter ego Jo March. Indeed, Meg's younger daughter Josie inherits Jo March's histrionic ambitions.

To the reader of *Jo's Boys* who remembers the first volume of the trilogy, there are many other reminiscences of *Little Women*. It is Jo who now asks Marmee's familiar question, "Girls, *have* you got nice pocket handkerchiefs?" Mrs. Jo refers openly to her "blood-and-thunder days" when she wrote thrillers anonymously to earn financial reward, and to the "old tin kitchen which used to hold her works." Dickensian allusions punctuate the chapters as they do in the earlier novels. Mr. March occasionally discusses Greek comedy with the serious-minded, as was ever his wont, and sometimes dilates on the Plato Club and Western receptivity to Eastern culture. Amy, whose prototype, Louisa's younger artist sister May has died, is quietly disposed of, the author writing: "Time seemed to have stood still with Amy." Now her fifteen-year-old daughter Bess becomes the replica of her mother. As for Meg's son Demi, he now works for "Mr. Tiber," a transparent disguise for Louisa's publisher Mr. Niles.

Even the history of *Little Women* is recalled, the time when "A book for girls being wanted by a certain publisher, she [Jo–Louisa] hastily scribbled a little story describing a few scenes and adventures in the lives of herself and sisters—though boys were more in her line—and with very slight hopes of success sent it out to seek its fortune. . . . The hastily written story, sent away with no thought beyond the few dollars it might bring, sailed with a fair wind and a wise pilot at the helm straight into public favor, and came home heavily laden with an unexpected cargo of gold and glory."

There are just enough threads from *Little Women* interwoven into *Jo's Boys* to make the remembering reader comfortable. There are even more threads from *Little Men*. Indeed, Chapter One of *Jo's Boys* briefly encapsulates the history of the original Plumfield boys and girls— Dan the wanderer; Nat the musician; the twins Demi and Daisy; medical-minded Nan—traces their predictable histories and skillfully sets the stage for what is to follow ten years later.

In the episodic style in which she excelled, Alcott devotes her chapters to the various characters in turn. Emil's Thanksgiving; Dan's Christmas; Nat's New Year—all present stories complete in themselves but related to the others. Nan comes to the rescue when Dan's dog threatens Ted; Josie, bent upon an actress' career, amusingly attracts the attention of a great tragedienne; the false report of the loss of Emil's ship devastates Plumfield; Nat sows mildly wild oats in Germany and pays his penance. Romance and flirtation are considered a part of education

and are permissible at Plumfield. Tom suffers an unrequited love for Nan; the romance of Daisy and Nat is
frowned upon until Nat earns his reward; Demi and Alice
are suitably and mutually attracted. "All these lovers and
weddings" permeate the pages of *Jo's Boys*.

Almost invariably the characters speak in character. Nan's
references are always medical ("I long for broken bones,"
she exclaims); Josie's are theatrical; Emil's nautical. Stuffy
still deserves his name. Both verbally and literally domestic Daisy attends to her muffins and dislikes "seeing women
on platforms."

Unlike Daisy, her Aunt Jo declares, "Yes, I'm going to
preach; that's my business." And preach she does upon
several occasions, championing work and plain fare and
"the good old-fashioned virtues," castigating nights of "riot"
with "painted girls," endorsing "self-knowledge and self-
control" as "the compass and pilot of the young." Although
there is little straight pedagogy at Plumfield, the "scarlet
strand" of virtue is held high.

Despite the cheerful platitudes and pietism—"moral pap
for the young"—despite the occasional condescensions ("We
Marches, though we have been poor, *are* . . . proud of
our good family. We don't care for money; but a long line
of virtuous ancestors *is* something to . . . be proud of."),
there is much in this novel that rings true and strong. The
author has not forgotten that "simple domestic scenes . . .
touch people's hearts and make them laugh and cry and
feel better." Nor has she forgotten her extraordinary skill
in painting character.

On one occasion Mrs. Jo remarks, "I'm tired of lovesick
girls and runaway wives. We'll prove that there's romance
in old women also." There is still much romance in Mrs.
Jo herself though the wild tomboy of *Little Women* has
become the matronly Mrs. Bhaer. Mrs. Jo still "carelessly" rumples "up her hair . . . just as she used to do
when a girl," still "gets into a vortex" of creative inspiration, and is sometimes as irrepressible as Jo March. The
once Ugly Duckling has turned into a Golden Goose "whose
literary eggs found such an unexpected market," but fame
and fortune have not altered her. She still identifies with
her boys although she has moved a long distance from the

wild young colt of *Little Women* bent upon total independence. Sometimes she wishes she had remained single,
but, as she explains to Nan, "My duty seemed to point
this way, and I don't regret it." At least one modern critic
has found Jo March Bhaer's calm acceptance of her destiny
factitious. Madelon Bedell writes: "Josephine Bhaer . . .
broods over her nest with a serenity that her creator
Louisa Alcott never achieved. We do not believe it. The
real person of Josephine March . . . is not to be found in
this aging matriarch." Perhaps not. The fact remains that
there was enough of Jo March left in the "aging matriarch"
to satisfy contemporary readers. As for today's critics, if
Mother Bhaer's apparent serenity arouses incredulity and
stimulates emotional discussion, that is all to the credit of
her creator and her prototype Louisa Alcott.

Still another character in *Jo's Boys* has aroused violent
critical reaction and interpretation. Daniel Kean, the "wild
boy" of *Little Men*, takes stage center in *Jo's Boys*, assuming a role of considerable significance. He is now the wild
young man, and during the decade that has elapsed since
Little Men he has tried sheep farming in Australia and
mining in California. He has shot a buffalo. Black Hawk
has given him a horse Octoo. His friends—his brothers—
are the Montana Indians who call him "Dan Fire Cloud."
Indeed, "Mrs. Jo often thought that Dan had Indian blood
in him, not only because of his love of a wild, wandering
life, but his appearance; . . . At twenty-five he was very
tall, with sinewy limbs, a keen, dark face, and the alert look
of one whose senses were all alive; rough in manner, full
of energy, quick with word and blow, eyes full of the old
fire." Bold and adventurous, a hunter, a jack-o'-lantern, a
firebrand, a black sheep, a colt not thoroughly broken, Dan
becomes the victim of his own hubris. Having killed a
scoundrel to protect a young friend, he is imprisoned for a
year. After his release he risks his life to rescue his companions in a mine disaster, and returns at last to Plumfield.
There his love of Amy's daughter Bess is regarded as
impossible and hopeless, "since light and darkness were
not farther apart than snow-white Bess and sin-stained
Dan." In the end he dies a hero's death, defending "his
chosen people" the Indians.

In the character of Dan, Jo's "most interesting boy,"
Madelon Bedell believed she had discovered Jo March's
alter ego, and in the "symbol-laden conclusion to Dan's
story . . . the hidden end of the *Little Women* legend."
Another commentator, Nina Auerbach, sees Jo's relation-
ship with Dan as "half-envious and half-erotic," reflecting
the irresolution behind the triumph of the "mother" and
perhaps her self-identification with her favorite black sheep.
In other words, Jo, as much of a wild hawk as Dan, fulfills
herself vicariously through him.

By introducing Dan's empathy for the Indian tribes, the
author not only rounded out his character but used him as
a medium to champion one of her own reforms. In 1885
the death of Helen Hunt Jackson, author of *Ramona*, gave
"a special interest to all Indian tales," and Alcott regarded
that novel as "a noble record of the great wrongs of her
chosen people . . . It recalls the old slavery days, only
these victims are red instead of black."

Through still another character in *Jo's Boys* the author
highlighted her favorite reform, feminism. For this purpose Nan, who becomes a physician and "a busy, cheerful,
independent spinster," is Alcott's torchbearer. Having had
to fight for her rights, Nan is protective of them. She is
ashamed of America for not enfranchising women, and
takes to the stump to demand a suffrage debate in the
legislature. "Do you believe in Woman Suffrage?" she asks
Jo's boys and, being Jo's boys, all are for it. There is
discussion of so-called "superfluous" women, and it is agreed
that "woman isn't a half but a whole human being, and can
stand alone."

In *Jo's Boys* feminist-related themes are touched upon,
from dress reform and temperance to co-education. In the
sewing circle organized by the March sisters, Mrs. Jo
gives little lectures on health, religion, politics, and "the
various questions in which all should be interested," reading extracts from books by women about women, including Cobbe's demand for the law's protection of abused
wives. In Plumfield's "little republic" Jo's girls occupy as
important a place as Jo's boys. In the pantomime of the
Owlsdark Marbles the words "Woman's Rights" adorn
Minerva's shield. As for careers versus marriage, Mrs. Jo

in one instance at least unhesitatingly endorses the former. Nan's career, she asserts, "shall *not* be hampered by
a foolish boy's fancy. In a moment of weariness she may
give in, and then it's all over. Wiser women have done so
and regretted it all their lives."

There is enough affirmation of feminism in *Jo's Boys* to
warrant historian Sarah Elbert's description of Laurence College as "a feminist Utopia graced with cooperative housekeeping and coeducation." Alcott endorses egalitarian
marriage and "makes spinsterhood a viable choice." Literary critic Joy Marsella sees *Jo's Boys* as an extension of
Little Women in regard to its espousal of feminism. She
writes: "Although the girls in *Little Women* become wives
and manage to give up, alter, or repress their youthful
ambitions, in *Jo's Boys* their daughters fulfill these ambitions" and enlarge their horizons. In an article entitled
"The New Woman Revisited," Carolyn Forrey remarks:
"A reader who knows Louisa May Alcott only as the author of *Little Women* might do well to look at *Jo's Boys*
. . . in which her sympathies for the New Woman are
quite evident. . . . Alcott fulfilled all the demands of the
sentimental domestic novel and did not reject the old
feminine virtues, but she thoroughly admired the New
Woman. She saw more than one path to woman's self-
fulfillment: old-style marriage and motherhood, marriage
and motherhood combined with a career, or a career alone
with no strings attached. . . . Woman's sphere is not nec-
essarily the home; woman's sphere is wherever she finds
it."

To the rights of women Louisa Alcott added in *Jo's Boys*
the rights of authors. In an amusing chapter, "Jo's Last
Scrape," she vents her antipathy toward the tribes of
autograph fiends and lion-hunters who have made her
their prey since the success of *Little Women*. "Suddenly
the admiring public took possession of her and all her
affairs, past, present, and to come. Strangers demanded to
look at her, question, advise, warn, congratulate, and
drive her out of her wits. . . . If she declined to open her
heart to them, they reproached her; if she refused to
endow pet charities, . . . she was called hardhearted, . . .
if she found it impossible to answer the piles of letters sent

her, she was neglectful of her duty to the admiring public; and if she preferred the privacy of home to the pedestal upon which she was requested to pose, 'the airs of literary people' were freely criticized." In one day Mrs. Jo is inundated with twelve requests for autographs as well as a poetic effusion beginning, "Oh, were I a heliotrope,/I would play poet,/And blow a breeze of fragrance/To you; and none should know it." An unabashed reporter for the *Saturday Tattler* intrudes upon her study; a group of admirers from Oshkosh demand a sight of the author; a young ladies' seminary camp on the lawn where they proceed to pick flowers and consume their lunch. To crown the day, one eccentric requests a grasshopper from the Plumfield garden and an old gown or pair of stockings belonging to Aunt Jo—this last to "put in a rug she's making" from a vest of Emerson's, a pair of trousers from Holmes and a dress of Harriet Beecher Stowe's.

However amusing these lunatic requests may be, they prompt Mother Bhaer to enunciate a credo on the rights of authors. In December 1885 Alcott wrote to a pedagogical correspondent: "If you can teach your five hundred pupils to love books but to let authors rest in peace, you will give them a useful lesson and earn the gratitude of the long suffering craft, whose lives are made a burden to them by the modern lion hunter and autograph fiend." In *Jo's Boys* she repeated her plea: " 'There ought to be a law to protect unfortunate authors. . . . To me it is a more vital subject than international copyright; for time is money, peace is health, and I lose both with no return but less respect for my fellow creatures and a wild desire to fly into the wilderness."

"Jo's Last Scrape" was related in Chapter Three of *Jo's Boys*. In the twenty-second, final chapter, the author disposed of her characters, delineating their futures tersely and ending her book. "It is a strong temptation to the weary historian," she wrote, "to close the present tale with an earthquake which should engulf Plumfield and its environs so deeply in the bowels of the earth that no youthful Schliemann could ever find a vestige of it." She refrains from that "melodramatic conclusion" and, "having endeavored to suit everyone by many weddings, few deaths, and as much prosperity as the eternal fitness of things will permit," lets "the music stop, the lights die out, and the curtain fall forever on the March family."

The author had described herself as a "weary historian." She was not only weary but still, after the loss of mother and sister, bereft. The brief preface she wrote for *Jo's Boys* on July 4, 1886, reflects her mood: "Having been written at long intervals during the past seven—an exaggeration—years, this story is more faulty than any of its very imperfect predecessors; but the desire to atone for an unavoidable disappointment, and to please my patient little friends, has urged me to let it go without further delay.

"To account for the seeming neglect of AMY, let me add that, since the original of that character died, it has been impossible for me to write of her as when she was here to suggest, criticize, and laugh over her namesake. The same excuse applies to MARMEE. But the folded leaves are not blank to those who knew and loved them, and can find memorials of them in whatever is cheerful, true, or helpful in these pages."

Like the preface, the dedication of *Jo's Boys* reflects a latter-day Louisa Alcott. This book was dedicated, not to family or friends, but to the author's physician Dr. Conrad Wesselhoeft.

At long last, *Jo's Boys*, illustrated only with the frontispiece of a bas-relief of the author, rolled from the press. Despite Mary Mapes Dodge's desire to serialize the novel in *St. Nicholas*, Niles objected, holding that "it is better for a tale to come out all together, as many read it in a magazine who would otherwise buy the book to our profit." The first printing consisted of 10,000 copies, and by the end of 1886, 47,500 copies had been printed. The prospect of *Jo's Boys* was no longer "uncertain."

Although most reviews would be favorable, "the first gun fired" objected to "Jo's Last Scrape" and prompted a self-defense that amounted to a literary credo. In a letter of October 3, 1886, Louisa wrote to her publisher: "You remember I asked you if it should go in, & you said, 'By all means, it's very good, . . .

"That was one reason for letting it stand, as the success

of L.W. comes from just that same use of real life & one's own experience. Another reason is that in no other way can the rising generation of young autograph fiends be reached so well & pleasantly, & by a little good natured ridicule be taught not to harass the authors whom they honor with their regard.

"If it is not good taste to put this part of Jo's life in print all the rest is a mistake also, for the best liked episodes are the real ones.

"I had my doubts, as people are particular about these small matters, but the young folks are the only critics I care for, & if they like it I'm satisfied."

Other reviewers questioned the feminist emphasis, one remarking: "The book is apparently intended to champion co-education, the uninterrupted acquaintance of boys and girls in their everyday life and a good comrade sort of marriage" rather than a "dignified and holy relation which brings sweetness and self-sacrifice to a woman's life." In another opinion, "no respectable boy would stand some of the abuse which several of these boys receive from their high spirited girl friends."

On the whole, however, the reviews welcomed the new Alcott book, the *Tribune* finding it a pleasant and innocent tale that would increase the author's popularity, the *Times* stating: "It has been some years since the best of our story writers for children has written anything, and the many early admirers of Miss Alcott, the fathers and mothers of to-day, will be delighted to meet once more their former acquaintances, those bright boys and girls who peopled her pages. In *Jo's Boys* the lads have grown older, as have the girls. But they are all as pleasing as of yore."

The original readers of *Little Women* and of *Little Men* had indeed belonged to an earlier generation. Now, with *Jo's Boys*, the author gave every evidence that her appeal would become perennial. Moreover, that appeal had broadened with the book to attract not only her accustomed readership but a more mature audience who would see in its pages the groundwork for intensive analysis. If the former delighted in its narrative, the latter found food for thought in its philosophy of life. Despite the difficulties Alcott had had in completing the book, despite her psychological reluctance to end the March saga, she had produced a volume of almost universal interest, one that encapsulated reminders of her earlier life while it upheld her present standards.

The curtain that had fallen on the March family would soon descend upon the Alcotts, both Bronson and his illustrious daughter dying in 1888. But the book that had completed a trilogy and marked a finale to the annals of the Marches would still be read, still be analyzed, still recall to later generations the lives and aspirations that had gone before.

SELECTED BIBLIOGRAPHY

WORKS BY LOUISA MAY ALCOTT

Flower Fables, 1855   Short Tales
Hospital Sketches, 1863   Sketches
The Rose Family. A Fairy Tale, 1864   Fairy Tale
On Picket Duty, and Other Tales, 1864   Short Stories
Moods, 1865   Novel: Revised Edition, 1882
The Mysterious Key, and What It Opened, 1867   Novelette
Morning-Glories, and Other Stories, 1868   Short Stories
Three Proverb Stories, 1868   Short Stories
Little Women or, Meg, Jo, Beth and Amy, 1868-69   Novel
    (Signet Classic 0-451-51814-4)
Hospital Sketches and Camp and Fireside Stories, 1869
    Sketches and Short Stories
Will's Wonder Book, 1870   Nature Story
V.V.: or, Plots and Counterplots, 1870   Sensational Nove-
    lette
An Old-Fashioned Girl, 1870   Novel in Little Women Series
Little Men: Life at Plumfield with Jo's Boys, 1871   Novel
    in Little Women Series (Signet Classic 0-451-51998-1)
Aunt Jo's Scrap-Bag, 1872-82   Six Collections of Short Sto-
    ries and Sketches
    I *My Boys*, 1872   Stories; II *Shawl-Straps*, 1872 Travel
    Sketches; III *Cupid and Chow-Chow*, 1874   Short
    Stories; IV *My Girls*, 1878   Short Stories; V *Jimmy's
    Cruise in the Pinafore*, 1879   Short Stories; VI *An
    Old-Fashioned Thanksgiving*, 1882   Short Stories
Work: A Story of Experience, 1873   Autobiographical Novel
Eight Cousins; or, The Aunt-Hill, 1875   Novel in Little
    Women Series
*Silver Pitchers: And Independence, A Centennial Love
    Story*, 1876   Short Stories

Rose in Bloom. A Sequel to "Eight Cousins," 1876   Novel in Little Women Series
A Modern Mephistopheles, 1877   Novel
Under the Lilacs, 1878   Novel in Little Women Series
Jack and Jill: A Village Story, 1880   Novel in Little Women Series
Proverb Stories, 1882   Short Stories
Spinning-Wheel Stories, 1884   Short Stories
Jo's Boys, and How They Turned Out. A Sequel to "Little Men," 1886   Novel in Little Women Series (Signet Classic 0-451-52089-0)
Lulu's Library, 1886–89   Three Volumes of Short Tales I *A Christmas Dream,* 1886; II *The Frost King,* 1887; III *Recollections,* 1889
A Garland for Girls, 1888   Short Stories
A Modern Mephistopheles and A Whisper in the Dark, 1889   Novel and Short Story
Comic Tragedies Written by "Jo" and "Meg" and Acted by the "Little Women," 1893   Dramas
Behind a Mask: The Unknown Thrillers of Louisa May Alcott, 1975   Sensational Novelettes
Plots and Counterplots: More Unknown Thrillers of Louisa May Alcott, 1976   Sensational Novelettes
Transcendental Wild Oats and Excerpts from the Fruitlands Diary, 1981   Autobiographical Fiction
The Selected Letters of Louisa May Alcott, 1987   Collection of Alcott Letters

BIOGRAPHY AND CRITICISM

Anthony, Katharine S. *Louisa May Alcott.* New York: Knopf, 1938.
Beach, Seth Curtis. *Daughters of the Puritans.* Boston: American Unitarian Association, 1905, 1967.
Bedell, Madelon. *The Alcotts: Biography of a Family.* New York: Potter, 1980.
Bonstelle, Jessie and Marian De Forest. *Little Women Letters from the House of Alcott.* Boston: Little, Brown, 1914.

Brown, Mary Hosmer. *Memories of Concord*. Boston: Four Seas, 1926.

Cheney, Ednah Dow. *Louisa May Alcott: The Children's Friend*. Boston: Prang, 1888.

Cheney, Ednah Dow, ed. *Louisa May Alcott: Her Life, Letters, and Journals*. Boston: Roberts Brothers, 1889, Little, Brown, 1928.

Clark, Annie M. L. *The Alcotts in Harvard*. Lancaster, Mass.: J. C. L. Clark, 1902.

Elbert, Sarah. *A Hunger for Home: Louisa May Alcott and Little Women*. Philadelphia: Temple University Press, 1984.

Fisher, Aileen and Olive Rabe. *We Alcotts: The Story of Louisa May Alcott's Family As Seen Through the Eyes of "Marmee," Mother of Little Women*. New York: Atheneum, 1968.

Gowing, Clara. *The Alcotts as I Knew Them*. Boston: C. M. Clark, 1909, 1980.

Gulliver, Lucile. *Louisa May Alcott: A Bibliography*. Boston: Little, Brown, 1932.

Herrnstadt, Richard L., ed. *The Letters of A. Bronson Alcott*. Ames: Iowa State University Press, 1969.

Linn, Edith Willis and Henry Bazin, eds. *Alcott Memoirs Posthumously Compiled from Papers, Journals, and Memoranda of the late Dr. Frederick L. H. Willis*. Boston: Badger, 1915, 1970.

MacDonald, Ruth K. *Louisa May Alcott*. Boston: Twayne, 1984.

Marsella, Joy A. *The Promise of Destiny: Children and Women in the Short Stories of Louisa May Alcott*. Westport: Greenwood Press, 1983.

Meigs, Cornelia. *The Story of the Author of Little Women: Invincible Louisa*. Boston: Little, Brown, 1933, 1968.

Morrow, Honoré Willsie. *The Father of Little Women*. Boston: Little, Brown, 1927.

Moses, Belle. *Louisa May Alcott, Dreamer and Worker: A Story of Achievement*. New York: Appleton, 1909.

Myerson, Joel, Daniel Shealy, and Madeleine B. Stern, eds., *The Selected Letters of Louisa May Alcott*. Boston: Little, Brown, 1987.

Papashvily, Helen Waite. *Louisa May Alcott*. Boston: Houghton Mifflin, 1965.

Payne, Alma. *Louisa May Alcott: A Reference Guide*. Boston: G. K. Hall, 1980.

Rostenberg, Leona. "Some Anonymous and Pseudonymous Thrillers of Louisa May Alcott," *Papers of the Bibliographical Society of America* 37:2 (1943).

Salyer, Sandford. *Marmee: The Mother of Little Women*. Norman: University of Oklahoma Press, 1949.

Saxton, Martha. *Louisa May: A Modern Biography of Louisa May Alcott*. Boston: Houghton Mifflin, 1977.

Shepard, Odell, ed. *The Journals of Bronson Alcott*. Boston: Little, Brown, 1938.

Stern, Madeleine B., ed. *Critical Essays on Louisa May Alcott*. Boston: G. K. Hall, 1984.

Stern, Madeleine B. *Louisa May Alcott*. Norman: University of Oklahoma Press, 1950, 1971, 1985.

Stern, Madeleine B., ed. *Louisa's Wonder Book—An Unknown Alcott Juvenile*. Mount Pleasant: Central Michigan University Press, 1975.

Ticknor, Caroline. *Classic Concord*. Boston: Houghton Mifflin, 1926.

Ticknor, Caroline. *May Alcott: A Memoir*. Boston: Little, Brown, 1929.

Ullom, Judith C. *Louisa May Alcott: A Centennial for "Little Women."* Washington: Library of Congress, 1969.